Standing outside in the rain with Claire last night, A.J. hadn't been thinking like a cop...

He hadn't been thinking of her as a witness who could break a case wide open for him, hadn't been thinking of her as an heiress who was way out of his league. He hadn't been thinking of her as a kid who was more than a decade younger than him and twice as innocent about the world.

He'd been thinking of Claire as a woman. A damn sexy, irresistible woman.

And she'd touched him. Those fingers had cupped his face and demanded he notice her.

He had.

Maybe not in the way she'd intended, but he noticed plenty. Clingy, wet silk, slender curves beneath his hands, dewy lips begging to be kissed. She'd asked him in every way without actually saying the words.

And he'd almost done it.

But common sense had prevailed. His training had prevailed.

So, no kiss. But he hadn't been right since.

Dear Harlequin Intrigue Reader,

This month you'll want to have all six of our books to keep you company as you brave those April showers!

• Debra Webb kicks off THE ENFORCERS, her exciting new trilogy, with *John Doe on Her Doorstep*. And for all of you who have been waiting with bated breath for the newest installment in Kelsey Roberts's THE LANDRY BROTHERS series, we have *Chasing Secrets*.

• Rebecca York, Ann Voss Peterson and Patricia Rosemoor join together in *Desert Sons*. You won't want to miss this unique three-in-one collection!

• Two of your favorite promotions are back. You won't be able to resist Leona Karr's ECLIPSE title, *Shadows on the Lake*. And you'll be on the edge of your seat while reading Jean Barrett's *Paternity Unknown*, the latest installment in TOP SECRET BABIES.

• Meet another of THE PRECINCT's rugged lawmen in Julie Miller's *Police Business*.

Every month you can depend on Harlequin Intrigue to deliver an array of thrilling romantic suspense and mystery. Be sure you read each one!

Sincerely,

Denise O'Sullivan
Senior Editor
Harlequin Intrigue

POLICE
BUSINESS
JULIE MILLER

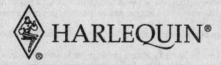

HARLEQUIN®

TORONTO • NEW YORK • LONDON
AMSTERDAM • PARIS • SYDNEY • HAMBURG
STOCKHOLM • ATHENS • TOKYO • MILAN • MADRID
PRAGUE • WARSAW • BUDAPEST • AUCKLAND

For Maxie Fireball Miller, my faithful writing companion.
You make me get up and walk, you always tell me when the
UPS man is here, you let me know when it's time to go get
the boy after school and you keep life interesting.

Thanks, too, to the humane society
for rescuing you. I'm glad you picked us to be your pack.

ISBN 0-373-22841-4

POLICE BUSINESS

Copyright © 2005 by Julie Miller

ABOUT THE AUTHOR

Julie Miller attributes her passion for writing romance to all those fairy tales she read growing up, and shyness. Encouragement from her family to write down all those feelings she couldn't express became a love for the written word. She gets continued support from her fellow members of the Prairieland Romance Writers, where she serves as the resident "grammar goddess." This award-winning author and teacher has published several paranormal romances. Inspired by the likes of Agatha Christie and Encyclopedia Brown, Ms. Miller believes the only thing better than a good mystery is a good romance.

Born and raised in Missouri, she now lives in Nebraska with her husband, son and smiling guard dog, Maxie. Write to Julie at P.O. Box 5162, Grand Island, NE 68802-5162.

Books by Julie Miller

HARLEQUIN INTRIGUE
588—ONE GOOD MAN*
619—SUDDEN ENGAGEMENT*
642—SECRET AGENT HEIRESS
651—IN THE BLINK OF AN EYE*
666—THE DUKE'S COVERT MISSION
699—THE ROOKIE*
719—KANSAS CITY'S BRAVEST*
748—UNSANCTIONED MEMORIES*
779—LAST MAN STANDING*
819—PARTNER-PROTECTOR†
841—POLICE BUSINESS†

HARLEQUIN BLAZE
45—INTIMATE KNOWLEDGE

*The Taylor Clan
†The Precinct

CAST OF CHARACTERS

A. J. Rodriguez—A legend in undercover work at KCPD. This son of a custodian used to be the one causing trouble out on the streets. Now he's the one taking the trouble right to the criminals' doorsteps. No matter what side of the tracks they live on.

Claire Winthrop—A sheltered society princess who'd like nothing more than to break free of her wealthy father's overprotective shadow to get a real job and have a real life. But witnessing a murder wasn't the type of reality she was looking for.

Cain Winthrop—Self-made multimillionaire. His love for his hearing-impaired daughter might get her killed.

Deirdre Gunn-Winthrop—Cain's second wife. She didn't marry for love.

Gabriel Gunn—He's ready to take over his stepfather's business empire.

Gina Gunn—Claire's stepsister. Is she on the fast track to earn her own cool million? Or is she after something else?

Marcus Tucker—Chief of Security for Winthrop Enterprises.

Amelia Ward—The office temp.

Peter Landers—An old friend on Winthrop's board of directors.

Rob Hastings—Executive hotshot with an eye on the boss's daughter.

Dominic Galvan—He always gets his man—or woman.

Antonio Rodriguez, Sr.—Former custodian at Winthrop Enterprises, whose murder is the only one his son, A.J., has never been able to solve.

Prologue

Detective A. J. Rodriguez sank low behind the steering wheel of his sleek, black Trans Am and peered over the restored leather dashboard into the neon glare and masking shadows of the drizzly Kansas City night.

He hated stakeouts. His coffee was cold, his bladder was full and his left shoulder ached from sitting still for so long in the damp, chilly air.

But he didn't complain. He'd given up the luxury of whining about the challenges and discomforts of life almost two decades ago.

Instead, with his endless patience and chameleonlike ability to blend in with his surroundings, he knew he was well-suited to such a job. That patience was a testament to his father's spirit and sacrifice, while his undercover expertise was a by-product of the years he'd wasted before coming to understand that Antonio Joseph Rodriguez, Sr. was a better man than any of the cool cats or hotshots on the street could ever hope to be.

A.J.'s father had been a better man than *he* could ever hope to be.

Static buzzed in the tiny earphone he wore beneath the black knit cap that masked his equally dark hair. His slow smile was the only movement giving any indication that his partner, Josh Taylor, was about to speak. "Hey, A.J. You got anything down at your end? This has got to be the slowest damn nightclub I've ever seen. I've only counted one couple going in during the past hour, and no one's come out. You think it's the band or the booze that sucks?"

"I'd say it's the two hours we've been watching the door."

"I'm supposed to be the comic relief, remember?" Since Josh was hiding out, too, his laugh was barely a whisper in A.J.'s ear. "Our informant said the meeting was at midnight. It's nearly that now."

"Give it time, *amigo.*"

For eight months, they'd had nothing but time, it seemed. Somebody was running drugs out of the Jazz Note, the umpteenth incarnation of a nightclub to occupy the same building in the tony arts and entertainment district of KC known as Westport. And while the club's current owner seemed legit, KCPD hadn't been able to pinpoint anyone who frequented the place often enough to make it a profitable distribution hub. The investigation had grown cold.

Until one of the patrons had been found stabbed to death in the men's room. Not just any patron. But Mort Firth, a two-bit dealer from the seedy KC neighborhood known as no-man's-land, who'd been infringing on someone else's territory. Suddenly, a case that had been the drug squad's purview for so long had been reassigned to homicide. And A.J. and Josh had been called in to investigate.

Mort had been the third small-time dealer taken out in a murder that wasn't gang-related in as many years. A.J.'s streetwise gut told him that the perp was no vigilante cleaning up the streets of KC. This was something bigger. An unknown scourge was moving in and killing off the competition.

Slowly, subtly taking over.

And it was up to KCPD to stop it.

A.J. spared a glance at his watch. Straight-up midnight. Their informant, Edgar Vaughn—Mort's former business associate—said that turf negotiations were going to take place at midnight at the Jazz Note between a dealer nicknamed Slick and an unknown suspect. All A.J. and Josh had to do was follow Edgar's dealer inside the club and find out whom he met with. One picture—and maybe a fingerprint and some eavesdropping—would be worth a thousand words when it came to breaking open the case.

The low-pitched hum of a well-tuned engine passed by and A.J. lifted his gaze in appreciation as much as curiosity. A pricey steel-gray sedan pulled into an empty parking space across from the Jazz Note. The car itself was polished enough to fit in with the neighborhood's cruise-by clientele of affluent baby boomers, yet nondescript enough to avoid drawing too much attention from the locals.

But the guy who climbed out didn't fit either category. His dark, pin-striped suit and the silver tie he adjusted as he scanned his surroundings weren't casual enough for the club. And no way was he one of the working class residents of the area.

Slick.

A.J. scooted up in his seat, his blood pumping quicker in even-paced anticipation. "Josh."

"I see him."

He didn't need Edgar to step from an alleyway and follow the dealer in for A.J. to know their man had arrived. With a brief glance up and down the empty street, he got out of the car, straightened his black leather jacket over the bulge of the guns at either side of his waist and strolled toward the front door of the Jazz Note.

"I'll come in through the alley entrance and try to spot him from that direction." Josh was moving, too.

Once through the club's glass door, A.J. paid the cover charge and slipped inside. His eyes quickly adjusted to the dark interior, though the heavy scents of smoke and alcohol were a little harder to get used to. He let the lazy beat of the electric bass onstage set the rhythm of his movements as he followed the suspect at a discreet distance. First, an uneventful trip to the men's room. Then to the bar.

Slick ordered a double scotch. Neat. His furtive glances over the rim of his glass before he bolted the amber liquid were a dead giveaway to A.J.'s trained eye. The man was nervous. Probably had never been to the Jazz Note before. Maybe had never even met his contact.

His nervous energy put A.J. on guard as he tailed Slick to an empty booth away from the stage.

A.J. found a seat at a table nearby and ordered a beer. With a wink and a decent tip for the waitress, he took an obligatory sip and tapped his foot in time with the soulful, driving music. Josh stood at the end of the bar, using the mirror behind the bartender to keep their man in sight.

A half hour later, the crowd began to thin out.

Slick was on his third scotch. And the mystery guest he was supposed to meet hadn't showed.

"Edgar's heading for the door." Josh's voice whispered over the radio. "You think we've been set up?"

A.J. had memorized the face of every person in the club, from the teenager bussing tables to the blind, balding maestro working magic at the piano. Something deep in his bones was trying to tell him that this didn't feel right. That there weren't enough people here for a club that played music this hot. It was as if he were watching a play, and each patron and employee was an actor carefully placed around the stage.

"I think our man's been set up." Suffused with an instantly wary energy that didn't change his outward appearance, A.J. shoved aside his warm beer. He used a subtle nod at the buxom waitress for a fresh drink as an opportunity to scan the room one more time. What he was looking for, he wasn't sure. Trouble. Someone else keeping a curious eye on their man. He tossed a five onto the table and whispered into his microphone. "You follow Edgar. I'll stick with Slick."

In the minutes that followed, the band played its last number and started to pack up. Odd. The lights didn't come up. There was no announcement about the last call for drinks—as if someone didn't want the few remaining patrons to move. Slick checked his watch and made a call on his cell phone that was more about cursing than conversation.

After hanging up, Slick downed the last swallow of scotch and shot to his feet. He grabbed his forehead and swayed a couple of steps as the booze hit him hard. Great. He'd fished his keys out of his pocket. Drunk drivers were about as high on A.J.'s list as drug dealers. As Slick staggered past him, he wondered if the waitress or bartender would say something. He wondered if he could stop Slick somehow without giving away his presence.

Hell.

A.J. blinked and cast the thoughts aside. This wasn't about a personal agenda. He had a job to do.

By the time Slick had stumbled through the front door,

A.J. was close on his heels. He lingered out of sight beneath the awning over the Jazz Note's door and kept his man in sight. "He's outside, Josh. Our boy's been stood up."

"I see him." Josh would be hiding somewhere in the shadows as well. "Edgar grabbed a cab about five minutes ago. He seemed pretty eager to get of here."

"I don't blame him. Something's going down."

Figure it out, A.J. Figure it out. He scanned every inch of the street, studied empty storefronts, read license plates, shook his head at the drunken man cursing the car that nearly ran him down in the middle of the street.

Slick dropped his keys to the pavement before squeezing them in his grip and unlocking the car door.

"Son of a bitch."

"Talk to me, A.J."

A.J. left the shadows. He reached for his gun, feeling the threat in the air like a hand at his throat. "We're gonna lose our guy."

"A.J.?"

"This is a hit."

Slick fell in behind the wheel and slammed the door.

"A.J.!"

A light sparked beneath the hood of Slick's car and the silver sedan exploded in a thunderous crash that slammed A.J. to the sidewalk and rained down a cloud of flying debris and rolling flames.

Chapter One

"Daddy..."

No. Though that had been the pet name Claire Winthrop had called her father all twenty-three years of her life, it wasn't professional enough for the request she intended to make.

Hearing the ding of the elevator only as a metallic buzz, she watched the lights marking each floor blink on and off above the doors as she rode up to the executive suites on the top floor of Kansas City's Winthrop Enterprises Building.

She rehearsed the beginning of her well-planned speech, trying to keep the excitement she felt from blurring the careful articulation of her voice. "Dad. The Forsythe School asked if I would be interested in working for them full-time next semester. As a middle school counselor. They're pleased with my volunteer work with the adolescents."

Opening her hand, Claire smiled at the proof of her success in her palm. A gold smiley-face pin with *Forsythe* etched into the back. It was probably gold-plated. Well, maybe just gold-colored since it had been a gift from the students themselves. But it was every bit as precious as her mother's pearls she wore around her neck.

Claire fastened the pin onto the lapel of her pink silk

suit. Her father hadn't been able to attend the school awards banquet that night; but then, he was such a busy man. That was the excuse she used, at any rate, to take the sting out of his dismissal of her need to work. She lifted her chin again, to watch the floor numbers fly by. She was proud of her paraprofessional and tutoring work with special needs preteens and teenagers. Thrilled to discover she had a knack for listening.

She almost laughed at that one. But her father wouldn't see the ironic humor. So she went back to practicing what he did understand—facts and numbers and a concise presentation.

Clenching her hands into fists to keep them still at her sides, she continued. "I would need to go back to school to earn my graduate degree, Dad. And take a test to be licensed for therapist's certification. But they're willing to pay for my classes. This is an opportunity for me to make a career for myself."

Too many Rs. Claire puffed out a nervous breath and raked her chin-length swath of hair away from her temples. Just as quickly, she smoothed the straight, champagne-colored strands back into place, covering up the tiny speech processors most people mistook for hearing aids that were hooked behind her ears.

She was always self-conscious when she spoke out loud, knowing her dull *R* sounds and practiced consonants were a dead giveaway to her hearing loss. But her father didn't like to sign. He claimed the visual expression only pointed out the shortcomings he already felt so responsible for. And while she could read lips, he needed to hear the actual words in order to communicate clearly with her. Speaking like a normal person would go a long way toward convincing him that she was ready to do more than volunteer part-time at the school.

Claire stretched her neck in the swan-like arch that fifteen years of dance lessons had given her. She closed her eyes and breathed deeply, straightening her petite body to its utmost height and easing the tension that had gathered in her muscles.

She could do this. She *would* do this.

Cain Winthrop might want his daughter to stay at home, host quiet dinner parties and stay out of the limelight until some handsome young man whisked her away to stay at *his* home to host quiet dinner parties and stay out of the limelight, but Claire had different plans in mind. She had the money, brains and desire to pursue any career she wanted—or ramrod the success of any charity. She could make a difference in the lives of people who needed someone to make a difference.

If her father would let her.

If he'd trust her to make smart decisions.

If he'd believe she could be safe in the world without his well-meaning protection shadowing her every step of the way.

But she had a lot of years of love and ingrained habits to overcome. Cain Winthrop was used to doing things his way. Running his business empire his way. Taking care of his daughter and stepchildren his way.

Claire intended to change that. Just a little. It was time to make a place for herself in the world.

Her way.

Feeling the gentle roll of her stomach that told her the elevator was slowing its ascent, Claire opened her eyes and watched the number 26 light up. She took a deep breath, clutched her purse beneath her arm and fixed a smile on her face. "Okay, Dad." She crossed her fingers and added a prayer. "Please listen."

The doors slid open onto the shadows of the twenty-sixth floor. The receptionist's desk stood empty and the waiting area was dark. Claire stepped out and turned along the plush carpet toward her father's suite of offices.

Even with the sharp bite of spring air outside to lure him to the family's cabin and the promise of fishing on Truman Lake, she knew her father would keep late hours until the weekend. She'd purposely waited until after her school dinner to pay him this surprise visit, allowing the office plenty of time to clear out so that they were less likely to get interrupted.

With a fortified sense of purpose, Claire walked past her stepbrother Gabriel's empty office and its dark interior. She strode past the senior vice-president's office and saw that Peter Landers had gone as well. Her stepsister Gina's office was dark. The corporate attorney's office, dark.

A chilling sense of unease tried to work its way beneath her resolve. She'd never cared much for dark places. She was already at a disadvantage, knowing she couldn't hear anything or anyone sneaking up on her. Not being able to see an approaching danger, either, could make her doubly paranoid if she allowed her fear to take hold.

As a young girl, trying to adjust to the cochlear implants inside her head, those bumps in the night that startled other children had been real terrors for her as distorted electronic sounds she hadn't learned to identify shrieked into her ears. It didn't help that the last actual sounds she'd heard had been her own screams of pain and loss as she battled the tropical fever virus that took 97% of her hearing and killed her mother.

Claire breathed easier as she rounded the corner and a soft glow of light greeted her with reassuring warmth. Beyond a private waiting area, she spotted the boardroom and her father's offices, all lit up. His faithful executive assistant, Valerie Justice, must still be working late as well, judging by the brightness flooding through her open doorway. Valerie wouldn't mind giving father and daughter some time alone. For twenty-odd years, she'd been nothing but discreet when it came to taking care of not just the family business, but the family itself.

Here, too, the carpeting gave way to the polished mahogany flooring her father had imported from Venezuela. The decor changed as well, as solid walls gave way to alternating black steel and clear glass panels, giving her glimpses of the interior of each room. A black leather seating group sat in the middle of a central waiting area, adorned by tropical plants, exotic animal prints and a custom-built aquarium nearly twelve feet long that divided the sofa, chairs and coffee table from the circle of private rooms.

Claire repeated the words inside her head, squelching the urge to sign them as well. *Dad. I've been offered a wonderful chance to—*

A bone-deep thud shook the floor beneath her feet and Claire halted in her tracks. She felt another vibration through the soles of her Manolo Blahniks and saw the water in the aquarium ripple against the side of the tank.

"What the…?"

Missouri hadn't had a big earthquake since the late 1800s, and there wasn't enough wind outside to make the steel-and-limestone building sway.

She glanced over her shoulder at the tunnel of darkness that filled the hallway behind her. Had a cleaning crew come in? Knocked over a bucket? Slammed a door? Was the security guard making his rounds early?

Had one of those unknown terrors just gone bump in the night?

Claire opened her mouth and turned to call out to her father. But she snapped it shut just as quickly and retreated into the shadows as a tall, black-haired stranger stepped into view beyond the open doorway to her father's office. The man's black suit and tie made him appear as little more than a silhouette against the cream-colored walls inside.

But there was no mistaking the gun he held in his black-gloved hands, or the methodic precision with which he unscrewed the long, tubular silencer from its steel tip and slipped both items into the holster beneath his jacket.

Oh, my God.

He'd shot someone!

Claire swung her gaze over to Valerie's office and back to her father's. The assistant hadn't run out to check on the noises. But with a silencer, maybe Valerie hadn't heard the shots.

Technically, Claire hadn't heard anything, either. The vibrations she'd felt could have been the concussions of the gun. Or a body hitting the floor. Or the bashing in of someone's head. Someone being shoved against the wall. A fight—

Stop it!

Tears pricked Claire's eyes. The breath stopped in her chest. But she forced herself to think rationally, to be aware of the danger at hand. Clutching at the pearls around her neck, she fought to dispel the image of her father, dead in his chair.

Nonchalantly standing there in her father's office, the

man in black stared down at his handiwork with cold, dark eyes. "I'll come back for the body."

Claire could read the promise on his lips clear across the waiting room. Body? Someone was dead. The man in black had just killed…

"Daddy?" she whispered the unthinkable thought, squeezing her fist so tightly that her necklace snapped.

A sharp gasp was the only curse she allowed herself as the clasp broke and pearls fell into her hand. She twisted to keep her elbow close to her body to catch the falling strand in the crook of her arm. Tiny knots kept most of the beads together in one string, but she contorted herself to catch two, three…but a fourth hit the floor, bounced off the hard wood and rolled away into the darkness.

To Claire's ears, there was no sound.

But in her mind, the bounce was deafening.

She whipped her head up to the lighted doorway. How loud was a single pearl? How good was the man in black's hearing?

How dead would she be if she were caught?

Concern for her father dimmed, and fear for herself blazed through her veins in full force.

Claire dropped to her haunches and crawled toward the aquarium, her instincts warning her to duck behind its thick mahogany base. Or maybe it was the pounding of her racing heart that made her suddenly too light-headed to stand. *Daddy!* She cried the word inside her head, knowing he wasn't there to help. She shoved the remains of the traitorous necklace inside her jacket pocket and tucked her legs beneath her, making herself as small as a child, hiding before the man turned and spotted her.

If it wasn't already too late.

Claire blinked and the tears spilled over to run down her cheeks. But she held her breath and disappeared from view between the jungle-size plants and their low, sheltering branches. She counted the seconds off silently in her head until her lungs burned and forced her to inhale.

With fresh oxygen came a fresh thought. He hadn't found her. He hadn't snatched her up by the hair or arm, or put a bullet through her head. She hadn't felt his footsteps through the floor or smelled him walking past, either.

Feeling safe for the moment, something new—something harder, tougher, angrier—slipped past her fear and grief, clearing her head.

With a bold sense of purpose, Claire scooted to the end of the aquarium and peeked through the camouflage of leaves. From this angle she could see the man with the gun. Above the partition that blocked his lower body from view, she memorized the shape of his face, the cut of his hair and every acne-pocked scar on his deeply tanned cheeks.

She swiped the tears from her cheeks and squinted harder, noting the movements of his long, thin lips. He was talking again. Having a conversation. Though the second person remained hidden from view behind a steel panel, she could interpret his pauses and nods.

At this distance, she couldn't hear the words. But then, Claire didn't need to.

"That's number four on your list," the man said.

Four dead bodies? He'd killed others? Why? Inching closer, she pressed her shoulder into the aquarium's base and eavesdropped with her eyes. Who was he?

The man in black frowned. His eyes narrowed as he tilted his chin. "You don't tell me when or where I do the job. When you hire me, all you have to know is that the job will get done." He smiled. It was a cold, evil thinning of his lips that twisted Claire's stomach into knots. "Think of it as insurance for both of us. You know that the people in your way have been disposed of. And I know you won't turn me in if someone figures out that you're the one behind all this."

Another pause. Who was he talking to? Who would want her father dead? Where was Valerie? Claire read the argument on his lips.

"Relax. I'm too good at my job for anyone to find me, much less find out who hired me." He buttoned his suit coat over his gun. "The last two will be eliminated once I feel the timing is right. In the meantime, I'll expect another deposit into my account for this one. By ten o'clock tomorrow morning. Or you'll find your name on my list. No charge."

His partner must have said something that displeased the man in black. His thready smile became an ugly frown.

"I'm worth every penny you're paying me. I never miss." When he leaned toward his unseen partner in crime, Claire backed away, as if the cold-blooded threat in his eyes was intended for her. "If I say I'll kill someone, they'll be dead. And I won't leave a trace."

Claire's breath rushed out in a gasp deep enough to stir the leaves of the ficus beside her. Quickly, she slapped her hand over her mouth. Had she made a noise? Had he heard her?

Though he didn't react as if he suspected he was being watched, when he turned to exit her father's office, Claire curled into a tiny ball and prayed to God that the aquarium, plants and shadows would keep her hidden from view as he walked past.

The man in black strolled by, his heavy size shaking the

floor beneath her knees with every step. She bowed her golden hair out of sight so that she felt, rather than saw, the second person—lighter in weight—hurry behind the hired killer at a faster pace.

Claire held her breath, closed her eyes and prayed. She couldn't make out the sounds of the elevator at this distance. So she hid there, hunching beside the aquarium, letting terror and grief hold her still long after the vibrations of the footsteps through the floorboards had faded. She waited until her thighs and knees began to cramp. Waited until she sensed that she had been alone for several minutes.

Then she slowly pushed to her feet. Her purse dropped into her shaky grasp as she stared down the long hallway into the darkness. Before fear made her foolish, before grief sent her into shock, Claire turned. On numb feet, she stumbled toward her father's office, praying for some sort of miracle every step of the way.

"Daddy?"

The steel door frame was as cold beneath her fingertips as the blood flowing through her veins.

Her father's chair was empty. She stepped inside and summoned her courage to walk around Cain Winthrop's immaculate desk and take a peek. Claire gripped the edge of the mahogany top, nearly collapsing with relief.

Then shock and compassion pushed aside the traitorous emotion. She wiped away her tears and knelt down as she fully absorbed the awful truth. There *was* a body on the floor, with two neat bullet holes piercing the heart and forehead.

Her father wasn't dead.

But Valerie Justice was.

"BUT, DAD, I'm telling you—I saw Valerie murdered!" Claire thrust her right index finger beneath her left palm, furiously signing the word for murder as she spoke. "That man shot her in your office. He had a gun. A silencer. I saw him."

"Slow down, sweetheart. You're slurring your words. I thought you said you saw a murder."

Still breathless from fear, the fastest drive of her life across the city and her run up the front steps of her family's Mission Hills home, Claire's frustrated sigh left her light-headed. She shrugged free of Cain Winthrop's placating grip on her shoulders and signed an emphatic statement. "I did."

"I thought you were meeting Rob Hastings for drinks tonight. After that school thing you went to."

Meeting the platonic friend her father had handpicked to become something more than a friend had completely slipped her mind. But, despite the stab of guilt she felt, even standing up a good friend didn't seem important now. She drew her palm across her forehead and closed her hand into a fist, signing the message, "I forgot."

"You forgot?" He scratched the top of his snowy white hair and shook his head. "Rob's a nice boy. I know he'll do big things with the company. It's not like you to go off on some wild goose chase when—"

"I went to see you!" Claire tamped down on her impatience and turned away. Sure, her father could communicate with her about manners and dating, but he refused to listen to her account of what she'd seen in his office.

After crouching behind the aquarium for several overwhelming minutes that had dragged on forever, then venturing forth to discover Valerie's body, Claire had decided to leave the Winthrop Building, risk a speeding ticket and drive home in record time. A regular phone was useless to her, and a cell only good if she could use text messaging. Somehow, she doubted reporting a murder to the police in a cutesy memo would get the immediate response she needed. In fact, she suspected they'd see it as some sort of prank.

She'd needed her TDD phone—Telecommunication Device for the Deaf. One she could speak into or type a message on that would be translated into a computerized voice at the other end of the line. A phone that would print out questions and conversation on a screen she could respond to.

Schooling her patience, Claire turned to face the familiar blue eyes. Urgent and scared hadn't gotten through to him. She'd try cool and rational. "Dad. Listen…"

She'd given up the whole *Daddy* thing as soon as she realized he wasn't taking her story any more seriously than the new guard at the front desk of the Winthrop Building had. And since she hadn't wanted to take the chance of running into the man in black or his unknown accomplice, searching the darkened hallways for a more familiar—more sympathetic—face to help her didn't seem like much of an option, either.

I'll come back for the body. Claire hadn't waited to witness that, too, or to become one of the well-erased *traces* he'd bragged about to his unknown comrade.

She articulated her words as succinctly as possible, carefully monitoring her volume and pauses through the speech processors behind her ears. "I know what I saw. I will never forget that man's face. I won't forget Valerie's, either. There was hardly any blood on her face or blouse. But her hair was caked with it in the back. It was pooling on the plastic mat beneath your desk."

"Please, dear. That's such a gruesome picture."

"Yes…it was." She took a step closer, curled her fingers around his sturdy forearm and begged him to listen. "I came here first to use the TDD phone—and because I knew you'd want to be there when the police arrive."

Cain Winthrop's indulgent expression sobered. "You're calling the police?"

"Yes." Hadn't she just signed it out and spoken the words? She'd been panicking in two languages and he still didn't grasp the urgency of the situation.

Shaking her head, Claire left her father and hurried into the study. She ignored the walls of books she loved and sat behind the walnut writing desk that had once been her mother's. Claire typed in the request for the police department's information line and waited for the computer to locate the number and automatically dial it.

The words scrolled across the screen as the operator picked up. "KCPD information hotline. How may—"

Her father pressed a button on the phone and disconnected the call. Claire shot to her feet. "Dad!"

"Don't call the police."

She read his lips in disbelief. "We have to. Valerie is dead in your office."

"Nonsense."

"Dad—"

"What's all the commotion in here?"

Claire heard the buzz of a new voice in her ears and groaned. She turned a silent plea to her father as the striking, fifty-year-old woman with frosted brunette hair joined them. If it had been difficult to get her father to believe her, it would be impossible to get any help from her stepmother.

"It's nothing, Deirdre." Cain explained away the argument between father and daughter. "Claire went up to the office this evening to surprise me, and I wasn't there. It's all a little confusing."

"I'm not confused. My ears might not work, but I have 20/20 vision. I live by what my eyes tell me. I know what I saw."

Deirdre signed the question, "I thought you were on a date with Rob Hastings."

Claire rolled her eyes and turned away. Maybe she should call Rob for help since everyone was so interested in him. "I'm calling the police."

"The police?"

Ignoring the metallic drone of Deirdre's shocked voice, Claire reached for the receiver. But her father blocked her path. "Sweetie, I'm only trying to protect you from embarrassing yourself." He gently pried the phone from her fingers and set it back in its cradle. "Valerie is on vacation in the Bahamas with that gentleman friend she met on her last cruise."

She watched his lips say the impossible. "No, she's not. She's—"

"I gave her a hug before she took off this afternoon. The temp who's replacing her for a couple of weeks was there when I called for my messages at six."

"But…" Claire's lungs deflated, along with her conviction. She sank onto the desk chair's brocade cushion. How could that be? She hadn't hallucinated since that fever she'd had as a child. She'd *seen* that man. Seen that gun.

She'd seen that dead body.

Her father's executive assistant could have been killed by mistake—a tragic case of being in the wrong place at the wrong time. The man in black and his accomplice might have come looking for her father, but found Valerie puttering about his office instead. The man she hadn't seen might have been Valerie's "gentleman friend." Maybe he'd taken her there on purpose to get rid of her in some kind of twisted love triangle thing. Or maybe Valerie had lied to her father and never really left the building. Maybe she was part of some conspiracy, some plot to take advantage of her father's wealth and worldwide trade connections, but her partners had betrayed her.

Why wasn't the great Cain Winthrop concerned about that?

And what about the list? *That's number four.*

The thin-lipped man with the pockmarked face didn't seem to be the sort of person who would make a mistake.

Neither was she.

Trusting instincts that no one else seemed to think she had, Claire pushed to her feet. There was only one way to convince her father that he or his company might still be in grave danger, only one way to convince him to get help. With a resolute sigh, she strode back into the foyer to retrieve her purse. The staccato tapping on the stone tiles beneath her feet told her that her father and stepmother were following her.

"Valerie must have come back for some reason, Dad. Deirdre, would you call Rob and make my apologies for me? I'll have to take a rain check on drinks." She turned to her father, ignoring the worry that deepened the creases beside his eyes. "I'm sorry. But we have to go back to your office. Right now. And I want you to call the police on our way over. I won't let this go until you do. Valerie's dead.

"I'll show you."

Chapter Two

Using the beam of his flashlight to guide his way through the dark offices and hallway, the man with the long fingers paused in his work. Caution, more than curiosity, guided him to the shiny gold disk that had caught his eye. Squatting down beside the potted ficus tree, he picked up a small gold pin. Cheap, by the weight of it. He turned the trinket over in his palm.

Forsythe.

He couldn't quite place the name, but he'd file it away in the back of his mind until he could.

Before he straightened, he lifted his gaze, studying the view from this vantage point. Interesting. A place to see, but not be seen. If anyone was of the mind to do so.

He'd been assured that the 26th floor would be abandoned after 6:00 p.m. That the cleaning crew wouldn't arrive until ten o'clock.

Was the pin a result of sloppy housekeeping? Unlikely, given the money and expectations tossed around this place. Was it just coincidence that someone had lost this pin on this night—in this place with a camouflaged view of Cain Winthrop's office?

In his business, it didn't pay to count on coincidence.

Had there been an uninvited guest at their meeting? A witness who could destroy years of hard work and cost him millions of dollars in potential profit?

His pulse didn't quicken at the possibility; his heart didn't leap into his throat. He closed the pin inside his palm and stood. This could be a problem.

The question was, did he tell his partner?

Or did he take care of it himself?

A.J. TUCKED HIS NOTEPAD AND PEN inside his leather jacket and knelt down to brush his fingertips across the polished sheen of the mahogany floor in the executive waiting area. While Josh did what he did best, and handled most of the interview questions, A.J. had taken his time to walk around the top floor and study every posh nook and imported treasure of Cain Winthrop's state-of-the-art decor.

He wasn't thrilled with the mix of eagerness and melancholy he felt at returning to the expensively hallowed halls of the Winthrop Enterprises Building. What had he been—seventeen? eighteen?—the last time he'd been here? He'd come in to see his father while Antonio, Sr. worked the night shift, vacuuming carpets and buffing floors, doing the minor repairs that kept the building in working shape.

He'd come here to bum money off the old man. Probably for something stupid, like the cigarettes he used to smoke or gas for the car he drove too fast and wrecked too often.

He splayed his fingers across the cool wood and admired the exotic decor, wondering if any of this was his father's handiwork. Wondering how many times his father's footsteps had crossed this floor.

Wondering why he couldn't have appreciated his father for the man he was until it was too late.

Eighteen years later, A.J. had finally come back.

Not to pay homage to his father, but to investigate a homicide.

Customarily, though, when two detectives were summoned to the scene of a murder, there was usually a dead body involved.

A.J. rolled the kink from his bum shoulder and pushed to his feet, squinching his face against the three itchy stitches that closed the gash along his left cheekbone. If it weren't for the location, he'd probably appreciate the diversion of a call. Even an apparent wild goose chase like this one was turning out to be. After the week of desk duty he and Josh had been assigned to following the explosion last month in front of the Jazz Note—which had sent him to the E.R. and stalled out their investigation into the drug dealer murders—A.J. was ready for a little action.

But coming to the Winthrop Building after all these years, looking Cain Winthrop in the eye and remembering the last words his father had spoken about the man, left A.J. feeling unsettled rather than relieved to be back in the game.

Despite the hysterical tinge in Claire Winthrop's distorted voice, she seemed absolutely sure that she'd witnessed a murder here. Both times he'd asked her to relate her story, she'd been clear and vehement about her facts—and unable to explain why Winthrop's office was spic-and-span tidy, with nary a bullet hole, speck of blood—or a body—in sight.

It wasn't the first time someone had reported a crime in the Winthrop Building that evidence said hadn't taken place.

No one had believed his father, either.

Well, one person had. One person believed Antonio Rodriguez's story enough to kill him.

A.J. lifted his gaze up to the vaulted ceiling and pondered the odds of something like that happening twice in the same location. No wonder he didn't feel right in his skin on this one.

There were too many secrets in this place. Too many lies. World-class players walked these hallways, as well as invisible men like his father had been. His father deserved better than what he had gotten. He deserved the truth.

So did Claire Winthrop. A.J. could feel something funny going on here all the way down to his bones. He couldn't put his finger on it yet, but he trusted that instinct more than what his eyes told him.

"I'm gonna make this right," he whispered out loud. He didn't know if he was making a promise to his father or Claire Winthrop or to the powers that be.

His determination might not show on the outside, but it was a vow he intended to keep.

"I don't mean to make light of the situation."

A.J. tuned in to the conversation across the waiting room as Josh followed Cain Winthrop out of his office.

"But could your daughter be mistaken in what she saw? She *did* leave the alleged crime scene. The guard downstairs said she was the only one who checked in for the 26th floor. Without his pass key to override the lock, no one could take the elevator to the penthouse floor. Maybe she got off on a different floor and we're in the wrong place."

The white-haired millionaire shook his head. "Everyone who works on this floor has a pass key. They wouldn't have to sign in, even after hours. But Claire would. If she said it was the 26th floor where she saw something, then I believe her. She wouldn't make a mistake about that."

Josh asked the right question. "Is there something she

would make a mistake about? Is it possible this is a cry for some attention? Or the repressed memory of another crime?"

"She's been known to have an active imagination, if that's what you're hinting at, Detective." Winthrop shoved his hands deep into the pockets of his charcoal wool slacks. When he pulled out his left hand, he was fiddling with something at the end of his key chain. "Claire lost her hearing when she was three. To the same illness that claimed her mother's life. She had a very lonely childhood. I know she filled her time with books and stories she made up inside her head. Sometimes she'd get so lost in her imaginary world that it was hard to reach her."

"So you think she's making this up?" A.J. strolled over and invited himself into the conversation.

Winthrop narrowed his gaze, studying A.J. as intently as he had when they'd first arrived on the scene and introduced themselves. "Are you sure I don't know you, Rodriguez? You look damn familiar."

So he was a dead ringer for his father. If the man had a good memory, he might be able to make the connection. But A.J. wasn't about to give Winthrop any information that might color his answers or affect his cooperation. He came up with an honest response and steered him back to the interview. "No sir, we've never met. You were telling us about your daughter?"

The older man shrugged, his expression perplexed. "I can't imagine why she'd be making up a story like this now. Those episodes were years ago, when she was a child. Tonight she seems so certain. But it's impossible. Maybe I should have called a doctor instead of—"

A.J. sensed the man striding up behind him and turned

before he heard the gruff interruption. "Cain. I should have been notified if there's a situation."

"Whoa, buddy. Who are you?" Josh stepped in to deflect the verbal attack with an easy smile.

The man in the corduroy blazer and jeans matched Josh in both height and brawn. But there was nothing easy about the grim set of his pale gray eyes or the blunt cut of his hair. "Marcus Tucker, Chief of Security, Winthrop Enterprises. Who the hell are you?"

A.J. didn't hesitate to square off against the bigger man. "Rodriguez and Taylor, KCPD." He flashed his badge and nodded toward the bulge beneath Tucker's coat at the side of his waist. "You got a permit to carry that weapon, Chief?"

The big man's cheeks ruddied as he schooled his temper. A.J. braced on the balls of his feet as Tucker wisely pulled open his coat to reveal the Smith & Wesson he carried. At the same time, he slowly reached inside the jacket to pull out his wallet and show his permit and ID.

The man was legit. But A.J. never relaxed his guard and Tucker never answered his question. Instead, the security chief pointed a blunt finger at his employer. "I shouldn't have to hear about a shooting on the premises from my contact at KCPD." He thumped his own chest. "*I* should have been your first call."

"You have a contact at the department?" A.J. asked.

"I have contacts all over the world, Rodriguez." Tucker sneered.

Cain Winthrop patted the air with placating hands. "Relax, gentlemen. Marcus, please. There *is* no situation." He glanced at Josh and A.J. "More of a misunderstanding, I think."

The pale eyes narrowed. "Was there or was there not a shooting?"

A.J. answered before Winthrop could discount his daughter's story again. "That's yet to be confirmed. But if you really are the top dog in security around here, then I'd start with your man at the desk downstairs. At least three unknown parties made it to the top floor without him being aware of their presence in the building. And when Miss Winthrop asked him to assist her earlier tonight, he refused to leave his post."

Tucker swung his gaze to Winthrop. "Is that true?"

"That's what Claire said."

That seemed to blow a hole in the chief's malign-the-cops-and-save-the-day routine. "Warren's new. He's still green about how we run things here and who we answer to. I'll take care of him. Miss Winthrop's okay, right?"

Cain nodded, though he didn't look entirely convinced.

After what passed for an apology to his boss, Tucker huffed up his chest and pointed another finger at the two cops. "I want to be copied on your report. Anything you find out about crimes on this property or against anyone associated with Winthrop, Inc. comes through me. Understood?"

Idly, A.J. wondered if Tucker would miss that annoying finger if he twisted it off the end of his hand. He'd taken down bigger blowhards before.

Josh grinned and vented the sarcasm that A.J. held in check. "I'll run your request past Captain Taylor. If he gives the okey-dokey, I'll trot that report right over to your office myself."

"Just do your job, Detective. And let me do mine."

Tucker pulled out his cell phone and stormed back down

the hall the way he'd come. No one said goodbye. No one seemed to miss him.

"He's a charmer," Josh joked.

"He might be short on personality," Winthrop apologized, "but he's well-qualified to safeguard an empire the size of Winthrop Enterprises. I do business on six continents, and he oversees security for all of it."

Maybe Chief Tucker could handle men across six continents, but he'd done a lousy job making one young, frightened woman feel secure in her father's own office.

And maybe his father's death wasn't the only reason A.J. was still here an hour after finding out there was no crime at the alleged crime scene. Claire Winthrop had reminded him of his youngest sister, Teresa, the night she'd been mugged on her way home from work. That same shock was in her eyes; the fear was in every darting glance over her shoulder. Something had spooked the young lady. No matter what the evidence said, Claire was afraid.

Of what or whom didn't matter. He supposed it was the big brother instincts in him. Or maybe some sort of continual atonement for not being able to prevent or solve his father's so-called accident. But A.J. wasn't going to walk away until he was sure that Valerie Justice wasn't really dead and Claire Winthrop wasn't in any real danger.

"Do you need anything else from me, Mr. Winthrop?" Pulling on her lightweight trench coat, Valerie Justice's replacement waltzed out of the office and joined them. She'd introduced herself as Amelia Ward, and Winthrop said she'd come highly recommended from the temp agency from which he'd hired her for two weeks. "I can't find anything that's missing in either your office or Ms. Justice's. The files and the phone logs all seem to be in the same order she showed me this morning. I've contacted the airline and the hotel in the Bahamas, as well, asking Ms. Justice to call us as soon as she gets the message."

The new boss offered her a reassuring smile. "Good thinking, Amelia. I'm sure everything will be fine. I appreciate you coming in so late. I'll see you in the morning."

"No problem, sir. I'm going to head back home and finish watching that movie I rented." She tucked her auburn hair behind her ear and offered Josh a smile that was more than friendly. "Unless the police need me for something else?"

Subtle.

Josh made a point of adjusting the front of his jacket and showing off his wedding ring. "I don't think so, Miss Ward."

Rebuffed by the big, blond cop, she turned her hopeful smile on A.J. "Officer Rodriguez?"

Not his type.

"It's Detective." He tapped his pocket where he'd stuffed his notepad. "But we're good. We have your name and number on file, and if we need anything more we'll give you a call."

She didn't quite take the hint. "Please do. Good night, gentlemen."

With a nod, Amelia sashayed down the hallway. A.J. watched her leave, but he wasn't noticing the purposeful strut of her hips. Instead, he was marking off the distance in his head because, for several steps before she turned the corner to the elevators, she'd completely disappeared from his line of sight.

I hid behind the trees and aquarium. I could see him, but he couldn't see me.

Claire Winthrop's words replayed in his head, fueling his curiosity. Marcus Tucker had been tall enough to remain in view as he walked the length of the hallway. But the top of Claire Winthrop's head barely cleared A.J.'s shoulder. Was she tiny enough to pull off what she claimed?

Leaving Josh and Winthrop to wrap up their conversation, A.J. drifted back to the doorway of Winthrop's office. He rose up on tiptoe, trying to make himself as tall as the man in the black suit Claire had described. *Nada.*

Even looking straight at the circle of pots and furniture, she could have hidden and watched the office without being seen. Why give that sort of accurate detail if she wasn't telling the truth? Unless she was in the habit of hiding behind potted plants and spying on her father?

Though her handicap and slender, petite build added a delicacy to her appearance, Claire Winthrop didn't strike A.J. as a woman prone to childish pranks. Maybe it was the designer suit or the careful way she chose and articulated her words that made her seem more grown up.

Or not.

"Miss Winthrop?" His voice fell on empty air as he turned into the interior of Winthrop's office. Maybe the boss's daughter did make a habit of playing hide and seek. She was nowhere to be seen inside here, either.

But he could hear her—rummaging around, mumbling to herself—on the other side of Winthrop's sized-to-intimidate mahogany desk.

Hooking his thumbs into the front pockets of his jeans, A.J. circled the desk and was greeted by the elegant sway of a pink silk bottom. *Bello.* His initial amusement at finding the proper, ladylike heiress crawling beneath her father's desk heated with something decidedly male as he watched the graceful shape bob up and down.

He made no apologies for enjoying the view, but heeded the voice inside his head that reminded him he was here on business. Unlike Amelia Ward's obvious flirting, this was no practiced seduction meant to entice. It was just a nice butt. Okay, a very nice one. One that moved with an innate sense of rhythm that seemed to match the pulse beating in his veins.

Ignore it, Rodriguez. He blinked and politely looked away. Whatever pleasures he might enjoy with the opposite sex, he knew they wouldn't be with the daughter of the man his father had once cleaned toilets for.

"Miss?" Despite her assertion that she could hear some sound, thanks to surgery and cochlear implants, A.J. raised his voice. "Miss Winthrop?"

She seemed inordinately engrossed with running her fingers around every inch of the plastic chair mat beneath the desk. Needing her attention, A.J. leaned down and tapped her on the shoulder. "Miss Winthrop?"

As soon as he touched her, she let out a yelp, smacked her head on the desk and muttered something a little less classy than he might have expected from the dainty heiress. She spun around and landed on her bottom in a graceful heap, rubbing at the back of her skull where she'd conked herself.

"Sorry." He squatted in front of her, bracing one hand on the desk above her head. Her blue eyes looked a bit dazed. Guilt instantly replaced both curiosity and amusement. He gently touched her shoulder, needing to do something to make amends. "I didn't mean to startle you. Are you hurt?"

She glanced down at his hand as if the comforting gesture surprised her. When she didn't pull away or protest,

he trailed his fingers up the side of her neck and found skin
as soft as the silk she wore and a racing pulse. Or maybe
that was his own heart rate speeding up with awareness and
concern.

"Do you need to lie down?" Her gaze darted to his lips
and searched them as if she couldn't quite grasp what he
was asking. "Miss Winthrop?" he repeated, reminding himself to focus on first aid and not the way her eyes pooled
and darkened as if she was having a hard time staying focused herself. "Are you hurt?"

He reached behind her head to probe for any cut or
goose egg. As he gently nudged his fingers into her hair,
his palm brushed against the small plastic hearing device
hooked behind her ear.

The instant he touched the device, she blinked her eyes
clear and pushed his hand away. "I'm fine."

Rightly denied the contact that had slipped beyond professional, A.J. sat back on his haunches. But he never got
the chance to apologize.

Instead, Claire Winthrop moved her fingers in a frantic
dance that he knew to be sign language, even if he didn't
understand the words. Fortunately, she spoke out loud as
she signed. "I think the mats have been switched."

The discovery seemed to excite her, judging by the flush
of color on her cheeks. A.J. grinned in relief and rose to
his feet. This woman wasn't hurt—he'd seen that distant
focus dozens of times in his sisters' eyes. Claire Winthrop
was preoccupied. Obsessed, even.

A.J. offered his hand to help her stand. "What makes
you say that?" When she didn't immediately answer, he
waited until she looked up into his face and repeated the
question.

"This one is worn around the edges and has wheel dents." She pointed out the damage. "I'm sure my father's was replaced within the last couple of months when my stepmother remodeled his office. This one should still be smooth."

Interesting eye for detail.

Seemed he couldn't help noticing a few details himself. About his witness.

After a moment's hesitation, when he thought she might refuse his assistance or continue her explanation, she laid her fingers across his palm, giving him a glimpse of the evocative contrast between her creamy porcelain skin and his callused, olive-tinted hand.

To his surprise, there was nothing weak in her grasp as he provided an anchor for her to pull herself to her feet. The pink suit and delicate features had given him a mistaken impression of fragility. This woman possessed a sinewed strength from the tips of her fingers to the length of her shapely calves.

"Detective…Rodriguez?" She pronounced his name carefully, slurring the *R*s with subtle *W* sounds. And while he mulled over the husky softness of her voice when she wasn't desperate with confusion or shouting with excitement, she dropped her sky-blue gaze to the clutch of their hands. "Thank you."

She hadn't signed, but A.J. understood the prompt and quickly released her. He'd held on a shade too long to be proper; his grip had been a little too snug to be polite.

Bad move, A.J. He shouldn't be noticing anything about Claire Winthrop except her reliability as a witness—which at this point was, unfortunately, questionable. He shouldn't care one damn whether the pampered heiress was offended or turned on by holding a working man's life-scarred hand.

It wasn't like him to get distracted from his purpose, not by any woman. Certainly not by Cain Winthrop's daughter. The job didn't allow it.

He wouldn't allow it.

He stuffed said workingman's hands into the pockets of his jacket and told himself he hadn't noticed the subtle perfume that clung to her hair and emanated from the heat of her skin, either.

Needing his space before his brain got addled with any more pointless impressions, A.J. strolled to the center of the room and placed the desk between them. "So you think the killer—"

"—and his accomplice," she insisted.

A.J. conceded the addition to her scenario. "The killer and his accomplice rolled up the body in the plastic mat and disposed of it? Then they put a new one in its place?"

"Isn't that a realistic possibility to explain why Valerie's not here?"

"Assuming Miss Justice is as least as big as you are, how do you smuggle out a body without being seen?"

"It's a big building. They took the freight elevator or the stairs. Only the security lights are on inside. The sky's overcast so there's no moon outside. I don't know." Her shrug was an easy enough sign to read. So was the quick snap of her fingers. "But we should be able to check the mats."

When she breezed past him and headed out the door, A.J. wondered if he was being polite or just plain crazy for following her and joining the search. At Claire's pace, it didn't take long to inspect every office on the floor to discover that there were no chair mats missing from beneath any of the desks.

He could almost feel her disappointment at a good idea

refusing to pan out. Her frustration was such a tangible thing in the stiff set of her shoulders and crossed arms that he wanted to say he believed her story, even though the possibility of a woman being shot to death in Cain Winthrop's office seemed more remote by the minute.

"How many offices are in this building?" he asked, knowing he didn't have enough of a case here to warrant pulling any manpower off the Slick Williams murder and other homicides for an extensive room-to-room search.

"Hundreds." She tipped the point of her chin at him, her blue eyes blazing. He recognized *that* look from his sisters, too. "And, yes, I'm sure I have the right room."

She looked about as dangerous as a kitten, all huffed up and ready to spit in self-defense. A.J. respected her right to a temper, but couldn't help smiling to himself at the notion she looked more cute than ferocious. "That wasn't what I was thinking, *amiga*."

Tiny fine lines appeared beside her eyes as she frowned. "What?"

She hadn't understood him. *"Amiga?"* Reading lips in English was amazing enough. He supposed translating a foreign language on top of that would confuse most people. "It's Spanish. It means *friend*."

"Oh. *Amiga*." She said the word again, touched her own lips as she repeated it, giving A.J. the feeling she wasn't most people. She'd just expanded her vocabulary and wouldn't miss that word again. "I'm bilingual, too."

"You seem to communicate just fine."

Her pale cheeks colored at the compliment. "It helps when someone really listens."

Meaning there were others who didn't listen to what she had to say? A.J. raised his guard a notch against his growing admiration for the woman. Maybe she had more of a reputation for making up stories than her father had indicated. Or maybe, like his own father had once told him, *Winthrop will ignore the truth if it doesn't suit his purpose. Or he'll change things to make them fit his truth.*

As a smart-ass teenager, A.J. had asked his father what he was smokin' to come up with that deep thought. Antonio, Sr. had shoved his only son up against the wall and warned him to watch his mouth. Maybe if he listened a little better, instead of putting so much noise into the world, *he* could see the truth. If he heard the truth, if he championed it, then men like Cain Winthrop and his *compadres* at Winthrop, Inc. would lose their power to control and ruin other people's lives.

His father, who had never once resorted to violence with his children, had been trying to tell him something important. But A.J. shrugged him off, called him *loco* and worse, ignored his warning and sped away in his muscle car.

It wasn't the first time his father had tried to teach him how to be a man.

But it was the last time.

Though A.J. knew his father's car, even as a burnt-out skeleton in the police impound lot, the coroner had needed dental records to identify his father's remains. His mother had needed a sedative, his sisters had needed a shoulder to cry on and he had needed to grow up and become the man his father wanted him to be.

He was still working on that last one.

With little more than a blink to betray the depth of guilt and hurt he buried inside him, A.J. shoved his hands into the pockets of his jacket and tried to hear Claire Winthrop's truth.

"Your father doesn't listen to you?" he asked.

Claire's cheeks paled again, giving him the real answer. "So what *were* you thinking, Detective? About the offices?" she asked, defending her father by refusing to condemn him.

A little spark of anger kindled deep inside A.J., disrupting the Zen-like sense of calm that kept his temper in check, his priorities straight and his desires under control. How could a father ignore his own child? Dismiss her when she needed his support? Antonio, Sr. never had.

But he was years beyond giving vent to angry words. His personal opinions were irrelevant to the investigation, anyway. So he did what he did best. He played it cool and let the witness and the facts take the investigation where it needed to go.

He shrugged off any awareness that he'd gotten too personal with his questions. "I was thinking more along the lines that your killers stashed the body somewhere else until they could come back and move it later."

Her eyes followed the movement of his lips, then lit with hope. "The supply closet."

He'd checked the supply closet earlier. No dead assistant.

But she was already hurrying across the reception area to a black steel door. A.J. followed at a more deliberate pace. Claire Winthrop wasn't looking for bodies. She was back to finding what she thought was the missing chair mat.

A.J. turned on the light for her and helped her move some chairs to uncover two plastic mats stacked on their sides against the wall. Her toes tapped an impatient rhythm as she tried to transform the items into a clue.

He tried to help. "Any idea how many are supposed to be in here?"

When she didn't answer, he realized she had her back to him and hadn't heard the question. As soon as he touched her shoulder, she spun around. Oh man, this was killing her. He could see the frustration carving squint lines beside her eyes. He could read what it was costing her to keep from screaming out loud in the tight set of her mouth.

"Who would know how many mats are supposed to be in here?" he asked.

He was fascinated with the way her eyes followed his lips whenever he spoke. It was an intimate connection that made him want to keep talking, that made him want to study her lips with equal thoroughness.

But Claire Winthrop was all about finding answers, not making a play for a world-weary homicide detective.

"Valerie would know. Or the chief maintenance engineer."

Bam. Finally, the wake-up call he needed. *Maintenance engineer.* No matter how she sugarcoated the term, Claire Winthrop was the daughter of a multimillionaire while he was the custodian's son. He had real crimes to solve, real victims to protect. A real world to live in.

He was done playing. It was late, he was tired and he was a damn lonely son of a gun for wasting even one moment feeling whatever the hell he was feeling for Claire Winthrop.

A.J. drew back the front of his jacket and hooked his thumbs into his belt, giving Claire a clear look at his guns, his badge and the seriousness of making a false report to the police. He needed the truth from her and he needed it now.

"How long were you gone tonight, Miss Winthrop? From the time you allegedly saw the murder to the time you returned to the 26th floor with your father?"

"I didn't *allegedly* see anything." Her temper spiked,

then dissipated just as quickly. "I don't know. I didn't check my watch until I got home. Maybe two hours. Maybe less."

Was that enough time to completely erase a crime scene? Or just enough time for a needy young woman to perfect an elaborate lie?

He waited for her to turn off the light and close the closet door behind her. "Since there's no body for us to look at, maybe you could tell me more about this man with the gun you saw?"

"I've already given a physical description to you and Detective Taylor."

"Tell me again."

"So you can catch me in a lie?" she challenged. Her probing eyes locked onto his.

Definitely not as fragile as she looked.

A.J. pulled out his notepad and pen to add credence to his request. "So I can find some truth to back up your claim."

Her defensive posture sagged on a weary breath.

"All right. One more time." He fell into step beside her and went back to Winthrop's office. "How tall are you, Detective?" she asked, turning to face him inside the doorway.

"Five-ten."

"Then I'd say this man was about six-one or six-two. He had hair as black as yours, longer, combed back. But his skin was pale. Almost sallow-looking. And there was acne scarring all over it." She closed her eyes for a moment, as if replaying the scene in her mind…or reviewing the details of her story. When her eyes sprang open, he was reminded again of just how blue they were—like a clear spring sky. "His suit and shirt were black, and his clothes fit as if they had been personally tailored for him. The man had money. But then I suppose professional hit men make—"

"Hit men?" A.J. slapped his notepad shut. His attention flashed back to the murder of Ray "Slick" Williams at the Jazz Note. That had been a professional job, not the work of some penny-ante thug guarding his territory. KCPD had even issued a profile on the type of man they were looking for.

Tall. Well-dressed. Probably wearing dark clothes to blend in with the shadows. Armed and extremely dangerous.

Hell. Had she read about Slick's death in the papers? Had he been about ready to buy into a crime because her story reminded him of his father's claim? Because her pretty blue eyes and articulate mouth stirred up a few hormones?

Being played for a fool didn't ruffle his feathers. Feeling any kind of attraction to the woman playing him did. "What do you know about hit men, Miss Winthrop?"

He wondered if she could pick up subtle nuances in vocal tones, or if he'd revealed something in his expression. Her shoulders went back and she crossed her arms in a classic defensive posture. "You don't believe me."

"There's nothing here to corroborate your story." This woman needed some help. But not the kind a cop could give her. "There's no sign of forced entry. No sign of struggle. No blood. No body."

But she wouldn't let the damn farce die. She paced the room, still searching for a way to make her story stick as she began to speak and sign again. "I could go down to your office to look through some mug-shot books. Or talk to a sketch artist. I have classes in the morning, but I could come in right after that."

Sure. Waste some more of his time.

But the taunt never left his lips. Instead, the phone on Winthrop's desk rang. On the second ring, Claire touched the receiver, as though using the vibrations to verify whatever sound she must have heard. "Daddy?"

It rang again before Cain Winthrop dashed in and picked up the receiver. "Winthrop here." His blue eyes nailed Claire's, warning her to pay attention. "Yes. I'll accept the charges."

The older man reached out for his daughter. He smoothed the hair across her crown, practically patting her on the head as if she was still a child. Then he smiled. "Thank God," he said into the phone. He wrapped his arm around Claire's shoulders and hugged her to his side. "Sweetie, everything's going to be okay. We can go home and forget all about tonight."

Her complexion blanched to a shade beyond pale as Cain delivered the truth A.J. had been pushing for.

"It's Valerie. She's alive and well and calling from Nassau."

Chapter Three

"Hey, I hear you caused quite a ruckus at the office tonight, Pipsqueak."

Claire dutifully stopped halfway up the cream-carpeted staircase to endure her stepbrother Gabriel's teasing. *Pipsqueak* had never been her first choice in the nickname department, but compared to six feet four inches of tall, dark and daunting, that's about where she measured up.

She'd always had to make up the difference in attitude. "Bite me, Gabe."

Clutching her purse and shoes in one hand, she trudged on past him in her stockinged feet. He quickly reversed his descent and backed up the steps ahead of her so she had to crane her neck to read his lips and continue the conversation. "It was that bad?"

Claire puffed out a frustrated breath. "I've been completely discredited by KCPD. Dad wants to send me to a spa to rest because he thinks I'm having some kind of breakdown. I broke Mom's pearl necklace. And Detective Taylor was friendly enough, but Detective Rodriguez…"

Detective Rodriguez what? How had her subconscious mind intended to finish that sentence?

He made her pulse beat a little faster because he always

seemed to be watching her with those unique golden-brown eyes? He entranced her with his beautifully sculpted lips, whether arched in friendly amusement, parted with concern or tight with disbelief?

Did the Latin detective linger in her mind because he was an older man? Mature? Experienced in life the way she'd never been allowed to be? Or was it because the jolt she felt at the simple touch of his hand was more intense than even the most passionate kisses she'd tried to share with Rob?

Heck. Rob and *intense* didn't even belong in the same sentence together. A. J. Rodriguez was everything Rob Hastings was not. Danger personified, judging by his compact strength and the stitched-up wound beneath his eye. Black leather and cold steel. No wasted movement. Deliberate in his speech.

Was she upset with A. J. Rodriguez for dismissing her claim? Or for revving up her dormant libido before he dismissed her?

"What did the detective do?" Frown lines had formed between Gabe's dark eyes, as if he was assessing the need to bring a few choice words or even legal action against Detective Rodriguez.

Thinking it best to keep her observations to herself, she stopped beside Gabe on the landing. She had plenty of other things to be upset about tonight. She didn't need her pseudo-big brother to overreact. "He didn't do anything. I started the evening on such a high note and then all this mess happened. I was just looking for a scapegoat to pin my frustrations on."

Her excuse seemed to appease his sense of family honor. He relaxed by straightening his tie against his starched collar. "The good news is that Valerie's okay, right?"

But Valerie *wasn't* okay. Claire raged against the futility of trying to convince anyone to believe the impossible. "If she's in Nassau, then what did I see in Dad's office tonight?"

"Apparently, nothing."

"I want that to be true, Gabe. But I know what I saw."

He lifted one eyebrow in an arrogant arc and shook his head. Dressed to close a deal, Gabe buttoned the jacket of his pin-striped suit and dismissed her like everyone else had. "You know, Claire, this game you're playing is probably upsetting to Cain on two levels. He's not just worried about you, but now he's got to have some doubts about Valerie's well-being. She's been his right hand at the company for a lot of years. Losing her would be like losing a part of himself. So give it a rest, okay?"

Though it clearly wasn't his intent, something in Gabriel's words triggered an idea that might help this all make sense. "Did Valerie have access to all of Dad's files? Did she know about his current negotiations?"

"She *does* know about them." Gabriel emphasized the present tense with a nod. "So does the rest of the board. You want to kill us off, too?"

"This isn't a joke."

"The hell it isn't." Gabe had moved beyond big brother into company man mode. He clutched her shoulders and hunched down to look her in the eye. "You need to forget this fable. We have a business to run. We have deals on the line, new hires to consider. Valerie's on vacation. She's safe. Now let it go."

Valerie knew the company inside and out. She knew her father's secrets and the family's history. There had to be a motive in there somewhere for killing her.

"I'm not trying to hurt Dad," Claire insisted, latching on

to Gabe's wrist and giving it a squeeze. If she didn't love her father so much, she might have already accepted what everyone else believed. "I'm worried about him. That man said there were other people on his list. What if Dad's in danger? What if you are?"

Gabe straightened with an exasperated smirk. "First, Valerie's dead, and now you're trying to knock off Cain and the rest of the family, too?"

"No—"

"I tried. I give up." Gabe leaned down and kissed her on the forehead before releasing her. "Goodnight, Pipsqueak. I have a meeting to get to."

Dismissed. Again.

"At this time of night?"

He was already loping down the stairs. At the bottom, he turned to doff her a salute. "I didn't say it was a business meeting."

Ah, yes, the life of one of Kansas City's most sought-after bachelors. "Have fun."

"I intend to."

As he strode out the front door, Claire summoned half a smile and headed for her room. Her stepsister Gina was probably out on the town, too. Seemed Claire was the only Winthrop heir who didn't have a life. No wonder everyone was so ready to believe she'd make up a horrible story about their dear friend and loyal employee being murdered.

Claire set her purse on the chaise at the foot of the canopy bed, then neatly placed her shoes inside her closet. She'd bet good money that A. J. Rodriguez had a life, too. Between his work and those poet's eyes—set in the middle of a face carved by classic Mediterranean ancestry and chiseled by real-world experience—his life would definitely be full of interesting adventures and relationships.

Her life wasn't full of anything.

She unbuttoned her skirt and stepped out of it as it slid to the floor. She tossed her jacket onto the bed, unhooked the shell she wore and slipped it over her head. The hose went next. Then the pearl earrings.

The pearls. "Oh, gosh."

Claire dashed back to the bed and dug inside her jacket pocket to find the strand of pearls and loose beads she'd managed to retrieve. She felt guilty at seeing the legacy from a mother she barely remembered in such sorry shape.

She pulled a velvet pouch from her jewelry armoire and slipped the pearls inside. Setting the pouch beside her purse she made a mental note to take them to the jeweler's shop tomorrow after school.

School!

Claire silently cursed the powers that be for ruining the good memories of what had happened earlier that night. In all the chaos, she'd completely forgotten to tell her father about the Forsythe School's offer to hire her as a full-time counselor. She'd forgotten to tell him about the honor the students had given her, naming her as their favorite paraeducator.

Hoping to recapture even a smidgen of the excitement that had thrilled her so earlier, she picked up her jacket to look at the pin. And frowned.

"Where…?"

She checked both lapels—looked at the material and crunched the pink silk beneath her hands to verify what her eyes were telling her. "Where's my pin?"

She dug into the pockets, wondering if she'd forgotten

that she'd taken it off earlier. Only, Claire didn't forget things.

"I want to wear it tomorrow to show the kids."

She dumped out her purse next, checked the bag of pearls. Then she was on her hands and knees, retracing her steps across the plush carpet. She was nearly frantic by the time she pulled a robe on over her slip and ran barefoot through the hallway and down the stairs. She ran past the door to the study where her father would be working or reading at his desk while Deirdre briefed him on the final plans for the party she was hosting tomorrow evening.

Nothing.

Claire rubbed her fingers against her temples, too late putting up a fight against the tension that throbbed inside her head. She didn't hallucinate murders. She didn't lose gifts. She didn't forget things.

Her Volvo.

Cinching the sash of chenille at her waist, Claire darted outside, down the steps misted with rain. The bricks were cold beneath her bare feet as she dashed around to the detached multicar garage beside the house. She punched the entry code into the keypad and hurried inside as soon as the lock released and the door went up. Inside, she switched on the light before closing the door to the night and the rain.

Claire wiped the dampness from her face and hurried past her father's Range Rover and stepmother's Lexus. She crossed the empty stalls where Gabe and Gina parked their cars and climbed in behind the wheel of her sensible beige Volvo. She turned on the interior lights and searched it from top to bottom.

"Where are you?" she muttered to herself, feeling her

self-assurance spinning beyond her reach. She crawled over the seats into the back and dipped her fingers into the seams between the cushions, checking impossible places for the missing pin she'd worn on her lapel.

Nothing.

Tears pricked the corners of her eyes and she gave in to the urge to lay her face in her hands and cry in weary frustration. She mentally retraced her steps from the time she'd signed her thank-yous at the podium during the banquet to the moment she saw that bullet hole in the middle of Valerie's forehead.

In between, she distinctly remembered pinning that gold medallion onto her lapel. There was no way around it. She'd have to go back to her father's office and search for the pin. And if she couldn't find it there, then she didn't even want to consider the possible explanations for its disappearance.

She didn't hallucinate. She didn't forget things.

Claire screamed at the thump on her car window and jumped halfway across the back seat. The flashlight beam shining in her face blinded her to the man outside. She slid her back clear against the opposite side as the door opened and a pair of khaki slacks and a gunbelt came into view.

"Miss Winthrop?" She heard the buzz of sound, but waited for the man to lower the light and for her startled fear to unstop her senses before she could see his lips and decipher his words. "Miss Winthrop? Is something wrong?"

Gradually, the words and the face of the estate's nighttime security guard came into focus. Claire pressed her palm against her racing heart and released a deep breath of recaptured sanity. "Aaron." She said the black man's name, reassuring him that she knew where she was and whom she was with. "You startled me."

"Sorry about that." He turned off the flashlight and hooked it back on his utility belt. "What are you doing out here?"

"I lost something. I was looking for it."

She became aware of the bare skin beneath her palm the same time Aaron's questioning gaze swept down to the thigh-bearing hem of her crumpled-up robe. Right. She might talk a good game, but sitting there crying, half-dressed in the back seat of her car in the middle of the night wasn't going to convince anyone that she wasn't crazy.

Quickly tugging her robe down to her knees and pulling the collar tight around her neck, Claire scrambled out of her side of the car. "I lost a piece of jewelry. A small gold pin."

He stood and closed the door, speaking to her over the roof of the car. "I haven't seen anything like that. But I'll keep my eyes open for it."

Claire summoned a smile to thank him. "Well, good night."

She felt the vibration of his footsteps through the concrete floor and knew he was jogging up beside her even before his fingers brushed her elbow. It was just a polite gesture to get her attention, but Claire flinched all the same and spun around.

"Sorry." He nodded toward her right ear. "I guess you couldn't hear me."

Guess she didn't know how to relax when the only person who might believe she'd witnessed a murder was the murderer himself.

But she felt a twinge of guilt as Aaron tipped the bill of his uniform cap in apology and held both hands where she could see them. "The rain's coming down a little harder now, miss. Let me grab an umbrella and walk you back to the house."

"That's not necessary. I—"

He opened the garage door to a curtain of gentle spring rain. She'd get soaked to the skin wearing what little she had on, and would no doubt have to explain that to her father. He'd be just as worried about her catching cold as he was about her making up gruesome stories of murder and cover-ups.

"Besides," Aaron explained, "Chief Tucker called and said I should keep an extra close eye on you tonight."

Security Chief Tucker? Claire frowned. "Why?"

"I didn't ask. I just obey."

Had her father ordered his security staff to watch over his handicapped daughter? Didn't anyone believe she could take care of herself? Think for herself? When would she be old enough for her family and friends and employees to start thinking of her as a capable, competent woman?

Resigned to the practicality of Aaron's suggestion, Claire linked her arm through his when he offered it and huddled against him beneath the umbrella. She fell into step beside him, her toes splashing through the puddles. "Thanks."

He said something back to her, but the rain muffled the sound receptors in her ears. She wasn't paying much attention to Aaron, anyway. Claire was more aware of the uneasy sensation that tickled the back of her neck and raised goose bumps across her skin.

Someone was watching her.

Maybe it was just the hypervigilance of the Winthrop security guard. Maybe it was the metaphoric weight of her family's smothering protection. Maybe it was the chill of the rain itself.

Aaron walked her up to the front door and stood on the

porch until she closed and locked the door behind her. Dutifully deposited back inside her sheltered ivory tower.

Claire shivered as she clutched her robe around her and climbed the stairs.

The feeling of being watched from the darkness never left her.

A.J. IGNORED THE FIRST TWO RINGS of the telephone to finish scrolling down the list of Winthrop Enterprises' holdings on his computer screen—Australia, Brazil, Italy, Mexico, Japan...

"Maldición."

He muttered the curse under his breath. Something about last night's events at the Winthrop Building still didn't feel right to him. So when he was done typing up the facts in his report, he'd done a little extra poking around. It had become almost a hobby of his over the years—digging up bits of information about Cain Winthrop and his import-export empire. He never knew when some nugget of info would bring him half a step closer to uncovering the truth about his father's death.

But reading through the corporation's annual report was turning into information overload. The business paid out a fortune through customs, but apparently took in nearly three times as much in profits. Jewelry, furniture, cars, collectibles—even exotic animals made the list of items the company transported across international trade lines. It was too much to make sense of in one sitting, with one set of eyes.

He'd have to get Banning to take a look at the report to see if Mr. Logic could narrow down the facts and figures into something that might actually prove useful—like a dirty little secret that money, time and power couldn't quite hide, or the name of a security specialist who terminated employees. Permanently.

But the detailed research would have to wait. Banning had gone to lunch with his wife Kelsey. Funny how newly-weds always seemed to have time for each other, no matter how busy their respective schedules might be.

A.J. looked across to the empty desk facing his. Hell. A man didn't have to be a newylwed to make time to spend with the woman he loved. His partner, Josh Taylor, had been married two years, had two little girls and still grinned like a lovesick puppy at the mere mention of his wife's name. He'd left by 11:30 to accompany his wife on some sort of newborn health checkup.

He couldn't afford to feel envy at his friends' happiness, though. What would be the point? A.J. didn't have time for a wife or a girlfriend. He'd date, get a little lovin' when both parties were willing, but he'd never get serious. His job demanded too much of his time; his work entailed too many risks.

So, while he saved some poor woman from certain heartbreak by remaining unattached, A.J. sat alone in a sea of empty desks.

He'd lost count of the rings and thoroughly depressed himself before he picked up the receiver. "Rodriguez."

"A.J." Maggie Wheeler, the desk sergeant with a body like Xena and the face of a farm girl, topped A.J. by two inches and worried him with the shadows in her hollow eyes.

"What's up?"

"There's a deaf woman here to see you. I told her you were on your lunch break and she said she'd wait. But she's pacing the floor by the elevators, so I thought it might be something important."

A.J. slid his gaze across the floor toward the main desk. Even though his view was blocked by several carpeted partitions, he could picture the petite blonde with the delicate features and surprisingly solid grip wearing a path in the floor on the other side. "Claire Winthrop?"

"Yeah." Maggie's surprise was evident. "You expecting her?"

"No. But send her on in."

"She's a pretty one, A.J. Is there something you're not telling—?"

"No." He cut off the friendly curiosity he heard in her voice and hung up. Maggie wasn't a gossip, but it would only take an innocent remark and Josh's sense of humor to create rumors of a whole sordid new love life between the taciturn cop with the stitches on his face and tattoos on his back and the virginal young heiress.

He knew how to put up with the teasing, knew how to put a stop to it if he needed to. But he had a feeling that Claire Winthrop wouldn't appreciate the joke.

A.J. stood, tucking his black T-shirt into his jeans and combing his fingers through the top of his thick, short hair. Not that he wanted to impress the prim and proper heiress. But it might be nice if he didn't scare her away.

Maggie appeared beside the partition that separated the elevators and check-in desk from the Fourth Precinct's Detectives Division offices. She pointed him out, and an instant later a flash of black slacks and gold jewelry hurried around the corner.

What the hell?

A.J. shifted onto the balls of his feet, his protective radar buzzing on full alert. Claire's blue eyes were wide and dark, boring into his. Her mouth was pinched into a thin line. Her fear was a palpable thing, a force he felt clear across the maze of desks between them.

"Claire?" There was no polite *Miss Winthrop,* no *How may I help you?* Was she hurt? Had she located a bloody chair mat? "What's wrong?"

He slipped around the desk to meet her partway and she ran right up to him. He planted his feet and grabbed her by the elbows to steady her as she latched on to his upper arms and curled her fingers into cotton and skin. She shook him, clung, pleaded with her hands as she rattled off her greeting. "I can't get anyone to listen to me. I looked all over my father's office. I talked to the custodial staff, nagged the office assistants. I've checked at home. At school. Everywhere. We have to find it."

"Slow down. Find what?" The body? Give it up already. He'd talked to Valerie Justice on the phone himself.

"The pin my students gave me. The Forsythe School's name is engraved on it. I can't find it anywhere."

He cupped his palms around the knit sleeves of her jacket, and the flex of muscle and bone underneath. "You want me to find a missing pin?

"No… Darn it!" She thumped his shoulder with a painless fist.

A.J. resisted the urge to grin at her ladylike curse.

"*He* took it! The hit man."

He saw little that was ladylike in the drill of her gaze.

A.J. quickly released her, damning his errant radar for tuning in to her frightened innocence instead of her crazy lies. "Miss Winthrop, I have serious work to do." He peeled her hands from his biceps and pushed them down to her side. "I will type up your deposition for you to sign, but it won't go any further than that because there's nothing to investigate."

As much as he wanted to find a connection between his father's death and her report, the facts just weren't there to make it happen. He turned away, wondering how far a man should trust his instincts and when he should stick strictly to the facts. Clearly, his dealings with Cain Winthrop's daughter had muddied his perception of what was real and what wasn't.

But Claire was nothing if not relentless. She snagged his arm and slipped in front of him before he could sit. "Please. Detective Rodri…Rod…" She caught her breath to slow her speech. She was struggling with the *R* sounds in his name. "Detective Rod…ri…guez."

Hell. Why not? "Call me A.J."

Her lips trembled with a sigh as she watched his own mouth say the words. "Thank you." Her breathing seemed to relax, her grip on him loosened and her fingers began a slow, no doubt unconscious massage across his skin. But those blue eyes never looked away. "Please, A.J. If he figures out that that pin belongs to me, he'll know I was there last night. What if he comes after me? Just because everyone else thinks I'm crazy, doesn't mean he won't believe me."

This wasn't about a missing piece of jewelry. The woman was truly scared. And that got to him more than it should.

A.J. tilted his face to the ceiling, still debating the wisdom of trusting instincts over facts. Claire braced herself against his arms and stretched up on tiptoe—to keep his mouth in view and the lines of communication open, he supposed.

Conceding to her need to see his beat-up features, A.J. looked down into her upturned face. *Pretty* wasn't exactly the way to describe her. The short nose was cute, the line of her jaw striking. Her lips, as expressive and finely drawn as her graceful hands, landed somewhere closer to sassy. There was barely a blemish on her creamy skin, not a wrinkle to be seen.

She was an interesting combination, refined by pure class. A smart man would never get tired of noticing the details about her.

Her hair had fallen back, exposing a pair of sapphire stud earrings and the hearing aids she wore in each ear. It was a sobering contrast, as bleakly evocative as the colors of their skin. Claire Winthrop was a rich woman, with every opportunity in the world at her fingertips. But she was oh, so vulnerable. She probably had dozens of people on the family payroll, lined up to help her, to protect her, to listen.

But she didn't trust any of them. She'd come to him.

She needed him.

The realization was both potent and humbling. And guaranteed to cause him trouble.

"A.J.?" His gaze flicked back to her mouth. "You're staring."

"I'm deciding."

MAN, HE WAS GOING to regret this.

Instincts won out over facts.

It was something about her hands, clutching at him with a needy force and sensuous artistry, he admitted, that seemed to seep through his skin and touch him deeper inside. Her words might not have been convincing, but her hands had finally persuaded him.

Claire Winthrop needed his help.

Without turning his head from the list of street contacts

he was analyzing, A.J. shifted his gaze to the glass that separated the bustling offices from Interview Room 3. Claire sat at the long table inside, surrounded by a stack of mugshot books. She'd left the blinds and door open, claiming she needed lots of light to see. But he wondered if she simply wanted a clear view to the world outside, so she wouldn't feel quite so isolated. She'd been working methodically for over two hours without complaint, slowly making her way through every page in every book until she found a familiar face.

He didn't really expect her to find anything. The majority of outstanding warrants were on computer now. And as the records division kept adding more information on convicted criminals, parolees and suspects to the KCPD and State of Missouri databases, some of the hard copy books were even getting to be out of date.

But one thing he remembered his father trying to teach him was that work kept the mind occupied. Busy hands and engaged minds created hope, and hope kept fear at bay. If looking at the faces of hundreds of convicted and suspected murderers from across the country made her feel useful instead of victimized—if doing *something* gave her any kind of hope—then he'd let her sit in that room all day long.

Definitely the hands, he mused, forgetting the list on his desk.

Even when she wasn't signing, Claire's small hands conveyed her emotions. The precise way she folded her fingers around her disposable coffee cup showed determination. When she flicked them through her chic cut of golden hair and rubbed her temples, he thought he detected frustration. She carefully grasped each page and turned it as if the stains of those men's crimes could be commuted through her fingertips from a photograph.

Some people might think he was reading more into Claire Winthrop's body language than a veritable stranger could. But he'd survived for years on the streets—first as a troublemaker, then as a cop—because he *could* read people. If he studied them long enough, he could almost tell what they were thinking. He could tell if they had secrets, if they wanted something. Sometimes, he could almost read their minds.

He could tell Claire was scared—of reality or of her own imagination, he wasn't ready to bet on yet. But she felt safe here at Precinct headquarters. She felt useful. She had hope.

And if hanging around here gave her a reprieve from the nightmares that haunted her eyes and made her cling to him, then she could stay. She could stay until she realized she didn't belong in his world. She needed to be at home in her mansion, with her designer clothes and heirloom jewelry. Where *Daddy* and his armed security team could listen to her stories and make her feel safe.

In the meantime, he'd do his job. He'd taken Claire's statement about the missing pin and added it to his report. He'd talked to Detective Banning and gotten the computer whiz to start digging up everything he could find on Winthrop Enterprises. A.J. had filled in his partner, Josh, on Claire's most recent concerns, tended to his other cases, and deflected the curious questions about the woman he'd sequestered away in Interview Room 3.

A wad of crumpled up paper pinged him in the middle of the forehead. "Yo, *amigo*."

A.J. glared across the adjoining desks at the amused smirk on Josh Taylor's face. That ass was having way too much fun minding *his* business. He was the senior partner here. Where was the respect? "Who taught you how to be a detective, *amigo*?"

Josh didn't miss a beat. "You, my friend. But you trained me to be your partner, not your replacement." He tossed a stack of manila folders across the desk. "Now quit staring at the babe through the window and help your partner do some work."

Babe? Is that how he saw Claire Winthrop? What happened to *victim? Crazy lady? Pampered rich kid? Heiress?*

A.J.'s gaze took a guilty swipe at the interview room. She was up and moving now, stretching her legs, arching her back and pulling her clothes taut over that sweet little rump.

Madre dios.

A.J. quickly looked away. She might be young, but she sure as hell wasn't any kid. He wished he hadn't noticed. Wished Josh hadn't put his subconscious thoughts into words. Now he couldn't deny them.

Claire Winthrop *was* a babe.

He hadn't been studying her with any detached, deductive analysis. His body knew the truth, at any rate. He'd been checkin' her out.

Though his reaction had already given him away, A.J. pretended that he'd only responded to what any red-blooded American male would see. "She's okay."

"She's more than *okay.*"

"I was graduating high school the year she started kindergarten."

"She looks all grown up to me."

Josh was looking? Thankfully, A.J. had a tight rein on his emotions, or else he might have snapped something about Josh already having a beautiful wife of his own, and to keep his eyes to his own damn self, before he realized the big *bastardo* was just trying to get a rise out of him.

A.J. wouldn't play. He forced out a calming breath. "You know where I come from. Check out her daddy's address. She's from another planet as far as I'm concerned. I'm just doin' my job."

"It's okay to be human like the rest of us."

"Uh-huh." Josh's good-natured gibe was a reminder that he wanted to keep his association with Miss Winthrop in the business-only department. A.J. thumbed through the stack of files on his desk. "You find something?"

Josh followed his lead and let the subject drop. "Check 'em out. I got my brother-in-law at the FBI to fax us rap sheets on alleged enforcers in the drug trade who've popped up on the radar across the country. Maybe if we could place one of them in the Kansas City area—"

"—we could find out who's trying to eliminate the competition and move their business into town."

They spent several minutes poring over the information, setting aside rejected files and putting together a list of suspects whose profile indicated the ability to kill by multiple means. Stabbing. Car bomb.

The smell of rich, dark coffee steamed past A.J.'s nose, alerting him to the woman at his side. Claire pushed aside a notepad and set a fresh cup of the hot brew on his desk. "I was getting myself a refill and thought you might like some." She held out a second cup. "Josh?"

His partner stood and reached across the desks to accept the gift from her outstretched hand. "Sure, thanks."

A.J. ignored Josh's less-than-subtle wink and angled his face toward Claire. "You didn't have to do that."

"No, but it's a nice gesture. You're welcome, by the way."

Who knew a person could sign sarcasm? It had to be the hands.

A.J. apologized for his rudeness. "Thank you. How do you sign that?"

Claire touched the fingers of her right hand to her lips and moved them forward, saying the word as she signed it. A.J. spun his chair to face her, touched his right hand to his mouth and imitated her. "Thank you."

But instead of approval or correction, Claire's eyes widened, focused at a point beyond his shoulder. Her cheeks blanched lily-white. A.J. clasped his hands around her slender waist, thinking she was about the faint. "Claire?"

Her gaze came back to his. She placed her hands over the top of his and held on as she forced her attention back to the open file on his desk.

"That's him."

Her fingers chilled against his skin. A.J. reached for the straight-backed chair beside his desk and sat her down before her legs gave way.

"Claire?" He glanced over his shoulder to see what she saw, then slipped his palm up to cup her trembling jaw. "God, you're like ice. Talk to me."

"That's the man in black."

A.J. scanned the bio at the bottom of the page. Dominic Galvan. Nicknamed "The Renaissance Man" of enforcers for his intellect and the variety of methods with which he killed his victims—making it virtually impossible for the authorities to profile him and track his MO. A man who, according to his case history, cared more about his perfect record of hires and hits than about the wealth he'd accumulated over his twenty-year career.

Perfect record.

No witnesses.

He snatched the grainy black-and-white photocopy and held it up for Claire to study one more time. "*This* is the man you saw at the Winthrop Building?"

She nodded.

He crumpled the picture in his fist and squeezed her knee. "Please tell me you're making this up. That you pointed out that picture because you're too exhausted to look any further."

"He's the man I saw in Dad's office." She started signing again. "Why? Who is he? You're scaring me."

A.J. tossed the picture across his desk to Josh. His partner had already risen to his feet in concern about Claire's reaction. He read the same information. "Son of a bitch."

Josh's reaction said it all.

A.J. suddenly had a very sick feeling that everything Claire Winthrop had told him was true.

She'd witnessed a murder.

"Josh. Call the D.A.'s office. We might have a case again."

"I'm on it. I'll call Sam and put him on alert, too." His brother-in-law worked in Kansas City's FBI field office and could mobilize an entire network of support if Galvan truly was in town. "What about her?"

A.J. leaned forward, touched her cheek, looked into her eyes and gauged the truth. Instinct beat facts.

"I believe you," was all he said.

Chapter Four

If she closed her eyes and used her imagination, Claire could almost hear the notes of Debussy and Strauss floating through the mansion.

Personally, she preferred the drama of an Aaron Copland suite or Tchaikovsky overture. Even rap music suited her tastes better. With its strong rhythms and unapologetic use of bass instruments, she could actually feel the music. She could imagine herself back on the stage at one of her ballet or modern dance recitals.

She pushed up onto the toes of her gray silk pumps and followed the imagined beat into the foyer away from the pungent smoke filling the conservatory. After dinner, her father, Gabe, and their guests who were interested, had retired to the music room to sample Japanese wines and the cigars from Cain's collection. She'd stayed long enough to be polite, but even with twenty-three years of proper decorum bred into her, she had to get away. She needed fresh air. Quiet. Something more meaningful to talk about than how many days she thought the spring rains might last.

She needed a reprieve from the uniformed guard who shadowed her every move. Aaron Barnette was a nice enough employee, but his presence set her apart from the others at the party and reminded her of the threat that might really be surrounding her.

A.J. wouldn't let her leave the precinct office that afternoon until he'd had a terse, to-the-point discussion with Marcus Tucker regarding the danger she could be in, the danger that might be closing in on her family. The security chief still wasn't buying Claire's story about Valerie being murdered, but he knew Dominic Galvan's name. His reputation. If the police suspected there was any connection between Galvan and the Winthrops…

Chief Tucker had shown up thirty minutes later to escort her home personally. Her father had greeted her with a hug and walked her upstairs. Then a guard had appeared outside her bedroom door. She saw more of Tucker's men patrolling the grounds. When the shift changed before their dinner guests' arrival, Aaron had become her new best friend.

Claire should be feeling better, now that her family was finally concerned about her claim. But all she felt was singled out, as if the spotlight shining on her had just gotten bigger and brighter.

To drown out the unsettling thought, she hummed louder and louder until she could feel the sound vibrating in her throat, and danced down the main hall toward the front of the house and the grand staircase. Her goal was her room, a bath, her bed—and putting an end to this relentless night.

As Claire rounded the corner to the foot of the staircase, two hands grabbed her from behind and hauled her back into the dim recesses beneath the stairs. Her startled yelp was muzzled by a hand over her mouth, and recognition of the familiar, cloying scent of a man's cologne.

"Rob!" The instant her toes touched the floor, she spun around and smacked her hand against Rob Hastings's laughing chest. "You startled me."

"Hey, blondie." He seemed disproportionately amused by an action that left her pulse pounding and her breath coming in short, deep gasps. He nudged her back against the gilded trim that decorated the white paneling and cornered her between his body and the staircase. "Grabbing you is the equivalent of jumping out and saying *boo* to your sister."

One, Gina Gunn was technically her stepsister, and two, if Gina enjoyed having her heart stopped periodically as some kind of teasing foreplay, then that was her business. And three—she flattened her palm at the center of Rob's chest and pushed him back a step—he'd have better luck wooing *her* with insults.

"I was on my way upstairs. With a major headache," Claire added for good measure. She straightened the neckline of her beaded silk jacket and tugged her hemline down to her knees, in case he saw a hint of leg or cleavage as an invitation to touch her again. "This really isn't a good time for me."

He slipped his arm behind her waist and pulled her hips against his. Apparently, he didn't think he needed an invitation. "But we haven't had a private moment all night."

"Rob." She wedged her arms between them. "I said 'No.'"

"You said it wasn't a good time," he corrected, lifting her chin so she could still see his bland green eyes and understand him. "Have you seen Gina?"

He put his arm around her and asked about another woman? He just wasn't scoring any points in the charm department. But her father had hired Rob for his logistics skills, not his charm.

She might have thought he needed to speak to Gina on a business matter, but Rob was just a little too ebullient for her to believe he was thinking business right now. "She went with Deirdre and some of the guests to tour the house. As far as I know, they're still upstairs."

Aaron appeared beside them as Claire tried to twist out of Rob's grasp. The security guard rested one hand on his billy club, the other on his gun. "Miss Winthrop, is everything all right?"

Rob shook his head and huffed out a saki-tainted sigh. "No problem, officer. Now get out of here."

Aaron stood his ground. "That's not your call, sir." His gentle brown eyes sought out hers. "Miss Winthrop?"

She briefly considered asking Aaron to show Rob the door. But it was just Rob, after all—six feet of business wizardry, buffed nails and boyish humor. She appreciated that Aaron was so conscientious about watching over her, but tossing one of her father's brightest young executives out into the rain probably wasn't the type of entertainment he wanted at his dinner party. With a reassuring nod, she sent Aaron back to his post. "He startled me, that's all. I'm fine. I'll be heading up to bed soon."

Once Aaron was out of earshot, Rob grabbed her by the shoulders and backed her up against the paneling again. He was flushed all the way up to the receding line of his cropped brown hair. "I remember when the hired help knew how to keep their mouths shut and look the other way."

"He's just doing his job."

"Well, I'm not giving a recommendation to Tucker if that guy ever needs one. I like to put the moves on my girl without an audience."

Rob made sure she saw the words before he leaned

down and nuzzled the side of her neck. Hmm. Nothing. Except the urge to offer him a breath mint and write out the lesson plans for her classroom visits next week.

Claire pressed her lips together to keep from giggling at the uncharitable thought. At the Fourth Precinct office this afternoon, A. J. Rodriguez had done little more than brush his fingers across her cheek and her body temperature skyrocketed. When *he* looked into her eyes and spoke, she had a hard time concentrating on anything *but* him. And his upper body did more for plain black T-shirts than any million-dollar ad campaign could ever do for Rob's Armani suits.

She squared her hands on the lapels of said suit and pushed. "Rob. Is there something you wanted? You said you were looking for Gina?"

"Gina can wait."

He leaned in to kiss her full on the mouth and she shoved harder. "Rob! Please. I don't want—"

"I know, I know." With a gut-deep sigh, he finally pulled back from his romantic overtures. "We have guests."

Technically, he was a guest, too. And though he'd made himself more at home than she'd like, Claire gave up the idea of making an early night of it and snatched at the excuse he offered. "We should get back to them."

Despite his answering smile, he made no move to let her pass. "I don't think your father would mind if we took a little time to play. I was looking for someone to share the good news with."

"What good news?" Right now, the only news she'd really appreciate hearing was that Dominic Galvan had been found—either dead, or trapped in some remote prison in Antarctica.

But since Rob didn't know the details of what she'd seen last night, she waited for him to speak. "Cain really liked the work I did with Gina setting up the nationwide distribution of our foreign wines. He even mentioned a promotion. I'll be sitting in at the board meeting tomorrow."

"That's great news. Congratulations."

Her feelings were genuine, but she wanted him to know that good wishes were as far as she intended to go with her congratulations. Claire signed to emphasize her words. "I appreciate your friendship, Rob. I'm glad to see good things happen for you. You've earned—"

He wrapped his smooth hands around hers to interrupt the message. "Come to dinner with me tomorrow night and let's celebrate. We'll go to the Adagio."

"I can't." She didn't want to stray too far from home or work and Chief Tucker's security detail right now. Not until A.J. could tell her something definitive about Galvan's whereabouts. Besides, joining Rob at Kansas City's newest four-star restaurant sounded like a serious date. "It wouldn't be right. I know Dad introduced us, and that you're hoping—"

"Do you have that school thing tomorrow night?"

Claire pinched her lips together to hold on to her patience. Did the man have to interrupt her every time she tried to explain that they would never be more than friends? She pulled her hands free. "The end-of-the-year awards banquet? That was last night."

She'd invited him to go with her. He'd turned her down, said he had an engagement he couldn't get out of.

"Good. Then you're free tomorrow night."

He missed the point.

The metallic sound of the doorbell buzzed inside her

ears, and Claire danced with the opportunity to escape. "I'd better get that."

He moved in closer. "Someone else will."

She backed against the banister railing. "This is *my* house."

"I could pick you up right after school. What's the name of that place? Freeman? Foreman?"

"The Forsythe School," Claire snapped, putting up her hands to block his chest from getting any closer to hers. "It's a private school for the hearing impaired. I've worked there a whole year now. I talk about it all the time, not that you listen! You've never visited it once. You've never asked about the work I do. You do *not* need to pick me up. I am *not* going to dinner with you. It's called the Forsythe—" her temper vanished on one shocked breath "—School."

Claire curled her fingers into her palms and broke contact. Saying the name out loud, without knowing where her pin was, without knowing who'd gotten a hold of it, made her feel as if she'd just shouted her name to the world. *I belong to that pin. I saw a murder. Dominic Galvan, come and get me.*

And then Claire became aware that she and Rob weren't alone. Her stepmother, stepsister and two of their Japanese guests had stopped halfway down the grand staircase and were looking over the railing. Deirdre's arched brow said it all.

Claire had been yelling. At a guest.

"I'm sorry." She wasn't sure whom she was apologizing to. Rob? The Japanese gentlemen? Her stepmother?

To make everything worse, her father had rushed out of the conservatory. "Is everything all right?"

Gabe, with Cain's oldest friend and Winthrop vice president, Peter Landers, followed behind him. Cain Winthrop stood in the hallway and stared at her with a look every bit as lost and guilt-ridden as the night they'd sat in the hospital and the doctor had told them she would never regain her hearing, but that there were procedures and therapies his money could buy which would make her life almost normal.

She barely remembered life any other way. For her, being motherless and hearing impaired *was* normal. Only, she'd never been able to convince him that she was okay with that. She'd never been able to convince him that she didn't hold him responsible for her handicap or her mother's death.

I'm okay, Dad. She made no sound; she simply signed the words.

Rob grinned at her, as if his indulgence could erase her humiliation and the pain she felt for her father. "So is that a yes or no to dinner tomorrow?"

He hadn't heard a word she'd said, hadn't clued in to a single bit of body language that screamed, *Go away!* She'd never slapped a man in her life, but if the gathering crowd wasn't already too curious, there would have been a first time.

"No."

A familiar sheen of thick black hair appeared beside Rob. "I think her answer's clear enough."

More startled than she by A.J.'s unexpected arrival, Rob spun around. "Who the hell are you?"

Claire's breath rushed out through a smile of relief. A.J. Where had he come from? Why was he here? She was almost ashamed to admit she really didn't care. "It's good to see you again," she signed.

Finally, someone who took her at her word. Someone who listened.

"I'll deal with you in a minute." Rob dismissed A.J. and blinked his eyes clear to focus on Claire. "Friday, then?"

A.J. spoke so she could read his lips. "She has plans."

He held out his hand to her. Claire hesitated only for a moment. Strong, sandpapery fingers closed around her own, and A.J. pulled her out of the corner. He smelled of rain-dampened leather and easy confidence, and Claire had no problem standing closer to him as he squared off against Rob.

"This doesn't concern you. Get out of here before I call security," Rob demanded.

"I wouldn't."

Rob seemed taken aback by the abrupt response.

A.J. was actually an inch or two shorter than his personally tailored opponent. But his compact body was in better shape than Rob's, and his brain was stone-cold sober. His refusal to be baited seemed to give Rob second thoughts about demanding anything from him.

Even Claire backed off half a step at the spooky calm that settled around A.J.'s broad shoulders. She would have pulled away entirely if he hadn't subtly altered his grasp to keep her at his side. He laced his fingers with hers in a grip that zinged along her sensitive palms, giving her the inexplicable feeling this timely rescue had a little bit of personal mixed in with whatever professional motives had brought him here.

Someone must have said something across the room— her father, no doubt, judging by the way Rob snapped to attention. Then his chin bowed in the slightest of nods. "Detective Rodriguez. My apologies."

"Hastings."

"What's going on?" Deirdre's glare was especially unwelcoming. She smiled to her foreign guests, then marched down the stairs. "Cain, do something about this."

Gina seemed to be the only one who didn't mind the arrival of the party crashers. Her stepsister's dark eyes glittered as she studied the new arrivals. A sultry pout settled on her lips as she winked and gave her a thumbs-up. "Nice work, Claire."

Claire's cheeks flushed with heat. Surely Gina didn't think that she and A.J...that he would... Laying a cool hand against her cheek, Claire ducked her head and reminded herself that A.J. was an earthy, experienced man of the world and she was...well...neither of those things.

But the chaos around her quickly took her out of her own self-conscious thoughts. Gabe argued with the seriously unsmiling blond man at the front door; Rob paced the foot of the stairs and mumbled under his breath. Peter Landers tried to play peacemaker, asking about lawyers and telling Cain not to worry. Deirdre seethed and six curious Japanese gentlemen pointed and chatted amongst themselves at the unfolding soap opera.

Without warning, that same sensation she'd felt last night when she'd come in from the garage shivered along Claire's spine. Someone was watching her. Maybe it was her imagination, creating spies where none existed. Or maybe it was the finer development of her nonauditory senses that made her hyperaware. She wrapped a second hand around A.J.'s and swung her gaze around the room, looking for that pair of eyes that would be colder, more hateful than the rest.

But these were her friends and family—they all loved her. They protected her. They weren't Central American drug enforcers with a list of murders to complete. They had their own arguments to fight, their own embarrassments to contend with, their own curiosity to appease. The only person actually looking at her was Rob, and she wasn't sure whether that pained look of resentment qualified as a threat or a pout.

Still, she couldn't shake the creepy feeling.

A.J. squeezed her fingers and rubbed his thumb across the back of her knuckles, as if she'd transmitted her anxiety into his hand. It was nothing more than a reassuring caress, low between their bodies, hidden from the rest of the guests. But the rough pad of his thumb injected warmth beneath the surface of her skin and short-circuited the fearful chills that had tried to sink their teeth into her.

He tugged on her hand. "There's someone I need you to meet."

Claire roused herself from her suspicions long enough to fall into step behind him. "Did you find Galvan?" she whispered hopefully.

The golden eyes told her no. "I wanted to see for myself if Marcus Tucker had made the arrangements I suggested for your protection." He eyed the uniformed guard at the door. "I'm glad to see he's beefed up security around here."

"He always posts extra guards when we host a party." Something flashed in those golden eyes, the first glimmer of emotion she'd seen. Her answer didn't seem to please him. "But Aaron is specifically assigned to me."

"Good." He masked his expression and invited himself into the circle formed by her father, Deirdre, Peter Landers, Gabe and the blond man. "Claire, this is Dwight Powers, one of our assistant district attorneys. He's taken a particular interest in your report."

"Mr. Powers."

"Ma'am." He swallowed up her right hand in a grip as strong and unyielding as the rest of him appeared to be. "I'm sorry to interrupt your evening, but Detective Rodriguez and I agreed that the sooner we could get this under way, the easier it will be to build our case."

Claire frowned. "What case?" She looked at Dwight, then to A.J. The comfort she'd felt from the touch of his hand suddenly became a trap. She extricated her fingers from his grip and hugged her arms around her waist. "Did you find Valerie's body?"

"No," the A.D.A. answered. His stormy, gray-green eyes took account of everyone around the room before settling on her father. "If we could have some privacy, sir?"

"We're all family here." Dwight's gaze returned to the stairs and Cain looked over his shoulder and bit back a curse. Their guests. He turned to his wife. "Deirdre, do you mind?"

"Cain!" She gestured to A.J. and Dwight, as if they should be the ones asked to leave. But her father couldn't be swayed. Turning with a huff on her high heels, Deirdre gathered the Japanese visitors. "Shoshiro? Hoshi?"

She spared one withering glance at Claire—for the ruination of her party, no doubt—before following them into the dining room and closing the door.

"Rob," Cain ordered. "You don't belong here, either."

"But I care about Claire as much as anybody here," he argued.

"Go."

Rob protested his dismissal by forcing a kiss onto Claire's cheek. "If you need anything, you call me."

Claire clenched her fingers to resist the urge to wipe the mark from her face. There was no need to answer him; Rob had already turned his defiant look on his boss. "I'm part of this business, Cain. And one day I will be part of this family."

Claire wasn't volunteering to help him with that goal.

"C'mon, loverboy." Gina's French-tipped nails closed around Rob's arm, practically petting him in an effort to soothe his temper. She tugged him back toward the dining room. "Don't worry, Cain. Rob and I will start talking up some of our shipping ideas with Watanabe's men."

"Thank you, Gina. I'm glad to hear someone making sense around here."

A simple nod to Aaron got him to step out onto the porch and close the door behind him. When Dwight asked about Peter, Cain shook his head. "He stays. Peter's my top adviser. He's been with me longer than anyone in the family." He held up the document in his hand. "Now tell me what this court order means."

"Very well." Dwight's deep chest expanded in a calming breath, as if he was about to present himself before a judge. "Dominic Galvan is wanted for murder in five states and four different countries. It goes without saying that when he shows up in Kansas City, both the district attorney and the police commissioner want to find him and put him away."

"And how does this quest of yours affect my family?" Cain asked.

"We believe we can force Galvan to reveal himself."

This was good news, right? But Claire was almost afraid to ask. They wanted something from her. That's why A.J. was here, why he'd played Sir Galahad to help her escape Rob's overzealous attentions, why he'd held her hand as if he cared. "How?"

"We're opening an investigation into the murder of Valerie Justice."

Dwight's announcement sparked another flurry of arguments.

"Where's your forensic evidence?" Gabe challenged. "Where's your body?"

Peter took a more rational approach. "Cain said he spoke to Valerie last night." He pulled his glasses down his nose and looked over the top of them at A.J. "Didn't you speak to her as well, Detective?"

"I spoke to *someone* on the phone." A.J. canted his hips to one side and pulled back the sides of his jacket, revealing his badge as he hooked his thumbs beneath his black leather belt. It was a relaxed stance, but the pinpoint focus of his golden eyes seemed to put her father on guard. "All I have is Mr. Winthrop's word that the woman's voice belonged to Ms. Justice. I've never met her and there's no recording to verify her identity."

Claire sidled closer to her father. Her lips parted in automatic defense of anyone who called him a liar. They snapped shut just as quickly under the intensity of A.J.'s brief glance. *She* was the one, in essence, calling her father a liar. They couldn't both be right. He couldn't have spoken to a dead woman.

Had the voice on the phone been Galvan's accomplice? And why wouldn't her father recognize the woman who'd worked at his side for so many years? Was he ill? In trouble? Covering for someone? Would he lie to discredit her, just to make the problem go away?

The same way he tried to make her handicap go away?

Confusion twisted her stomach into knots. She retreated from the circle of family and friends who had always taken such perfect care of her. To some of these people, she was still a lost, lonely little girl. To some, she was window dressing, a decorative prop. To some, she was…oh God. Those golden eyes, filled with apology, had locked on to hers.

Bait.

The knot in her stomach slid halfway up her throat and choked her.

She'd trusted A.J. Became strengthened by his belief in her. She'd wanted to do something useful with her life, serve a purpose. He wanted to use her, all right.

"You're launching an investigation based on rumors," Gabe accused.

"For God's sake, Cain," Peter interrupted, already pulling his cell phone from inside his gray suit. "Call Valerie and put an end to this. I'll have Marcus fuel up the company jet. We'll fly her home ourselves."

The debate around Claire escalated and overlapped and blurred into one big buzz of indistinguishable noise. Pain spiked through her head, the result of pure stress and fatigue. She was suddenly awash in a sea of faces with moving lips that flapped too fast and made no sense. It was as if her hearing implants had shorted out. Or her patience. Or her sanity.

She jerked and cried out at the warm vise that cinched itself around her left wrist. She saw it before she recognized it. Darker skin against her own. A.J.'s hand.

His voice seemed crystal clear.

"I need to speak to your daughter for a moment. Police business."

HER FEET were moving. A.J. opened the front door and ushered her out into the damp night air. The stocky frame of Dwight Powers slid in behind them to block the door and, with a firm click of the latch, no one tried to stop them.

Chilled drops of rain hit Claire's cheek and nose, waking her senses as though she'd been in some kind of trance. The light spring shower spotted her jacket and stuck dots of silk against her skin. A.J. nodded off Aaron's concern and pulled Claire down the steps behind him. They jogged into the moonless shadows beneath the fir trees that lined the driveway.

"What are you doing?" Claire twisted in his grasp and tried to stop, but her heels sank into the rain-softened dirt. One shoe caught and plucked itself off her foot. She tumbled forward and smacked into A.J.'s back. Ignoring the instant impression of heat and hardness beneath the damp leather, she pushed away. "Where are we going? Where are you taking me?"

He said something as he glanced over his shoulder.

"What?" Claire crushed a handful of butter-soft leather in her fist and yanked on his sleeve. In the moment he slowed, she grabbed his jaw between her hands and forced him to look at her. The stubble of beard beneath her palms was as soft and prickly as the pine needles beneath her stockinged foot.

"It's too dark out here to read your lips when you're moving like that," she protested. Her elbows sank into his chest as she leaned in closer. His hands settled at her waist, scorching her beneath the thin layers of silk that separated them. Blinking the rain from her lashes, she focused on the droplets of moisture that clung to male lips that were so close to her own, close enough to kiss.

If she'd be so bold.

If she didn't think he'd laugh at her naive efforts.

If she wasn't so frustrated with every male on the planet, so confused about truth and lies that she wasn't sure she could even trust what her simmering body thought it wanted.

"Claire."

His lips said her name with elegant artistry. The subtle movement of his jaw teased her sensitive palms. The rain dripped from the trees between them, but she no longer felt it. A.J. pursed his mouth and touched his tongue to the rim to wipe away the gathering drops, and her own lips parted with a hopeful, needy sigh. His fingers shifted their grip at her waist, dipping lower, over the swell of her hips. Anticipation gathered in the tips of her small breasts and made them feel larger, heavier. Cotton and man expanded before her eyes as A.J. took a deep breath of his own. He was pulling her closer, dipping his head. She stretched up on tiptoe. Lights flashed behind her eyes.

He was pushing her away. He straight-armed her, setting her flat on her feet. "We need to get out of the rain."

The mood was broken.

Frustrations of different sorts, and a dose of major embarrassment made her temper short. She felt the rain now. "Then why drag me outside to get soaked?"

"You were about to jump out of your skin in there."

"So bullying me around out here is the cure for being bullied around in there?" She propped hands on hips still warm from his touch and tilted her chin to hold his probing gaze.

"*Madre dios.*" A.J. swiped his hand down his face, taking the moisture and her errant fantasies with it. Then he snagged her hand and pulled her along behind him again. "C'mon."

He cut through the trees to a low-slung sports car that was just as black and shiny as his hair. Without the canopy of branches to shelter them, the rain fell harder, plastering her hair against her scalp and wetting the beaded silk atop her breasts. He opened the passenger side door, palmed the crown of her head and helped her climb inside.

"Where are we go—?" The slamming of the door cut short her demand.

A.J. disappeared through the row of fir trees. Moments later, she was still peering into the rain-shrouded darkness when something moved in the shadows and he reappeared as if he'd materialized from the night itself. He jogged around the hood of the car, opened the door and dropped into the seat behind the wheel.

"Here." Before she could ask a thing, he held out her rescued shoe like a peace offering. "I tried to wipe off the mud."

The cover was stained but the shoe was intact. Claire wrapped her hand around it and accepted the gift. "Thanks."

"I don't know how you women walk in those things."

"I don't know how other women do it, but dancers walk on their toes, so I'm used to it. And I can use the extra height."

He raked his fingers through his hair, sluicing away the water and leaving it outlined in a haphazard disarray against the darkness outside his window. "You're a dancer?"

"Trained for years in ballet and modern dance. Now I teach an occasional class and do it for exercise."

"That explains the muscles."

He'd noticed muscles on her? Was that good or bad? How did she respond to that? And why did her fingers itch to smooth his hair back into place?

After several moments spent dripping and trickling in

silence, Claire still couldn't seem to catch a normal breath. Though she suspected her nerves had more to do with the moisture-intensified smells of leather and man filling the car's interior, she still asked, "Um, do we have to sit in the dark?"

"Sorry." A.J. stuck the key in the ignition and started the car. The engine hummed to life with a powerful purr. Claire felt the smooth vibrations like a light, gentle, completely thorough massage. Once he turned on the dome light, she finally began to relax. Before she knew it, she'd sunk back into the seat that was every bit as comfortable as her reading chair.

She cradled the wet shoe in her lap and trailed her fingers across the supple black leather that covered the armrest. "Nice car."

"She's no limousine, but—"

"It's a nice car." She repeated the compliment more succinctly, wondering if he hadn't heard her, or if he didn't believe she could appreciate the obvious workmanship and painstaking care that kept the interior so sleek and spotless.

"She's all right. It's a Trans Am. My dad owned one like it about twenty years ago. I've been fixing it up."

So the car was well-loved, too. It was a surprisingly sentimental admission for a man of so few words to make.

But they hadn't come out here to talk dancing or cars or family history. Claire crossed her arms beneath her breasts, shivering at the cool air from the vents breezing across her wet clothes. "Are we going somewhere?"

"We're here." He reached across the dashboard to turn on the heat. The blast of warmth was a shock to her skin, and a riot of goose bumps popped up in visible protest along her exposed forearms.

Those golden eyes missed none of her body's instantaneous reactions to the temperature changes. With a curse of something she couldn't quite make out—more Spanish, perhaps—A.J. shifted in his seat. Moving with concise efficiency in the car's compact interior, he peeled off his jacket and draped it around her shoulders. He tucked it shut across her chest, then retreated to his side of the car. Turning sideways in his seat, he rested one arm on the wheel and one on the bent knee he propped on the center console between them.

"Better?" he asked.

Claire found herself in a strange new world inside the Trans Am. The overhead light reflected off the windows and ignited glints in the wet muss of his hair. Her body temperature rose as the air from the heater filled the car. His jacket, shaped by broad shoulders and years of wear, and still warm from the heat of his body, cocooned her like a soft embrace.

"I'm better." She wasn't just talking about the temperature. "It was getting a little crazy in there, wasn't it?" Huddling deeper inside the leathery scents of car and jacket and man, Claire realized she wasn't signing. She hadn't even been paying close attention to how well she was articulating sounds. "Can you understand me okay?"

He nodded.

She stayed huddled in the comfort. "I appreciate the rescue, but there are dozens of rooms in the house. We could have stayed dry if you wanted to find a quiet place."

"I needed somewhere private to talk. And I like to stick with what I know. Where I'm comfortable. This was the closest piece of personal space I could think of."

"Oh."

The vague sense of unease triggered by his words intensified as she focused in on the black steel gun strapped inside the holster on his waist. He wore a smaller weapon, with a shiny silver handle, on the opposite side of his belt. The badge and muscles and lack of a smile in between reminded her that this was no friendly stroll through the rain, no secret rendezvous to explore the sensual awareness still sparking along each nerve ending.

"You want to talk about Dwight Powers treating Valerie's disappearance as a murder investigation." She closed her eyes, but the memory of the bullet hole in her friend's face was already chilling her from the inside out. "You think I'm a handicapped, sheltered rich girl who doesn't know anything about the real world and how cruel it can be. You want to know if I can handle the questions, the spotlight."

She tried to look out her window, but in the reflection, she realized she couldn't escape the probing omniscience of A.J.'s golden eyes. "You want to know if I'll stick to my story. If I can live with the pressure from my family to make this whole situation just go away."

He brushed his fingers beneath her chin and turned her to face him again. "Say the word, and we don't do this. I'll talk to Powers and we'll keep you out of it."

Wasn't the investigation as much his as the assistant district attorney's? Claire couldn't hear the inflection of his words, but she squinted to catch the meaning in his expression and interpret it. There was something more here. "But?"

He released her chin and boldly reached inside the jacket to find her hands and pull them in between his. "Galvan may already be after you."

His blunt answer stunned her for a moment. But as he

leaned toward her across his knee and gentled his stern expression, Claire realized on a sobering breath that she already half believed him. How else could she explain the feeling of being watched? "You think he knows that *I'm* the one who saw him?"

"Maybe he found that pin, or his accomplice did. It wouldn't take long to connect the school name to you. You reported the crime, you've been to the precinct office, you've talked about it with your family. He might not know what you saw, but he'll figure out soon enough that you were there. That's not neat and tidy, the way he likes things."

An invisible weight bore down on Claire's shoulders. "So instead of innuendoes about there being a witness, you want to throw my name in his face?"

With a single finger, A.J. reached up and smoothed a sticky tendril of damp hair off her cheek. He tucked it behind her ear, brushing against the speech processor there, exposing the receiver inside her ear. Claire caught and held a self-conscious breath. He glanced at the device in curiosity, but didn't avert his eyes in polite embarrassment or pull away.

"I don't like putting innocent people in the line of fire. Powers thinks that if we're as bold about this as Galvan is, it will force his hand. He'll have to move more quickly than he likes. Hopefully, Galvan will make a mistake. We'll see him coming, and we'll be ready."

The safety of anonymity. The guilt of doing nothing. Twenty-three years devoted to family duty and easing her father's concern. The untapped desire to make a difference in the world.

Claire's breath slowly eased out. "What do *you* think?"

"I think he's right. Galvan won't leave town as long as there are loose ends." A.J. withdrew his touch and sat back, as though he didn't want to influence her decision. But those eyes, and the potential danger of what he was suggesting stayed with her. "The plan is to let Marcus Tucker use his fabled security team to keep an eye on you while KCPD raises a ruckus and waits for Galvan to show his hand."

"I have a question."

"Ask. Anything."

"What if you don't see him coming?"

Chapter Five

The man stood in the darkness and peered through the rivulets of water streaking down the windowpane.

"Yes, I see them." He spoke into the cell phone in one hand, and in the other, he flipped the cheap gold Forsythe pin between his long fingers.

That detective was smart. He hadn't turned on the interior light of the black Trans Am until the two had done enough talking and breathing and who knew what else to fog up the windows and blur the view of anyone who might be watching. He listened to his partner's concerns, knew he had a right to be worried. But he wasn't. Yet.

He'd love to hear what was going on inside that car. A lecture? A plea? A seduction? The man in the darkness almost laughed aloud at that one. Claire Winthrop didn't have it in her. Her father's bank account was the sexiest thing about her, and cold, hard cash, tempting as it was, couldn't warm a man's bed at night. Her proper, virginal ways couldn't, either.

But his partner had no sense of humor.

"She's daddy's little girl. I don't think she has the backbone to go through with it. And the D.A. has no case without her."

The man on the phone disagreed in two languages.

"I don't care what you like—you're not in charge of this operation. I pay you, not the other way around." Though his partner did have a point. They'd been at this for too long to risk discovery. "Let me do what I can to discredit her first."

He moved closer to the window, but kept himself hidden in the shadows of the unlit room. The windshield in the black Trans Am was clearing. Rodriguez had done some gallant thing with his jacket, and Claire was no doubt eating it up. Was it just Kansas City's finest taking care of one cold, wet citizen? Or was there something personal going on between them? He'd have thought a woman like Gina Gunn would be more the detective's type.

The man at the window smiled in remembered satisfaction. Now there was a woman with real fire running through her veins.

"The deal with the police officer? I don't know. He does seem familiar. The name, too. I already have my men putting together a dossier on him. We'll figure out his game."

No, he wasn't worried.

"I've used Winthrop Enterprises with scarcely a hitch for a number of years now." Gathering his patience on a controlled sigh, he continued. He didn't like to explain himself. "Valerie tried to change the arrangement on us. Whether she thought she was doing it for love or money makes no difference. She wasn't in one hundred percent, so she needed to be out." He squeezed the pin in his fist, bending it with his strength. "I won't let some stupid girl stop me from getting what I want, either."

His partner made a suggestion, and his face creased with a wicked smile. "You are a clever son of a bitch, aren't you? Yes, I can arrange that. But nothing else for now. Give me another twenty-four hours to handle this without drawing any more attention to the project. We'll still be on schedule to eliminate the others, and no one will be the wiser."

And after twenty-four hours? "If nothing changes, we'll add them both to your list."

A.J. ZIPPED INTO the dark blue coveralls that masked his gun and purpose, and adjusted the prescription-free glasses on the bridge of his nose. Picking up the tool box he'd borrowed from the custodian's closet, he went out to the granite steps that led up to the Forsythe School's main entrance and began replacing one of the iron hinges that anchored the retractable security gate.

The students were arriving now, drawing up to the front walk in yellow school vans, being dropped off by parents who foisted umbrellas and jackets on them for later in the day. To A.J.'s surprise, the students were just as noisy and talkative as any other group of young teenagers. Though their hands flew as quickly as their tongues, they were happy to reunite with friends they hadn't seen for several hours, eager to complain about homework assignments, anxious to share about boys and gossip and their favorite team.

He stooped over his work, keeping his back to the two plainclothes security men sitting in their parked car next to Claire's beige Volvo. He had to give Marcus Tucker his props for assigning a dedicated security team to watch over her, but the two suits could have done a better job of blending in. They were drawing plenty of attention from protective parents and curious students alike, who clearly knew every vehicle in the parking lot and were bound to notice an unfamiliar face on the premises.

Besides the undercover detail, he'd spotted a uniformed guard stationed outside Claire's office, and a second one patrolling the hallways. A.J. had done his homework; he knew Tucker's men had foiled kidnappings in foreign countries. They kept the paparazzi and disgruntled employees away from the Winthrops and their associates. He knew that no serious harm had come to any member of the family. They were well-qualified to guard the heiress.

But A.J. felt a personal stake in keeping Claire safe while his partner Josh and several other detectives from the Fourth Precinct went to work locating Valerie Justice's body and flushing out Dominic Galvan. Claire's name was bound to surface in the investigation. And because Galvan was out there somewhere, looking for the witness who had seen his face, A.J. was here.

He wanted Galvan and the secrets at Winthrop Enterprises to be revealed. But to do that with a clear conscience, he needed Claire to come out of this in one piece.

He'd promised her last night in the car. The same car that still smelled of lavender and class from the woman who'd been inside it with him. Just like his jacket this morning retained her scent. Just like his memory refused to shake the unprofessional images that stayed with him from last night.

Standing outside in the shadows and rain with Claire, A.J. hadn't been thinking like a cop. He hadn't been thinking of her as a witness who could break a case wide open for him, hadn't been thinking of her as an heiress who was out of his league. He hadn't been thinking of her as a kid who was more than a decade younger than him, and twice as innocent about the world.

He'd been thinking of Claire as a woman. A damn sexy, irresistible woman.

Yeah, he'd been riled at the sight of her backed into a corner by Rob Hastings—trying to be nice while keeping her feisty temper in check. A temper which, it seemed, she didn't have any trouble unleashing on him. Who'd have thought a woman with Claire's fragile beauty could have so much energy stored up inside her?

It seemed *he* was the one losing control last night, and that just didn't happen. Knowing what Dwight Powers was about to dump on her, listening to her family talk about her, all around her, but rarely straight to her, A.J. had sensed that Claire's composure was about to break. His own patience was about to blow.

So he'd grabbed her, escaped with her. Maybe he'd been rescuing himself from his own frustrations at seeing her treated like that. But she'd touched him, dammit. Those fingers, that skin—soft on the surface, like steel underneath—had cupped his face and demanded he notice her.

He had.

Maybe not in the way she'd intended, but he noticed plenty. The tight nipples budding beneath clingy, wet silk, slender curves of muscle beneath his hands, dewy lips begging to be kissed. She'd asked him in every way without actually saying the words.

And he'd almost done it.

But common sense had prevailed. His training had prevailed.

Marcus Tucker's Humvee pulling into the driveway up to the house had prevailed.

So, no kiss. But he hadn't been right since.

Even with this morning's overcast sky cooling the air

with the promise of more rain, A.J. felt hot and itchy inside his skin. He had to get that woman off his emotional radar, or he'd be more of a hindrance than a help to her.

The insistent tug on his sleeve startled A.J. from his guilty introspection.

"Is it broken?"

A.J. rarely responded to anything with a *huh*. But he was thinking one as he looked down into the studious eyes of the young man in jeans, braces and hearing aids.

The boy signed the question again, then pointed to the hinge. "Is it broken?"

The kid slurred his words a bit more than Claire did when she spoke, but that wasn't what confused him. What threw him was that he'd been so distracted from his work that a sixth grader with shaggy brown hair had gotten the drop on him.

For a moment, he stared down at the drill and screw bit he held in his hands as though he couldn't remember how they got there. But his years on the streets made him a master of faking cool, even when he wasn't really feeling it.

He nodded. "Looks like vandalism." He pointed to the bent metal and gouged-out concrete behind it, but kept his face toward the kid—the way Claire had taught him—so he could be understood. "Someone tried to pry off the hinge. I have to remove it and replace the anchor so a new screw will stay in."

The kid nodded sagely at the explanation, then shook his head. "No one would want to break into our school. It's old. It stinks in the basement. I hate when we have to go down there for tornado drills. My big brother says there are bodies buried down there. That's why it's so dark."

"Yeah?" Sounds like something he would have said to tease his younger sisters about twenty years ago.

"I think they just need to change the lightbulbs. My dad says it would be cheaper to build a new school than to keep fixing up this one." He stuck out his hand. "I'm Zach, by the way."

"A.J." Impressed by the kid's confidence as much as he was amused by the rapid-fire change of topics, A.J. shook his hand.

"You're new."

"I'm temporary." The precinct captain had given him the go-ahead to put all of his time in on the Winthrop investigation as he saw fit. "I volunteered."

"What happened to your face?"

Police stakeout? Car bomb? Dead man? "I was in a car…accident."

A sniff of lavender buzzed his radar on full alert.

"Zach." The buffed, blunt-tipped nails of Claire's hand appeared on the boy's shoulder. God, he loved those hands. "Are you bothering this man?"

"Hi, Miss Winthrop." Zach barely had to tilt his head to look Claire in the eye. "This is A.J. He cut his face in a car wreck and he's temporary."

"Is that so?" Despite the authoritative look in her eyes, Claire flashed the boy a smile that would have gotten A.J. to class every day of the week. "Run along, Zach. You don't want to be late for first period."

Zach said goodbye and ran inside to catch up with a friend. "Sorry, about that. He can talk your ear off."

"I'm a good listener."

Her sweet smile turned into a frown of concern. "Are you going to tell me what you're doing here?"

"My job."

"That's a little vague, isn't it?" She hugged her arms

across the front of her blue tailored jacket, tucking her hands away to speak without signing. Her form of whispering? "Did something happen with Galvan?"

A.J. wanted to reach out and soothe the worry lines that creased beside her eyes. Fortunately, he had his dusty hands full of tools, making it just doable to keep the conversation professional and his cover intact. "Josh and some friends from the precinct are already stirring things up this morning. They're paying visits to known contacts of Galvan and the cartel he works for. Detective Banning, another good man, is doing in-depth research into your friend Valerie, trying to come up with a connection between the two."

Her matter-of-fact sigh tugged at his conscience. She swung her gaze straight out to the two bodyguards keeping watch from their car. "That explains them." Her blue eyes came back and nailed him. "It still doesn't explain why you're here, dressed like a janitor."

For a brief moment, A.J. wondered if Claire saw any distinction between a woman of her class and a man who got dirt under his nails while he scraped out an honest living. When he was young and angry all the time, that kind of garbage used to really set him off. But he was a mature man now. And Claire's personal opinions—would she have been so eager to kiss a janitor, or the son of a janitor?— didn't matter. This was about work. It was about Dominic Galvan. It was about serving and protecting *every* citizen of Kansas City.

Even the pretty, stubborn—rich—ones.

"I'm glad your dad is springing for all the extra protection. I don't think you can be too safe where Galvan is concerned. But ultimately, you're KCPD's responsibility. You're a witness to a murder, so we're going to keep an eye on you."

"You mean there are more of you around here? I don't want to put these children in any danger. And some of them don't respond well to disruptions in their routine."

"That's why it's just me." He squeezed his fingers around the drill in lieu of taking her hand. "Keeping a low profile should be less disruptive. And being on the inside, I can stay close to you. Closer than you'll probably even know."

He thought he detected a shiver go through her body. But she tilted her chin at a determined angle and stretched her body to a posture of graceful strength. "And what am I supposed to do while we wait for something to break on your case?

"I've got your back, Claire. Just go about your day as you normally would. You won't even know I'm here."

She glanced over her shoulder at the last handful of children entering the building. "You'll keep them safe, too?"

One man keeping watch over nearly two hundred students and staff? It was a mighty tall order, more like impossible. But it was the promise Claire needed to hear. "I'll try."

He held himself still—didn't blink, barely breathed— while those blue eyes studied the sincerity of his words. "Try hard, A.J. Try very hard."

Then she turned and walked into the building with a couple of girls who immediately welcomed "Miss Winthrop!" into their animated conversation. A.J. slowly released the breath he'd been holding.

Claire seemed more natural and relaxed around these kids than she had in that fancy silk dress and pricey house last night. She was scared, yes. Cautious in a healthy way. But she wasn't anybody's victim in this place. And here, no one overlooked her.

Something eased a little in his chest at the revelation.

At the last instant before she disappeared inside, A.J. remembered to scan the grounds and parking lot to see who else might be watching her as well. He cursed his lack of focus. Watching for Galvan or his accomplice should have been his first priority. He buzzed the drill and went back to work.

He definitely needed to refocus his radar.

YOU WON'T EVEN KNOW I'm here.

Claire could have laughed out loud at the absurdity of that promise. A. J. Rodriguez was too darn hot to ignore. Even with the bulky coveralls and thick black glasses—that did nothing to disguise his beautiful eyes if you really looked—the man exuded strength, calm and something her limited relationship vocabulary could only describe as sexy.

He'd lurked on the fringes of her awareness all morning—sweeping the floor outside her room, replacing the cracked window pane outside the principal's office, joking with Mr. Lavery, their regular custodian.

But no one else seemed to think he was out of place. Volunteers were nothing new to the school, so teachers and students alike had quickly welcomed him, then moved on with their usual routines. Maybe, in some karmic aspect of the universe, A.J.'s presence was keeping any hint of danger at bay. There were no men in black lurking about the grounds, no weird phone calls, nothing out of the ordinary whatsoever.

Except the extra thump her heart seemed to give every time she caught a glimpse of him.

Claire squeezed her hands into fists inside the pockets of her linen jacket and surveyed the lunchroom. She needed to move beyond her fascination with the man and concentrate on the danger at hand. At the very least, she needed to concentrate on the two young men butting in line ahead of the rest of their class.

Shaking her head at the effects of budding testosterone on the adolescent male's ability to follow the rules, Claire made her way through the rows of tables. One push had already led to another before she tapped each boy on the shoulder and signed, "Where do you belong?"

She was escorting the two eighth graders to the end of the line when the fire alarm went off.

Every muscle clenched at the first dull honk of warning in her ears. As if pierced by a gunshot, she clutched her stomach and gasped out loud. She whipped her head around, checking every window, every exit, for Dominic Galvan. *A.J.?*

She nearly shouted his name out loud.

But the startled, even frightened, looks on the students' faces snapped her back to the reality at hand. She didn't have time to be afraid or wait for anyone to rescue her.

By the time most of them had noticed the visual warning signal, Claire had taken a deep breath and slowed her racing pulse. She told the two boys to head outside and quickly moved down the line to sign instructions to the other students.

With the direction of the other lunchroom monitors and kitchen staff, most of the students were filing out the doors onto the basketball courts behind the school. But their fire drills had always been conducted during class time, and the students had a practiced route following their teacher from their room to an assigned area outside. The odd timing told everyone that this was no drill. This mass exodus was less orderly, and with the classes all mixed up, counting heads to make sure everyone was outside would take longer.

Claire pointed students toward exits, offered calm reassurances. By now, there were so many panicked cries and nervous talking that her processors could no longer distinguish the sound of the alarm. As she quieted the students and kept them moving, she made a visual sweep of the cafeteria and connecting hallways. Everyone seemed to be heading in the proper direction. Except…

A flash of movement down the corridor caught her eye. A glimpse of blue jeans and the soft close of one of the doors leading down to the basement.

Oh, no. One of the students had mistaken the fire alarm for a tornado alert.

He was going deeper into the building instead of outside to safety.

"Anywhere but the basement," she mouthed. Dread crept in and courage seeped out on a long, low breath. There were no flashing alarm lights in the basement. In fact, there were few lights, period. There was plenty of storage space and old pipework, two abandoned bathrooms and a heavy iron furnace that no longer worked but was too heavy to remove.

It smelled of mold and dust down there, and she hated the darkness. It was the last place in the world she wanted to go.

Yet, because these children were her responsibility, she grabbed a flashlight from the office and went after him.

BY THE SECOND BUZZ of the fire alarm, A.J. was moving.

Where the hell were Tucker's men? Surely to God they didn't take lunch breaks?

All at once?

But the sedan parked next to Claire's Volvo wasn't just empty. It was gone.

A.J. ran.

He dropped the trash bag he carried and unzipped his coveralls to put his gun within easy reach. He rounded the corner of the building and slowed to a quick, steady gait so that he didn't panic any of the students filing out the front door.

His first instinct was to locate Claire. A fire alarm was a classic diversionary tactic. He'd left her inside, working the lunchroom with a couple of parent volunteers so the teachers could take a break. He scanned over the heads of kids, looking for a grown woman who was just a few inches taller. She should be out here. Now. With them. Safe.

Tucker's men should be all over her right now.

But there were no bodyguards. There was no Claire.

A.J. pushed his way upstream, against the current of evacuees. He spotted a familiar pair of braces and tapped the young man on the shoulder to stop him. "Zach, have you seen Miss Winthrop?"

"Last I saw, she was in the cafeteria, heading out the back door with some of the other kids."

"Thanks." A.J. bounded up the steps.

"Hey, A.J.! Wait!"

Schooling patience that was in short supply, A.J. turned to see Zach charging up the steps after him. He put out his hands to catch the boy. "Whoa, *amigo*. You can't go back in there." He nodded toward the woman coming up the steps behind them. "You need to stay outside with your teacher."

Zach shook off the order. He glanced over his shoulder, then back at A.J., spilling his information so quickly that it was almost indecipherable. "I forgot. I saw Miss Winthrop come out of the office with a flashlight. The teachers don't need flashlights when there's a fire. The only time they need flashlights is during a tornado. And that's because we go down to the stinky basement."

Definitely a diversion.

"Thanks, Zach." A.J. squeezed the boy's shoulder.

"You're not really a custodian, are you?" Zach asked before A.J. could get away.

The kid didn't miss a trick. With his chameleonic ability to don a persona and blend in just about anywhere, A.J. had duped criminals who were now in prison for life. But a twelve-year-old?

A.J. debated for all of three seconds before putting his finger to his lips in a hush sign that could be understood in any language. "I'm a cop."

Zach mimicked the gesture in man-to-man understanding. "Is Miss Winthrop in trouble?"

"Not from me."

Zach bopped down the steps to rejoin his class, leaving A.J.'s cover intact.

He'd deal with the incompetence of Tucker's men later—and question why talking to a twelve-year-old boy made him think of his father.

But he had to find Claire first.

Thunder rumbled in the gray clouds overhead, an ominous portent of danger. But A.J. wasn't thinking of the coming storm as he pulled off his glasses and ducked inside the building.

WHY THE BASEMENT? *Why the basement?*

The question droned in Claire's head as she left the

meager light on the landing inside the door and descended into the remodeled wrestling pit the Forsythe School called a basement. Her world grew dimmer with every step. The repetitive snarl of the alarm faded and fell silent as her senses got swallowed up by the maze of shadowy objects and darkness before her.

She searched the wall with the beam of her flashlight for the switch and flipped it up. A single bare lightbulb came on at the far side of the low-ceilinged room, at the base of the stairs leading up to the pit's opposite exit. "Figures."

Her fear of those things that go bump in the dark swirled around her and tried to take hold. The smells of dust, tainted by damp and darkness, stung her sinuses.

Crinkling her nose, she tried to recall the clean, leathery scents of A.J. and his car. It was enough of a distraction to remind herself that she didn't have time to be afraid.

Pointing her flashlight at the ceiling, Claire reached up to check the light at the base of the steps where she stood. Maybe the darkness was as simple as a bulb needing to be replaced. Or maybe it just needed to be tightened. Or… there was no lightbulb.

Claire frowned. If there wasn't a lost child and the threat of a burning building, she'd have marched back up the stairs instead of venturing forward into the fearful cliché of every horror movie she'd never been able to sit through.

"Hello?" She stepped off the last stair into the darkness. There was little point in calling out if the blue jeans she'd seen going downstairs belonged to a deaf child. But talking gave her something to focus on while her pulse beat with the insistence of the fire alarm blaring upstairs. "It's Miss Winthrop. You need to come upstairs with me and go outside with everyone else. There's a fire."

She swept the beam of her flashlight back and forth across the stacks of storage crates and broken desks slated for repairs. She flashed her light past the abandoned furnace that sat like a hulking black hole against one wall. Not to check for signs of a frightened child, but to reveal her own presence. The students were trained to respond to the lights in emergencies, whereas a hearing child was trained to respond to the sound. But she called out, anyway. "Where are you?"

Her flashlight showed a clear pathway across the floor to the opposite stairs. She'd cross the basement by herself first, and then hurry upstairs and come back with a hearing teacher if she couldn't locate the child.

The shadows gathered around her feet as she checked the two shelter areas that had once been locker rooms. Her imagination conjured scrapes of sound and whispers of stale breezes. A chill wrapped its icy fingers around her ankles and crept up her legs.

Run! her phobia shouted, trying to tell her that fleeing this dank, horrible pit was the only antidote that could warm her, sustain her. "C'mon, kid, where are you?" she whispered.

Claire braced her hand atop one of the old, broken desks, then snatched it back when her fingers stuck in the tacky, damp layer of dust that coated the surface. Curling the sticky fingers into her palm, she leaned around the end of the stack and shone her light into the space between the desks and the wall. "Don't be afraid," she warned, hoping she'd find a huddled child.

Empty.

The darkness won. A breath of air whispered across the back of her neck, standing her hair there on end and flooding her skin with goose bumps. "Who's there?"

She swung around with the light, catching a glimpse of a moving shadow, darting from one gloomy corner to the next. Her heart stopped for an instant, then thundered back to life, hammering at the walls of her chest.

She was out of here. She couldn't do this alone. She needed help.

"I'll be back!" she shouted, needing reassurance herself.

Desperate to orient herself in the darkness, she trailed her fingers along the stacks of desks, uncaring of the grunge that caught beneath her fingernails. The light at the far stairs marked the most visible escape route. Needing light as much as she needed her next breath, Claire hurried her steps.

One. Two. Something hard smacked against her right forearm. Claire screamed. Pain bloomed up to her elbow and tingled down into her fingers. The flashlight flew from her grasp and skittered away into the darkness. "No!"

Long fingers closed around her throbbing wrist and yanked her around. Blackness in the black. A fleeting impression of one shadow, darker than the rest, almost tall enough to brush the ceiling. Another hand encircled her throat. Leather gloves. They were soft against her skin. The fingers inside that glove were not.

Claire gasped for air, kicked out, clawed.

The shadow lifted her up onto her toes. The glove squeezed.

But in the instant she knew she couldn't breathe, the vise around her neck stilled. Her heels hit the floor and the shadow shoved her, hard.

Claire careened back into the desks. She hit one with her shoulder blade and tumbled to the floor with it. Her hip smacked into concrete and the desks toppled around her, onto her.

She covered her head and curled into a ball to absorb the blows. But almost as soon as the vibrations of wood and metal hitting concrete stopped resonating through her bones, the hand snatched her again.

Claire made a fist and came up swinging. The punch landed with a satisfying flinch of the man's shoulder. But his grip on her arm didn't budge. She opened her mouth to scream, but the sound caught and rasped in her throat. Every imagined terror that had haunted her in the darkness assailed her.

Valerie Justice with a bullet in her head and her chest.

A man in black, whose heavy footsteps vibrated across the floor.

Death, coming to take her the same way he had taken her mother.

Panic welled up inside her, stealing her breath, cancelling out common sense. Claire cursed being small and deaf and too sheltered and rich to have ever learned how to fight for herself.

The shadow spun her around, and suddenly she was locked up against something solid and warm. A hand covered her mouth, muffling whatever sounds she could make. Her flailing arms were pinned to her sides, her back and bottom pressed tight against muscle and bone.

Not a shadow. A man.

Claire shimmied and twisted, but there was nowhere to go. Something warm and moist brushed the rim of her ear. Deep, insistent tones murmured into her brain.

Her panic shorted out on a single, delayed discovery.

No gloves.

The hands that held her were callused and warm and bare against her skin and lips. The hard body that molded itself to hers took shape and form—matching and surpassing the images she'd only observed. His scent, a hint of leather blended with the earthy appeal of soap and hard work, filled her nose with each panicked breath.

Not any man. A.J.

"Shh, baby. It's me." She couldn't be sure of the words he whispered against her ear, but she heard them in her soul.

"A.J." She went limp with relief and his hold on her eased, changed. It was no longer his strength overpowering her, restraining her. It was his strength supporting hers, cradling her in a tight embrace.

The fear that had fogged her brain cleared enough to let her know her surroundings again. The lone light was off. But, like before, the light from the landing at the top of the stairs provided enough illumination for them both to get a glimpse of the door swinging shut.

The shadow who'd attacked her—the man in black— was escaping.

Claire felt the tension in A.J., the poised tiger ready to pounce on his prey. But he held himself still, for her. He stayed rooted to the spot, holding her tight, his lips pressed to the charging pulse beneath her ear, whispering words she could only feel.

But Galvan was getting away.

She reached for his hand where A.J. had palmed it against her hip. "Go. Go after him. I'll be okay."

There was no hesitation in his movements. There was no time to regret her brave words, either. Without ever breaking contact with her entirely, A.J. took her hand in his and pulled her along behind him. They crossed the basement, ran up to the landing. He pulled out his black gun and pushed her behind him before nudging the door open a crack. Claire curled her fingers into a handful of navy coveralls and clung to the sheltering wall of his back.

She peered around his shoulder into the flashing alarm lights, but the hallway was empty. Claire could hear sirens now, but she suspected the firefighters wouldn't find anything but a mess of broken desks in the basement.

A.J. hurried to the closest exit and led her outside, into what passed for light beneath the clouds brewing in the sky. The tension she felt in his coiled muscles never relaxed. He was scanning the grounds, and those all-seeing eyes weren't finding what he was looking for. She actually jumped when his gaze finally dropped and landed on her.

"Are you hurt?" he asked.

Claire shook her head and reached up to tuck her hair behind her ears as nerves still worked their way out of her system. "Just scared."

"Madre dios." The curse was followed by a string of foreign obscenities she couldn't make out. But his grim expression made their meaning clear. He holstered his weapon, then reached for her right hand. Cradling her forearm, he pushed up her sleeve and inspected the purplish, palm-sized welt on her wrist. "He got to you. That son of a bitch got to you."

"It could have been worse." Gentle as his touch was, there was something angry roiling in the depths of A.J.'s eyes that left her wanting to stroke the tight line of his mouth or give him a hug or say something wise to ease emotions that seemed almost too much for him to contain. But since she didn't know how to help him, Claire pulled away and tugged her sleeve back down to her wrist. "I think he must have heard you coming. That's when he ran."

"Did you see the guy's face? Was it Galvan?"

"I didn't really see him. He was tall enough. He wore jeans and something dark on top. But I think…" Fear clawed at the tatters of Claire's emotional energy. She took a step back toward the building. "Wait. There was a child down here. I saw him go…" Her feet stopped and her voice trailed away. She hugged herself tightly around her waist, feeling useless and foolish and completely at Galvan's mercy. There was no child. "I'm such an idiot," she murmured out loud. "Such a naive idiot. He lured me down there to…to…"

"Come here." A.J. made sure she read his intent before wrapping his arms around her and pulling her up to his chest. Palming the back of her head, he pressed her nose into the juncture of his neck and shoulder. Claire nuzzled into the gap that caught his warmth and scent between his collar and throat. Her own hands snuck around his waist and latched on tightly, huddling as close to the security of A.J.'s embrace as he'd let her.

The hand at her throat had meant business. If A.J. hadn't shown up when he had—if he hadn't come looking for her in the first place, then she might be a little more than beat up around the edges. She'd be more than terrified.

She'd be the next name on Galvan's list.

She'd be dead.

Chapter Six

The Fourth Precinct conference room had been taken over by a brain trust of detectives and investigators coming together to pool information, turning the bright white walls and long oak-topped tables into an organized hive of activity resembling a command center.

"So we've got his attention?" Assistant District Attorney Dwight Powers was practically slathering at the mouth at the report that Dominic Galvan had surfaced to pay Claire a visit.

If the guy smiled once, if he even so much as smirked, A.J. was going to go over there and take him down. Fortunately for Powers's sake, and for A.J.'s professional standing as a police officer, the A.D.A. never smiled. Never. It was one of the traits that made him such a tenacious opponent in the courtroom. Of course, a man who'd lost everything the way Powers had probably found little to smile about in life.

But if the big man in the blue suit took one iota of pleasure in putting Claire up as a pawn again to bring in Galvan—if the A.D.A.'s plan put one more bruise on her fair skin—then A.J. intended to forgo both compassion and professional courtesy and lay the man flat on his ass.

But Claire was holding her own. She answered each of his questions about the attack clearly and concisely, despite her nervous habit of tucking her hair behind her ears, then just as quickly smoothing it back in place to hide her sound transmitters and speech processors.

Obliquely, A.J. wondered why she was so self-conscious about a handicap that wasn't truly a handicap for her. Claire was a far better communicator than he'd ever be. Words and emotions came easily to her, and she could express herself in two ways. Three, if he counted those pretty blue eyes that had reprimanded him, desired him and revealed her trust. How the hell men like Rob Hastings or her father could ever ignore the truth in those eyes was beyond his comprehension.

Right now, those blue eyes revealed fatigue, wariness— and a glow of determination that was the only thing keeping A.J. on his side of the room, while Dwight Powers grilled her and took notes on the other.

"Boo."

With merely a blink and a shift of his gaze, A.J. looked sideways at Josh, who pushed a fresh cup of coffee into his hand. A.J. took a long drink from his cup before responding. "I saw you coming."

"Sure you did." Josh sat on the back table and crossed his arms, imitating A.J.'s position. "Nobody's gonna hurt her here."

That made A.J. turn and look at his partner. "Am I that obvious?"

"Nothing is ever obvious with you, *amigo*." Josh nodded to acknowledge Merle Banning walking into the room and coming over to them. "I've just gotten to know you well enough over the years that I can tell you're off your game."

He raised a hand before A.J. could defend himself. "Now, mind you, you're so much better at reading a scene and keeping your cool than the rest of us, that you're still gettin' the job done. Claire's in one piece and we're building a solid case against Galvan." A.J. sipped his coffee and let him talk. "The word I'm getting on the street is that outside help was called in to do Slick Williams's murder. Probably Mort's, too. Galvan fits the profile. And you, partner of mine, came close to nabbing the guy today."

Josh leaned in for a conspiratorial whisper before Banning joined them. "But the day A. J. Rodriguez drinks his coffee with milk and sugar is the day I know something—or someone—has finally gotten under your skin."

A.J. looked down into his mocha-colored drink, just now tasting the liquid in his mouth and realizing it lacked the rich, bitter flavor he liked. "Touché, *amigo*. But it's guilt that I'm feeling. Yeah, maybe she stirs a few hormones, but I'm more concerned that an innocent woman has gotten dragged into something way too dangerous. She's gonna get hurt. More than she has already if we're not careful. I've got enough on my conscience."

"Don't worry." Josh wasn't buying the explanation A.J. wanted to believe. "Your secret's safe with me."

"And what secret would that be?" Merle Banning joined them, donning his glasses and opening the manila folder he carried. "That you've got your eye on Miss Winthrop?"

Was everybody talking about it? A.J. stood. He was just doing his job. He shouldn't feel anything for Claire Winthrop; he didn't want to feel anything. So what if she fit so perfectly against his body that she could have been made for him? So what if her innocence spoke like salvation to the cynical soul inside him? So what if every cell in him burned with the urge to kiss her in exactly the way she'd asked him to last night?

That didn't mean he cared about the woman.

But Josh was shaking so hard with barely contained laughter that he had to set down his coffee before it sloshed over his hand. He pointed at Banning, who had the temerity to be grinning behind his folder. "He's the smart one around here. I can't help if he figured it out, too."

A.J. crossed to the trash can by the door and dumped his drink. "Just tell me what you found out about Valerie Justice and the Winthrops, and I'll forget that you two—whom I outrank, by the way—ever had this conversation."

"Yes, sir," Josh and Banning echoed in unison.

Right, like pulling rank wasn't another indication that Claire Winthrop was shattering more than his stereotyped beliefs about the heartless arrogance of the wealthy class. He let his gaze slide across the room to Claire and Powers. Damn. She was staring right back with a question in her eyes. Had she been able to lip-read any of their conversation? He didn't want to have to explain anything like *hormones* or getting under his skin.

Not when he didn't understand it yet himself.

He tore his gaze away and would have even turned his back on those perceptive eyes, but he was even less thrilled to have Banning face her. If there was anything gruesome, or revealing about her father and his business, in what he'd uncovered, A.J. didn't want Claire to find out by "eavesdropping" across the room.

"Your report?" he prompted.

Banning rattled off his facts about the Winthrop holdings in a way that helped A.J. understand the vast scope of international trade routes, customs treaties and domestic distribution networks that would certainly interest the men Dominic Galvan usually worked for. Drug trafficking and terrorism had tightened import/export regulations throughout the country. Kansas City, with its international airport and convergence of major rivers, railroads and highways, offered opportunities for the enterprising criminal to transport drugs or launder money. It could be an especially lucrative opportunity if some of those restrictive government regulations could be handled by someone within Winthrop Enterprises.

"Do we have proof anything like that is going on at Winthrop?" A.J. asked. Had his father discovered something illegal at the company eighteen years ago? Antonio, Sr. had been trying to tell him something about Cain Winthrop in his cryptic advice all those years ago.

"Not specifically," Banning answered, drawing A.J.'s focus back to the case at hand. "But it makes a hell of a motive if someone on the inside hired Galvan to silence anyone who stumbled across the operation. Or who wanted out."

"The hits on the street would tie in to that theory," A.J. reasoned. "Galvan's killing off the competition."

"It can't be any small coincidence that we've got eyewitness testimony putting him in the Winthrop Building," Josh added. "All the trails are starting to lead back to Claire's daddy."

Even the death of A.J.'s father. He processed that nugget of information and filed it away to handle later. "What else?"

Banning filled them in that Valerie Justice had checked in for her flight to Nassau, but that the seat assigned to her was resold—indicating she was a no-show or had changed flights. "The hotel in the Bahamas hasn't seen her. And as far as I can tell, no boyfriend has checked in, either."

"Do we know the name of the boyfriend?"

"The hotel lists his reservation as Sid Greenstreet."

"Like the old movie actor?" asked Josh.

Banning nodded. "I followed the records trail back to the cruise where Ms. Justice supposedly met him. There was no Greenstreet on the passenger manifest or the crew."

"So we've got someone using an alias." A.J. shook his head. Another twist to a case that got more complicated by the minute. "Or a boyfriend who never really existed."

"Right. And why go to all that trouble creating a fictitious affair if she didn't have something to cover up?" Banning closed the file. "I'm looking into her personal and financial records next. In the meantime, CSI sent Holly Masterson with a team over to Valerie's apartment to see if forensics can turn up anything there. You want me to follow up on this Greenstreet?"

"Did you say Sid Greenstreet?" Claire raised her voice to be heard across the room. Dwight Powers stood when she did and followed her across the room.

Josh and Banning exchanged looks, questioning whether their prize witness had suddenly developed telepathic abilities. But A.J. knew the trick before Powers explained. "Miss Winthrop has been demonstrating her lip-reading proficiency to me."

The detectives stepped aside to form a circle to include Claire and the A.D.A. Her frown worried A.J. "Why were you talking about Sid Greenstreet?"

"You've heard of him?" he asked.

"I'm not sure I've seen any of the actor's films, but I know the name. That's the code name Marcus Tucker's security team uses whenever they're escorting a high-profile client in or out of the country for the company. Like Mr.

Watanabe, who was at the party last night. The security detail referred to him as Mr. Greenstreet." Claire looked up at A.J. "Is that helpful?"

He looked at Powers, who looked at Banning, who looked at Josh. When Josh completed the circle of unspoken suspicion, A.J. connected the dots out loud.

"Maybe Ms. Justice was doing a little escorting of her own. It'd be a perfect way to smuggle Galvan in and out of the country to do his work."

"WHERE'S MY daughter?"

A.J. heard Cain Winthrop's bellow through the closed door of the conference room, and quickly glanced down at Claire to see if she'd heard him, too.

But she was still defending the man to him and Dwight Powers. "I don't think my father would do any of the things you're suggesting. He wouldn't sell drugs. He'd go bankrupt before he'd allow his company to be used that way."

"Your father isn't the only one with access to the 26th floor," Powers reminded her. "It could have been another Winthrop board member who was in that room with Galvan. That's why I recommend a safe house. All the suspects in this case know you."

Finally, Powers was saying something A.J. could agree with. Claire needed to be locked up, away from her family and so-called friends, away from their influence. Until Galvan was off the streets, and his accomplice identified, she wasn't safe, even in her own home.

"I want to see Rodriguez!" So, Daddy Winthrop remembered his name. Though A.J. doubted Claire's father had made the connection between the new detective and the old custodian yet.

"I don't care who the hell you are," another voice barked. "You'll follow procedure, or you're either out of my precinct or in my jail cell." Captain Taylor was getting into it out in the main room now. A.J. kept his gaze carefully focused so as not to alert Claire to the confrontation.

"I can't believe that." Her fingers reached for her hair and first tucked it behind, then fanned it out over her ear. "The members of the board are friends, family. None of them would want to hurt me."

Screw denying Josh's suspicions about him having feelings for Claire. A.J. took her hand and laced their fingers together, offering her something to cling to besides her own doubts and fears. Her strong, eloquent fingers latched on and held tight.

A.J. squeezed, trying to soften the impact of his words. "You didn't believe that anyone could want to hurt Valerie, either."

Claire's hand went cold in his grasp. "You're saying that someone in my own family…? That someone who was at *my* home last night hired Galvan to kill me today?"

The bruises on her wrist and collarbone—where that bastard had hit her, shoved her, strangled her—seemed to darken before A.J.'s eyes. The attack had scared the hell out of him, and left him seething with an anger he hadn't felt since his father's senseless death. He rubbed his thumb across the back of her knuckles in lieu of reaching out to touch one of her injuries and apologize for ever letting her out of his sight.

"We're suggesting it's a strong possibility."

"That's why I'm having Josh make the arrangements to put you in a safe house under twenty-four-hour watch," Powers added. "If you've got a better idea of who brought

Galvan to Kansas City and that list of whom else he wants to kill, I'm listening."

Claire stood in mute shock, considering the change her life was about to take. No school until this was over. No contact with her family. They were taking the sheltered princess out of the castle she'd known her whole life and sticking her in a nondescript house in an uneventful part of town, with no servants, no outside contact and—this was the part A.J. suspected would drive her stir-crazy—no chance to help her kids at Forsythe.

A firm rap at the door signaled to A.J. that the confrontation with her father was about to come inside. Reluctantly, he released Claire's hand. This was not going to go well. "Your father's here."

Captain Taylor opened the door and stuck his head inside. "You ready for this, Rodriguez? The man has the right to see his daughter."

A.J. simply nodded.

The captain backed out of the doorway and Cain Winthrop charged inside. "Where is she? Is she all right? Claire?"

"Daddy?" Without hesitation, Claire ran to him.

"Sweetie. Thank God you're all right." The white-haired man in the three-piece suit scooped her up in a hug and held on tight.

The way a father should, A.J. thought silently, relieved to see the happy reassurance in Claire's expression. Winthrop held his daughter close and rocked her back and forth, *the way a criminal keeps his enemy close at hand,* he thought with less charity.

It was a cruel scenario to consider—a father marking his own flesh and blood for death. Sacrificing what he claimed to love so that his business would thrive and his butt would stay out of prison.

A.J. had seen worse than that in his time. But what was really sticking in his craw now was the idea of how much further out of range a relationship with Claire would be if he wound up having to arrest her father.

He shouldn't even go there. He was already too old for her, too working-class and—he could make a pretty good guess—too experienced. Any one of those factors should dissuade him from thinking anything lusty or tender or remotely personal about Claire. Factor in that the people she cared about were the people he was investigating, and a relationship just wasn't gonna happen.

"You." Claire dropped to her feet and pushed her way around her father. Marcus Tucker filled the doorway, his unsmiling eyes taking in the flush of her cheeks and the primly upraised index finger that was about to point out the error of his ways. "I thought you were supposed to be some crackerjack security expert. But your men allowed a known criminal—a murderer, no less—to get inside a building with nearly two hundred innocent children. I thought you were supposed to stop Galvan, not let him endanger my kids."

A.J. twisted his lips together, resisting the urge to cheer her on. Man, he loved that sassy temper of hers. She wasn't such a lady through and through, the way first impressions might indicate. He'd planned to lambaste Tucker about how royally his men had screwed up their protection detail. But Claire, who was half the size of Marcus Tucker, had the situation well in hand.

"If A.J. hadn't been there to scare him off, who knows what might have happened."

"I'm sorry you were hurt, Miss Winthrop," Tucker apologized, his voice a monotone of rehearsed words that lacked sincerity in A.J.'s point of view. "But mistakes happen. I assure you, they will not happen again. I intend to personally oversee your safety from here on out."

"Too little, too late, don't you think?"

Cain laid a hand on his daughter's shoulder. "Rodriguez saved your life?"

"Yes." Though Claire couldn't pick up on the distant, almost confused tone that had quieted his voice considerably, Winthrop must have conveyed something in his touch. She turned to face him, a question drawing fine lines beside her eyes. "A.J. was the one who came down to the basement to get me, not Mr. Tucker's men. What is it, Dad?"

A.J. held his relaxed stance as Cain looked at him, searching his face as if really seeing him for the first time. Was a familiar connection trying to click into place inside his memory?

"Rodriguez." Cain mouthed the name, frowned. Then, before anyone could comment on his strangely distracted behavior, the CEO sucked in a deep breath that pinched his nostrils. He swung around toward Tucker, coming back to the moment, clearly steamed at his employee. "I thought I told you to assign bodyguards to Claire."

"I did." Tucker puffed up to his full height, reminding everyone he was the biggest man in the room. "A four-man team—two in uniform, two in plainclothes. Stationed inside and outside the building."

A.J. wasn't intimidated by bluster. "Who were nowhere to be found when Galvan showed up."

Cain wasn't too pleased with the truth. "Is that right?"

"He's a tricky man to spot, Mr. Winthrop. My men must

have been on patrol. I ordered them to do periodic sweeps of the grounds and the school building. One of them was to have your daughter in view at all times."

"And with all that searching and viewing, Galvan still got to her?" Uh-oh. Daddy was ticked off at Tucker's incompetence.

"Look at that bruise on her arm, sir. Apparently, Detective Rodriguez didn't spot him in time, either."

"I don't pay Rodriguez to protect my daughter!"

"Placing blame serves no purpose here, gentlemen." Now Powers wanted to get into the verbal fray?

Claire stood between Tucker and Winthrop, her palms on her father's chest, trying to urge him away from a fight. "Dad, please. I'm fine. Really."

A.J.'s chest drifted forward, every protective instinct in his body set to reach in and pull her out from the middle of the argument. But Cain beat him to it.

Ignoring her protest, Claire's father grasped her by the shoulders and tucked her to his side. "I pay you a hell of a lot more than you're worth, Tucker, if you can't keep my baby girl safe."

"If she hadn't insisted on maintaining her usual routine—"

"Your men screwed up."

"I take full responsibility—"

"Fire them."

The order shut Tucker up for a moment. Just long enough to set his lantern jaw and curl his bottom lip into nonexistence. "Those are *my* men, Mr. Winthrop. I will deal with them in *my* way."

"Do I still pay your salary?" Cain asked.

"Yes, sir."

"Fire. Them." Cain Winthrop was a man used to having his own way. "Come along, Claire. I'll take you home."

She twisted out of his grasp and backed a step toward A.J. "I can't go with you."

"Of course you can." He reached for her hand. "We'll send someone for your car."

She tugged herself free and retreated another step. Automatically, A.J. put out his hand to warn her of his presence behind her. His fingers brushed against the back of her waist and stayed when she didn't startle or flinch away. "I rode with A.J., but that's not the point."

Dwight Powers made the point. "She's going to a safe house."

"She's not going to testify against Galvan."

"Yes, I am!"

Cain wiggled his fingers in a "come here" gesture. "No. You will come home and—"

"I'm not your baby girl anymore."

Bam.

Silence filled the room, consuming the oxygen and replacing it with tension. A.J. felt the cost of Claire's defiance clenching in the small of her back. He flattened his palm at the spot, offering his unspoken support. With an infinitesimal movement, she leaned into the brace of his hand and something shifted inside him. At that moment, a bond was forged, one that A.J. would never willingly break.

Claire had allied herself with him. Against her father's control. Against Marcus Tucker's incompetence. Against a Central American hit man and a mysterious, so-called friend who wanted her dead.

If his fingers curled a little farther around the nip of her waist to turn the friendly contact into something more personal, he couldn't help it. A. J. Rodriguez wasn't a man who did anything halfway.

Oddly enough, Claire was the one to break the silence. She started signing, though she hadn't used her hands to speak until now. "I haven't been a *baby* for years. I'm old enough to make my own decisions. If it's the wrong one, then you have to let me live with my mistake. And learn from it. You have to let me grow up."

"I know. It's just that..." Cain lifted his hands and began to sign slowly, as if his fingers were rusty from disuse. "You remind me so much of your mother. I didn't do a very good job taking care of her. I promised myself I'd do better by you."

"Then let me do this. It's the right thing. You know it. You know Valerie's gone. And I can help put away the man who killed her."

Winthrop flinched, as if his daughter's words had struck a nerve. But just as quickly, his expression grew stern. "It's too dangerous. If *this* decision is a mistake, it could cost you your life."

"I'm not planning on dying, Dad." She smiled a serene reassurance that almost had A.J. believing they had nothing to worry about.

"But you saw Galvan's face. He's tried to kill you once already."

Marcus Tucker apparently saw an opportunity to redeem himself. "I will guard her myself, sir. Use every man and precaution at my disposal. I'll make this right."

Cain dropped his hands to his sides. "Somehow, Marcus, that doesn't make me feel any better."

"KCPD will be handling Claire's security," Dwight Powers confirmed. "So that we don't risk any communication leaks—however inadvertent," he added for Tucker's benefit. "We don't want Winthrop Enterprises involved."

Marcus protested the issue being taken out of his hands. "My team—"

"Shut up, Tucker." Cain dismissed the burly security chief and turned his attention to A.J. "Are you in charge of this safe house?"

"I'll be one of the men assigned to it, yes."

Winthrop stroked a finger across Claire's cheek. "She's never been away from me for more than a few days at a time. When she was sick, I stayed at the hospital with her. Even when she was at college, I saw her nearly every weekend."

"With all due respect, Mr. Winthrop, this isn't about you."

He felt Claire catch and hold her breath as Winthrop's gaze dropped to her waist, taking note of A.J.'s hand on his daughter. But he made no indication of displeasure or approval. "No, it isn't. Keep her safe, Antonio."

He lifted his gaze and looked dead-on into A.J.'s eyes.

A.J.'s grip tightened around Claire's waist, the only outward indication of the emotions coursing through him he allowed. "You know who I am?"

"I know who your father was. A good man."

"Yes, sir, he was."

"He was more than a custodian, you know."

"What do you mean?"

Winthrop paused. "His death was tragic. So unexpectedly tragic."

Was that sympathy? Or a warning of some kind?

The possible answer left A.J. raw and unsettled. He kneaded an unconscious rhythm against the flare of Claire's hip, until her small, strong hand covered his. Her

GET FREE BOOKS and a FREE GIFT WHEN YOU PLAY THE...

777

Lucky 7

Just scratch off the silver box with a coin. Then check below to see the gifts you get!

SLOT MACHINE GAME!

YES! I have scratched off the silver box. Please send me the 2 free Harlequin Intrigue® books and gift for which I qualify. I understand I am under no obligation to purchase any books, as explained on the back of this card.

382 HDL D7W2   **182 HDL D7XG**

FIRST NAME | LAST NAME

ADDRESS

APT.# | CITY

STATE/PROV. | ZIP/POSTAL CODE

7	7	7	**Worth** TWO FREE BOOKS plus a BONUS **Mystery Gift!**
🍒	🍒	🍒	**Worth** TWO FREE BOOKS!
♣	♣	♣	**Worth** ONE FREE BOOK!
🔔	🔔	🍒	**TRY AGAIN!**

www.eHarlequin.com

(H-I-04/05)

DETACH AND MAIL CARD TODAY!

The Harlequin Reader Service® — Here's how it works:

Accepting your 2 free books and gift places you under no obligation to buy anything. You may keep the books and gift and return the shipping statement marked "cancel." If you do not cancel, about a month later we'll send you 6 additional books and bill you just $4.24 each in the U.S., or $4.99 each in Canada, plus 25¢ shipping & handling per book and applicable taxes if any.* That's the complete price and — compared to cover prices of $4.99 each in the U.S. and $5.99 each in Canada — it's quite a bargain! You may cancel at any time, but if you choose to continue, every month we'll send you 6 more books, which you may either purchase at the discount price or return to us and cancel your subscription.

*Terms and prices subject to change without notice. Sales tax applicable in N.Y. Canadian residents will be charged applicable provincial taxes and GST. Credit or debit balances in a customer's account(s) may be offset by any other outstanding balance owed by or to the customer.

If offer card is missing write to: Harlequin Reader Service, 3010 Walden Ave., P.O. Box 1867, Buffalo NY 14240-1867

BUSINESS REPLY MAIL
FIRST-CLASS MAIL   PERMIT NO. 717-003   BUFFALO, NY

POSTAGE WILL BE PAID BY ADDRESSEE

HARLEQUIN READER SERVICE
3010 WALDEN AVE
PO BOX 1867
BUFFALO NY 14240-9952

NO POSTAGE
NECESSARY
IF MAILED
IN THE
UNITED STATES

touch calmed his body, but even that deliberate physical contact couldn't staunch the questions and suspicions spilling from his soul.

But Cain either wouldn't or couldn't talk about it. Tempting A.J. with just enough information to make him anxious to learn more, Cain leaned in, kissed Claire and pulled her away from A.J. for one more hug. "Just keep my baby…keep my daughter safe."

"YOUR TWENTY-FOUR HOURS are up. Your plan failed."

The man with the long fingers disentangled himself from the naked woman in his bed and climbed out from beneath the covers to take the call in relative privacy. He stood at the hotel window, pulled aside the curtain and looked out the Liberty Memorial, spotlighted against the starless night atop the next hill. He lifted his gaze to the eternal flame that burned atop the columnar structure and wondered how much longer he'd have to endure the peculiarities of his hired assassin.

"I told you not to call me."

"I don't care about your little tryst. She's not the woman I'm worried about."

He glanced back over his shoulder at the sleepy woman, pushing her hair out of her eyes as she sat up and let the covers slide down to her waist. His body stirred at the intentional display of bare breasts. She was willing to do anything for him. Or, more accurately, for the money and power he could share with her.

She'd come as soon as he called, to be with him for a few hours before daylight and the next phase of his well-orchestrated plan fell into place. He'd needed the sex, needed to get the frustration of a very trying day out of his system.

He didn't need to be dealing with Galvan's muck-up. He turned back to the Memorial. "Ramon Goya is sending a shipment along with the coffee we're bringing in from Tenebrosa tomorrow. I need to be able to tell him we can distribute all of the product without any interference. How are you coming with the last two names on the list?"

"You do not understand, *compadre*. There is no one else on the list until I finish this job. I have my reputation to protect. The Winthrop bitch is cozier with the cops than ever now. Trying to spook her did no good."

"You took it too far."

"I didn't take it far enough. I should have snapped her neck and been done with it. But you wanted to play games. She isn't changing her story, and now that cop is attached to her at the hip."

"I'm not worried about Rodriguez. He's just a man. He has a weakness we can exploit if we have to. I'm not worried about Claire's testimony, either."

"It wasn't *your* face she picked out of a police report."

"Darling? Are you coming back to bed?" The woman's voice jarred against his ears. "I'll have to leave soon."

"And you know damn well, *compadre,* that if anything happens to me, yours will be the first name on my lips."

The man with the long fingers headed back to the bed to assuage more of his frustrations.

He was losing his taste for such decisions. Who'd have thought getting rid of a glorified secretary could cause so much trouble? Killing Valerie had been a matter of silencing a team member who'd unexpectedly developed a conscience. But for an extra quarter of a million dollars, she'd find a way to keep her mouth shut. He didn't need to live with that kind of blackmail. He didn't need the inside information she'd once provided for him. The woman in his bed would see to that now.

All he needed was for Ramon Goya to be happy. And to do that, he needed Galvan to finish the job he'd been hired to do.

He slipped into bed and let the woman put her hands on him. Claire was just a kid. She wasn't a street thug or a dealer or the competition like the other names on the list. She wasn't even a part of the company that had become such a profitable enterprise for him over the years.

But she'd been in the wrong place at the wrong time. "Do it."

He disconnected the call, knowing Galvan intended to kill Claire Winthrop, no matter what he said.

He'd deal with his conscience later.

Chapter Seven

Even in the nice part of town, stakeouts sucked.

A.J. sipped on his cold black coffee and watched the two boys zoom past on their bicycles. They found the deepest puddle of water on the sidewalk to hydroplane across, splashing water up onto their bikes, themselves and the neighbor's lawn. It looked like a great way to spend a drizzly Saturday afternoon after being cooped up all week in school.

He wished he could take his car out to the country and find an old blacktop road where he could take it up to speed and kick back some water himself. But his wild days had ended years ago, and *carefree* hadn't been a part of his vocabulary since he'd gotten that sobering call from his mother eighteen years ago.

Your father's dead, A.J. Wherever you are, come home. I need you to be a man now.

He'd been grown-up ever since.

But maybe all those years of undercover work and watching his back—all the times he'd watched his partners' backs because he knew that's what kept a cop alive—were starting to tell on him. Life was passing him by. Fun and laughter and letting loose weren't a part of his life anymore, not to any real extent.

Maybe that's why he'd been so restless lately. He set his coffee in the cupholder between the Trans Am's bucket seats and let his gaze slide over to the dark gray, L-shaped ranch house behind the white brick retaining wall and evergreen bushes.

She was in there. With Reed and Henley, sharing her smiles and working those hands with elegant precision whether she was washing dishes, playing cards or reading a book. Maybe that's why Claire's youthful vitality held such appeal for him. He needed something more than work in his life. He needed something more than duty in his heart.

He needed to play cards and trade smiles and…get his head back in the game.

Silently cursing his uncharacteristic flights of fancy, A.J. pulled his cell from the pocket of his leather jacket and called the precinct.

"Josh. When you get to the safe house, why don't you bring me something decent to eat. And some black coffee."

"You're at work early, *amigo*. Our shift doesn't start until one." He could hear the creak of Josh's chair as he sat up straight at his desk and swore. "Or have you been there all night?"

"I've been here thinking." A twelve-hour stakeout gave a man little else to do.

"I'm thinking you need to seriously get with this woman and get her out of your system."

"Whatever. Now that you're done assessing my love life, Dr. Phil, could we talk police business?"

"If you insist." Did the big guy have to sound so cocky. "Banning found three different bank accounts in which Valerie Justice has been depositing around $10,000 a quarter for the past few years. Winthrop was generous with his bonuses, but not $40,000 a year worth. She was into something else."

"Any leads on the body yet?"

"Nothing at her apartment. Though Holly Masterson said Valerie had a male visitor within the past week."

"Sid Greenstreet?" Talk about a longshot. If they could place Dominic Galvan with Valerie before the murder, then they could build a pattern of familiarity to back up Claire's testimony.

"Holly's typing the DNA of the semen sample this morning. But if Galvan isn't in the system, there's no way we can get a match."

The boys zipped back by on their bikes, and A.J. saluted when they waved. The gray house with Claire inside remained quiet and unassuming.

"Can we place Galvan at any of the dealer murders yet?"

"We've got a couple of DNAs from the stabbing victim scene we can cross-match. But you know there wasn't much left when Slick's car exploded."

"I know." A.J. checked the rearview mirror to probe the crescent-shaped scar tissue that glowed pink against his olive-tinted cheek and beard scruff. He'd had the stitches removed yesterday. "But there's a connection there, I know it."

"I thought that's what made him the Renaissance Man—that there was no pattern. If he is responsible for all the dealers' deaths, then he's just as adept at explosives as he is at hand-to-hand combat."

"He's pretty handy with a gun, too." A.J. tried to relax and let his brain think of new possibilities. "What kind of man would have expertise in all those areas? And be in good enough shape to maintain that career for twenty years."

Josh went with the flow. "You mean like a navy SEAL?"

"Or a SWAT team member. Special Forces. Who's to say Galvan hasn't had that kind of training?"

"You want me to check with Tenebrosa to see if Galvan has a military record?"

Taking the investigation in a new direction reenergized A.J.'s sleep-deprived body. For the first time in a lot of days, he began to think they were making some progress. "State police. Mercenary. Rebel forces. Tenebrosa's been in a civil war of various drug cartels for almost thirty years now. Why wouldn't he have that kind of background? If so, somebody's got to have an address for him. A phone number. A means to contact him when he's due a pension check, or somebody wants to rehire his services."

He heard the grin in Josh's voice. "You think any of them would keep medical records? If he's former military, he must have had a physical somewhere along the way."

"Put Dwight Powers on it. He can clear through the red tape faster than we can. Good thinking, partner."

A.J.'s renewed energy matched the hum of the engine that turned the corner of the street. There was a lot of horsepower under that hood. But when the car passed by, he was less impressed. The body of the dinged-up Chevy needed some work and a coat of paint. Something in red or black, more in keeping with the sound of the engine.

The sound of the engine.

A.J.'s senses sharpened. He pinpointed the license plate and tried to get a look at the hunched-up driver.

He'd heard that engine before.

The faded beige Chevy pulled into a two-story house down a ways. The driver, wearing a black stocking cap and reflective orange hunting jacket, climbed out, stretched, then rubbed at the small of his back as if he'd been driving a long time. A.J. watched him shuffle around to the trunk of the car and unload a duffel bag, a tackle box and some fishing poles. The poor guy had either eaten his catch or come home empty-handed.

But A.J.'s instincts wouldn't let him feel any sympathy yet. He started the Trans Am's engine and let the power of the car flow through him. "Josh. Before you come down, run an ID on a '78 Chevy Malibu. Plate number six-eight-Charley, four-tango-three."

"Something going on?"

The man unlocked the front door and trudged inside. He was shorter than Galvan, stockier than Claire's description. But the bulk of that jacket and equipment could camouflage a lot, and A.J. hadn't gotten a good look at his face.

He slipped the Trans Am into gear and idled past the driveway to get a better look. "And get me the family name of 7520 Fairway."

They'd better come from a long line of outdoorsmen, or he was going to go knock on the front door and introduce himself.

"That's catty-corner from Claire's location. You need backup?"

"Not yet. But stay close to the phone."

He hung up, pulled around the corner and dialed the safe house number. The facts said a tired fisherman with a wannabe stud car had just come home from a long, uneventful trip.

But those instincts were screaming he'd need backup soon.

"No. Like this."

Claire reached across the sofa and curved Officer

Reed's index finger into the proper position. "Think of the shape of a cursive X when you write it on paper. Without the slash mark. That's it." She signed the last two letters of the alphabet. "Then *Y. Z.*"

She heard a distant, metallic rendition of the "William Tell Overture" that she'd learned to identify as the telephone. When Officer Henley went into the next room to answer it, she knew it was something official. The cops guarding her these past forty-eight hours had learned quickly enough not to let her "see" their conversations. Though she preferred to know what was going on around her, they'd done their best to keep her from being alarmed or upset by such phrases as "possible sighting", "get her to the safe room" or "her father knows better than that."

Pretending the exclusion didn't make her any more edgy than two days of confinement already had, Claire hitched up the legs of her tan linen slacks and curled them beneath her on the sofa. She picked up the soda from their carry-out lunch and took a sip.

"*S-E-X-Y.*" Claire laughed at Mike Reed's adolescent efforts to spell words in sign language. "You think my girl-friend will be impressed? Now how do I say, 'You sexy thang'?"

"At least you're not learning the cuss words." She set her drink on the end table beside the paperback novel she'd been reading and showed him a few phrases that might score him some points.

"Pretty. Woman." She wanted to know what Henley's phone call was all about. Had there been a break on the case? Had Galvan been caught? "Sweetheart." Mike imitated her sign. She really wanted one o'clock to get here so she could see A.J. again.

Not that he used any of his guard-duty time to flirt with her or even get better acquainted. But she felt safer when he was around. Not just from the threat of Galvan. But safer in her own skin. Calmer. Stronger. More confident about who she wanted to be. When A.J. was around, Claire didn't feel handicapped—by her hearing loss or her money or her family name.

She was just Claire.

He'd dismiss it as a crush, no doubt. But she was falling for him. Because he made her feel normal. He made her feel as if her opinions mattered. He made her feel like a woman, not a girl.

He made her feel. Period.

"Show me another one." Mike was still looking to impress his girl. Claire wondered if advising him to just listen to his girlfriend the way A.J. listened to her would make any sense.

But Mike wanted the flash, not the substance. "How about this one?" She curled her right hand into a fist, then extended her thumb, pinkie and index finger into a combination of the letters *I-L-Y*. "I love you."

"Hey, now let's not get carried—"

A vicious concussion of sound ripped through the air outside. Loud enough for Claire to hear the thunderous explosion, powerful enough to shake the sofa beneath. "What—?"

In the next split second, the glass in the living room windows shattered and flew into the room, shredding the curtains and giving Claire a glimpse of fire and metal sailing into the air across the street.

"Get down!" The force of the blast tipped her off balance, and she was halfway there when Mike grabbed her and dove to the floor. He covered her with his body as he pulled out his gun.

Claire heard screams and shouts, from inside the house and out, but nothing made any sense. Mike was on his hands and knees, dragging her toward the archway that led into the windowless interior of the house.

She climbed to her knees to crawl for herself. Tiny aftershocks from the explosion vibrated through her palms. A chunk of the pinewood arch frame splintered before her eyes. Mike pushed her back down to the floor.

Oh God.

"Henley!"

She knew that sound. Not again.

Officer Henley appeared in the archway. A bullet struck him in the neck above the collar of his Kevlar vest and down he fell.

"No!" Claire screamed and reached for the fallen man. Mike grabbed her by the collar and thrust her back against the base of the sofa. A cushion exploded above her head and stuffing snowed down on them.

Mike was on his radio. "We have a security breach. Shots fired! Officer down!" He shoved the radio into her hands. "Stay put."

"But I can't—" He didn't wait for her to explain that she might not be able to pick up any of the responses from the airwaves. He crawled on his belly toward the closest window. Another shot gouged out the floor beside him. "Mike!"

Propping his back against the wall, he cinched up his protective vest, rose to his feet and turned to peer through the tatters of curtain still hanging in the frame. His body jerked and his knees crumpled.

"Mike!"

He threw himself against the wall and sank to the floor, clutching his shoulder as a circle of crimson bloomed on his white sleeve.

"Get to the safe room!" he ordered between clenched teeth. "Get out of here." He shoved his gun and his good hand through the open window and started firing. "Now!"

Claire couldn't tell if the grit stinging her eyes were tears or debris. People were dying for her. They were dying!

Getting out of there would be the surest way to remove them as a target and spare their lives.

Pressing her belly flat to the hardwood floor, she crawled beneath the coffee table and dragged it along on top of her toward Henley's body. "I'm sorry. I'm so sorry," she whispered, reaching out to touch his still hand.

Another shot broke a leg of the coffee table and tilted it over her back. Splinters pricked her bare ankle and pierced the top of her feet. Instead of crying out, Claire scrambled over Henley's body and tumbled into the hallway. A bullet followed her through the archway and lodged itself into the wall across from her.

Oh God, what was she going to do?

She needed A.J. She needed to think.

She swiveled her head back and forth, seeing the promise of easy escape through the front door just a few feet away. But Mike said to head for the safe room—the interior bathroom down the hall toward the kitchen.

Desperate instincts made her want to do more than just run and hide. Rising up on her knees, she used all her strength to grab Henley's vest and throw herself back to drag the lifeless body into the hallway with her. A couple more tugs and she'd hauled him around the corner.

Another bullet sprayed chips of wood and plaster beside her head. Claire swiped the grit from her cheek and ripped open the Velcro on Henley's vest. His blood seeped onto her fingers as she pushed the metal-lined nylon over his head, then rolled him from one shoulder to the next to remove his vest.

She slipped the Kevlar over her head and ducked as a shower of glass rained down from the top of the front door. Was that a ricochet? Had the shooter changed his location? Could he move that fast? Dammit! Wasn't anybody stopping Galvan?

Barefoot and bleeding, Claire asked Henley to make one more sacrifice. She pulled the gun from his limp hand and crawled down the hallway. It was heavier than she'd expected. And cold. She hadn't expected the metal of the gun to be so cold. She didn't know who the hell she was going to shoot—she didn't even know how to use the thing.

But she wasn't just going to die. She wasn't going to be a very nice good girl about this and let Galvan win without a fight.

She couldn't hear or feel the shots any longer, but something made her turn. Rolling over onto her bottom, she squeezed the gun between both hands and caught a ragged breath. The wood around the front door's dead bolt exploded. And then the whole thing was flying toward her.

Claire screamed. She raised the gun. A man in dark clothes rolled across the floor. She found the trigger.

He lunged toward her. "No, Claire!"

"A.J.?"

His hand closed around the gun and shoved it out of harm's way as his body tackled hers.

Too stunned at the recognition, too numb with fear, too

blinded by the adrenaline still pumping into her system, Claire could only wrap her free arm around his neck and hold on as they slid across the floor and bumped to a stop against the wall.

He folded his body around hers, squeezing her in a life-affirming embrace. He clung to her with his arms and legs. He pressed his rough cheek against her own and made sounds—whispers of air, brushes of lips—deep and potent against her ear.

"A.J. A.J."

By the time she could chant his name and thank God that he had come to save her, A.J. was rolling to his feet and dragging her up to his chest. He hooked his arm around her waist and half dragged, half carried her down the hallway toward the door that was hanging from one hinge. He lifted her over Henley's body, placing himself for a split second between her and the open archway.

And then her feet were on the concrete steps and the cool wet grass and she was running. They ran straight for the black Trans Am, parked like a car wreck in the middle of the lawn. The exhaust told her the engine was still running as A.J. opened the door and dumped her inside.

He ran around and climbed in. A bullet smacked against the windshield, and he shoved her head down between her knees as a web of cracks rippled outward from the tiny hole. A.J. shifted into gear and stepped on the gas, slamming Claire against the door as the wheels caught in the grass and mud and the car lurched forward. They bounced over the sidewalk into the street. From the roar of the engine through the floorboards and the acrid stench of burnt rubber, she knew that the car had found traction and they were flying through the streets.

By the time A.J. massaged the back of her neck and urged her to sit up, they were turning out of the residential area onto a busy, four-lane street. He drove with calm assurance through the other cars, his speed matching the flow of traffic and blending in. She watched the landmarks go by and knew they were heading downtown toward the heart of the city.

"Henley's dead," was all she could think to say.

A.J. nodded. "Better buckle up." He glanced toward the straps beside her and Claire dutifully complied.

She watched him holster his gun and pull out his cell phone in one fluid motion. He punched in a number, then wedged it between his ear and shoulder to free one hand to reach across the car and touch her cheek. His fingers shook as he brushed them across her skin. He smoothed the hair away from her eyes and tucked it behind her ear. Claire hugged her arms around the bullet-resistant vest she wore and wanted to cry.

Not because she was hurt. Not because she was scared. Not because Dominic Galvan had killed one cop and wounded another trying to get to her.

She wanted to cry because A.J. had tears in his eyes.

But he blinked them away and turned his face into an emotionless mask as soon as someone picked up the other end of the line.

"The safe house has been compromised." She read the words clearly on his articulate mouth. "Repeat. The safe house has been compromised. I'm going under, Josh. I'm taking Claire with me. I'll contact you when I can."

He listened to something Josh said and nodded.

"Always, *amigo*." He turned. Golden eyes met blue across the car. "I'll watch her back, too."

"What does all that mean?" she asked, once he'd disconnected the call and tucked the phone back inside his jacket. "Going under?"

"It's you and me now, *amor.*" He reached across the console and laced his fingers through hers. Claire held on with both hands. "*I'm* your safe house."

Chapter Eight

A.J.'s damn hand was shaking as he shoved his key into the lock and opened his apartment door.

He held Claire around the waist, shielding her between his body and the door. He knew Galvan hadn't followed them. He'd driven too fast, taken too many shortcuts for even the best of trackers to pursue them. She still wore that damn Kevlar, and he was armed to the teeth with both his weapons and the service pistol she'd taken off Jordan Henley.

But he still felt the threat, hanging like a shroud around his shoulders. His mind had replayed a perpetual loop of images of that Chevy Malibu blowing sky-high, shattering the windows in every house for half a block. The gunshots had hit next. A high-powered sniper's rifle used for only one purpose—to kill.

The fisherman in the dark gray house. Dominic Galvan. Able to pick off every moving object in the safe house from his vantage point on the second floor.

Claire had been one of those moving objects. Bullets were flying. He'd heard her scream over Henley's phone and had floored it. He had to get to her. By the time he'd shot through the lock and busted his way inside, she was armored and armed—and hurt.

The danger of the gun pointed his way was almost an afterthought when he saw all that blood on her. Her hands, her feet, her neck. He thought she'd been hit. He knew she was dying. *No! No way. No damn way!*

He'd gotten her out. He'd gotten her to safety—for the time being. But he still couldn't erase those images.

He could smell it on her now. The coppery tang of blood. Twelve years on the force, most of it on the streets in undercover work, he'd seen plenty of blood. Even his own. He'd turned off his emotions and dealt with it.

But his stomach twisted into a big, queasy knot at that smell on her.

The dead bolt finally turned. A.J. opened the door and pushed her inside.

"Wait here," he instructed, refastening the bolt and the knob lock before slipping from room to room to pull every blind and double-check that every window was secure.

When he came back to the foyer, she was rooted to the same spot, huddled inside his leather jacket. Barefoot and small and shaking, as the shock wore off and the chills set in.

The first things he reached for were her hands. He pulled them from that perpetual clutch across her stomach and held them out between them, palm up, palm down, inspecting them for any cuts or bruises.

"Are you hurt?" He rubbed his thumb across the back of her knuckles, flaking away the blood that had dried there. Not her blood. He thanked the saints who had protected her.

Her eyes darkened like indigo pools against her pale skin as she watched him kneel at her feet. Splinters here. Scratches. All things he could fix.

But he couldn't right now. His hands were still shaking. He'd almost lost her.

A.J. rose and tunneled his fingers into the tangled fall of hair at her temple. He snugged it behind her ear and swore at the blood staining her lobe and the transmitter nestled inside her ear. Where she was most vulnerable. The rage in his gut poured out through his veins. He barely held it in check behind his tightly clenched teeth. "Did he hurt you?"

"He didn't shoot me," she murmured, closing her hand around his wrist to pull him away from the sensitive spot.

It was barely a cut, just a nick on her scalp. But the blood on her snapped the last of his control. "Where else did he hurt you?"

His hands were on her neck now, on her shoulders. He pushed aside his jacket and dropped it to the floor.

"I'm fine. There's nothing serious—".

But he couldn't hear her words. There was blood on the Kevlar. He ripped open the Velcro at each side and pulled it off over her head and tossed it aside. His own pulse thundered in his ears. "Where are you hurt?"

His hands were on her waist, at her hips, up and down her arms and up to her neck again. He was rougher than he should have been, needier than he wanted to be.

"A.J."

And then her hands were on him. Those strong, beautiful—bloodstained—hands were on his face. Framing his jaw and forcing him to look her straight in the eye the way she had beneath the trees that night of the party. "I'm okay, A.J. I'm fine."

He heard the words, knew that she believed them. But he needed a different kind of proof.

With a gut-deep sigh that wrenched through his chest, he raked his fingers into her hair, tilted her head and kissed her.

At first it was just his lips on hers, learning their shape, seeking their taste. He took advantage when her lips parted on a soft breath. Thrusting his tongue inside, he discovered the textures of a mouth that could light up his soul with a smile, stir up his amusement with its sass—and set him on fire with its pliant demands beneath his own.

Dammit all, she was kissing him back! Like she meant it. It was no tentative exploration, no submissive acquiescence. Her welcome acceptance of his passionate need humbled him, hardened him. She chased away the fears and anger with her questing fingers and throaty whimpers.

Claire's hands were on his face, in his hair, around his neck. She stretched up on tiptoe, asking for more, and A.J. obliged by palming her butt and lifting her. He leaned into the door, pinning her hips with his own, freeing his hands to skim along her sides and catch his thumbs beneath the swells of her breasts. They were small, but full, and hot to the touch even through the clothes she wore.

A.J.'s blood thundered through his veins and pooled behind the zipper of his jeans. He squeezed his thumbs between their bodies and flicked her taut, pearled nipples. Claire moaned in her throat and he instantly moved his lips to the spot.

"I don't want you to be hurt," he whispered against her skin, forgetting she couldn't hear. "I need you to be safe." He touched her again, and when she hummed with husky pleasure, he laved the softness of her throat and absorbed the vibrations underneath.

"A.J.," she breathed, twisting her hips to find some release and rubbing herself against his erection. "A.J.?" She froze for a moment, suspended in time with her thighs clutched around his. His arousal seemed to surprise her, please her, inspire her. Her cheeks blushed a healthy shade of pink, and she wasted little time digging her fingers into the short crop of his hair and directing his mouth back to hers. "A.J."

Lightning arced between them. He claimed her open mouth with all the frustrated desire he'd denied himself for too many long days and nights. He pulled her away from the door and wrapped her up in his arms, still holding her just as close.

She was pure temptation—unhindered by her innocence and as greedy with need as he seemed to be. He kissed her hard and deep, extracting a promise from her that she was, indeed, in one piece.

But as the strength in his arms waned, and his fears for her ebbed to a manageable concern, sanity returned. He remembered about breathing, and discovered that Claire's chest was moving in and out just as deeply and erratically as his own. A.J. lowered her feet to the floor, and in the ultimate demonstration of self-control, he tore his mouth from hers and ended the kiss.

He was the experienced one. He knew where an embrace like that was headed. Taking Claire Winthrop to his bed on their very first kiss sounded naughty and perfect, but it didn't seem like the mature or professional thing to do. Though his body had been more than willing to teach her everything she wanted to learn about making love, the rest of him needed something else.

So he hugged his arms around her, letting one hand find a home on her hip, the other in her hair. Her arms settled around his waist, and with a deep sigh that eased the last of the turbulent emotions inside him, she lay her cheek against his shoulder and snuggled close. A.J. rested his chin in the crown of her silky hair and let the fact she was bless-edly alive and virtually unharmed sink in.

They stood like that for several minutes, and A.J. had the foolish notion that he could go on holding her forever.

But that embrace had been a brief storm. Maybe another would come their way. In the meantime, life went on. And he'd made it his responsibility to see that her life went on for a very, very long time.

"I didn't mean it to happen that way," he apologized, tipping her chin up to read his lips. "But I'm not sorry I kissed you."

"I'm not, either. Sorry, I mean."

He brushed his fingertip across the swollen lips of her sweet, forgiving smile. "I didn't exactly leave you much choice."

"It's okay, A.J." She caught his fingers in hers and stilled his guilty caresses. "I was scared, too." Her hand slipped up to cup the side of his face. Her eyes sparkled with a hopeful trust he wasn't sure he deserved. "Now? Not so much."

Then she was pulling away, unbuttoning the bloody collar of her blouse and tugging it away from her skin. "Where's your bathroom? I need to get out of these clothes and clean up."

"Around the corner on your left. I'll set out a towel and something to wear."

A.J. hooked his thumbs into the pockets of his jeans and watched her until she disappeared from his line of sight. He didn't move until he heard the water running, and then he had to keep moving or he'd go nuts thinking about that finely tuned body all naked and soapy inside his shower.

I was scared, too. Too.

So she knew he wasn't as big and bad and cool under

the collar as the image of himself he'd learned to portray over the years.

That intuition about people she had was a force to be reckoned with. How else could a twenty-three-year-old virgin be wise enough to figure out the secrets of a thirty-five-year-old man?

THERE WASN'T ANYTHING too gentlemanly about a strip club where mostly naked women danced on the bar and beefy bouncers tossed out anyone who didn't order regular drinks or give big tips to the waitstaff. But the Riverfront Gentleman's Club, where A.J. and Claire had gotten temporary jobs under the fake names of Joe and Kiki, was loud and busy. And nobody asked a lot of questions.

"I saw the news." Dwight Powers sounded just as pissed off as A.J. had been when he'd seen Claire's face plastered across the television screen in the employees' workroom. "I've already called all the stations and the papers. You won't see it again."

A.J. poured a couple of drafts of beer and set them on the waitress's cork-lined tray at the end of the bar. With his cell wedged between his ear and shoulder, he managed to make change at the register, keep track of his conversation with Dwight and scan the patrons of the club to make sure one particular waitress was always in sight.

"You'd think Winthrop had a death wish for his daughter, posting a reward like that." Once again, A.J. wondered just how close to home Dominic Galvan's accomplice at Winthrop Enterprises was to Claire. "All of Kansas City's going to be looking for her now."

"He's a father, A.J. As far as he knows, the safe house was compromised and an attempt was made on Claire's life. According to the news, she's on the run and lost or lying dead somewhere. He just wants her back in his arms." The heavy breath on the other end of the line warned A.J. that this topic might be hitting a little close to home for Powers. But either the man was made of stone, or he was the consummate professional because the A.D.A. glossed right over the awkward pause. "You've tied my hands by not letting him know she's with you."

A.J. shook his head. He was absolutely firm on this. "I don't trust anyone but you and Josh right now with that information. Someone had to leak the location of the safe house. Galvan's either got someone inside at KCPD, which I doubt, or his accomplice has enough influence to tap into our most private information lines."

Marcus Tucker came to mind. He had enough covert training and shady *security* associates to uncover that kind of information. Hell. Maybe it was Winthrop's snooty wife. He'd be willing to bet she'd do just about anything to get what she wanted. And she certainly hadn't been a friend to Claire at that party. Then, of course, there was Daddy. Maybe the grief-stricken father was just an act, and his public pleas to find his daughter were a heartless ploy to track down the one person who could destroy him.

"I put through your request to Tenebrosa. Their governmental army is going to send whatever they have in Galvan's medical file. I'm not expecting much. But I had another idea."

"Yeah?"

"We can run the semen sample from Valerie Justice's apartment against DNA from members of the Winthrop Board of Directors."

A.J. stopped, with a whiskey bottle poised above an

old-fashioned glass. "Brilliant idea, but they'll never agree to that."

Powers laughed, but it was more of a gloat than real humor. "Leave that to me. You have your talents, Detective, and I have mine."

A.J. finished mixing the drink. He was beginning to think there might be something to like about the Assistant District Attorney. There was certainly something there he could respect. "You're not someone I want to play poker with, are you, Powers?"

"I've heard the same thing about you, Rodriguez."

After A.J. hung up, he wiped down the bar and started unloading the clean glasses from the back. His internal radar knew the instant Claire had changed directions out on the floor and was heading toward the bar. He went down to the tarnished brass bumpers that separated the waitress station from the rest of the bar and watched her approach.

She looked nothing like the champagne-haired heiress with the silk suit and cultured pearls he'd seen on the news. A bottle of brown wash had dulled the color of her hair, and his black-framed glasses obscured her face in an eccentric, coyly intellectual kind of way.

But the blue eyes were the same, and those articulate hands still made his pulse rate do crazy things. Even when one finger was pointed squarely at him, and the wag on the end of it indicated her patience was frazzling. He did his best not to smile.

"You do know I've never waited tables before?" She plopped the tray down on the counter. "That's the third set of drinks I've gotten wrong tonight."

A.J. practically had to read Claire's lips to hear her over

the raucous catcalls and loud music that swelled to the big finish of Debbie Demure's pole dancing number.

"I don't think experience matters here."

In fact, one look at Claire in that sexy street-punk outfit of hers and the manager had hired them on the spot. A.J. couldn't resist making his point. He circled the end of the bar and cozied up to her. It didn't hurt their cover to let everyone in the place know that she was off-limits. Sliding his hand around her waist, he palmed a delicious expanse of soft, supple skin, revealed between the loose, low rise of his jeans on her hips and the tied-up hem of his old Led Zeppelin T-shirt.

"Trust me. Just smile and don't spill whatever you do serve them."

"Very funny." She swatted at his shoulder, then massaged her hand across the spot as if she thought she'd done some damage to him. "But I can't hear anybody. And it's too dark in here. Between that and the flashing lights, it's hard to read what they're saying. I feel like an idiot."

"Hey." A.J. drifted half a step closer and let his hand slide against her warm, silky back. He brushed her hair away from her temple, exposing her naked ear. The delicate pink shell almost looked as if it belonged on someone else without the transmitter and speech processor attached. But since her hearing aids were probably Claire Winthrop's most identifiable feature, he'd asked her to remove them. "I thought you were going to look at this as some kind of adventure."

"Yes, but I'd like it to be a successful adventure. You said you only had enough cash to pay for the room we rented this week."

"We're not hurting for money." But, maybe to an heiress who was used to mansions and champagne, living in a studio over a tattoo parlor was hurting pretty bad.

"I'd like to at least buy a change of underwear and some food to eat."

"I can spring for those," he assured her. He'd quickly nixed her offer to pawn her jewelry or call her bank that afternoon. Both transactions were easy to trace. Any amateur sleuth, much less a man of Galvan's experience, could find her by placing one phone call.

"But I want to help. I'm part of this investigation, too." She curled her fingers into the front of his shirt, but it was more reprimand than caress. "You and your friends are putting your lives on the line for me. Some of them are dying for me. If all I can do to help is put some money on the table so we can eat, then that's what I'm going to do."

"Okay, *amor*. Okay." She'd made him sound a little like her father just then, and he wasn't too sure he liked the comparison. "You're in charge of food. As long as you blend in and don't draw attention to yourself—and you run for cover the instant I tell you to—you're welcome to help in any way you want on this investigation."

Her chin perked at an indignant angle, as if she was surprised she'd won the argument. "Thank you."

A.J. finally let himself smile. "Now go out there and be the best damn cocktail waitress you can be."

"Smart-ass."

Man, he hadn't been called that in a lot of years. Her teasing subtracted at least a decade of life experience off his conscience.

"You know, Kiki," he emphasized her alias to let her know he was playing, "I don't think your hearing loss is your biggest handicap. I think it's that temper of yours."

Her mouth opened to argue; he silenced it with a kiss. Then he gave her curvy rump a little swat and sent her back onto the floor.

Too many years on the force still had him scanning the club for anything or anyone that looked out of place. But he couldn't seem to stop smiling.

Undercover work had never been this much fun.

CLAIRE LIMPED into the women's dressing room after using the toilet and sank with a groan into the first empty plastic chair she could find. Who knew that after all those years of dance training, she would be too out of shape to survive one seven-hour shift on her feet?

Toeing off the tennis shoes she'd borrowed from A.J., she curled a foot into her lap and rubbed the swollen arch. Her first night as Kiki the cocktail waitress had been more of an ordeal than she'd expected, and it had given her a taste of both the allure and constant tension of undercover police work. She hadn't solved any crimes. But no one had tried to kill her, either.

It had been interesting to see a whole new part of Kansas City. And though a couple of touchy-feely customers had spooked her a little with their suggestive gestures and comments, she'd learned how a friendly smile or an extra wiggle of her hips could turn a dollar tip into five. The spilled beer and mixed-up drinks had been embarrassing. Flirting with A.J. had been fun. And—ow! she stretched out her leg and pointed her toes—running on her feet all night had been painful.

But Claire was as proud of the thirty-two dollars she'd earned in tips tonight as she was of her college degree. Because she'd earned them both completely on her own.

One of the exotic dancers who'd performed onstage in little more than a thong and some feathers waltzed into the room on her three-inch heels, pulled on a white terry cloth robe and slipped into the chair beside Claire. "I said, aren't you the new girl?"

Claire hadn't heard her come in, didn't know she'd spoken, but she could see the greeting reflected in the lighted mirror over the dressing table in front of them. "I'm Kiki."

"Debbie Dunning." Debbie peeled off her metallic silver wig and shook a plain brown ponytail down the center of her back. She misinterpreted the reason Claire kept watching her in the mirror. "Demure's my stage name. I figured it was a pretty good joke. Nothing about what we do here is demure."

Claire nodded. She got the joke.

Debbie surprised her by suddenly turning and leaning over to inspect Claire's foot. "Problem?"

"I don't know how you do it, dancing all night. My legs and feet are killing me." She'd carefully avoided difficult sounds, and articulated as clearly as she could without hearing her own speech patterns.

"Here. Try this." Debbie dug through an oversize tote bag on the counter and tossed Claire a tube of eucalyptus-scented foot lotion. It was one hundred percent easier to read her words straight on instead of backward in the mirror. "The right size of shoe would help, too. Who do those big boats belong to?"

"A…" She'd almost slipped and said A.J. "A friend. Joe."

"Your boyfriend, the bartender? He's a cutie."

More like a sexy demigod, but that opinion was for her own private fantasies. "Yeah."

Not terribly eloquent, but apparently sufficient to keep

the conversation going. Claire missed bits and pieces of it because Debbie kept looking in the mirror to remove false eyelashes and what looked like a week's worth of makeup. Claire pretended to concentrate on massaging the soothing lotion into her feet to cover her seeming inattention.

"…your own shoes?" A.J. had said there wouldn't be a lot of questions in a place like the Riverfront. But she didn't feel any threat from Debbie. The dancer seemed to be making an effort to be friendly, so Claire answered in kind.

"I, uh, lost my shoes." Stretching the truth was a new experience for her. "I left them at…the last place I stayed."

Apparently, it wasn't unheard of in Debbie's world for a person to not own her own pair of shoes. Sad.

"What size are you? In shoes?"

"A six."

Debbie got up and disappeared through another door. When she reappeared a minute later, she wore a pair of jeans and a tank top, and carried a pair of white running shoes. She handed the shoes to Claire. "Here. One of the girls who used to work here left them behind. They should work for you."

"Are you sure?" With a wave of her hand, Debbie gave her the go-ahead. As soon as she tied them on, Claire felt the arch supports kick in. "Heaven. Thanks."

"No problem. We girls have to look out for each other down here on the riverfront." She suddenly looked away. Claire missed the words, but she understood the "hold on a second" gesture. Debbie fished a cell phone out of her bag and answered it.

Girls lookin' out for each other, huh? Had Claire just made a friend? She tried to think back to another time when she'd hit it off so quickly with another woman. Certainly not with her stepmother. And she and Gina's lifestyles were so different, they barely passed as friendly acquaintances.

She liked this independence. She liked Debbie.

Debbie waved her fist in the air, startling Claire from her reverie. The other woman was pleading with the person on the phone. Tension radiated from her posture as she collapsed into her chair and stuffed her phone back in the bag.

Claire hadn't caught any of the conversation, but something had clearly upset her new potential friend. After waiting what she thought was a polite length of time, she asked, "Are you okay?"

Debbie nodded, but the reflection of red-rimmed eyes in the mirror told Claire the truth.

"What happened?"

"That was the professor from one of my classes." She looked at Claire, debating whether or not she could be trusted. With a heave of her shoulders Debbie stood. Claire got up, too, trying to keep Debbie's face in view as she started to pace. "I failed my chemistry test….me retake it. But if I didn't have enough time…when will I have time to study for the retake? I'll get behind in everything else and…work every night."

A stripper in a chemistry class? It sounded about as farfetched as an heiress serving drinks in a strip joint. Maybe she and Debbie had more in common than either of them realized.

"What are you studying?"

"Nursing. I'm close to getting my practical nursing license. I'd like to go to school full-time and become an RN, but that takes money." She threw up her hands. "So I work every night and don't have time to study."

Claire had never *had* to work before tonight. Of course, there had been a lot of firsts in her life this week. First murder scene, first car bomb, first kiss from a man who could make her forget everything else except that kiss.

Her blood heated at the memory of that passionate affirmation of life in A.J.'s apartment. That needy admission of fears and reassurances, that volatile exploration of mutual hunger.

She felt as if she'd spent twenty-three years living in a plastic, baby-doll world. But like Debbie Dunning, she was learning about living in the real world. She loved it. She felt richer out here. More alive. More aware of everything she stood to lose if Dominic Galvan found her before KCPD found him.

Hating how that man could get inside her head and erase the joys and textures she was just now beginning to discover about living, Claire fought to recapture the camaraderie she'd felt with Debbie. "Is there anything I can do to help? You know, girls lookin' out for each other?"

Debbie seemed surprised that Claire had asked. But she shook her head and pointed to the clock on the wall. "Look. Sorry I dumped all that on you." She pulled on a denim jacket, slung her bag over her shoulder and retreated toward the club's rear exit. "I have to run to get to the bus stop before the line stops running. See you tomorrow?"

Without her makeup and costume, Debbie looked more like a co-ed than an exotic dancer. She felt more like a friend. "Sure."

She stopped with her hand on the doorknob and waited. "Aren't you going to answer that?" Claire frowned at the question. Debbie glanced to a point behind Claire's shoulder. "Your boyfriend?"

"Oh." Claire spun around and found A.J. standing in the open doorway behind her, wearing his leather jacket and carrying the hooded sweatshirt he'd loaned her. She wondered how long he'd been knocking and whether or not Debbie had picked up on her inability to hear him. "Joe."

"Everything okay in here?" He looked from her to Debbie and back to her, the look in his eyes telling her that he'd stood outside the dressing room door long enough to be concerned.

"Fine," Claire reassured him. "Debbie and I were just getting acquainted."

There must have been some sort of exchange because A.J. nodded. "Same here. Good night."

Then he closed the distance between them. He draped the sweatshirt over her shoulders and held it together at the neck while she pushed her arms into the overlong sleeves. But he wasn't being gallant or solicitous, he was getting close enough for her to read his warning without him being overheard. "Be careful who you make friends with. There's a price on your head, remember?"

"Debbie isn't the enemy. She wouldn't hurt me."

"All she has to do is mention to the wrong person that she saw a woman who looks like Claire Winthrop at the club where she works. The fortune hunters will show up in droves and Galvan will be right there with them."

He hooked his fingers around her upper arm to lead her out of the dressing room. But Claire dug in her feet.

"Wait. You have to walk Debbie to the bus stop." A.J. glared. She glared right back. "It's the middle of the night. This isn't the greatest neighborhood. She isn't safe by herself."

"Did you hear anything I said?" He planted his hands

on his hips and ignored the pun. "*You* are my responsibility. Not anyone else. I can't leave you here by yourself."

"Then I'll walk with you."

"I don't want you out after dark."

He'd run out of choices. "If I was in Debbie's place, you'd want someone to escort me, wouldn't you? Please?"

For all of about two seconds, Claire questioned whether or not A.J. was the hero she thought he was.

She'd never doubt him again. With a muttered phrase she suspected was both Spanish and graphic, he grabbed her hand and headed for the exit. "C'mon."

Ten minutes later, they were waving goodbye to Debbie as she climbed onto the well-lit bus and found a seat.

As soon as the door closed, A.J.'s strong arm settled around Claire's waist and urged her into step beside him. "Now we get you home safe and sound."

Claire skipped to get a step ahead of him, then turned and blocked his path. Impulsively, she braced her hands on his chest and stretched up on tiptoe to kiss his cheek. "Thanks for being a good guy."

"Yeah, well don't let that get around, okay?"

He tried to look so tough. But the crinkling of laughter at the corners of his eyes gave him away.

His hands had crept beneath the sweatshirt to the bare skin at her waist, searing her with his heat. The leather of his jacket was soft beneath her palms, and he was harder underneath. It seemed the most natural thing in her brand-new world to haul herself up by a handful of leather and meet him halfway as he bent his head to kiss her again.

His lips moved over hers in a sure possession that warmed the night and kindled a longing deep inside her. Less explosive than the kiss at his apartment, more deliberate than the quick peck inside the club, this kiss spoke of intent.

He tasted warm and male. The rasp of his beard stubble tantalized while the stroke of his tongue soothed.

But the fumes from the bus, shifting into gear and pulling away, stung her nose, breaking the spell.

With a self-conscious laugh at their public display of affection, Claire ducked her chin to her chest and pulled away. That embrace would go a long way toward convincing any onlooker that "Joe" and "Kiki" were a real item. But the hour was late, the sky was heavy with rain, and A.J. had said he didn't want her outside after…dark.

The heat that had drizzled through her froze and locked up the rhythm of her heart.

The corner streetlight was on. A.J. was beside her. But suddenly Claire was awash in goose bumps, afraid of that unseen thing or person in the dark.

She felt the eyes. She felt *him*.

He was watching.

"How…?" She spun around. The bus was already a block away, the faces on board mere silhouettes in its well-lit windows. Was it one of the passengers?

"Claire?"

She looked across the street to spot a wino in the alley. But the only thing he was watching was the inside of his crumpled brown sack.

"Claire." A.J.'s hands were hard on her shoulders.

She lifted her gaze to the black and broken windows of the warehouses on either side of the street. But brusque fingers grabbed her chin and forced her to look into golden eyes instead. "Talk to me right now," A.J. ordered. "What is it?"

"I can feel him watching me. Us. He's here."

Chapter Nine

"What do the symbols stand for?"

Claire sat in the bed, the pillows propped against the wall behind her since there was no headboard. She'd thumbed all the way through the year-old catalog of collectible knives and swords that passed for reading material in the tiny, one-room apartment. There was no TV, no deck of cards. The clock on the bed stand glowed nearly 3:00 a.m., but she was restless and couldn't sleep.

By far, the most interesting thing in the furnished walk-up was the man sitting at the table near the window. Like Claire, A.J. had stripped down to basic clothes for the night. She wore his T-shirt and her panties; he wore his unsnapped jeans and nothing else she could see.

He'd been sitting there, facing the door, his back to her, working with machine-like diligence for the past forty-five minutes. He'd cleaned all three guns, holding them up at arm's length and checking his aim against the chair he'd wedged beneath the doorknob. He wore a small, silver gun in a Velcro strap around his ankle. He'd stuck another in the gap at the back of his jeans. He was clipping the big black gun—the Glock, he'd called it—into his holster in the middle of the table.

"Are you expecting an invasion?" But the lame attempt at a joke bounced off his shoulders as if he was the one with the hearing loss.

"The tattoos on your back—" beside the scar on his shoulder that was too round and perfect to have been anything other than a bullet hole "—they look Chinese. What do they mean?"

It was a beautiful back. Muscled and golden and smooth. Framed by broad shoulders and sturdy triceps, and adorned by three blue-green hieroglyphs of skin art.

While she could appreciate the aesthetics of that back, and feel intimate parts of her respond to his blatant masculine beauty, what struck Claire most was how hard and unyielding that back had become. And how cold she felt that that was all he allowed her to see.

"What does A.J. stand for? Dad said he knew your father. Antonio. Are you Antonio Junior?" She tossed the catalog onto the floor and pulled her legs up beneath her, pretzel-style. She tucked the sheet and blanket up over her lap and wondered how air, so thick with tension, could feel so cold. "I've never had a good nickname. My stepbrother calls me pipsqueak, but I don't really care for that. My middle name is Landers, after my mother's maiden name. But C.L. doesn't roll off the tongue very well. And Claire, well, you can't shorten that into anything, so I've always just been…Claire."

Though not quite a storm, the hard, steady rain falling outside muffled what sounds she *could* hear. But she didn't think there was anything to listen to.

"Dammit, A.J.! Are you even answering me?" Frustration, fueled by fear, erupted inside her. "I can't see what you're saying. I can't hear you." Too strong to be contained by patience or decorum, her emotions flashed along every nerve, then burnt out just as quickly, leaving her weary and cold and shaking. "All I can feel is him watching."

After a long, endless moment when she thought he might be cruel enough to leave her alone in her soundless world, A.J. turned in his chair. Above the grim lines of his unshaven face, he looked at her, but without the golden fire she was used to seeing in his eyes. "They stand for peace, strength and honor. I'm Antonio Joseph, like my father. Now go to sleep, Claire."

"I can't. You're scaring me. Working with all those guns. Not talking."

"You should be scared. I'm losing my edge. Galvan's already gotten to you twice. He killed a good man who stood in his way. Tonight, we were out in the middle of the sidewalk, with at least a dozen vantage points for Galvan to get a shot at you. And what was I doing?"

Being a nice guy? Celebrating life? *Loving me?*

Apparently, none of those things.

"I was standing there like a horny street punk, feeling like I'm all that, thinking about getting laid, instead of getting you out of sight and keeping you safe. That should have been my first priority. That should *be* my first priority. Always."

The idea that he'd been thinking about having sex with her stunned her, pleased her. The idea that he hated having had that thought destroyed her pleasure.

"You can't stay up all night," she countered, trying to argue with reason instead of her battered emotions. "You can't be on watch twenty-four hours a day."

"Galvan doesn't sleep."

"Of course he does. He's human like…" Well, not like

anybody else. A.J. was speaking metaphorically, of course. Galvan would never give up his pursuit. Not until she was dead. Or he was.

Oh, God. Claire caught a breath that lodged painfully in her chest. Was that what this game of undercover hide-and-seek would eventually come down to? Some kind of standoff, shoot-out, last-man-standing tragedy? A confrontation where she or Galvan or both of them would be dead? Or A.J.? Other cops and innocent bystanders—like her students? Like Jordan Henley?

Her breath seeped out and tears stung her eyes. "I don't want you to die for me. I don't want anyone else to die."

A.J. stood and picked up the gun and holster from the table. On bare feet he crossed to the squarish brown sofa. He lifted one end and turned it so that it sat perpendicular to the front door. "To serve and protect. It's what I do. I'm not a punk anymore. I'm a cop."

He sat at the far end of the sofa and swung his legs up so that he could lean back against the armrest and face the door. He set his Glock right beside him on the cushion.

Claire swiped away the tears that dotted her lashes and listened to what he was telling her. Really *listened.*

He had to do his job. He had to be responsible. He didn't think he'd done very well at either task. He intended to rectify those mistakes and do what he considered to be the right thing.

Or die trying.

Peace. Strength. Honor.

Symbols of a man who was more than a badge and a gun. Symbols of character, commitment, belief.

"You're more than a cop," Claire stated quietly. "You're more than some tool of justice or guardianship or death.

You're also a man. A brother. A son. A friend." *You're someone I love.* "You can't beat yourself up because you slid into one role more than another tonight. Being a cop is your job. And I think you're damn good at it. But it's not who you are."

"It's who I have to be."

She ignored the dismissive finality in his eyes. Claire Landers Winthrop had been dismissed one too many times in her life—and never by someone who needed her more.

"You're not coming to bed?" Okay, so there was a little snap to her voice. They'd already discussed how to fit two people on the small double mattress, with one of them on top and one beneath the blanket so they couldn't get into any kind of compromising position. But he preferred to be uncomfortable and alone.

"No." He adjusted, fluffed and finally tossed the throw pillows off the sofa. "I'm fine to sack out here. I want to keep a close eye on you."

The few feet that separated them across the room seemed farther away than the prospect of Dominic Galvan turning himself in to the police. A feeling—intuition, perhaps—swelled inside her, making her feel wise beyond her experience. A.J. didn't want to be alone. He just thought he had to be.

Trusting that instinct, taking a chance, she climbed out of bed, untucked the yellow blanket and folded it up in her arms.

"What are you doing?" She sat down on the edge of the sofa, facing him. "Claire?"

She lay her head against his chest and stretched out beside him on the sofa, pulling the blanket up over them both. "Is this close enough?"

She held her breath, feeling the thunder of his heart beneath her ear, lying there as still as A.J. was beneath her. She rode the deep sigh that expanded his chest. But only when she felt his lips in her hair, and his arms around her, did she snuggle into his heat and close her eyes to sleep.

AMELIA WARD WAS a pretty thing, bustling around the 26th floor in a skirt that was a tad too short to be professional, but just right to remind him why he'd traded in Valerie Justice for a newer model.

She was well on her way to becoming a permanent fixture in the office, provided she passed the Deirdre Winthrop test and kept her hands off Deirdre's husband. In public, at least. He didn't think Deirdre cared too much what Cain did with his private life, so long as nothing embarrassed her, altered her position of power, interfered with her checkbook privileges or kept her children from inheriting the millions of dollars she thought they deserved.

If Amelia had any designs on the boss, thus far she had been discreet. It didn't hurt that she had learned the Winthrop systems quickly and was damnably efficient. Especially during a crisis—like murder investigations and missing daughters and postponed board meetings.

The Chairman of the Board was finally back on track— at his urging, of course. He earned a lot of money coming up with good ideas and playing the game so that it appeared the company always came first—and that the family was the company.

Even this impromptu board meeting had been his suggestion. Business as usual. That was the ticket to assure investors and trading partners that all was well at Winthrop, Inc., despite the attempt on Claire's life and her subsequent disappearance. Keep the company running as normally as possible. Beyond dispelling rumors and taking some of the public scrutiny off the missing heiress, he'd suggested that busy hands would help keep their minds from brooding on horrible thoughts about how Claire was doing and where she might be.

He settled on the black leather couch in the lobby beside Gina Gunn and pretended an interest in the colorful fish swimming in the aquarium. All of the board members and a couple of guests were on hand—pacing the lobby, reading the paper, prepping for the meeting. Peter Landers. Gabriel and Gina Gunn. Marcus Tucker. Rob Hastings. Amelia Ward.

Cain had called them together to discuss the Japanese offer—and Dwight Powers's attempt to take the murder investigation in a new direction. The damn D.A. thought he was so smart, using the excuse of the board's travels into Third World countries and suspect nations as a reason to subpoena medical records—including DNA samples. Something about verifying their passport identifications in the interest of Homeland Security. The corporation's attorneys would have him laughed out of court by the time they finished their appeals.

Of course, it would go a long way to promote company and family morale if everyone voluntarily supplied a DNA sample to prove they had nothing to do with Valerie's death—pardon, he meant alleged death, of course. By the time they found her body, any trail leading to him would have grown cold.

And how easy would it be to reach into his private petty expense fund and pay off some lab technician to point the DNA match another way? Maybe even toward Galvan. His obsession with Claire was getting tedious. Ramon

Goya was waiting, with millions of dollars worth of "imports" for him to distribute. If he could get rid of Claire, he could get Galvan back on task.

"Are you sure?" Amelia's animated response on the phone in her office caught his attention. It was a unique mixture of excitement and anxiety that attracted the other board members as well. "Un-huh." He stood and watched her show a little more thigh as she bent over her desk to scribble something on her notepad. "Give me your address. If this pans out, the company will send you a check."

"Amelia?" She was clearly agitated about something.

"Hold on a sec." The secretary covered the receiver and turned to wave them over to her door. "This is someone who claims to know where Claire is. They must have seen the item on the news before it was pulled. Should I tell Mr. Winthrop? He'd want to know about his daughter, but if it's a prank, he doesn't need to be disturbed and upset anymore than he already is.

"What should I do?" She looked at each board member, gathered outside her doorway.

"I'll take care of it."

She handed him the phone.

A FAMILIAR FIGURE slid onto the stool at the end of the bar. "Does your mama know you're workin' in a place like this, Rodriguez? A strip joint?"

"Cole Taylor." A.J. grinned and reached across the bar to shake hands and butt fists with his former partner and oldest friend. "Can't you read? The sign out front says Exotic Dancers."

"Oh, so it's a classy place." Cole combed his fingers through his short dark hair and turned to watch the dancer onstage pop one of the balloons on her chest. "I'd better start absorbing the culture."

A.J. laughed at the easy give-and-take they'd always shared. "Forget my mama. You turn that stool back around this way or I'm gonna call your wife."

Cole put up one hand in surrender and then pulled a five-dollar bill from his pocket. "Well, since she can kick my butt, on second thought I think I will just sit here and have a beer."

A.J. picked up a glass and pulled a draft. "So how is Victoria?"

"My wife is healthy and happy, thank you very much, and so's her husband."

Right. Another friend on the force who'd learned how to be a cop and love a woman without shortchanging either role. A.J. just wasn't seeing how he and Claire could make anything work once this mess was over. If they survived this mess. If he didn't get her killed or his heart ripped up in the process.

A.J. tossed a coaster onto the counter and served Cole his beer. "This one's on the house, *amigo*."

Cole accepted the drink, but slid the fiver across the bar. "Thanks, *amigo*. But I really want to pay for this one."

A.J. understood that tone. He knew the look in the eye. They'd both worked undercover for too many years for him not to recognize the signs that told him this surprise visit was actually a contact call—a way for a cop on the inside to communicate with the department without jeopardizing his cover.

Angling his back to the other patrons at the bar, A.J. picked up the bill and flipped it to read the phone number and note on the other side. *Body Found.*

A charge of adrenaline quickened A.J.'s heartbeat. "You kiddin' me?"

Cole raised his glass in a toast as the music ended, and a smattering of applause and whistles marked the end of the performance. He fit in with this lowbrow crowd like a pro. But as he played the role of good ole boy, he talked all business. "Police dogs located Valerie Justice in one of the landfills south of town. You can call Holly Masterson at that number—she's doing the autopsy this evening. Josh says she's heading up the CSI team assigned to the case."

"I know her." A.J. stuffed the phone number into his pocket. He needed to talk to Holly to find out if there was any forensic evidence they could use against Galvan in order to take the heat off Claire as the key component of the D.A.'s case.

Another part of him just wanted to take a look at the body to see what Claire had seen. To help him understand what she'd gone through. He wanted everything to be exactly as she described so he could go back to her father and stepfamily and handsy, wannabe boyfriend and shove it down their throats that Claire didn't make up stories. She had a good head on her shoulders and an even bigger heart inside her. And the next time any one of them ignored her or dismissed her, then he...hell.

He wouldn't do a damn thing. She was getting pretty good at standing up for herself and being heard. She could take care of herself without his help.

"So which one is she?" Cole's probing gaze pulled A.J. from his gloomy mood. "I want to meet the woman who finally put you off your game."

"Who says I'm off my game?"

Cole didn't believe the bravado act any more than he

did. "This is me you're talking to." He wrapped his hands around his glass and leaned over the bar to whisper. "Between what Josh tells me, and what I've seen tonight, you're distracted. The A.J. I know doesn't get distracted."

The A.J. Cole knew would never have endangered a witness's life because he was too busy kissing her. He wouldn't have let personal feelings get in the way of doing his job—he wouldn't have acknowledged even having personal feelings.

"I'll get the job done," A.J. reassured him.

He'd been telling himself that very thing, over and over, ever since waking up this morning with Claire in his arms. With her snuggled up like a contented kitten on top of his chest, her legs tangled with his, he'd slept the most peaceful sleep he'd ever known. She'd smelled better than the millions of bucks she was worth. And when she'd stirred against him, her hip had nestled against his groin, her breasts had beaded through the thin cotton shirt she wore to brand his chest. Her hand had slid across his shoulder and curled around his neck as if she was dreaming and wanting the same thing his thoroughly awake, lust-starved body did.

"You're doing it again," Cole teased. Maybe it was a friendly warning.

A.J. needed to forget about peaceful nights and passionate mornings. With Claire, at any rate.

"I'll get the job done." He stated the vow more firmly, though he wasn't sure he completely believed it, either.

A.J. spotted the thick, black glasses and ballerina's posture heading toward the bar with an empty tray. "Here she comes. Hey, Kiki."

"Kiki?" Cole asked.

A.J. winked. "She picked it out herself. Said she always wanted a cool nickname. It beats C.L."

"What's C.L.?"

C.L. Claire Landers Winthrop. A.J. frowned. Why hadn't he considered the importance of a name before?

Claire set her tray at the waitress station and leaned against the brass railing. "I need a red beer and a draft."

"Is Peter Landers a relative of yours?"

Her eyes widened with surprise. "That came out of left field."

"Is he?"

"Uncle Peter's my mother's brother. He introduced her to Dad back when the business first started taking off. She loved to travel. So did he. I think if she had lived that Dad would never have settled down to an office job."

"Does Peter do the traveling now?"

She shrugged. "A lot of it. But so do Gabe and Rob and Gina. Why?"

"I'm not sure. I never made the connection between his name and yours before."

"Winthrop prides itself on being a family business." She spouted what sounded like the company motto, then tilted her head toward Cole and shifted her eyes, covertly reminding him that they weren't alone. "But I didn't think we were supposed to talk about that stuff here."

"He's okay." A.J. let his half-formed thought about her uncle's name go until he could figure out whether it was a useful piece to the puzzle surrounding this investigation. He prepped the drinks while he made the introductions. "This is Cole Taylor. Josh's big brother. A lifetime ago, when he first made detective, I used to be this guy's partner. Cole, this is…Kiki."

"I thought you looked familiar." Claire accepted Cole's handshake and smiled a friendly greeting. "You're like a dark-haired version of your brother, Josh."

"I'm the better-looking version of my brother."

They both laughed. But Claire's smile quickly flatlined, and she glanced back and forth from Cole to A.J. "Why are you here? Did something break on the case?"

A.J. considered the note in his pocket, but hesitated to share the information. Out here where they'd have an audience, anyway. Claire would either be elated by the news that there was finally some physical evidence to corroborate her story, or she'd be sickened by the gruesome details regarding the autopsy of a friend.

"A.J.?" She reached across the bar and touched his wrist. She shook her head, catching the slipup. "I mean Joe? What's happening?"

A.J. closed his hand over hers and squeezed, silently asking her to be patient. "Deliver your drinks, then meet me in the back by the janitor's closet."

She tucked a strand of hair behind her ear, then quickly fluffed it back into place, even though there was nothing to hide. "Okay, now I'm really worried."

He patted her hand and let her go. "Deliver the drinks."

With a hesitant nod, she picked up the tray and threaded her way through the patrons who were beginning to fill in the tables closer to the stage for the next performance. A.J. knew he didn't have to wait until she was out of earshot to speak, but he waited until she was at her table and occupied with the customers before coming around the bar to speak with Cole in hushed, urgent tones.

"You say Holly's doing the autopsy right now?"

"She's probably finished by now and typing up her notes."

"You got any plans for the next hour or two?"

Cole grinned and threw a twenty-dollar bill on the counter. "I thought you might ask that. Go ask your questions and find your answers. I'll stay with Miss Kiki."

Besides Josh, Cole was probably the only person he'd entrust Claire's safety to. "Don't let her get hurt."

"Go, already."

"Remember everything I taught you."

All pretense vanished from Cole's expression. He'd always been able to read people. And right now, A.J. had the feeling his old friend was reading more than he was willing to admit himself. "She's really gotten to you, hasn't she?"

A.J. didn't know how to answer that. He wasn't sure he was ready to assess just what that answer might mean. He had to keep his focus on the here and now. On the case. On helping Claire survive.

The only answer he could give was to reach out and squeeze Cole's shoulder. Then he gave him a swat on the arm as if he was sending his first-string player into the game. "Just don't let her get hurt."

A.J. found Claire pacing the back hallway. When he first saw her, she was walking away from him and he allowed himself a second to enjoy the view. She wore a pair of clingy tank tops over his jeans that were baggy and revealing on her. The clothes hugged her lean torso and emphasized the rounded swell of her hips and bottom.

As refined and ladylike as he knew she could be, this was the real Claire Winthrop as far as he was concerned. Proud of a hard night's work. Sassy. Tough. Sexy and real. And as trusting and vulnerable as he was cynical and worldly-wise.

Cole had him pegged.

He was well and truly sunk with this woman.

"A.J." She spun around and caught him staring. But she was worried enough about something that she charged right up to him, taking no notice of his pensive mood. "You're not going off to do something crazy, are you? With all those guns? What did Cole say?"

Her fingers curled around his shoulders and he let his hands go straight to where they wanted to, settling around her waist. "I'm going to go do my job, and I need you to stay here with Cole so that I don't have to worry about Galvan hurting you while I'm gone."

"I want to go with you. I thought we were a team."

A couple of the dancers dashed back and forth at the end of the hallway between numbers, and A.J. realized this place might not be private enough. The door to his left beckoned, mocked. The plastic sign glued to the center read Custodian.

"Let's go in here." He didn't even want to consider the symbolism as he opened the door, turned on the light and ushered the heiress inside.

The smells of paint and ammonia stung his nose, and there was barely enough room for the two of them to stand together and turn around. But the door shut out the loud music and curious looks, and gave him the opportunity to tunnel his fingers into her hair, lift her onto her toes and steal a kiss. And then another one. And then it wasn't really stealing because she looped her arms around his waist and parted her lips and kissed him back.

"A.J." Just one more. "A.J., what—?" One more.

Drawing on the strength of the cop and ignoring the needs of the man, A.J. lifted his mouth and inhaled a sobering breath of cleanser-tinted air. He pulled Claire into his chest and palmed the back of her head, cradling her beneath the crook of his chin.

With a sigh, she settled against him, fitting their bodies together in perfect unison. But as much as he loved holding her, he knew the clock was ticking.

Leaning back, he cupped her face between his hands and tilted it up so she could read his words. "KCPD found Valerie's body. I need to go to the police lab to gather whatever information I can from the autopsy."

"What am I supposed to do while you're gone?"

"Be safe. Stay alive." He combed the hair back from her temples and traced the pretty shells of her ears with fingers that trembled with tightly suppressed need. "Be here for me to come back to."

She moved her hands up to his jaw, stroked the planes of his face and lips, soothed the new and fearsome emotions that truly did have him off his best professional game. That same Madonna-like serenity that had gentled his self-doubts and eased his guilt last night reached out to him again.

"I'll be here," she promised.

He gathered her in his arms and hugged her tight.

How was he ever going to let her go and get his life back to business as usual when this was over? He couldn't picture himself going to parties like the Winthrops hosted, and Claire's bright light certainly didn't belong in the dark world where he made a living.

He didn't want to lose her. He didn't want to lose this.

With his emotions as twisted up as they were, he knew that losing Claire was going to hurt like hell. But deep inside, at the core of what made him a man, A.J. knew that Claire getting hurt—or killed—would destroy him.

He forced himself to pull away so that they could communicate once more. "My instincts tell me we're closing in…that something big's about to break. Now I have to go get the facts to back that up."

Claire nodded her understanding. "The more you push, though, the more likely Galvan and his accomplice will push back. Right?"

Some of his streetwise mentality was rubbing off on her. "Cole will watch over you. I trust him with my life. I'll trust him with yours." He tweaked her chin between his thumb and forefinger to make sure she paid attention to his warning. "You do not leave this building. You do not go off by yourself anywhere. If any of the customers give you any trouble, you tell Cole. If you get the feeling you're being watched again—"

"I'll be good." Her reassuring smile almost made his fears go away.

Almost.

"I know. It's the other guy I'm worried about." God, she was still smiling. "It makes me nuts to know that somebody wants to hurt you. I need you to be safe."

Claire nodded, maybe understanding more than he wanted her to. "And I need you to find answers. Find out why this is happening to me, A.J. Make it go away. I want my life back."

That was one promise he intended to keep. Even if he wasn't a part of it. "Give 'em hell, tiger. Anybody tries to hurt you, you give 'em hell."

"A couple of hours, right?"

"Cole will keep you safe."

"A.J., I…" She grabbed a handful of his T-shirt. An unvoiced thought chinked a frown across her lips.

"What?"

She smoothed everything back into place, including her smile. "Just hurry back."

He leaned in for one last, quick, passionate kiss that promised her everything he had to give.

And then he was gone.

Chapter Ten

"So you've known A.J. a long time?"

Claire set her tray on the bar next to Cole and allowed herself to climb up on the stool beside him for a five-minute break. After a couple of nights of being "on" for the customers, and running herself ragged to do a good job, she was finally learning how to pace herself. During the performances, most of the men didn't want to be disturbed while they lived out some fantasy watching the women onstage. That was when she could take a breather and not worry about reading lips or mixing up drinks. When the number was done, then she'd go check her tables.

But tired feet weren't the main reason she sat down. A.J. had already been gone for the two hours he'd promised, and she was starting to get an antsy feeling that something had happened to detain him.

"We go back a lot of years." Cole smiled as if he was flirting with her, but Claire knew it was part of the act. "He was my training partner when I first made detective. He's got the best instincts of any cop I know. He can take care of himself."

Was she that obvious? "So you think he's okay?"

Cole had blended in like any of the other customers, but

like A.J., she'd also noticed a wariness about the man. Cole was much taller and built on a stockier scale than A.J., so he carried himself differently. But there was something about the eyes that was the same—always looking, always alert, always seeming to know right where she was any time she looked at him across the club floor.

"I think that nose of his is on the trail of something that'll give the good guys an advantage on this case."

"What can Valerie's body tell him?"

Cole shrugged. He might not know all the details of the crime, but he could speculate. "If there's still a bullet in her, then we can trace the gun. Its make, who sells them, who's bought one recently. If there was any struggle, she might have trace DNA of her killers on her. If there was no struggle, that tells us she knew her killer—someone she wouldn't suspect would harm her."

Claire refused to believe someone in her father's own company, or her own family, would want to harm her. That thought scared her more than knowing a hit man was after her. Dominic Galvan was the enemy she knew. But there was someone much more treacherous closer to home— someone she trusted. Someone who had no qualms about betraying her. Who in her circle of family and friends was capable of murder? Or if not actually pulling the trigger, of being callous enough to pay someone to do it for them?

The crowd of patrons filling the dimly lit room suddenly didn't feel as disinterested as they had just a moment ago. The tipsy party atmosphere of the room took a malevolent turn. *What?* she wanted to scream. *Who are you? Why are you doing this to me?*

She turned and scanned each table and booth. Everyone seemed focused on the woman onstage or the drink in his hand. But her arms prickled with goose bumps and her breath caught in her chest. *He* was here. Watching her. Again.

"Hey." Claire gasped out loud at the hand on her knee. As soon as she recognized Cole, he pulled his hand away. "Easy. What is it?"

Freaky paranoia? Shot nerves? "You don't think anything's happened to A.J., do you?" She couldn't do this on her own. She didn't want to be on her own.

Cole's posture didn't relax. Her suspicions had put him on guard. "He's coming back. I've never known him to fail at his word. What's wrong?"

She looked into the seriousness of Cole's eyes. *Never known him to fail.* Is that why A.J. was so hard on himself? Did he think he had to be the perfect, quintessential cop twenty-four hours a day?

Claire knew he was much more than that. But if failure wasn't an option, then how could he ever take a chance on happiness? On love? On her?

Why couldn't he just be the man she loved? The man who needed to learn to love himself a little better.

She'd almost blurted it out before he left. *I love you.* But the janitor's closet wasn't the right place for such declarations, and her timing had sucked. He'd been anxious to leave—to pursue the case. And…oh hell. "I think somebody's watching me."

Was it the bachelor party just coming in? Someone hidden in one of the secluded booths?

Claire couldn't see, and she wasn't going to get a chance to because Cole stood and pulled her up in front of him, blocking her view of most of the bar, or rather, blocking their view of her. "Let's go." He kept his hand on her shoulder and nudged her toward the back rooms. "A.J. said to…"

"He said what?" Cole had turned his head. They were still moving. "I couldn't see—"

At the tap on her shoulder, Claire screamed out loud. Cole pulled her behind him as he pushed someone out of the way. The volume of the music and din of voices must have drowned out her scream because no one but Cole seemed to be reacting to her panic.

"Wait." Claire twisted in his grip, needing to see who'd accosted her. "Debbie?"

Debbie Dunning wasn't dressed for work yet. Her plain clothes and unadorned face made it easy to read the tension that had her wound tighter than her stage garters. "Kiki, I need to talk to you."

A gentle shove stopped Cole long enough to check on her friend. "What's wrong? Did your professor give you more grief over that test?"

Debbie's gaze darted about the club as she waved that topic aside. "It's about a guy."

Cole was moving again, taking her away. "You'll have to finish this conversation another time, ladies." They were in the back hallway now, her legs pumping in double time to keep up with him. "The first rule is to get you out of sight, then we'll contact A.J."

Debbie had run to catch up with them. She planted herself in their path. "Claire, you have to listen."

Claire?

She froze.

"That's right." Debbie grimaced in apology. "I know who you are. I recognized you off the TV last night in the dressing room. The shoes made me think you were on the run. And," she cringed, "I think I made a really big mistake."

"What mistake?"

"You're gonna hate me."

"What mistake?" Cole insisted.

Debbie flinched at the big man's threat. Needing information more than she needed protection right now, Claire laid a hand on his arm and tried a calmer approach. "What did you do, Deb?"

Keeping a nervous eye on Cole, she answered. "I called your father's office and said I knew where you were."

"You talked to my father?" A moment's concern quickly passed. Looking at Debbie's expression, there was a bigger problem here. "Who did you talk to?"

The problem was bigger than she'd imagined. "He's on his way here. Right now."

"Who is?"

"I didn't get a name. Except for the secretary, Amelia something. This guy just said he handles these kinds of affairs for Winthrop Enterprises. I thought I could use the reward money for my classes. But then I thought about how you listened to my sob story and made sure I got home okay, and I realized a girl can't rat out her friend. So I called the office back and said I'd made a mistake. But this guy's like a bad date who won't take no for an answer."

She paused to catch her breath and sped on. "I'm sorry. But this guy said he was coming to either find you and take you home where you belong, or he was gonna find me to see what kind of sadistic slut would get your family's hopes up when they're suffering like they are over your disappearance."

Claire squeezed Debbie's hand. "He threatened you?"

"Don't worry about that. I've heard worse." Claire was getting more and more disenchanted with her family and their circle of friends by the minute. "I just wanted to say I'm sorry and give you a heads-up so you had time to get out of here before he comes. I kind of figured you didn't want to be found."

"I can't leave." A.J. had warned her not to. Galvan was out there, waiting for her. But if another enemy showed up here…She turned her head to include Cole. "If I'm gone when A.J. gets back, he'll freak."

"He'll understand. Your safety comes first."

"He'll blame himself." She might not know a lot about men, but she knew that much about A.J. She didn't want to be any more of a burden on his conscience than she already was.

Wait a minute. *Give 'em hell, tiger. Anybody tries to hurt you, you give 'em hell.*

What was the message there? Don't wait for someone else to tell her what to do or to fight her battles for her. Stand up for herself. Be her own person. All those clichés had to come from some piece of wisdom somewhere.

A.J.'s words had her thinking she could take care of herself. That *he* believed she could take care of herself. She could fight this. "I don't want to run," she murmured out loud.

The idea that she could make a difference both thrilled and frightened her. But she could do it. A.J. believed she could do it. For her life—and his sake—she wanted to try.

"I don't want to run," she stated with more conviction. She tugged on Cole's arm. "I'd be able to recognize whomever Debbie talked with on the phone. If I could get a look at everyone who comes in here tonight, we'd know who Galvan's accomplice at Winthrop, Inc., is. Then we could force him to turn in Galvan."

"We don't know that's who Debbie talked to. It could just be a concerned friend," Cole argued. "But the idea is to keep you hidden. If someone else can find you, then Galvan can, too."

"I'm staying."

"No way. I am *not* explaining you getting hurt to A.J."

Claire shook her fists. "I am sick and tired of people telling me what I can and cannot do. I don't need permission to be who I am. I don't have to make my choices based on what someone else thinks Claire Winthrop ought to be."

With a frustrated sigh, she tucked her hair behind her ears. And left it in place. Neither of these people was her enemy; she shouldn't take a life's worth of frustrations out on them. She was thinking more clearly, signing as she spoke this time. "I'm sorry. But I'm the only one here who knows the Winthrop people on sight."

"Maybe that's why one of them wants you dead," Cole pointed out. "What if he spots you before you see him?"

"I could hide."

"Where?" Debbie asked. "There isn't any place secluded in this joint where you could still have a view of the customers."

The best view of the customers.

The germ of an idea formed. A.J. had reputedly taught Cole everything he knew about undercover work. Maybe Claire had picked up a few tips from the master, too.

"What if I hide in plain sight?" She looked into Debbie Dunning's coed face. "Can you fix me up like I was going onstage? With the wig and the makeup?"

"A disguise?"

"Yes."

Debbie's guilt eased into a smile and she grabbed Claire's hand. "C'mon, girlfriend."

A.J. LOCKED THE DOOR of his Trans Am and jogged across the parking lot to the front door of the Riverfront Gentleman's Club. Sneaking in the back way to avoid questions from the manager about his four-hour coffee break was less important than getting to Claire as quickly as possible. He'd been gone almost two hours longer than he'd promised her.

Punctuality was probably another trait highly prized by corporate giants like Winthrop Enterprises, Inc. But in police work, when the pieces of a case started falling into place, a good cop stuck with it until he found his answers.

Bless Holly Masterson's eye for tiny details.

Valerie Justice had been as neatly killed and disposed of as Claire had described. She'd been a beautiful woman in her fifties. The bullet holes had been efficiently placed to kill instantly and make a minimal mess. Though there'd been no plastic mat found with her body, Holly's team had discovered patterns in the pooling of the blood in the body—as if Valerie had been rolled up like a tamale filling and cinched in tight.

Unfortunately for the killer who had rolled her up and transported her to the landfill, he'd left an unintended calling card. Mixed in with Valerie's expensively dyed and permed hair, Holly had found a thin, straight black hair with the root intact to establish DNA. Holly's team had already retrieved a matching hair from the gray house where Galvan had positioned himself to kill Claire.

Thank God the man needed Rogaine. Now all they needed was a sample from Galvan himself and Dwight Powers had a case he could run with. The focus of the prosecution would be the pattern of forensic match-ups at both crime scenes, not the testimony of Galvan's sole surviving witness.

It was news enough to share. Progress enough to give Claire hope that there was an end in sight.

But the most telling clue—pressed into the stiff, bloated skin at the back of Valerie's neck—was the perfect imprint of a man's ring. As if it had turned palm-inward and cut into her skin when he lifted the body to dispose of it. If the killer hadn't done such a thorough job of wrapping up the body, decomposition might have taken the clue with it.

Holly had taken a picture of the marking from every angle, and A.J. had sketched a drawing in his notebook. Four angled lines at the center of a circle, with two small squares at either side.

According to Claire, Galvan wore black leather gloves.

His accomplice at Winthrop, Inc., apparently did not.

He'd find the hand that wore that ring. And he vowed that hand would never hurt Claire again.

A.J. shoved open the door, wanting to stride inside as if he owned the place. But common sense dictated that, as usual, he draw as little attention to himself as possible. It took a few moments for his eyes to adjust from the natural darkness outside to the garish strobe and spotlight swirling up on the stage.

The music was too loud, but it had a spicy salsa beat that seemed to match the pulse in his Latin blood. His chin started an unconscious bob to the rhythms playing in the background. With his hands hooked into the pockets of his jacket, he lingered in the shadows at the back of the club and scanned the bar and tables for the petitely sexy *mamasita* who served the wrong drinks and had a kickin' ass.

When the big man materialized out of the shadows beside him, A.J. didn't react. He'd worked with Cole for too many years to not recognize him by scent or silhouette. "I have good news, *amigo*."

"I have news, too." His former partner's oblique statement put the first suspicious chink in A.J.'s positive mood.

He still hadn't spotted Claire, but Cole wouldn't be standing here for a friendly chat if something had happened to her. "I've got a way to nail Galvan. And a new lead on the accomplice."

"I've got a lead on the accomplice, too."

A.J.'s chin stopped bobbing. What kind of investigating had Cole been doing? He was supposed to be watching Claire. The second blow to his mood was a big one. He focused his gaze and swept the room again. "Where is she?"

Cole raised his hands in friendly surrender. "First, let me say that I think you and I share an affinity for stubborn women."

Panic rose like bile in his throat. "Where is she?"

For a second, he thought Cole wasn't going to answer. Friendship be damned—if he didn't tell him what had happened to Claire, he was going to take him down at the knees.

Then he realized that Cole *was* telling him. With his eyes.

A.J. followed the direction of his gaze. Trepidation turned to curiosity. Curiosity became a shameless jolt of testosterone as he watched the limber dancer with the bright cheeks and lips do a vertical split against the pole at the middle of the stage, while her giant red-feathered fan kept all the good stuff teasingly hidden from view.

A.J. looked beyond her to the stage entrance to find Claire. The drums of the Latin tempo music became more of a headache than a dance as his patience wore thin. The stripper onstage pirouetted away from the pole, flipped her feathers and wiggled the little strip of red lace that graced her fanny.

"*Madre Dios.*" A.J. muttered a good chunk of his Spanish vocabulary as he headed for the stage.

A big hand closed around his arm and stopped him. "Don't do it," Cole warned.

A.J. whirled around. "This is what you call taking care of my woman?"

"Easy, A.J. She's undercover."

"What?" Some *bastardo* reached up and stuffed a bill in Claire's panties. "Hey!"

"She says it's a trick she learned from you."

His virginal heiress was the hottest damn thing to ever strut the runway at the Riverfront Gentleman's Club. And she learned *that* from him? "That's a load of bull. Get her off the stage."

"She's hiding in plain sight."

A.J.'s wiring shorted out at Cole's choice of words. He'd said that to Claire, hadn't he? Take the heiress undercover into his world. Alter their appearance, change their jobs, assume a new persona.

Hide in plain sight.

His engine revved back into gear as the import of Cole's words registered. "Hiding from what?"

THE LAST BEAT of the rhythm pulsed through Claire's bones. She let out a whoop and tossed her fan onto the stage.

"You're a natural." Debbie shut the curtain behind her and grinned. "I can tell you're a dancer."

Claire pulled out the money that had been tucked into the various strips of elastic she wore and pushed it into Debbie's hands. "Here. For school tuition. Or groceries or whatever."

Debbie pushed it back. "You earned it."

Claire waved the money aside. "You need it more than I do. Besides, that's not why I went out there."

Hugging her arms around her middle, between the bra and tap pants she'd borrowed, Claire balanced on her three-inch heels and followed Debbie down the steps toward the dressing room.

"That was a little weird at first. Okay, a lot weird. It probably helped that I couldn't hear all the comments." The adrenaline from all she had done and seen was still pumping through her system. "But then it was just like a workout. It was exhilarating. Nerve-racking. And I was victorious!"

Debbie glanced over her shoulder. "You saw him?"

"Yes. That leering, bug-eyed monster. He probably thinks he's earning points with my father by trying to find me. I can't believe he's working with Galvan, though. I wouldn't think he could afford to pay him. Unless he's got some other business on the side I don't know about. Where's Cole? I have to point him out."

The enticing scent of well-worn leather stopped her at the bottom of the stairs. A black jacket and jeans stepped out of the shadows in the hall. Claire looked into piercing golden eyes and shivered. The flow of adrenaline bottomed out.

This was bad. This was very bad.

"A.J."

He wasn't smiling. He wasn't talking yet, either.

Nerves kept her tongue going. "Are you okay? You were gone so long, I was getting worried. Did you find something useful?" She thumbed over her shoulder toward the stage. "We had an opportunity here, so I…" Her voice trailed away and she made a lame effort to smile. "Are my lips moving?"

"Cole's outside, escorting Rob Hastings down to the precinct. I don't know if he's guilty of anything more than annoying me, but Josh and Cole will ask him some questions." He shrugged off his jacket and draped it around her, covering her bare shoulders and arms in its A.J.-scented warmth. He overlapped the opening and held it in place with his hands, masking her body. "Hastings isn't your man. There's still somebody else to worry about at Winthrop, Inc."

Claire clutched the lining of the jacket and shivered. But Rob Hastings had tracked her down. He'd tracked down Debbie, at least. He'd seemed right at home with the vulgar, leering crowd of men trying to glimpse more than lace and feathers during her performance. He was greedy enough, ambitious enough, base enough to be her villain. But A.J. seemed so sure he wasn't. "How do you know?"

"Police work." He spared a glance over her shoulder. "Debbie, could you give us a minute?"

Debbie tapped Claire's arm. "Is that okay?"

She nodded. Her friend seemed glad to disappear in the face of A.J.'s dour mood, and on the surface, Claire supposed she couldn't blame her. But she saw something beyond the ominously quiet facade, beyond the tough-guy temperament.

This was the A.J. who'd held her last night on the sofa. The one who had tears in his eyes when she'd almost died at the safe house. This was the man who didn't want to feel anything as deeply as he did, and whose cool and aloof facade was cracking open wider and wider as those emotions emerged.

This A.J. pulled off her red-feathered wig and mussed her mousy brown hair back into place. He hugged her close to his chest and whispered sounds in her ear she couldn't understand. It was easy to sense that he needed to hold her, and Claire had no intention of denying him what gave her such comfort as well.

A minute or so later, when he pulled away, he actually grinned. "So you liked doing the striptease, huh?"

"Exotic dance," she corrected with a matching smile. "It was kind of fun," she had to admit. "But I don't think I want to make a career of it. I tried to do a Gypsy Rose Lee-ladylike routine. Tease them a lot, without really showing much. I don't think I was really that good at it."

"You were damn good at it, *amor.*" The hint of jealous propriety in his expression warmed her down to her toes and made his next order sound all the sweeter. "Now go put some clothes on. I need to take you home."

Claire washed her face, then pulled her jeans and shirts on over her red dance costume so she could take her own underthings back to the apartment to wash out. She wore A.J.'s jacket out of the club, and when he didn't ask for it, she didn't offer. It was warm and soft and it felt a little like him holding her again.

Besides, she'd never be adverse to seeing what his upper body could do for a plain black T-shirt.

The night was dark and overcast as it had been for the past week. With the club closing for the night, the customers were starting to file out to their cars or line up at the curb for a taxi to pick them up.

"You want to wait here while I pull the car around?" he asked.

Let's see. The dark? Or the drunks? Half the lights in the parking lot were out, and the nearest street lamp was a block away. Claire crooked an eyebrow. "Do you mind?"

He pushed her back a step into the circle of light pouring through the club's open front doors. "As long as you don't move from this spot."

"Deal."

With his black hair and black shirt, A.J. quickly disappeared into the darkness of the parking lot. Claire swallowed the lump of insecurity in her throat. She knew he was out there, she just couldn't see him. She hadn't been abandoned.

Still, Cole was gone. She didn't see Debbie anywhere. She hadn't even gotten the satisfaction of giving Rob Hastings a piece of her mind. Calling Debbie a slut. Ogling over "Kiki's" salsa ballet performance when he had supposedly come to the club to find Claire Winthrop. Yeah, he cared a lot about her family. A.J. hadn't explained how he knew Rob wasn't Galvan's accomplice, but then he hadn't told her anything about the autopsy yet. She hoped he'd found something that could put them on the offensive to go after Valerie's killers—instead of feeling like running and hiding were their only options for survival.

The first taxi pulled up to the cab stand, then another. While she waited for A.J., Claire huddled inside his jacket and distracted herself by reading snatches of conversation from the departing patrons.

"I am so wasted."

"Dude, your last night as a single man is over."

"My wife can just…"

"…hot little tamale." She grinned sheepishly at that one. The first cab left and another pulled in. The driver climbed out and pulled his cap low on his forehead. The cars were starting to line up in the parking lot.

"Give me my keys!"

"You're not driving."

"What is that crazy guy doing?"

Claire turned to see who the young man was making fun of.

A.J. charged out of the darkness, pointing down to the pavement. "Get down!"

Nothing funny about that.

He ran straight toward her. "Get down!" Claire's knees hunched, almost obeying. Some people were nervously curious, others oblivious, to his warning.

A.J. waved his arms, shouting to the entire crowd. "Everybody get down!"

And then he was upon her. "Claire!"

A light flashed beneath the hood of the abandoned taxi.

A.J.'s arms whipped around her and slammed them both to the sidewalk as the night exploded.

Chapter Eleven

Third time's a bitch, A.J. thought, gritting his teeth at the fiery pain burning through his left thigh.

He was learning to hate the sound of a well-tuned engine. Out in the parking lot, away from the noise of the crowd, he'd heard the unique pitch of that same powerful hum that had preceded Slick Williams's death and the diversionary explosion at the safe house.

The car bomb was an empty shell, the taxi in front of it on fire. People all around him were screaming, moaning, silent.

But he was only interested in two of them. "Claire? *Amor?*"

He pulled the costume glasses off her face and tossed them aside. Her dazed eyes blinked in a slow, unnatural rhythm. He cradled her head in his hands, checking for signs of injury. She had a lump the size of a walnut on the back of her head—probably from his linebacking effort to hit the sidewalk. He cursed himself in two languages, then said a prayer in both.

"Talk to me, *amor.*"

He stroked her face, willing her to respond. She was so still beneath him, but he hadn't moved yet. Galvan was out there somewhere, waiting for his shot at her.

A.J. raised his head and risked a look. This place was a disaster. The light from the fires made the shadows beyond them even darker and harder to assess. People ran out of the club to join the chaos of wounded and possibly dead patrons and passersby. There were people with too much booze in their systems to deal with shock or pain in any logical way. He saw a few good Samaritans, a few hysterics, and plenty of places to hide amongst them all.

Black hair, black eyes. Scarred-up face. A.J. had only seen Galvan in a scratchy black-and-white photograph. How the hell would he find him in all this?

He shifted to one side and hissed at the pain that radiated up and down his leg. He pulled the cell from his pocket and hit 9-1-1. His situation report was brief and graphic, and all response units were soon on their way.

Claire suddenly lurched beneath him and moaned. She shoved at his chest and he tried to adjust his weight without aggravating the shrapnel in his leg or exposing her to Galvan's line of sight. She tried to suck in a deep breath and winced. "Oh God, it hurts to breathe. My head."

"Claire?" A.J. ignored his first aid training and kissed her quick and hard on the mouth. "Tell me you're okay."

"Did that taxi blow up?" She pushed her bangs off her face, then reached up and did the same for him. "My chest feels like a ton of bricks landed on it."

"You probably had the wind knocked out of you. I clobbered you pretty hard."

Her cheeks were pink again, her eyes clear. "My head hurts."

"I'm afraid that's my fault, too."

"I think you just saved my life, so quit talking about this being anybody's fault."

He couldn't help grinning in relief. She was going to be just fine if that bossy mouth was any indication.

"Oh, my God." Now she was looking around, frowning, pushing at his chest to sit up. "I'm okay, A.J. Let me up. We have to help these people."

"You help no one but yourself," he ordered. "Galvan's here."

"Did you see him?"

"Not yet."

"I think I did, getting out of the cab. Black ball cap. Light dress shirt, untucked."

"That description fits half the people here."

She twisted frantically beneath him, trying to observe the crowd from her obscure vantage point, jostling his leg between hers. Something caught and jerked. A.J. swore.

"What's this?" She uncurled her fingers beside her face and gasped. "Blood. But I'm not…" Her eyes flashed at him. "You're hurt."

"It's just a scratch."

"You are so full of it." Her anger was touching, her concern humbling, her burst of strength entirely unacceptable. "Claire."

But she was agile enough and he was hurt enough that she managed to sit up. "There's a first-aid kit behind the bar."

"You're staying put."

She was getting up.

Propped at this angle, it was hard to maneuver his leg. By the time he'd pulled himself to his feet, she'd slipped out and run inside the club. "Claire!"

Pulling the gun from his ankle holster would only panic the victims, and it was already war zone enough to keep track of everyone's movements. Galvan would take advantage of the situation and lose himself in the crowd. Light shirt. Dark cap. A.J. had to stay sharp to spot him. He had to stay close to Claire to keep her safe.

She was running back to meet him by the time he'd limped through the door. If she wanted to play doctor, then fine, but they were going to do it someplace more secure than the middle of the sidewalk.

"In here." He pulled up one of the bouncer's stools and sat behind the cashier stand.

Sirens wailed in the distance. Help would be here any minute. But until he saw somebody with a uniform and a gun to back him up, he would unstrap his Beretta and keep it in his hand while Claire knelt beside him and inspected his wound.

He winced as she probed the side of his leg. "It looks like part of a mirror." She looked up at him. "Should I pull it out?"

"If you can get it in one piece." She removed his jacket and tossed it on the table beside him. Then she peeled off one of her tank tops and wound it around her hand to protect herself. "It'll bleed when you pull it out," he instructed, "so be ready to pack it off."

She angled herself one way and then another, trying to decide the best vantage point. "I'll have to cut your pant-leg away to get to the wound. Oh, God, A.J. I'm so sorry. This is going to hurt."

"Just do it. I'm tough."

She touched her hand to his face and blessed him with a wry smile. "I'm not."

When she turned her back to him and knelt out of earshot, he whispered, "You're tougher than you know, sweetheart."

He looked at his jacket on the tabletop, took note of the sandpapery scrapes that abraded a shoulder and the length of one sleeve. If she hadn't have been wearing his coat, that would be her skin, and he'd be doctoring...

"Son of a—" A.J. bit off the curse as the shard of mirror popped free.

Claire pressed her shirt against the wound to stanch the bleeding and A.J. decided that at least the pain was good for keeping his senses sharp. She wrapped gauze around his thigh to keep the pack in place. "I think you need stitches."

A.J. nodded. "Just tie it off. It's not vital. The bleeding will stop."

Snapping her fingers, Claire shot to her feet. "Debbie's a nursing student. She'll know how to do the stitches."

"No." She was already around the counter and out the door to save his sorry hide. "Damn."

A.J. slipped the gun into his waistband and pulled his shirt over it as he limped out the after her. "Claire?"

She stopped to speak to a man sitting and holding his head. She squeezed another man's hand. Though she had sense enough to stay low to the ground, she called for her friend and worked her way across the battlefield—as if she was Clara Barton—staying too many damn steps ahead of him.

The final whoop-whoop of a siren told him the first police cruiser had arrived. Two men in blue suits got out and started to organize, ask questions. As an officer on the scene, he should go over and make a report, but he had to catch up to Claire first.

An ambulance arrived, then fire engines and another cruiser. The place was crawling with even more people than before. Facts said more cops on the scene would improve crowd control. His instincts told him the extra people just gave Galvan more places to hide.

"Claire?" Screw the pain. He'd bleed right on through the makeshift bandage and double-time it to get to her.

He spotted Debbie Dunning, over in the parking lot, kneeling beside an injured man. Claire had spotted her, too. A.J. turned to cut her off and get her safely back inside, or maybe in the back of one of the cruisers.

Light shirt, dark cap. *Son of a bitch.*

"Claire!"

Damn it, she couldn't hear him.

Black hair, black eyes.

Dominic Galvan stepped out from the shadows and fell into step behind her, his quicker pace closing the gap between them. No! A.J. ran. His leg screamed in protest and buckled, but he shoved himself back to his feet as soon as he hit the pavement.

"It's Galvan! Claire!"

He pulled out his gun and took aim.

The next few seconds unfolded like a nightmare playing in slow motion to draw out its torturous images.

Claire finally turned.

She saw him. Saw the gun.

Saw Galvan.

Her footsteps stuttered. She gasped. Retreated.

Galvan pulled a knife from the folds of his shirt and kept coming. Damn Renaissance Man. Trained to kill any way he wanted.

"Police, Galvan! Drop it!"

Never breaking his stride, the hit man turned his head toward A.J., giving him a look into the cold, conscience-less black eyes Claire had described so perfectly.

He wanted A.J. to see him. Wanted him to see Claire's terror. Wanted them both to know he would win.

"Gun!" The two blue suits pulled their weapons and shouted at A.J. "Drop it!"

"I'm KCPD," he responded, knowing they wouldn't let him reach into his pocket to draw out his badge until he set down his weapon. And that wasn't gonna happen.

Claire stumbled toward him. "That's Galvan! That's him!"

A.J. had a clear shot. "Galvan!"

Debbie Dunning stood up beside her patient to see what all the commotion was about. She stood up right in the line of fire.

"*Madre Dios.*" A.J. cocked his elbow and pointed the gun away from the innocent bystander.

The blue suits were on him by then, taking the Beretta, kicking his legs apart, ordering him to the ground.

"Get your hands off him!" Claire shouted. She snatched at the arm of one of the officers, who shook her loose and warned her aside.

"No, sweetheart, don't fight them."

But she hadn't seen his words. "He's on your side! Detective A. J. Rodriguez, KCPD." She pointed to the parking lot. "That's the man you need to arrest."

But he was gone.

By the time the uniformed officers had checked A.J.'s badge, returned his gun and apologized for drawing on a ranking officer, Dominic Galvan was long gone.

He'd slipped, like a wraith, back into the night.

DESPITE THE CANE he carried, Claire propped herself beneath A.J.'s left arm to support him as he walked, long after the ER doctor who stitched up his leg had declared him officially sound and ready to return to light duty after a good night's rest.

She braced her hands at his waist and back and took a bit of his weight—not because he still needed her assistance to get down the hallway from the elevator to his apartment, but because she desperately needed to hold on to something solid and reliable or she'd go raving mad.

Fear, exhaustion, frustration, guilt—they taunted her from every corner of her mind. Like those unseen terrors that haunted her in the night, images from the past week tried to creep in and push her over the edge.

But A.J. was her lifeline to the light and sanity of the real world, and she was hanging on for all she was worth.

And since he'd had his arm around her shoulders or her hand in his almost every moment since they'd left the Riverfront Gentleman's Club, it seemed as if he needed something to hang on to, as well.

Dozens of cops, uniformed and detective alike—plus a couple of FBI agents and one assistant district attorney, from the sound of things—had shown up after a single call A.J. made from the hospital to his partner, Josh Taylor.

"I need help, *amigo*."

He couldn't bring down Galvan, unmask an accomplice, protect Claire—and fill out all the paperwork, he'd tried to joke—by himself anymore.

Claire nearly cried when she saw how many of A.J.'s friends and fellow cops had turned out to set up a watch around both the city block and apartment building so he could have time to rest and recuperate. Others had gone to the office to process reports, others to the Riverfront Gentleman's Club to take witness statements. Seemed they knew the same secret she'd discovered. That the quiet man on the force, the chameleon of KCPD, the veteran detective who'd trained some of the best in the business—was much more than a good cop.

He was a good man.

A.J. unlocked the door and showed her inside. He bolted the door behind them and took her hand to lead her into the living room. She'd hardly noticed the place when she'd been here before. But the sun was dawning in a clear sky for the first time in a week, and its rays filtered in through the window to warm the pale turquoises and rich dark earth tones that defined the comfortable Mediterranean decor.

"This is nice."

"I can't take credit. My sisters did the decorating. Said I needed more than plain white walls and a cot to make this livable."

"They have good taste."

"You sure you don't want me to take you home?" he asked.

"I'm sure." One, there was the little matter of not knowing whom she could trust at her father's house and who wanted her dead. And two, she worried that once she left A.J., he'd find some noble reason not to invite her back.

"Hungry?"

"Starving. But I think I'm too tired to eat."

"How about a drink?"

"I could use some water."

"Coming up." She watched him stow his unused cane in the corner beside a silk plant and walk into the kitchen. His limp was barely noticeable now, though the green hospital pants they'd given him to replace the jeans they'd cut off were a definite reminder that he'd been hurt.

Trying to defend her.

Claire squeezed her eyes shut, then opened them just as

quickly, hoping the mental pictures would go away. A.J. running to save her. Putting himself between her and a bomb. Standing at the ready to kill the man who terrorized her, giving up his chance in order to protect the innocent bystanders around him.

Innocent bystanders *she'd* endangered because Galvan didn't seem to care how many people he hurt or killed in his quest to have a perfect hit record. Imagine finding that listing in the *Guinness Book*. Claire laughed, but her teeth were clenched and it hurt her throat.

"Here you go." A.J. handed her a bottle of water and pointed to the overstuffed sofa and chairs. "Make yourself comfortable. I figure I've got about twenty-four hours worth of favors called in for us to get some uninterrupted time to relax."

She'd bet it was more like twenty-four years, but didn't have the energy to argue the point with him. She perched on the edge of the brown-and-cream brocaded couch and opened her water. "Your friends seem to really like and respect you."

"Yeah, go figure." A.J. sank into the chair across from her and propped his leg up on the ottoman before opening the orange juice he'd brought out for himself.

She took three sips of water in the weary silence that followed. Two nights ago she'd had to fight through his good intentions and misconceptions to earn the privilege of sleeping in A.J.'s arms. Last night there'd been no sleeping. Just destruction and pain. This morning didn't seem to be dawning with anything resembling hope.

"They seem nice." She tried one more time to make conversation.

"Yeah."

At least he hadn't turned his back on her. But the silence in her ears left her with little to respond to besides her guilty memories and the fears that made her weary. She screwed the cap back onto her water and noticed the dried blood caught beneath her nails and cuticles.

A.J.'s blood.

He'd needed nine stitches because of her. One taxi driver had lost his life. Because of her.

She flicked her thumbnail beneath another nail and tried to pry the flakes of blood from beneath it. Nineteen people injured in the blast, six of them critically enough to be admitted to the hospital.

Picturing Galvan's cold black eyes, taunting her, telling her he could get to her whenever he wanted, made Claire's breath catch in her sore lungs. The knife he'd flashed hadn't been a threat, so much as a promise. He could hurt her in any number of ways. A gun, a bomb, a knife…

Claire rubbed at her cuticles now. The blood wouldn't go away. Killing her was a game to Galvan—maybe the ultimate challenge with A.J. thrown into the mix. He could—and intended to—make her suffer.

He was succeeding.

Claire shot to her feet, startling A.J. enough that he swung his injured leg to the floor. "Could I use your shower again?"

"Sure."

"I feel dirty and grimy."

He stood and took the water from her tense grip. "You remember where everything is?"

She nodded, though she hadn't really seen his words. "I'm exhausted, but I can't relax."

"You don't have to explain. Go on." He nudged her

elbow and turned her toward the hallway and the bathroom around the corner.

A.J. handed her a towel and washcloth and closed the door behind her, leaving Claire alone in the middle of the tan-tiled bathroom. With rote, robotic movements, she dropped her towel onto the back of the toilet and reached into the shower stall to turn on the water to let it heat up. She wanted to fill the room with heat and steam and let the water cleanse every pore on her body.

She toed off her shoes and kicked them beneath the sink. Untied the leather thong that held up A.J.'s jeans and let them slide off her hips to the floor. Stepping out of them, she stretched her arms over her head to pull off her shirt.

Debbie had loaned her the two tank tops. This one was smudged with dirt and sweat, and the other had been so caked with blood—A.J.'s blood—that the ER attendant had thrown it into the trash.

"I'll buy you some new clothes, Deb," she promised her absent friend. She reached behind her back to unhook the red lace bra. "I'll replace your costume. No, I'll pay for your classes so you don't have to go back to that place."

But she'd forgotten the bra didn't have a hook. So she slipped the straps off her arms and twisted to pull it off over her head.

Maybe she should pay to fix up the club. She could dip into her trust fund and buy some new lights for their parking lot. Offer to buy a new cab for the city. Pay some sort of restitution to all the people who'd been hurt because she'd had the dumb luck to finally choose a night to stand up to her father, and had stumbled upon a murder instead.

People were putting their lives on the line for her. Getting hurt. Dying. And it was all her fault. All her...

The bra's elastic caught in her hair and plucked at the knot on the back of her scalp. Tears pricked her eyes at the sharp jolt of pain.

And then they kept falling. And falling.

Claire hugged her arms across her breasts and stood in the steam and cried.

There must have been a knock, maybe a soft word that she never heard. It was the whisper of cool air across her heated skin that told her the door had opened.

A.J. had stripped off his T-shirt. His guns and holster had been put away. He stood there in nothing but the hospital pants that reminded her of everything she hated about all this. His chest was smooth, his breathing steady, but his beautiful mouth was lined with worry.

She'd put that there, too, no doubt.

"I thought I was doing the right thing." Her breath stuttered through her chest and her chin trembled with embarrassing vulnerability when she tried to apologize. "I didn't want you to get hurt. I didn't want anyone to get hurt. Why are so many people getting…?"

But his arms were around her now. Her cheek was nestled against the beat of his heart. His hands held her gently, securely, and she wept.

Maybe he spoke to her, she didn't know. But she was too emotionally spent to protest when he shucked off his pants and briefs, opened the shower door and led her inside.

The spray of the water was a shock against her bare back. Claire whimpered and nuzzled her face into his chest. Moving with her, he eased her back under the water, drawing slow circles across her back and massaging his fingers at her nape as the hot water sluiced over the top of her head and cascaded over her shoulders and breasts and in between them.

More minutes passed, and the warmth of the water began to seep inside her, warming her blood and bringing her back to life again. She finally released the grip of her arms and slid her hands slowly around A.J.'s water-slicked flanks and back. She latched her fingers behind him, pressing her tender breasts against the unyielding hardness of him. She closed her eyes and kissed a curve of muscle, savoring the perfection of the contact between them.

Claire held on when his hands left her. She opened her mouth to protest, but her throat was still raw with the tears she'd shed. Then he palmed her hip and guided her forward a step as he retreated. The angle of the water changed, hitting her square in the back. When strong, gentle fingers tunneled into her hair and began a slow, easy massage across her scalp, she understood.

The manly scent of something spicy and clean teased her nose and made her want to smile. No girly shampoo for this guy. Bubbles tickled along her neck and ran down her spine. He was gentle around the bump on her head, but more firm at her temples, easing the tension of a crying headache.

When he was done, he slipped his finger beneath her chin and tilted her face to his so she could read his intent. Claire simply nodded. With her fingers still anchored at his waist, she trusted him enough to lean back against him and let her head fall back under the water to rinse her hair.

Her arched back exposed her breasts to the steamy spray of water—and to the hungry intent of his golden gaze. His pupils dilated at the proud display and her breasts tingled and tightened beneath the caress of the water and the fire in his eyes.

She caught her breath with a mixture of fascination and

hope as he dipped his head and kissed the swell of one breast. His lips were tender, firm—warmer than the water that fell around them. His overnight beard stubble was a tickly rasp that danced across her skin and made her shiver. A.J. softened the overload of friction with a flick of his tongue.

The tips of her breasts knotted and thrust, demanding more than her inexperience knew how to ask for. At the unspoken invitation, he closed his mouth over one distended tip and swirled his tongue around it. Claire clutched her fingers into his back and gasped at the sheer, raw pleasure that coursed through her body and rushed to the point of contact. He treated the other breast to the same seductive torment, tutoring her body in the thrilling responses to this man's touch.

His hands followed the path of the water down her back and cupped her bottom. He squeezed and lifted and dragged her hips into his, revealing the thrilling response of his own body.

Claire moaned in her throat at the intimate contact. He lifted his head to kiss that spot. She opened her mouth to catch her breath, and A.J. covered her lips with his own.

Blossoming, unfolding beneath the driving force of his mouth, Claire moved her hands to frame his face. With her unskilled touch, she slicked her palms across his jaw, pressed her thumbs at the corners of his lips. She angled his mouth one way, then another, finding each way she loved to be kissed, learning that every way offered something wonderful.

His tongue slipped inside and danced with hers. Finding the matching rhythm, Claire swept her hands around his neck and into his hair, lifting herself into his kiss.

Warmed by water on one side, by man on the other—and by an awakened passion that set everything on fire in between—Claire felt the fatigue of the past few hours wash away. The guilt, the fear, the frustrated rage that had overwhelmed her receded at the roving exploration of A.J.'s hands, the consuming heat of his kisses, the friction of his body moving against hers.

A hungry, desperate instinct thrummed through her veins at a feverish pitch, knowing what she wanted even before her mind could acknowledge it. This was about cleansing, strengthening, renewing. But she didn't know how to ask. She didn't know how to give voice to what her body and soul were yearning for.

When A.J's hands left her, she thought it was too late, that she'd missed her chance, misread his intent. Her heart pounded in her chest and she cried out in protest.

But then she felt the rough stroke and the washcloth against her back. He was bathing her, completing what she hadn't even been able to start. Her heart squeezed tight, then swelled in her chest at the strength of his will and body. He had always taken care of her, always protected her—in ways she'd never even known a woman could need. His consideration made her want to cry all over again. His example made her want to do the same for him. If she could. If she knew how.

A.J. kissed her lips and stepped away. She braced her hands on his shoulders as he knelt before her to brush the soapy cloth across her stomach. He slid the red panties she still wore off her hips and down her legs. He'd kiss a spot, then wipe it clean. The water rinsed away the soap, but her skin still tingled with each press of his lips. He kissed her hip, her thigh, and nuzzled close to the heart of her, draining her of sensation except for the pressure pooling at that potent spot. Just when she thought her knees might give way, he turned her around and scrubbed her backside.

The cooling spray of the shower splashed her face, reviving her from the raging heat that pulsed through her body in a sensuous Latin rhythm. She gasped at the nip of teeth on her bottom, swallowed a mouthful of water and sputtered it out with a new purpose in mind.

Rising to the challenge of that playful bite, Claire turned and snatched the washcloth from A.J.'s grasp. She urged him to his feet and reversed their positions so that he stood beneath the spray, blocking all the water but the splatters off his body. She filled the cloth with shower gel and boldly returned the favor.

Student became teacher as she washed his body, cleansing him of fear and guilt as she washed away the grime of a long day and night. She taught A.J. that a nip at the jut of his chin tickled him. A kiss to the newly healed scar on his cheek made him tremble.

She brushed the cloth over his flat bronze nipples and watched them perk up. She ran her palms over them. She felt a groan vibrate through his chest, and discovered he liked that touch even better. Claire rinsed his chest, then tasted them, swirling her tongue around each taut temptation until he lurched the same way she had.

Claire stooped down to tenderly wash around his wounded thigh, then froze. She was at eye level with the unmistakable proof of his desire. His aroused member seemed shocking at first, maybe even frightening in the slick, pulsing strength of it. But A.J. was also a thing of beauty. Something inside her clenched and wept at the obvious stamp of want and need. Pressure ran to her extremities and poured into the heart of her. Her arousal was less overt, but no less potent.

Feeling awed, but more confident, Claire began to think that maybe her inexperience in life—and with this—wasn't necessarily a drawback. With the right man, the right moment, the right purpose, maybe she could be what *he* needed. Maybe she could provide the same strength and will that he'd given to her.

She stood, closing a soapy hand around his sex. When he thrust into her hand, Claire gasped. She was startled at first, then awed by the sheer power that a man and woman could hold over one another.

The passion, the promise in A.J.'s eyes locked onto hers, and Claire knew this was it. There was no turning back. She didn't want to.

The water had grown cold, but A.J. folded his arms around her and merged their bodies into one steaming kiss.

Then the water was off, a towel was around her. A.J. picked her up and carried her into his bedroom.

There'd been no words, none spoken at any rate, until he laid her on the bed. A.J. left the towel between them and lay down beside her, throwing one thigh over both of hers. He smoothed the hair from her face, tucked it behind her ears. A drop of water beaded at the tip of his nose and dripped onto her cheek. He smoothed the spot with the pad of his thumb and Claire felt the tender gesture deep inside her.

"Are you sure you want me to be your first, *amor?*"

She wanted him to be her only.

Claire answered with a smile and a nod and the clutch of her hands urging his mouth down for a kiss.

In moments, the towel was gone and she was sinking

into the pillows and covers beneath the good, solid weight of the man she loved.

"There might be some discomfort," he warned. "Even pain. And I don't want to hurt—"

"You won't hurt me. Only if you stop."

"No, Claire, *amor.* I don't want to stop."

And then his hands and lips were on her mouth, her breasts. She smoothed her fingers along his wet, strong back, kissed him on his chin, his throat. His fingers tested her, and she moaned at the sweet, sweet torture of his hand. "That feels good. So good."

When he slid inside her, Claire was beyond feeling if there was any pain. She was too consumed by the utter rightness of it all, the completeness of feeling him stretching her, filling her.

Then A.J. began to move. She quickly caught on to the rhythm of the sensuous dance, feeling the beat of every note build in intensity with each touch, each thrust. And when that noiseless crescendo reached its climax, Claire tipped her head and cried out. A.J. kissed her throat and she held on tight as he drove into her one last time and made the dance complete.

For one hazy moment, drifting along in the echoes of the dance that still trembled through her body, Claire remembered some old wives' tale about this making her a woman now. But she smiled in serene contentment against the cooling pulse beat in A.J.'s throat, knowing something those old wives never could. He'd made her feel like a woman long before their very first kiss.

This made her feel like *his* woman.

Afterward, cleansed, sated, but exhausted beyond reason, they crawled beneath the covers. A.J. tucked their naked bodies together, her back against his chest, his hand on her breast. His knee wedged between hers and his lips nuzzled against her ear.

And skin to skin, soul to soul, healing heart to healing heart, they slept.

Chapter Twelve

"Better?"

A.J. watched Claire drift into the bedroom in her grace-ful ballerina's walk, toweling her hair dry. He'd thought she'd look lost in his terry cloth robe, but she'd cinched it at the waist in such a way that the vee-shaped collar re-vealed an enticing stretch of creamy, cool skin, and the bunching at her hips only reminded him of the womanly curves underneath that had welcomed him with such sweet, soul-stealing abandon.

"I was fine before," she smiled, lighting up the room, if not quite assuring him that seducing a virgin was the best way to offer her comfort or find solace for his own emo-tional needs. "What's this?"

She hooked the towel over the doorknob and crossed to the bed to inspect the tray of sandwiches, chips and salsa he'd prepared while she was in the shower. "Breakfast in bed didn't seem appropriate at one in the afternoon, but I wanted to do something…"

To thank her? To beg forgiveness? To ask her to make love all over again?

If that was the case, then this setup was pretty lame. He should be buying her diamonds or taking her around the world. But then he supposed Claire Winthrop had enough money to buy however many diamonds or trips she wanted for herself. He didn't think he could compete in her world, and she had no business staying in his any longer than necessary.

"That's sweet. Thank you." She dropped a quick kiss on his lips, then scooped up some salsa with a chip and popped it into her mouth. "That's good," she said, as she chewed.

She crossed to the dresser and started combing her hair with some of the women's toiletries that Maggie Wheeler had brought by an hour ago. There was a new outfit in the closet, too.

A.J. hadn't gotten any further than emptying his pockets and pulling on a pair of jeans after his shower. The cut on his leg was little more than a dull ache now, and he was rested enough to be thinking beyond the moment again. Earlier this morning, there'd only been Claire and the fact that she'd needed him. She'd been too tired, too scared, too everything to go on. When he'd heard the water running, but hadn't heard her step inside, he knew something was wrong.

She'd needed comfort, and the only thing he had to offer was himself. But it seemed to be the only thing she'd needed. Seeing her naked, touching her, tasting her—and A.J. had known that she was the only thing he would ever need.

But that was this morning. This was now.

Dominic Galvan was still out there waiting to strike— to destroy Claire, consequently destroying him. He needed to be thinking like a cop now. They needed to come up with a plan of action—something that involved him going after Galvan while Claire was holed up someplace safe.

"Is this your family?"

Claire's innocent question jarred A.J. away from his

professional intentions. He stood and came up behind her to look over her shoulder at the last family portrait the Rodriguezes had ever taken together. "That's us. My mother Sofia. My sisters Émilia, Luisa, Ana and Teresa."

"And your father, Antonio." Claire traced her finger across the silver frame on the dresser. He felt that gentle reverence as if she'd stroked his skin. "You look like him. Now, I mean." She looked up to meet his gaze in the mirror. "You looked like quite the tough guy back then—long hair, earrings, leather."

"I was in a gang for a couple of years." Her blue eyes widened and her lips parted in surprise. "Yeah, I'll bet having that on my résumé impresses the hell out of your father."

"What?" She turned around to look him straight in the eye. "What does Dad have to do with it?"

A.J. shook his head, feeling a trace of that same resentment that had driven him to make all the wrong choices growing up. "Do you have any idea how different we are, Claire?"

"Do you resent the fact that I'm rich?"

"Do you resent the fact that I'm not?"

She shrugged. "I hadn't really thought about it."

Damn those eyes of hers. She was innocent enough to have really not considered the culture clash between them. Their ages, their backgrounds, their future prospects.

She might not see it now, in the rosy afterglow of losing her virginity, or the nebulous peace and quiet of a well-guarded, twenty-four-hour respite from Dominic Galvan. But there was no chance that she could make any long-term commitment to him. She'd have to give up too much. She'd have to put up with too much.

A.J. reached around her and picked up the photograph. "Do you see this man here?" He pointed to his father. She nodded. "He worked for your father. Years ago."

"Dad said that at the police station—that he knew your father. That sort of rattled you." She clutched the robe together at her throat. "I don't think I'd seen you react to anything like that before."

"My father was a custodian in your daddy's twenty-six-floor high-rise. He swept his floors and emptied his trash. And every night your father would pass him by without a backward glance because my father was beneath him."

"That's not true." Of course she'd defend her father. "Dad has always made a point of knowing everyone who works for him—from his closest friend on the board of directors to the men on the loading docks at the airport. If he doesn't know them by name, he knows their jobs, he knows their supervisor. And he'll always be courteous and friendly."

"Would he invite the son of his custodian over to the house for a family dinner?"

Claire frowned. "A.J., why are you doing this? I thought we just shared something very special, and you're spoiling it."

"You're right." He set down the picture and walked back to the bed. "It was great sex."

"Sex?"

Though in his heart, he knew it had been an act of love, not of lust, he let the coarse statement stand. "Claire, sweetheart, this has been a very trying week for you, and we've had some close calls. That can distort—"

"You better the hell not be saying I'm some kind of snob. That I get my thrills by slumming around with the first working-class guy who'll fall into bed with me." She grabbed him by the elbow, demanding that he turn to face her. "I don't care where you come from—what you were like as a kid—what your father did for a living. If anything, I admire you even more because you had it tough. And look what a good man you turned out to be. A well-respected detective, a valued friend. You're a man who saves lives, a man who puts others before himself. At least, I thought you were."

"I'm a cop, Claire. I'm never going to be anything more than a cop." He shook off her hand, then snagged her by the shoulders. "I'm never going to be as good a man as my father."

"What?" He saw the anger drain from her expression, felt the tension ease beneath his hands.

A.J. released her and stalked to the far side of the bed. He swiped a hand across his jaw and wondered why the hell he was pushing her away when holding her close was the only thing that had ever made the pain go away. Probably because he was smart enough to know that there would be no forever. Eventually, she'd see him for what he was or wasn't. And without the threat to their survival binding them together, there'd be nothing to keep them from drifting apart.

And that would hurt. It would kill him to lose Claire.

"Tell me about your father, A.J." He heard the bed creak as she sat behind him. He squeezed his eyes shut at the gentle balm of her voice. Damn it. She was going to be sweet and understanding about this.

With a surrendering sigh, A.J. sank onto his side of the bed. He braced his elbows on his knees and his forehead in his hands. Then he pulled one knee up on the bed and turned so she could read his lips. "My father was killed when I was seventeen. He burned to death in a car accident—supposedly, he was hit by a drunk driver."

"Supposedly?"

"There was no one in the other car. No one could have survived that kind of collision and fire and walked away. I always thought it was a cover-up. That he'd been killed somewhere else, and then the accident was rigged to hide the true cause of death."

"That's awful."

He raked his fingers back through his hair, seeing the blackened skeleton of that burnt-out Trans Am in his mind. Knowing in his heart that he'd never lived up to his father's expectations. "A couple of days before he died, my father tried to tell me that he was in some kind of trouble—that there were men who wouldn't be too happy with him if they found out he knew something."

"Did he say what it was?"

He shook his head, damning himself the way he had for eighteen years. "He tried to tell me, but I was such a damn punk back then I wouldn't listen. He was always on my case, trying to get me to be a better man—no, just trying to get me to be a man, period. I thought it was some other stupid piece of advice he was giving me. I didn't listen. And then he was gone. I've been trying to figure it out ever since. But I can't."

"Oh, A.J." Her soft gasp weighed upon his soul.

He shook his head, feeling the tears clutch at his chest. But he couldn't shed them. "He was always trying to teach me to do the right thing. To listen more than you talk, and to tell the truth when you do open your mouth. To stand up for those who can't stand up for themselves."

The bed shifted as she moved across it. "But you do all those things."

"I didn't use to. It took a good man dying for me to change."

"You were a kid." He flinched as her cool hands splayed across his back. "That's not who you are anymore." Her glorious hands swept around his shoulders and she hugged him from behind. "I know your father would be so proud of the man you've become. I'm proud of you. You're a man of peace. Of strength. Of honor." She pressed a kiss to his shoulder—three times, marking each tattoo. "That's why I love you."

A.J. went still.

I love you. They were the most beautiful words he'd ever heard.

And nothing had ever scared him more in his life.

With a quick twist, he reached around and pulled her into his lap. He realized this argument wasn't about teaching her a lesson, teaching her why they couldn't be together. It was about admitting to himself why he never wanted to be apart.

He caressed her face, stroked her lips, touched her delicate ears. "I look at you, and I'm ashamed. Look at all you've overcome. You lost your mother, your hearing. But it hasn't jaded your heart. You knock yourself out to help everyone else when you have every right to be taken care of yourself. You've tried to do the right thing from day one on this case. It can't be easy to stand up to your father. You knew Galvan was dangerous, but you reported the crime, anyway. You—"

"Shut up." She pressed her fingers over his lips and silenced him. "Just shut up."

She replaced her fingers with her mouth and A.J. held her tight and absorbed the guilty pleasure of her kiss. He slipped his hand inside her robe to caress her breast. Her hands touched his face, his shoulders, his chest. She opened her mouth in loving welcome and he seized advantage of the gift. She loved him. She might be a fool, but he was an even bigger fool for believing it.

A.J. needed her, and Claire denied him nothing.

In a shameless matter of minutes, he'd slipped out of his jeans. He straddled Claire across his lap, pushed the robe to the floor. He entered her in one long thrust and fell back onto the bed to savor the feel of her soft, warm body closing down around him. In this, there were no differences between them. Not age, not money, not secret shames.

He played with her breasts as they bobbed above him, but he was too far gone to make this last. He rubbed her with his thumbs and pulled at her thighs and plunged into her slick, welcoming heat, then watched her cry out in pleasure as he poured himself out inside her.

She collapsed atop his chest and he held her tight.

"Te amo, amor," he whispered in her ear, knowing she couldn't hear. *"Te amo."*

A FEW HOURS LATER, A.J. parked his Trans Am in the street across from the Winthrop Building and climbed out. He buttoned his tweed jacket over his T-shirt and gun and circled around the hood to open the door for Claire.

In her blue silk suit, she looked a lot more suited for the boardroom confrontation he expected than he did. But Claire had convinced him to face her father and the board on his own terms. So, armed with the knowledge from the investigation, and his tenuous faith in Claire's claim about being any man's equal, A.J. escorted her into the building and made their way up the elevator to the twenty-sixth floor.

Amelia Ward tried to stop them first. "Miss Winthrop. Detective." She hurried across the mahogany tiles to reach them before they reached the black steel doors of the executive boardroom. "It's so good to see you. Is everything all right now? Your father was so worried. Is he expecting you? The board members asked not to be disturbed. They're trying to figure out what to do about Mr. Hastings. He was arrested, you know. Something about lewd behavior and resisting arrest."

Claire wore her sound transmitters and speech processors again, so she heard every word. She politely stopped when Amelia dashed in front of them to bar the door. "Miss Ward, you do realize that your predecessor was killed because she was loyal to the wrong person, don't you?"

The executive assistant gulped. "I shouldn't be loyal to your father?"

"I hope you are." She nudged the redheaded woman aside. "He'll want to see me."

A.J. bit his lip to keep from smiling at the cutting tone. Claire had the makings to be every bit the corporate shark as the other members of her family were. If that's what she wanted. In a week's time, he'd learned Claire Winthrop would shine at whatever she wanted to be.

He opened the door and Claire marched inside. The grumblings at the interruption were quickly replaced with gasps of shock and shouts of joy.

"Claire." Cain Winthrop was the first to rise. He hurried down from the head of the table and scooped her up in his arms, kissing her cheek and hugging her tight. "Oh, baby, baby. Dwight Powers told me you were all right, but I couldn't believe him until I saw you with my own eyes. I missed you, baby, I missed you."

"Dad. I told you I didn't want to be called *baby.*" He set her on the floor and pulled back to inspect her with his eyes.

"I know, sweetie. I know, I know. I'll work on it, I promise." He pulled her in for another hug. "I love you. I'm just so happy to see you safe again. Does this mean you're coming home?"

A.J.'s blood froze as Cain curled his arms around his daughter and patted her back. On his left hand he wore a gold signet ring, with four lines of gold overlaying the ruby underneath. Four angled lines, like the murderer's imprint on Valerie Justice's neck.

A *W.*

Winthrop.

More than anything, A.J. wanted to rip those hands away from Claire. But they hadn't come here to make any outright accusations. They'd come to lay out a few facts about the murder to force the accomplice's hand.

Cain Winthrop's hand.

The man his father had said would change the truth to suit his purpose. The truth was, he had a hand in Valerie Justice's death, and his own daughter was the eyewitness who could put him in prison for life. Accessory to murder. Conspiracy to commit. The list of crimes went on and on.

Was Antonio Rodriguez, Sr. just another name on Winthrop's hit list? Had his father uncovered the man's crimes years before and been silenced? Would he lose the woman he loved to the same conspiracy and cover-up?

A.J. stood back while the others around the table—her Uncle Peter, her stepbrother Gabriel, Gina Gunn, Marcus Tucker—all gathered around to greet her.

Claire was the one to push the group aside and take a seat at the table. "Dad, Peter, everyone—A.J. and I have uncovered some very interesting pieces of information about Valerie's murder."

"Oh, honey, do you want to talk about this now?" Peter Landers asked. He slipped on his glasses and sat at the end of the table opposite Cain. The other board members filled in in between. No one asked A.J. to sit. He didn't mind; he preferred the advantage of easy movement among all these corporate predators. "Maybe you should go home for a rest. Let us take care of this."

Claire shook her head. "Valerie's murder concerns me more than any of you because I'm the one who saw it." Seeing she had everyone's attention, she continued. "There's a hit man in Kansas City named Dominic Galvan. He's from—" She turned to A.J., more for effect, he thought, to show she'd been working with the police. "What's the name of that country?"

"Tenebrosa," he answered. "In Central America. It's a country known for its civil wars and illegal drug exports."

"I saw his name in the news," said Gabe, thumbing through the pages of a report in front of him. "What do drugs and a hit man have to do with us?"

Gina shook her head. "I've never heard of him."

"I think one of you knows him very well." Claire's statement generated a buzz of questions in the room that she quickly silenced. "One of you was also here the night Valerie was murdered. One of you hired Galvan. And I—" She reached for A.J.'s hand, and he could tell from her grip that her confidence wasn't one hundred percent in place, despite her brilliant performance. "*We* have a way to prove it."

Marcus Tucker shoved back his chair and circled the

table. "This is your doing, Rodriguez." He jabbed that stubby, annoying finger in his face. "This is absolute slander. None of us are guilty of anything except trying to do what's best for the company and this addle-brained daughter whose imagination—"

A.J. snatched that finger and twisted, earning a curse as he shoved against Tucker's shoulder and drove the bigger man to his knees. "One, Miss Winthrop has a better grasp of the real world and how to live in it than anyone in this room. And two, if you ever insult her in front of me again, I will break your finger."

Releasing Tucker, A.J. stepped back, knowing the security chief would want some payback. He charged forward one step, but seemed to think better of any rash action, considering their audience and the fact that A.J. didn't budge. "I didn't mean anything by it, Miss Winthrop." He looked to Cain to include him in the apology. "I'd just like to know where you're gettin' these so-called facts that can prove one of us is working with Galvan."

A.J. felt Claire's eyes seek him out before dropping the bombshell. He nodded his support.

"I know it's a rather indelicate subject, but one of you was having an affair with Valerie. It ended just before she died. We believe that's why she was killed. She knew something about illegal goings-on at the company—probably using our import and customs agreements to transport drugs into the country from Tenebrosa and distribute them. KCPD thinks there are some local murders tied in with the drug smuggling—getting rid of the competition, I believe, so they could be distributed without local interference.

"Valerie was a woman scorned. And she wanted revenge. She probably threatened to expose her lover as the man who's been using Winthrop, Inc. to make himself a very rich man."

Gina's cheeks blanched, then dotted with color. "That's why Dwight Powers wanted the semen samples. To prove which of you men slept with Valerie."

"I slept with her," Cain confessed, his gaze touching his daughter and stepchildren.

"What?"

"Dad?"

"Cain." Gabriel's protest wasn't one of shock. It was more of an accusatory sneer as he stood and crossed the room to his stepfather. "You son of a bitch. You cheated on Mother?"

"Only once. The day Valerie disappeared." Cain rose and faced his stepson, but his stony expression didn't reveal whether he was apologizing or justifying his actions. "You know your mother. Or maybe you don't because you're out gallivanting around town every night—or flying off on a business trip so you don't have to spend much time with her."

"Don't you dare insult—"

"I am a grown man. I've built an empire out of nothing. I knew true love once—with Claire's mother—but it was snatched away from me far too soon when she died. I don't need to be managed or manipulated. I need to be loved and accepted and supported as I am." He turned to include Gina in his explanation, as if he saw a pattern in the family genes. "All Deirdre sees are deals and dollar signs. I'd love to retire to our cabin on the lake. But that doesn't suit your mother's social calendar."

He turned to Claire next, addressing her mention of the DNA, maybe even apologizing for not being the father he'd hoped to be for her. "Valerie and I had been friends for many years. In some ways, I think she always understood me better than either of my wives." He paused. "She'd been dropping hints for a number of weeks that she wanted to make things more personal between us. I set it up with Marcus to make it appear that Valerie was traveling with her beau to the Bahamas.

"She went to the airport, but then came back to hole up in her apartment for a week. She said she'd be at my disposal—whenever I could get away, whenever I needed her." Cain shook his head despondently.

"I knew Deirdre wouldn't suspect anything if she thought Valerie was out of the country."

He sank back into his chair. A.J. took note of how tightly Claire gripped the arms of her chair. She wanted to go to her father. But she held back, letting him spill the rest of his story. "The day Valerie disappeared—the day she died—I went to her apartment. I let her seduce me. Hell, I didn't put up any fight. I talked about divorcing Deirdre and the possibility of committing to something more serious with Valerie."

"You'd divorce Mother?"

He waved aside Gina's protest. "I didn't love Valerie, but I could relax with her. I went home when we were done to think about whether I could make any promises to her. And that's when Claire stormed into the house, claiming Valerie was dead. It had only been a couple of hours since I'd seen her. I was thinking about changing my life for her. And then she was gone."

His gaze touched on each person at the table, begging forgiveness. "When Claire said Valerie was dead, I knew it had to be a mistake. Val had sworn to stay hidden away—

to be discreet so that no one would guess our intentions. I had Amelia call, pretending to be Valerie. I wanted to get to Val's apartment, speak to her myself—find out why she'd risk discovery, find out if she'd betrayed me—before the police got involved. If she was at the office that night, she was up to no good."

Peter Landers stood and cleared his throat before sauntering to the door. "You know, this is all playing out like a gripping *Murder, She Wrote* rerun. But I have better things to do with my time." He turned to Cain. "Pull yourself together and don't confess to anything else until I get our lawyers here. I'll post Rob Hastings's bail as we discussed. I still think we should turn him loose as a liability and let him mount his own defense. But that's the board's call."

He leaned down and kissed Claire's cheek. "It's good to have you back, dear. Even if you are spouting nonsense." He crossed to the door, pausing to look down his nose at A.J. "Detective, I think you've brought enough harm to this family. May I suggest that the next time you pull a stunt like this, you don't involve Claire."

Marcus Tucker followed Landers out the door with a huff.

"Damn you, Cain." Gina shot to her feet and hurried around the table to catch one of the men who'd exited. "Wait. I want to talk to you."

Gabriel Gunn buttoned his suit jacket. "I thought we were family, Cain. I don't know if Mother will forgive you for this." He pressed a kiss to the crown of Claire's head. "Good to have you back, pipsqueak. Rodriguez."

After the last board member had left, Cain Winthrop spoke. His gaze seemed distant, as if focused on the past. "You know, Rodriguez, years ago your father came to me and told me a very similar story. He said he'd overheard Valerie late one night, talking with someone on the phone about a shipment from Central America. Said he could tell from the conversation that it was something illegal—she was bypassing a customs inspection and talking about making a deposit of money in a coded account. But I didn't believe him. I trusted my family not to hurt me or the company."

A.J. held himself perfectly still as Cain told him what he'd suspected all along. "Someone believed my father's story, and didn't want him to tell anyone else."

Cain nodded. "I always wondered about that car wreck. The timing…"

"A.J." Claire pushed her chair back and stood beside him. "What are you saying? That the same man who killed Valerie killed your father?"

This was it. He was going to lose her. But his quest for justice overruled the needs of his heart.

With a rueful sigh, A.J. touched her face one last time. Then he circled around her, walked up to Cain Winthrop and held out his hand for the damning evidence. "Mr. Winthrop. May I see your ring?"

"YOU CAN'T ARREST my father. That's not what we agreed to." Claire hustled after A.J. down the hallway toward the elevator. His partner Josh had already put Cain Winthrop in handcuffs and taken him downstairs. "You said if I talked long enough about everything you suspected that one of them would reveal something. You could trace their actions and see who contacted Galvan."

A.J. paused long enough to turn so she could read his lips. "Your father revealed plenty. He was with Valerie that afternoon. He suspected she was using him and his company. He had no alibi."

"He didn't kill her. And he wouldn't let anyone try to kill me."

"He's got the ring, Claire. And DNA will match him up to Valerie's bed."

She tugged at his arm to stop him. "That's your proof?"

He dangled the marked plastic bag with the gold ring inside. "The facts say he's our man. The markings on this ring match the imprint on Valerie's neck. Made after her death. It shows he picked up the body and moved it. Now we're going to get your dad to hand us Galvan." He reached for her, but she scooted away. Her rejection didn't seem to surprise him. If anything, it set the shape of his mouth into a grimmer line. "I'm sorry it turned out this way. But at least you'll be safe now. You won't have to run or hide anymore. I told you—I needed you to be safe. No matter what it cost me."

She couldn't believe her father was a murderer any more than she could believe A.J. hadn't been using her all along.

All that they'd been through, all that she'd given him—had been for nothing. He was a cop, through and through, just like he'd said. And all the good she'd seen in him, all the trust she'd shared, didn't mean a damn when it came down to doing his job.

Everything inside Claire was breaking. Tears stung her eyes, but she refused to cry. "No wonder you didn't believe we had a future together. It didn't have anything to do with our ages or the money or where we come from."

She looked into those beautiful golden eyes for the last time. "You think my father killed yours."

Chapter Thirteen

Claire waved to Aaron on her way up the porch steps. Between KCPD and Marcus Tucker's armed security team, she should be plenty safe in her own home.

It was a tragic bit of depression that had her thinking she wouldn't care if Dominic Galvan did find a way through all of the guards protecting her. She'd lost her father. As a result of his actions, she was pretty sure she was going to lose her stepfamily. And she'd lost A.J.

She tossed her purse on the stand in the foyer and crossed the marble tiles into the library. She paced the room, digging through her memories of the past week and trying to figure out where she'd made her first mistake. Was it trusting A.J.? Giving him her body? Her heart? Was it thinking a naive, sheltered woman like her could stand up for herself and make a difference in the world?

With her students? With a friend's death? With a man who couldn't see he was every bit the man his father had wanted him to be?

She should have stayed in her small, rarefied world. Let her family take care of her problems for her, let them make choices for her—in men, in careers, in friends.

A.J. had encouraged her to think for herself. He hadn't

acted like she was an ungrateful fool when she expressed an opinion or disagreed. He shared his burdens with her, albeit reluctantly, believing she could handle them, believing she could make them more bearable.

If she'd stayed in her own little world, she wouldn't be hurting now. Her father wouldn't be in jail. And A.J. wouldn't be carrying a truckload of guilt on his shoulders.

But she was a different person now. Smarter. Tougher. She was the woman she was always meant to be.

She wasn't a woman who surrendered to obstacles in her path. A.J. had to be wrong about her father. There had to be some proof she could find to clear his name. He hadn't killed Valerie and he wouldn't have killed A.J.'s father, either. There had to be a way to get through to A.J.

Claire sat at her desk and kicked off her shoes. She turned on the TDD phone to check for messages and wound up dialing the Fourth Precinct.

"Detective Rodriguez, please." She flipped the switch to speaker phone and watched the words scroll across the screen.

"He isn't available right now. May I take a message? Or would you like to leave something on his voice mail?"

"Voice mail, please." What she wanted to say couldn't be trusted to a pink slip of paper. She wanted A.J. to hear it in her voice—at least she hoped he could hear what she had to say.

She touched the screen as his message played across, and wished she could hear the real thing.

He'd been the real thing.

She was going to clear her father, and she was going to find a way to get A.J. back. It's what the new and improved Claire Winthrop would do.

"A.J.," she began. "It's Claire. I know talking isn't your best thing, but I think we need to. I'd at least like you to listen to me. I love you, A.J. How do you say it in Spanish? *Te amo?* I don't want to lose you. I don't want to lose my father, either. And maybe you weren't mine to begin with—I mean, not really. Sheesh."

The machine recorded the sound of her frustrated sigh and Claire shook her head. She stood up and walked away before she rambled off any more tiresome clichés. She raised her volume so the phone would still capture her voice. "Anyway, call me when you get a chance. I'll be—"

A sharp chill washed over her, leaving her covered in goose bumps and shaking. She could feel the eyes. She could feel the hate. *He* was here. Watching.

Claire spun around and frowned in recognition. "Uncle Peter."

How long had he been standing there? She glanced beyond him into the foyer, peeked at the stairs, looked through every window. No. It couldn't be. Peter had loved her mother. He loved her. But the sensation had stopped. Maybe she'd just imagined that paranoid feeling, or she'd picked up on the strain that marred her uncle's features. "What is it?"

Peter Landers's steel-gray hair had been fluffed by the wind, and a frown carved two deep grooves into his forehead, above the bridge of his glasses. "Have you heard?"

He crossed straight toward her. The purpose in his stride made her hug her arms across her middle and pull her shoulders back to gain every inch of height she could summon. "Has something happened?"

"I'll say." He gripped her by the shoulders, squinched

his mouth into a frown, then took a deep breath. "Galvan found out that your father was arrested. I guess he thought Cain was going to turn him in." He stopped, closing his eyes as if he couldn't go on.

Seeing his pain, feeling the urgency coursing through his fingertips and into her arms, Claire shook off her suspicions and laid a hand against his lapel. "What is it? What did Galvan do?"

He opened his eyes and looked deep into hers. "There was a bomb at the police station. The Fourth Precinct office, where they took your father."

The Fourth Precinct? Cold, numbing fear turned her veins to ice. "Is A.J. all right?"

"A.J.!" Her uncle's kindly old expression darkened with a forbidding look. He plucked his hands off her with a tiny shove, as if he was suddenly sickened by her touch. "A.J.? What about your father? Don't you want to know how he is?"

Claire tucked her hair behind her ears, then just as quickly fluffed it back into place. Thoughts of the carnage at the Riverfront Gentleman's Club and of Jordan Henley's death flooded her mind. "Of course, I do. Is he hurt? How many people were injured? Was anyone killed?"

"I don't know the details yet, but we should go. I'll drive you."

"I have a car. I can drive."

But he beat her to her purse. He picked it up and held it out to her, his temper short with concern, no doubt. "My car's parked right out front. Let's go."

For a few interminable moments, Claire couldn't move. She couldn't think or feel or see anything beyond Peter's outstretched hand.

And the gold signet ring, just like her father's, that he

wore on his third finger. A twenty-five-year service ring honoring his tenure at Winthrop Enterprises. A ruby embossed with a gold *W*, its angles raised high enough to leave its mark on a dead woman's neck.

Claire drifted back a step without taking her purse. It couldn't be. Could it? Her lungs didn't seem to be working right. She thumbed over her shoulder, grasping at the first excuse that came to mind to put distance between herself and her uncle. "Just let me get my shoes."

She hurried back to the desk and sat. Thank God, the screen was still transmitting; it had picked up almost every word of their conversation. Taking her time to slip her toes into her shoes, Claire typed in a message so Peter couldn't overhear. *S-O-S.* No, that's not what cops responded to…*9-1-1.*

She lifted her head and called to her uncle over the top of the machine. "I can drive, really."

An uncharacteristic impatience flared. "I said I'd drive. Your father may have been taken to the hospital by now. We should hurry."

"Are we taking your Lincoln Continental?" she articulated for the recording.

"What?" Peter frowned. His gaze slipped to the machine, he remembered what it was now. "You stupid bitch. I worked hard to keep you alive. But now you deserve everything you're going to get."

As he stormed into the library, Claire shot to her feet. "Come get me, A.J.," she whispered and disconnected the call before Peter picked up the machine and threw it against a wall of books.

He gripped her wrist in one smooth, long-fingered hand that had never been anything but kind to her before and hauled her up against him, twisting her arm behind her back. Pain radiated through her shoulder as he shoved her toward the front door. "Now smile real nice for the guard outside, and I'll tell Galvan not to shoot him."

Through clenched teeth, she begged, "Don't kill anyone else. Please."

She raised her gaze and found Peter staring down at her. With cold, empty eyes. Eyes that would let a brother-in-law go to prison for him. Eyes that would sell drugs or kill a colleague who threatened to betray him. Eyes that a man like Galvan would do business with.

Claire swallowed past the lump of dread in her throat. This was bad. This was really bad.

He pulled out his cell and punched in a number. Claire didn't have to guess who answered on the other end.

"I'm bringing you a gift. And this time, I want you to get it right."

A.J. CIRCLED THE INTERROGATION room table for the umpteenth time. Something wasn't right here.

Figure it out, A.J. Figure it out.

Had he jumped to the wrong conclusion? His instincts were screaming at him, but he just couldn't make out what they were trying to say.

He wondered if that chilly look of betrayal in Claire's eyes was affecting his judgment. God knew how dead he felt inside, knowing that doing his job had cost him a chance at her love. Justice for his father felt pretty empty right now, compared to the joy he got from one of Claire's smiles. Or the redemption he'd felt buried inside her welcoming body. Or the healing grace he'd felt each time she'd touched his face or defended him against his own self-recriminations.

But Cain Winthrop had no alibi for the night of Valerie's death—beyond claiming to be at home alone. He and Valerie had a history. He'd insisted that Claire had made up the whole murder story in the first place. He had enough money spread through enough banks in enough countries to account for illegal trading and money laundering a dozen times over.

He had the damn ring.

Claire's instincts claimed her father was innocent. Could A.J. trust hers when he couldn't trust his own anymore?

"Park it, Rodriguez." Dwight Powers's deep voice interrupted his turbulent thoughts. "We've got our man. When Winthrop's lawyer is done explaining the difference between life in prison and twenty years with the possibility of parole for cooperating with us, we'll have Galvan, too."

A.J. splayed his hands at his hips and looked at the attorney. "I don't see how a father could allow his own child to be hunted like that."

Powers shrugged. "That's probably why he broke and confessed. I'm not looking a gift conviction in the mouth."

"Technically, he confessed to having an affair with the victim, not to murder. We don't have a witness to place him at the crime, and everything else is circumstantial."

The A.D.A.'s eyes narrowed. "Are you rethinking this?"

"Yeah." A.J. pulled his tweed jacket off the back of his chair and slipped it on. "After all we've been through, this was too easy to get Winthrop. Just too damn easy."

"You think he's being set up?"

"Or he's protecting someone."

A.J. pushed open the door. There had to be something he was missing here.

"Where are you going?" Dwight called after him.

"To do some police work."

"MADRE DIOS." The slew of curses that followed in both Spanish and English alerted A.J.'s partner, Josh Taylor, along with Merle Banning, Captain Taylor and a half dozen other cops still on the floor, that something had gone beyond wrong. "He took Claire. That son of a bitch took Claire."

It was the first time most of them had seen A. J. Rodriguez lose his cool.

A.J. listened to the end of the recording one more time. "I'm coming, *amor.* Be safe. I'm coming."

Josh was the first to ask. "Talk to me, *amigo.*"

A.J. slammed down the phone. "I need a plate number for Peter Landers's Lincoln Continental. I'm sure it's new. And then I need to know its twenty ASAP." If they could locate the car, he could put his hands on the real killers. If they could locate Claire… Well.

Claire wanted to talk. He'd talk until he was hoarse if that's what the woman wanted. He just needed the chance to be with her. To prove himself. The chance to speak the truth in his heart.

Where would Landers take her?

A.J. closed his eyes and breathed slowly, in through his nose and out through his mouth. Quieting his emotions, he tuned out all the noise of the world and listened.

His eyes popped open. He knew. "I'm coming, *amor.*"

"Is there a situation?" Dwight Powers had come out of the interrogation room.

"Don't book Winthrop." A.J. was already backing toward the elevator doors, checking the clips on both his Glock and Beretta. "Run your numbers on Peter Landers's accounts. And find out if he thinks Cain Winthrop is responsible for his sister's death."

"The plate is Beta-Delta 1-5-6," Banning called out. "Black Lincoln. I've got the APB out on him now."

"Keep me posted. Send units out to the landfill. That's where they got rid of the last body." They weren't going to do it again.

Josh suited up to follow his partner. "What are we looking at, A.J.?"

Kidnapping, attempted murder, tampering with a witness, drug smuggling—hell, putting his hands on Claire was crime enough.

"If I don't come back with Peter Landers, that means I'm dead."

THE FIRST GUNSHOT hit his windshield and A.J. swerved into the oncoming lane.

He cursed in his head, but concentrated on his driving. A KCPD helicopter had spotted the Lincoln Continental, and confirmed its destination. He'd caught up with the car on I-71, cruising south at a speed nearly thirty miles over the limit. It was a dangerous game to play on this rainy night.

Between the swipe of the wiper blades, the lightning strikes that lit up the night and the swirling red and white lights of his dashboard siren, A.J. could pick them out. All three of them in the front seat. Landers, Claire and Galvan.

His petite, brave beauty was sandwiched between two killers. That meant she was still alive. Whatever plans for elimination Galvan had designed for her this time, he hadn't carried them out yet. It was all the chance A.J. needed to drive harder.

Thankfully, this late at night, in the wet, unfriendly weather, traffic was scarce. As the highway curved well out

Police Business

of the city, it cut through a maze of hills, low-lying creeks and eroded gulleys.

The Continental had a powerful engine and negotiated the dips and hills without losing speed. But speed was what his Trans Am had been built for. He'd spent years and a small fortune rebuilding this car to become the hot rod his father had always dreamed about. But he'd run this baby into the ground if it meant keeping Claire alive.

With a deep, steadying breath, he pressed his foot on the accelerator and crept up behind them.

Galvan stuck his arm out the window and fired off another round of bullets. A.J. swerved, compensated, and with its low center of gravity, he quickly regained control of the car.

They were getting close to the landfill now. The stench of the place hung heavy in the damp atmosphere and leaked in through the vents. The smell of it burned his sinuses and kept his senses sharp. If they reached the dump site before him, he'd lose any advantage. Two of them on foot in the darkness with a hostage, instead of one enemy vehicle.

A.J. floored it. "Hold tight, *amor.*"

He gritted his teeth and braced for the impact. Thunder crashed in his ears as steel rammed steel. The Trans Am's front end buckled and ground against the right front tire. The Continental fishtailed across the wet pavement, then spun in 360s again and again and again.

"Claire!"

The Continental sailed off an embankment and flew through the air until gravity caught it and sucked it down. The black monster crashed to earth. It bounced, flipped, caught in the watery muck of the landfill below and lurched to a halt.

A.J. skidded his last three wheels onto the shoulder and jammed his car into park. He was out of the car, Glock in hand, sliding and scrambling down the hill into the rain-soaked night even before a door opened on the twisted frame of the Continental.

"Police! Freeze!"

The instant he saw Landers's bloody sleeve at the open door, A.J. grabbed a fistful of it and dragged him out, face-down onto the stinking mountain of wet garbage. He pressed his gun to the back of Landers's head. "Stay down!"

"You'll never get away from this, Detective." Landers's speech slurred from the gash on his scalp, but he had enough temerity to turn his head and taunt him. "You will lose one way or another."

He stuck his knee in Landers's back and flattened him. "I said stay down! And I'll take this as evidence." A.J. worked the gold signet ring from Landers's finger and stuffed it into his pocket, finally making the connection to the mole on the Winthrop board that Claire already had.

"Claire!" he shouted, peering through the dark and the rain to see the car's dark interior. An instant thought of how much she'd hate it out here in the stinky blackness of this stormy night was eclipsed by the worry that she wasn't answering. He hoped they had just taken away her hearing devices and nothing more. "Claire!"

He glanced up the hill to the empty highway above. Where the hell was his backup? The storm had probably grounded the chopper. He'd outdriven everyone else to catch up with Landers.

"Claire!" he shouted one more time, pulling the hand-cuffs from his belt and ignoring his fear.

"Give it up, Detective. She's already dead."

"Shut up!"

The minute it took to cuff Landers was a minute too long. By the time A.J. had scrambled to his feet, braced his gun and swung around into the car, the Continental was empty. He swore against a backdrop of Landers's laughter. "Claire!"

Rain beat down on him, plastering his hair to his forehead. It hit the dirt and fill with a noisy cadence, making it virtually impossible to hear anything beyond his own voice. He'd left his flashlight up in the Trans, so visibility was next to nil.

Hunching down, he kept his back to the car for protection. He pulled his radio from his pocket and called it in. "Suspect on foot with hostage. Armed and dangerous. I repeat, armed and dangerous. I need some backup down here, boys."

A flash of lightning pinched off his pupils, temporarily blinding him. "You'd better not hurt her, Galvan." A.J. tried a little blindman's bluff taunt of his own to track them down. "Or on my father's name, you are a dead man!"

Then A.J. closed his eyes and prayed for a miracle. "Talk to me, sweetheart," he whispered, thinking of all the times he and Claire had communicated without words. "Talk to me."

It came to him first, like a flutter of breath on the wind. A ripple of sensation along the back of his neck that had nothing to do with the rain dripping inside his collar. A footstep. A drumbeat of sound. A pulse of rhythm that could only be felt, not heard.

Glock in hand, A.J. shimmied around the car and peered into the dapple of light and shadows created by the storm and abstract carpet of bottles, junk furniture and trash bags.

He listened for the telltale sounds that would lead him to Claire. Maybe it was her footsteps, maybe it was the path of the storm leading him. Maybe he simply followed his heart.

He found them, a quarter of a mile away, trying to get back up onto the highway. Galvan was trying, anyway. Who knew what kind of moves a dancer had in her when she wanted to escape a professional assassin? She twisted, she slipped, she kicked, she squirmed. It looked as if her hands were bound together because Galvan used the ligature between them to drag her to her feet, haul her up beside him, punish her for her lack of cooperation.

Damn it.

"Galvan! Let her go!"

Claire's tormentor turned and fired and A.J. dove for the ground. Chin-deep in pungent leftovers, A.J. stayed low and covered his head as the bullets thunked in the mud and exploded the plastic and paper around him. When the fusillade stopped, he was up and running, pursuing them at a parallel course, closing in on them as they climbed to a higher level toward the road and solid ground.

Closer. Closer. A.J.'s lungs grew accustomed to the stale air and expanded to give him a boost of energy. "Claire!"

She never answered, never screamed. She must be gagged as well. Galvan was tiring, dragging Claire up the incline beside him. He reached behind him and fired random shots A.J.'s way, but nothing came close.

Twenty yards away, A.J. stopped, stilled his breathing and took aim. But then they were climbing again, and the way Claire kept moving, he had no clear shot.

Damn. There was only one way to do this.

A.J. changed direction and charged, straight up the muddy slope. He leaped at Galvan and braced himself for the jolt as they hit the ground. The impact knocked Galvan's gun loose and it skittered away into the darkness. But the Renaissance Man was trained to kill in any number of ways and the fight was on.

Like a couple of street toughs, they did whatever it took to survive. They wrestled at the top of the incline, traded punches. When a knife materialized in Galvan's hand and he lunged, A.J. deflected the thrust. Before his forearm recognized the slice of pain, he tangled their legs together and twisted, throwing them back to the ground. The two tumbled and fought and slid down the hill.

Galvan landed face-first in the muck, and his startled gasp for air gave A.J. the split-second advantage he needed to push to his weary feet and pull out his Glock. "Enough, Galvan. You're under arrest."

A.J.'s chest heaved in and out with the effort to breathe. His gut was sore, his arm burned, and he was going to have one hell of a shiner come morning. Galvan rolled over on his back, spitting muck and water and blood from his mouth, slicking back his hair and grinning like an arrogant son of a bitch.

A bolt of lightning flashed, illuminating Claire long enough to give A.J. a reassuring glimpse of his feisty she-tiger, ready to wield a two-by-four despite her taped wrists. He barely had time to smile at her and the light had disappeared.

"So, Rodriguez," Galvan spoke from the ground, demanding A.J.'s full attention. "You will go down in history as the man who silenced Dominic Galvan."

Galvan kicked the gun from A.J.'s hand. He rolled, reached to retrieve it. A.J. spun around, pulled the second gun from his holster. Galvan rose on one knee, took aim.

A.J. fired.

A moment later, A.J. holstered both guns and checked the dead man to see that he had no pulse.

A.J. stood and walked off the distance between him and Claire. He took the board from her grasp and tossed it aside, pulled the knife from his pocket and cut her free. He cupped the back of her neck in his palm and kissed her, communicating in a way that had never needed any translation. "I got your message."

Epilogue

Four months later

Holding Claire Winthrop-Rodriguez's hand tight in his, A.J. hurried out of the church, dodging bubbles and ribbings and good wishes from friends and family alike.

He kissed his mother and all four sisters. He shook Cain Winthrop's hand. He traded hugs and jabs with his best man, Josh, and his oldest friend, Cole. Peter Landers didn't receive an invitation at his holding cell, nor did his former mistress, Gina Gunn. But Dwight Powers took a break from prepping the prosecution's case to attend.

A.J. appreciated them all, but he only had eyes for his wife. "C'mon."

They dashed down the stairs to the wedding present Claire had gotten for him—a trimmed-out classic black Trans Am. His father would have loved it. His father would have loved Claire.

As he stuffed the silky folds of Claire's elegant white dress around her in the seat, A.J. wondered how long it would take him to get that thing of beauty with all the buttons off her. When he got in behind the wheel and closed the door, the first thing he did was rip off the black bow tie and unhook his collar. The second thing he did was reach for his wife.

Claire came to him willingly, the way she always had, accepting him and loving him even when he hadn't been able to accept himself. She tumbled into his arms, her eloquent fingers making him crazy with every touch, her beautiful lips soft and demanding against his.

The hoots and catcalls and applause from his friends at the Fourth Precinct finally reminded A.J. to come up for air.

He moved his fingers the way she had taught him and signed, "I love you, Claire."

She smiled and answered, "*Te amo,* Antonio."

He kissed her one more time, then started the car and sped them on their way toward their new life together. A counselor and a cop. The new benefactor of the Forsythe School and its part-time, volunteer handyman.

Instincts won out over the facts. Yeah, maybe he was a little old for her. But she made him feel young. Maybe they came from two different worlds. But they had a lot in common—a passion for salsa music, a passion for each other.

A.J. loved Claire. And she loved him right back.

Every instinct in him said that this was the right thing to do.

Case closed.

* * * * *

Coming in September 2005...
Get CORNERED—a Signature anthology featuring three brand-new suspenseful novellas from Julie Miller, Linda Turner and Ingrid Weaver!

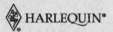

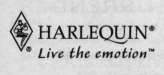

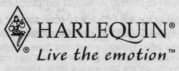

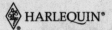

"Look. I truly do need a favor, Emmy. If you do this one thing for me, then...then we would not be even. Not even close. I would owe you, big time."

Emerson lifted her head and stared at her speakerphone.

Yes, bumping into him had been nowhere near as horrible as she'd imagined it might be. Yes, the ache she'd once felt any time she even thought his name was long gone. But pushing it any further was tempting fate.

Unless...

Unless this was actually an opportunity. A chance to be absolutely sure that no matter what life threw at her, she would be okay.

"No promises," she said, "but give me the gist."

"Can do. I need you to be my date."

Emerson may have snorted. And coughed. At the same time. Leading to a rather unladylike choking noise.

"Actually, strike that," Holden said. "What I am truly in need of is someone to accompany me to an upcoming dinner. And I was hoping you might be the one."

Dear Reader,

The question I am asked most often when people discover I am a writer is, "Where do you get your ideas?"

For me, the ideas are the easy part. Song lyrics, news headlines, funny stories overheard in cafés (be careful, a writer might be listening). Yet it's often the smushing together of two—or more—arbitrary, unconnected thoughts where the magic happens.

The idea for this story came about by way of the '70s song "Heartache No. 9." I had written it down years ago, the title alone sending me down a glorious rabbit hole—a heroine who looks upon heartaches like a cat with nine lives and, after her eighth major heartache, fears the ninth may herald her doom. But it didn't have weight, purpose, heart until I stumbled upon a video of a woman at a wedding lifting her glass of champagne in a blithe salute after not winning the bouquet toss. At that moment, Emerson Adler was born.

So thank you to the scraps of paper, the backs of receipts, the bar coasters that have sacrificed themselves to the gods of Big Ideas.

Happy reading!

Ally
xxx

The Wedding Favor

Ally Blake

HARLEQUIN

Romance

HARLEQUIN®

Romance™

ISBN-13: 978-1-335-40718-4

The Wedding Favor

Copyright © 2022 by Ally Blake

Harlequin Enterprises ULC
22 Adelaide St. West, 41st Floor
Toronto, Ontario M5H 4E3, Canada
www.Harlequin.com

Printed in U.S.A.

Australian author **Ally Blake** loves reading and strong coffee, porch swings and dappled sunshine, beautiful notebooks and soft, dark pencils. Her inquisitive, rambunctious, spectacular children are her exquisite delights. And she adores writing love stories so much she'd write them even if nobody else read them. No wonder, then, having sold over four million copies of her romance novels worldwide, Ally is living her bliss. Find out more about Ally's books at allyblake.com.

Books by Ally Blake

Harlequin Romance

A Fairytale Summer!

Dream Vacation, Surprise Baby

The Royals of Vallemont

Rescuing the Royal Runaway Bride
Amber and the Rogue Prince

Hired by the Mysterious Millionaire
A Week with the Best Man
Crazy About Her Impossible Boss
Brooding Rebel to Baby Daddy
The Millionaire's Melbourne Proposal

Harlequin KISS

Faking It to Making It
The Dance Off
Her Hottest Summer Yet

Visit the Author Profile page
at Harlequin.com for more titles.

My books are not the books they are without my wonderful writerly friends—those suppliers of laughter, bastions of empathy and lighters of creative fires. This story owes so much to Kali Anthony for her boundless love of romance and dazzling "glitter bomb" light bulb moment, and to Amy Andrews for her spit take–worthy NSFW insights and invaluable word sprints. I am so grateful for you both.

Praise for
Ally Blake

"I found *Hired by the Mysterious Millionaire* by Ally Blake to be a fascinating read... The story of how they get to their HEA is a page-turner. 'Love conquers all' and does so in a very entertaining way in this book."

—*Harlequin Junkie*

PROLOGUE

THE FIRST TIME Emerson Adler's heart broke she was ten years old.

Well, ten years and one day to be exact. Her actual birthday had been wondrous—her dad surprising her, and her mum, for that matter, with a caramel-coloured fluffball in the shape of a cocker spaniel.

The bigger surprise had come the morning after, when her dad had roused her from her sleep before the sun was even up, tweaked her on the nose, called her his favourite girl, and said, "Life ebbs and flows, kiddo. When it feels hard, remember it'll be okay. It always gets better."

Then he'd kissed her hair and walked out the front door. Never to return.

Emerson's mum had coped by turning her naturally cheerful nature up to eleven, starting a mini-orchard in their small back yard as a symbol of "growth", hugging her daughter a hundred times a day, and adoring Pumpkin, the puppy she'd had no say in taking on. Throwing in the occasional telling words of wisdom of her own, such as, "Take care when falling in love, as things that fall often end up broken." As if quips and dauntless sunshine might make her daughter bombproof to the shock she herself had endured.

Unfortunately, as it turned out, that first heart-break had created some kind of crack in the space-time continuum, making young Emerson a conduit for heartache.

So many heartaches that she—like a prisoner scraping tallies in the walls of her cell—had kept count. Of the big ones, especially. The ones that took something from her. That changed the course of her life. Though in lieu of fingernails on con-crete she'd used a pen with a pom-pom on the end, and a dedicated notebook with a sparkly cartoon cactus on the cover.

Heartache Number One: ten years old.

Dad left. Obviously.

Heartache Number Two: eleven years old.

Mrs Abernathy, the teacher who gave her extra stars on her homework and seemed to know when her mum was not feeling quite as sunny as usual, had also upped and left! Retired, they said, but how could she be sure?

Heartache Number Three: twelve years old.

Kailey Deluca, best friend, turned up on the first day of high school with a new haircut, new earring holes, new boobs, new clothes…and new friends. Totally awful.

And so the Heartache List had gone on.

That was its name, scrawled in big black bubble writing on the front page, begun in reaction to:

Heartache Number Four: fourteen years old.

A devastating, unrequited high school crush which had soon morphed into a detailed, annotated roadmap penned in a special notebook, ruling and shaping Emerson's decisions in the hopes she might one day figure out how to make sure she never broke her heart again.

And then…

Heartache Number Eight: twenty-five years old.

Her beautiful mum passed away, after a breathlessly quick battle with cancer.

After that there would be no *Heartache Number Nine.* For surely it would be the end of her.

This story starts nearly two decades on from that seminal heartache.

The Heartache List, with its spiky cactus cover and pages filled with detailed ramblings and deeply felt promises, has long since gone.

Emerson no longer has need to keep track of heartbreaks, for hers is a meticulously curated life, vigilant in its setting of boundaries. She enjoys a small crew of trusted friends. Work at Pitch Perfect, her very own bespoke recruitment firm, is immensely satisfying. Her life is no longer fettered by the assumption that it all may be whipped out from under her at any moment.

For she knows that everything comes to an end eventually. Opportunities, employment, favourite restaurants, favourite lipsticks, relationships. The trick, she has discovered, is in the accepting and the moving on.

It is a warm spring day on the glorious Mornington Peninsula of southern Victoria, and a wedding has taken place. The bride, Camille, is Emerson's very best friend in the entire world, and the groom, Phillip, is an utterly lovely guy who would not dare break his bride's heart—due, in no small part, to the fact he'd have Emerson to deal with.

Dusk is settling over the gorgeous reception marquee perched at the edge of a forest a short drive in from the coast. Birds flutter and chatter as they fill the sky, following the last rays of the sun. And the air tastes like the first lick of spring after a long, cool, coastal winter. It brings with it the scent of impending change.

While inside the marquee, Emerson has no clue that her comprehensively fortified heart is about to be put to the ultimate test…

CHAPTER ONE

THE TIDE OF anticipation rippling through the crowd was palpable, voices ascending, glasses clinking, dresses shimmering in the buttery light of a marquee strung with enough fairy lights to bring a plane safely home on a cloudy night.

All the single ladies—along with a handful of convivial and unattached guys—stood in a loose group at the edge of the dance floor, shifting from foot to foot, jostling for position, eyes sharp on the deviously grinning bride who stood alone beneath a spotlight waving her lavish bouquet back and forth like some kind of lure.

Emerson Adler alone remained immune to the collective fervour.

As Maid of Honour, Emerson felt duty-bound to at least *appear* as if she was taking part. Though the bride was hardly what one might call traditional. Emerson's place card read "Best Woman/ Sister/Wife" and her dress—as chosen by the bride—was less pastel eighties prom, more backless glittery bronze *va-va-voom* Vegas hostess. The bride was nothing if not extra.

Speaking of the bride... Camille planted her bare feet, backside wiggling dramatically as she readied to make the toss, and the rowdy crowd held its collective breath. Then a *whoop* split the evening air as the bouquet arced high in a tumble of white roses, orchids, moonflowers, and faux pearls.

The group surged up and to the left—like a rugby scrum, only better dressed. While Emerson and her glass of warm bubbly took a deft step to the right.

The bouquet landed atop a shelf of groping hands, then bounced—once, twice—leaving those in the bullseye in an entangled heap on the parquetry floor. Finally, like a whale breaching the surface of a stormy sea, Bernadette, sweet younger cousin to the bride, leapt to her feet, brandishing the bunch as if it were Excalibur.

Congratulations ensued before the competitors moved off to reclaim their partners, their drinks, their chairs. While Emerson sighed in contentment, happy that she'd navigated that whole affair with subtle aplomb.

Or so she thought, till she caught the bride's gaze across the crowded room.

Camille, being Camille, grinned broadly as she waggled a *naughty, naughty* finger Emerson's way, clearly finding Emerson's mini-rebellion hilarious.

Emerson offered a sly shrug, lifted her bubbly in salute, downed the lot in one gulp, placed the empty glass on the tray of a wandering waiter, found a gap in the crowd, and took it.

Camille's bark of laughter was loud enough that

it could be heard above the band, who'd just her-
alded their return to the stage with a clash of cym-
bals and blurt of a trumpet.

"Dance with me, Emmy!" one of Phillip's
groomsmen begged as she slipped by.

Emerson took his hand, spun deftly beneath
his arm, and let go, before disappearing into the
throng, stopping only when she reached her desired destination—the empty, moody, dimly lit,
back corner bar, half hidden behind a screen of
stripped willow.

Catching the eye of the bartender, Emerson
motioned to the fresh tray of glasses filled with
golden bubbles. Chewing on a toothpick and dry-
ing wine glasses by hand, he lifted his chin the
barest amount in confirmation. Not a chatty one.
Perfect.

While the soft strains of moody, forties jazz
filled the marquee like smoke, bringing the slow
dancers to the floor, Emerson plonked her clutch
bag on the bar, leaned her back against warm
wood, and took a moment to herself for the first
time in what felt like days.

Without busy work keeping her occupied, it
wasn't long before she noticed the uncomfortable
feeling that had grown in her belly, incrementally,
as the day had gone on. Not hunger. She'd had the
fish, and the chocolate mousse. More as if her in-
nards were being pickled in something bittersweet.
More as if she felt a little…downhearted.

It made no sense, for the wedding had gone off without a hitch, the ceremony whimsical, the after-party decadent and joyful.

So why these...*feelings*?

If the Heartache List had taught her anything, it was that *feelings* were messy and perilous. Far better to keep them squished deep down inside where they might shrivel up and die due to acute lack of oxygen.

And yet, as she watched the crowd on the dance floor part, right as Phillip swept Camille into his arms and twirled her about, before hauling her close and slow dancing as if they were the only people in the room, and her two favourite humans move on to the next stage of their lives in real time, a stage that would no longer include her, Emerson dropped her hand to her belly and the— dare she even think it—*ache* therein.

"Then again," she muttered, "maybe it was the fish."

Shaking off the feeling as best she could, Emerson rolled her shoulders, closed her eyes, and drank deeply, the bubbles biting winningly at the inside of her throat on the way down. She nudged a high heel off one foot, releasing a small sound of relief as she stretched her toes, twirled her ankle and—

"Emmy?"

The voice calling her name, invading her moment of sanctuary, was a masculine one, deep, rumbling, and lit with the expectation of conversation returned. "Emmy Adler? Of East Kew High? Or, more particularly, the cracked hard plastic chairs outside the guidance counsellor's office?"

Emerson took a small breath before twisting to face the interloper now leaning back against the bar beside her.

Used, as she was, in her work as a professional recruiter of human resources to determining first impressions in a blink, Emerson took mental bullet points: tall, great hair, hell of a jawline, beautiful suit, exceptional tailoring required to contain those mighty shoulders, slow smile tugging at the corners of a wide mouth, rather lovely crinkles at the edges of a pair of magnetic eyes the colour of a coming storm—

All too late a skitter of warning thundered its way down Emerson's back, knocking against the bumps in her spine like a pinball.

The jaw, the shoulders, the stormy eyes, the *cracked hard plastic chairs outside the guidance counsellor's office*—they belonged to none other than Holden Roarke.

Aka *Heartache Number Four*.

Emerson's eyes skewed to the dance floor, seeking Camille—the very person who had bought the sparkly cactus notebook in which the Heartache List had been etched, right after the guy now standing beside her had broken Emmy's teenaged heart.

Holden's voice cut through the fog. "It is Emmy Adler, right? If not, then the words echoing disastrously inside my head must sound like the most dubious line."

Realising that, bar bolting for the exit, there was no way out of this moment but through, Emerson forced a neutral smile onto her face, then held out a hand, as if this was all cool and normal.

"Holden Roarke," she said, her voice admirably even. "Yes, it is me. Though I go by Emerson. Mostly."

"Emerson," he said, smiling into her eyes, her name sounding like an endearment in that low, slow, velvety dark voice. "Mostly."

Then he took her hand in his. Encompassing, cool, good pressure, she'd have given him a big tick next to the "handshake" box if she was taking him on as a client. Though the shimmer of warmth that shot up her arm as he held her hand was overkill.

But he was not a prospective client. He was a guy who had, at one time, made her cry into her unicorn pillowcase simply because he existed.

Emerson let go first, her hand springing back as a zing sparked from his hand to hers. A zing that seemed to spark in his eyes as well. Though that was more likely from the fairy lights. There really were a lot of them.

Wishing she'd waited a minute before mainlining a glass of champagne, Emerson pushed her near empty glass across the bar.

The bartender, finding within himself a sudden burst of helpfulness, slid a full one her way.

"How long *has* it been?" Holden crooned. Well, he didn't croon exactly, but he had the kind of voice—all warm and deep—that, when combined with the acoustics in their little alcove, made it sound just so.

When Emerson blinked, rather more slowly than was natural, the bartender coughed, his eyebrow flickering, a knowing smile growing around his toothpick.

Emerson narrowed her eyes meaningfully at the guy, then turned her back on him to shoot Holden a quick, bland glance. "How long? Aeons, at least."

"That long?" Holden asked. "And there I was, thinking it had only been ages."

Unfortunately, Emerson's quick glance had somehow stuck, meaning she was forced to bear the full brunt of those stormy blue eyes crinkling in that very particular, effortlessly charming, entirely discombobulating way that had put her under his spell all those years ago.

Aeons. Ages. Once upon a time, when she'd been a dreamy young thing, desperate for some guy to see her oodles of wondrous potential.

Emerson grabbed herself by the metaphorical collar and yanked herself back to the present, only to nearly topple sideways, having forgotten she was wearing only one shoe.

Stomach swooping, she white-knuckled the bar behind her and glanced down at the floor to find no sign of her own missing heel, only a gleaming, Holden-Roarke-sized shoe cocked roguishly out in front.

"Having a good time?" Holden said, his shoe kicking back further, so that the toes faced the ceiling.

"Of course," she said through gritted teeth as she swept her bare toes behind her.

"Big fan of weddings?"

"A fan of *this* wedding," she managed as she sank a little lower, her toes searching a little farther.

"Mmm. I'd put good money behind the bet you have no plans to star in one of your own anytime soon."

Now manically searching for her shoe so she could extricate herself as quickly as possible, Emerson muttered, "Now, *that's* a dubious line."

After a beat, Holden burst into laughter, the sound deeply relaxed and entirely unselfconscious. "I wouldn't dare. If I *did* dare, I'd hope I had better material."

Emerson's foot stopped mid-search as she realised what she'd just intimated.

Of course, it hadn't been a line. Even at sixteen he'd smiled with ease, made eye contact and held it, listened when people spoke. At fourteen she'd mistaken it to mean something other than what it was, and had been proven mortifyingly wrong.

She would not be making that same mistake twice.

"I'd hope so too," she said, holding eye contact to show just how undaunted she was. "Or you'd be the kind of guy who'd follow up with a little, *Hey, aren't you the Maid of Dishonour?*"

Holden's smile was broad. And when he turned his body towards her he blocked some of the light. "Then I'd come at you with a little side-eye and a dare—fifty points for a kiss with a stranger in the cloakroom, a hundred for landing the bride's garter, twenty-five points for getting Aunty Verna sloshed."

"Poor Aunty Verna. Seems a tad low."

"Turns out it's not that hard."

His smile grew, yet again, and she felt her mouth kick into a quick smile of its own, despite itself. Damn those eyes, with their lovely crinkles. And zillion lashes. How could she have forgotten about all those lashes?

"How many points for making a bridesmaid blush?"

Emerson blinked her eyes back into focus as she felt heat creep into her cheeks. "Now, that's definitely a line."

This time when his smile flashed, she glimpsed canines. "Not at all. A purely academic exercise, as we stand here together, a part of the festivities and yet not. Outliers in arms."

Before Emerson could unpack all that, the bartender piped up with, "If blush is a euphemism for what I think it is, two hundred and fifty points, at the very least."

As one, Emerson and Holden turned to face the bar.

Emerson asked, "That much?"

"I've done a lot of weddings. And a lot of bridesmaids." With that the bartender moseyed off to serve someone at the other end of the bar.

"That, ladies and gentlemen, is a line," said Holden.

"And from such an unexpected source." Out of the corner of her eye, Emerson saw Holden slowly lift a fist, knuckles out. What choice did she have but to bump it back?

A waiter came by, grabbed the tray of bubbly from behind the bar, readying to swish it out into the crowd. It took half a millisecond for Emerson to decide to nab another glass. For her shoe had obviously disappeared into some alternate dimension and she'd just fist-bumped Holden Roarke. Bubbly seemed the only sane choice.

"I've been thinking," said Holden, looking back out into the crowd. "If I was a line guy, you'd know it."

"Would I, now?"

"I wouldn't throw them out there without a care.

I'd take my time. Curate them, incessantly. Until I had a small but specific set. Instant classics. World class. Legendary."

He's more playful than I remember, she thought. What she said was, "Settle down, Casanova, I get it. If you *had* taken it upon yourself to hit on me, I might never have recovered."

Her eyes were on his when he smiled—a slow, deliberate lift of the corners of his mouth. A wave of heat swept from her cheeks to her toes.

"What are you doing here, Holden?"

He blinked. "At this very moment? Having an unexpectedly delightful exchange with an old acquaintance. You?"

Emerson didn't let the sudden rough edge to his voice distract her. "I know the guest list back to front and you're not on it."

"Open yourself up to the universe and the universe provides, don't you find?"

Emerson coughed out a laugh. For no, she did not *find*.

Holden leaned in, as if about to bestow upon her a secret, and she caught his scent—freshly cut grass, bubbling brook, warm male skin.

"My earlier quip, such as it was," he said, "was in reference to the fact I've never seen anyone less interested in a bouquet toss."

Emerson followed the lift of his glass, to see the bouquet in question now waving its way through the crowd, a snake of conga dancers falling in behind.

Oh. Her spare hand moved to her neck. "Was I that obvious?"

"Not at all," he said, gathering his glass back towards the snowy white shirt straining against acres of broad chest. "You were the very picture of discretion. I just happen to have a keen eye for understated insurrection. I'm a bit of an expert, you see. Years of experience given to the cause. It's not often I spot a kindred spirit, then there you were."

There she was. Holden Roarke's kindred spirit. It was all she could do not to burst into laughter.

Holden's eyebrow lifted, slowly, in question. As if it was her turn to say something.

"Yes," she said, her voice a little breathless. "I mean no. It's not my thing. Not even in my top hundred."

"Fighting over a used bunch of flowers?" A pause to give her an extra centimetre of smile. "Or marriage?"

"Both," she shot back.

"And not a moment's hesitation," he said, his voice tinged with awe.

She shrugged, unapologetically.

Holden Roarke's stormy blue gaze followed the move, landing on her bare shoulder for a beat, before moving to the shift of a dangly diamante earring against her cheek, then sweeping back to her eyes with such a rush, Emerson felt herself sway. And it all happened in a single heartbeat.

It was all too bizarre, standing like a flamingo, under a starfield of romantic fairy lights, with *Zoot Suit Riot* blasting in the background, as she talked marriage with the man who had dashed her teenaged heart into a thousand tiny little pieces.

"Now, what do we have here?" Mr Heartache murmured, placing his drink on the bar before dropping to an easy crouch, reaching under the closest barstool and coming up with her shoe. Just like that.

His gaze dropped to her feet—well, one foot, for the other was tucked away inside the matching four-inch heel. "Yours, I presume?"

At which point Holden Roarke dropped a knee, and held out a hand.

Emerson blinked, the ridiculousness factor having just turned up to eleven. Enough that she actually gave her arm a quick pinch.

Wobbling on her one heel, Emerson snapped her fingers at Holden. "Up. Up, up, up. I can do it myself."

"I have no doubt," he said, his gaze stuck on hers. "Yet here I am, shoe in hand, knee in the dust, willing and able to do you this small favour."

That voice of his—deep, unhurried, and laced with humour—wound around some delicate, unprotected part of herself she was too flummoxed to keep locked down.

A small favour. Over in a jiffy.

"Fine."

Taking great pains not to feel like freaking Cinderella, Emerson looked away as he slid his hand along the soft, sensitive underpart of her foot, leaving prickles and shimmers in his wake, before his long, strong fingers moved to curl around her ankle. At which point the prickles and shimmers rushed up her calf, the back of her thigh, higher, as if connected directly to nerves, muscles, tendons, the very marrow of her bones.

Five hundred points, she thought, *at the very least, for making a Maid of Honour blush. No euphemism required.*

Then it was over before it began, with Holden shucking the heel neatly into place and gently lowering her foot to the ground. Entirely G-rated. No lingering touches, or signs of fetishism. Just a guy helping a girl he'd once known, out of a jam.

Though when Holden stood, sweeping to his feet with a whoosh, dragging a hand through his hair leaving thick, dark tracks in its wake, he had noticeably more colour in his cheeks. Was it possible the prickles and shimmers weren't hers alone?

Emerson shook her head. She'd lived half her life since Holden Roarke had broken her heart. Had survived several shiny new heartbreaks since. Those collective experiences building up the phenomenal resistance she had today. Yet, standing here beside him, it was if she'd learned nothing at all.

Now that she had both shoes on, it was time to vamoose. "Look, this has been—"

Emerson cut herself off when Holden spun dramatically to face the bar, his fingers tightening on the wood, as if he was thinking about leaping over the thing.

Intrigued, despite herself, she asked, "What's happening right now?"

Holden's jaw twitched. "Did she see me?"

"Did who—?"

A high-pitched voice called from the crowd, "Holden!"

Emerson followed the sound to find Bernadette, bouquet gripped in her hand as she battled her way through the dense crowd now dancing to a wild, fast, jazz rendition of *Dancing Queen.*

"Holden! Where are you?"

"Ah. So that's how you got in. You're here with Bernadette," said Emerson, mad at herself for the sting that brought on.

He shook his head. "We met half an hour ago when she tried to slip her room key into the pocket of my suit pants."

Emerson coughed on her surprise. "Front pocket or back?"

Holden's mouth twitched before he turned her way, his voice low, and intimate, as he asked, "Why? Is one worth more points than the other?"

"Goes without saying. But, actually, don't tell me. I've known Bernie since she was eight." A thought. "Do you still have it? The key?"

"No, I don't have the *key*. I tactfully declined." He sounded abashed. Which was unexpectedly… adorable.

And finally, for the first time since he'd ambled up to her and said her name, she felt the dynamic shift. This she preferred, by far. "I'm not sure you were as clear as you imagine you were. In fact, it seems congratulations might be in order."

Frowning, Holden leaned in a little closer in order to pick up her voice, his upper arm making contact with hers.

"She won the bouquet," she said, eyes flicking between his. Meaning she caught the moment his hunted look dissipated and a glint took its place.

Their arms still touching, Emerson could feel the man's body heat. The rise and fall of his breaths. Their faces were close enough she could make out the swirls of blue and gusts of grey around his deep, dark pupils. Count those glorious lashes, including the one that had fallen to his cheek.

She would *not* lift her hand to sweep that lash away. *She would not.*

Her voice was a little husky as she said, "Don't think, just because I am not into the bouquet-toss-winner-is-next-to-marry thing, you can't be all for it. Truly. More power to you."

Slowly, as if time stretched, Holden's eyes seemed to narrow, even as the eye crinkles returned, deepening deliciously. Till his expression turned wolfish. And very, very grown-up. "Emerson."

"Mm-hmm?"

"You know that small favour I did for you, not too many moments ago?"

"Favour?"

"Helping you with your errant shoe. I'd be hugely grateful if you'd allow me to ask for one in return."

Emerson felt, with every fibre of her being, that she ought to say no. To give him a light, chummy punch on the arm, wish him luck, then go on about her Maid of Honour duties for the rest of the night.

But his words, simple and respectful, hooked her, like a claw in a buttonhole.

"What do you need?"

The man grinned—the move so bright, so joyful, she felt it in the backs of her knees. Then he turned, lifted his arm over her head, and placed it behind her along the bar, so that she found herself tucked against his big, warm, hard body, wondering how the heck she'd ended up there.

Bernadette's big doe eyes lit up as she spotted Emerson, before she slipped through a gap in the crowd and was upon them. "Emmy!"

"Emmy?" Holden murmured.

"She gets to call me whatever she wants. She's special."

"There you are!" said Bernadette.

"How you going, Bernie?" Emerson asked.

"I'm wonderful. Such a gorgeous wedding! And you look amazing. That dress! *Phwoar*." Only then did Bernie seem to spot Holden. "Oh, hi! I was looking for you! And there you are too!"

"Here I am too," he said.

Then he shifted, just a fraction. Enough that Emerson felt surrounded by the guy. On all sides. Trapped in a haze of his scent, his warmth, his shelter.

For all that he presented as relaxed, it was suddenly all too clear that it was an act. Calculated misdirection. An ocean of energy pulsed through him, deep, rich, barely contained. Ready for anything.

"Look!" said Bernadette, oblivious, holding out the bouquet and waving it under Holden's nose as if it might put him in her thrall. "I won!"

"We saw. Hell of a leap you have."

On the "we" he lifted the arm he'd positioned behind Emerson, his fingers curling around her elbow on her far side. So aware of him was she, Emerson had been waiting for it. Her body primed for his touch before he'd even moved.

Which was when she heard the alarm bells go off deep inside her, echoing, as if they'd been ring-ing for some time but she'd only just begun to notice.

Bernadette pointed the bouquet towards Emerson, nearly poking her in the eye with a rose. "Hey, do you know Emmy?"

Holden's hand slid up Emerson's arm to find her shoulder, then the back of her neck. There, his thumb shifted back and forth over the small covered button holding the halter neck of her dress in place as he said, "*Emmy* and I go way back."

Emerson nudged an elbow into his side, his wince evidence she'd hit the mark.

Bernadette's eyes grew wide and she said, "Now it all makes sense." After which she gave Emerson a big, slow almost-wink, then she spun on her heel, gaze dancing over the crowd as she called, "Barry! Barry!"

And then she was gone, the air around them fluttering back to normal, like leaves in the wake of a whirlwind.

"Barry?" Holden asked, removing his hand from the back of her neck, the hairs there lifting, as if reaching for his touch.

"One of Phillip's hundred-odd groomsmen," she said. Then, "A hundred and fifty points, at least." She felt Holden's grin even though they were both still facing the crowd.

"Far more cache than a mere guest," he added, his voice a low burr.

"Oodles."

"So we actually did *her* a favour."

"Gosh, I hope so. If she remembers even half of it, she's going to be mortified."

"No need. Only way to find out if someone you like likes you back is to be a little brave."

Unable to help herself, Emerson glanced at Holden's face, expecting a glint of humour. But his expression, as he looked into her eyes, was keen. Direct. It nudged against some soft, unprotected part of her.

Then the music changed. Slowed. A sigh coming over the crowd as the opening strains of *The Way You Look Tonight* began to fill the space. A spotlight hit a disco ball, which sent shards of warm light scattering over them both.

Feeling warm and a little light in the head, for one moment, a single breath, Emerson opened herself up to it. To the full force of him. To see if, after all this time, she could.

Time seemed to stretch, the sound of the band muffled, and everything at the edges of her vision became a blur. Her breath turned a little slow and viscous, her skin tingly and tight. She may have even felt herself sway towards him, just a smidge.

Turned out, despite excellent inroads into self-actualisation since she'd moved on from the Heartache List, testing was a form of sadomasochism.

Emerson pulled herself back from the brink, just, and asked, "How did you end up here, Holden?"

He watched her for a few long, drawn-out moments, before a smile tugged at the corners of his eyes. "Ours is not to reason why, young Emerson. Ours is but to enjoy what is, in fact, a damn fine band, pretty good plonk, and excellent company, all on someone else's dime."

Her dad's voice suddenly floated up out of the deepest recesses of her memory. *Loosen up, little one, so you don't snap. It'll be okay.* He would say *It'll be okay* quite a bit, her dad. As if that might make up for any number of disappointments.

Funny that she'd thought of him now, while talking to someone else on her Heartache List. Funny ironic? Or funny cautionary?

Before she could decide, Holden took a distinct step away from the bar. "I've been keeping you. I'm sure, as Maid of Dishonour, you have many duties."

"Many," she agreed, breathing out hard. "Lots. A plethora."

A crease, like a super-dimple, formed at one corner of his mouth, heaven help her.

"It was really good to see you again, Emerson." He nodded, as if surprised by the truth of his own words. "Now I must be off, perhaps even to indulge in my newfound respect for a good pick-up line."

"Or perhaps not," she offered.

He touched the side of his nose in agreement,

before dipping an invisible cap, and ambling back out into the fray.

Mere seconds later, Camille burst through the edge of the crowd. So much for finding a quiet corner.

Camille held up her middle finger. "I broke a nail. Help me before I snag."

"On it." Very glad to have a purpose, a distraction, Emerson found an emery board in her clutch bag, then grabbed Camille's outstretched hand and buffed away the ragged corner.

"Whoa. Slow down, honeybun! Everything okay?"

Emerson eased back before she buffed the nail clean away. "Did you know Holden Roarke was here?"

Camille's eyes popped. "What's that, now?"

Emerson waved a hand at the crowd. "Holden Roarke—aka *Heartache Number Four*—is out there. Right now." Possibly trying out dubious lines on unexpecting—and unresisting—guests.

Camille growled, "Phillip."

"Phillip?" Emerson asked.

Camille took her hand back and nibbled on the nail. "Okay, so Phillip banged into the guy a couple of weeks back at some ex-uni networking thing where Holden was the guest speaker. Turns out they went to uni together for a tiny bit before Holden dropped out. Did you know that? That he dropped out? No, unlike the rest of us you don't keep tabs on those who did you wrong. Anyway, apparently he's some app design genius—infamously retired in his early twenties when he sold his first app for zillions, so I guess it's more like he 'dropped up' than 'out'. Everyone at the networking thing was drooling over him from a distance, while Phillip being Phillip walked up and said, 'I'm getting hitched, you should come!' Thankfully—for Phillip's sake—Holden politely refused, so I figured it best to leave it at that rather than stir everything up for you unnecessarily. I had no idea he'd actually come!"

Emerson puffed out a don't-worry-about-it breath, surprised to find her lips were slightly numb. After nursing one glass of champagne all evening, she'd somehow gone through a few in a short burst.

Camille's eyes narrowed as she peered out into the crowd. "I've done enough bride stuff today. I'm now on keep-Holden-Roarke-away-from-my-beloved-Emerson duty."

"We already spoke. And it was fine. I'm a big girl. I handled it."

Camille's eyes skewed back to Emerson's. "Of course you did. You're a brilliant, mature, magical unicorn." Then, "So, what was he like? Smarmy? Flirty? A douche? Ground down by the weight of the world? Still a total hunk, or has the middle-aged spread hit early? Often does with the big guys."

Emerson let go of a sigh before she even felt it coming.

"Really?" Camille said, drawing out the word. "That good, huh? Hey, remember that time I thought I saw Kailey Deluca at a shopping mall, two tiny, screaming children clinging to her knee-high Ugg boots?"

Kailey Deluca, aka *Heartache Number Three*, aka Emerson's best friend in primary school, who'd dumped her on day one of high school.

"If she hadn't turned weird we'd never have found one another, and would not be standing here, together, right now." Camille's hand slid through the crook of Emerson's arm and they leaned towards one another, skulls gently knocking. "Thank you for being my best woman. No one else could possibly have fitted that title. Much less that dress."

Emerson glanced down at her slinky sparkles. "It is quite a dress."

Camille grinned. "Has it worked?"

"In what way?"

"Did you not wonder why I allowed you to look hotter than me on my wedding day? I was hoping some dashing friend of Phillip's would man up and sweep you off your feet, then you'd fall in love and be as deliriously happy as I am. Then we could buy houses side by side and have babies together…" She stopped to take a breath. "Was that too much to ask?"

It seemed Emerson wasn't the only one sensing change in the air. Her heart squeezed—not an ache, but it was close.

She held Camille's face between her hands and gave the cheeks a wiggle. "The night is still young; who knows what it might yet bring? Now, is this a party or is this a party?"

"It's a party!"

With that Emerson downed the last drops of her third—or was it fourth?—bubbly, grabbed Camille by the hand, and together they boogied out onto the dance floor.

Where the rest of the night slid by in a beautiful, ache-free blur.

CHAPTER TWO

HOLDEN'S GAZE GLANCED off the minutiae of a wedding done and dusted, cake stand empty bar a few stray crumbs, tablecloths no longer centred, centrepieces pilfered by light-fingered guests.

He righted a chair that had fallen to the ground, as Barry—the groomsman young Bernadette had taken a belated shine to—came out of nowhere to slap Holden on the back for the umpteenth time of the night.

"Last man standing!" said Barry. Then, "It was really good to meet you, mate. Don't be a stranger." When Barry looked ready to move in for what looked to be a teary hug, the remaining groomsmen descended, midway through the umpteenth rendition of *Sweet Caroline* of the night, and dragged Barry out of the marquee's gently flapping exit.

And all was quiet once more.

The noise and light had done an admirable job of drowning out Holden's thoughts, but the moment they could they returned with a flourish, unhappy memories, unprocessed regrets...all of them wrapped up in this damn city.

He had meant it when he'd declined Phillip's generous invitation, for he was back in the country for a limited time and a specific purpose and had every intention of getting the hell out of Dodge the moment he was done. Then the weekend had whipped around, and with it hours of dead time looming before him.

An hour-and-a-half drive to Sorrento—late enough to miss the ceremony, early enough to fill the evening with the perpetual blur of cheerful company, innocuous conversation, blunting distraction—had seemed just the ticket.

It had delivered. Not two minutes had passed all night long without him finding himself cornered.

You're that app guy, right? Heard about you. Are you really retired?

Ostensibly.

As good as it sounds?

People were usually happy with a quick, *Yes*. They didn't want to hear that dreams of sitting on a beach for the rest of time lost their lustre faster than expected. That sitting still in any place for too long made that place feel like any other.

Or perhaps that was just him. The chase the thing that drove him, rather than the spoils.

So-and-So said you live in Sweden/San Francisco/Singapore. Or are you home for good? Some new opportunity we could get in on?

A sage smile, some linguistic prevarication, and flipping the questions their way was the fastest route out of that rabbit hole.

At least the chatter had ably filled the time.

Till the bouquet toss. More specifically, the

woman glinting darkly at the edge of the group, blithely refusing to partake.

While everyone else shifted and shuffled, she'd seemed so unruffled. Above it all. No, not *above*. Extrinsic. Enjoying their enjoyment, but not a part of it. As if—despite that dress with its gravity-defying architecture, and magical fabric sparking light in a thousand directions, despite her loveliness even beyond the bewitching dress—she believed herself unseen.

Something had uncoiled inside him then, some flicker of recognition, as she watched the world as if from the other side of the looking glass.

He'd had no intention of approaching her, his plan being to take the path of least resistance. Then someone had called out "Dance with me, Emmy!" as she'd stalked past.

Swap the glossy waves for wild curls, and the tiny bag clutched in her hand for a unicorn backpack, and it was Emmy Adler—his one-time hallway buddy.

How could he not say *hello*? And then, after finding her unexpectedly crisp and zesty, like that first hit of lime in a glass of iced water, how could he not stay? For, surely, she would be the most perfect distraction of all.

A chatter of voices broke into Holden's reverie as the clean-up crew bustled through the marquee entrance hauling trolleys of supplies and packing crates. He lifted a hand to intimate he'd move out of their way.

A glance at his watch showed it was a minute before midnight, and he had a long drive ahead.

Picking his way around the detritus, he made it to the exit when he heard a commotion. He turned to find Emmy, an open magnum of bubbly in one hand, the heels of her shoes dangling from the other, her clutch bag under her chin as she bore down on the cleaners.

"Let me help," she insisted. "Do you have spare gloves?"

A murmur from one of the cleaners was followed by, "I know. Such a great wedding. Though bittersweet, you know?"

The cleaner nodded, while also clearly looking for a way out.

Holden worked his way around the maze of tables and chairs. Long drive or no, he wasn't going anywhere till he knew she was okay.

"My very best friend in the whole wide world," Emmy continued, her voice lifting. "My sister by choice if not by blood, just stepped onto a conveyor belt that runs perpendicular to my own."

When she pointed off into the distance her bag dropped to the ground, and she sank to pick it up. The cleaner saw his chance and bolted.

"I didn't expect this. Not today," Emmy muttered from her crouch. Then she lifted her hand—the one holding her shoes, not her bubbly—to her heart. "The ache, right here. I thought I was done with all that. That the List had made me immune."

"The list?" Holden asked.

Emmy looked up, her eyes wide, her mouth a comical "O". Her voice was a stage whisper as she said, "Holden Roarke. There you are again. And how on earth do *you* know about the List?"

Holden held out a hand. She offered up the near empty bottle for him to use as leverage to get her back to her feet.

"You're taller than you used to be," she said, punctuating her accusation with a slow blink of those big bright eyes of hers, a rare, mossy green, fringed by insanely long lashes and tinged with mistrust.

Holden bit his lip to stop himself from laughing. "Only because this time you're completely barefoot. Now, what's this about a list?"

She waved her shoes towards him, nearly blinding him with a heel. "You can't use it against me, if that's your nefarious plan."

Holden held out both hands in surrender. "I have no plans, nefarious, dubious, or otherwise."

"Good. All that matters is that, while my heart might feel a little squidgy right now, I will survive this. The List taught me that. Where is everyone?" She looked around.

"We're it. Camille and Phillip left some time ago."

"Yes, they did." Emmy lifted her bottle in salute,

only to find it was empty. She slowly placed it on a table by her side, the way she unwound her fingers from the neck almost ceremonial.

Then she took a step sideways, teetering so that Holden reached out to cup her elbow, to steady her. Soft, smudged, and slanted, she looked up at him.

"Gosh you smell good," she said, breathing deep. Then, "Camille made me wear this dress. So we could have babies together. Then *you* turn up smelling like fresh cut grass. It really isn't fair, considering my insides already feel like a soufflé on the verge of collapse."

Holden tried to keep up, he really did, but it was a lot, what with her leaning against him, smelling rather lovely herself. *Citrus,* he thought, *citrus, and some wholly female concoction she wore on her skin. Or maybe it was her skin. All on its own.*

"Apologies?" he murmured.

"For what?"

"I have no idea." Holden took the opportunity to lean back, so that he might breathe air not filled with her. "While your current lack of a filter is extremely enjoyable, I think the clean-up crew would love to see the back of us. Come on, let's get you home safe. Unless…"

Holden looked around to see if there were any other stray guests. "Unless you came with someone?" He wasn't entirely surprised to find discomfort in that notion.

"Are you kidding? I get a thousand trillion points for *not* bringing a plus one."

"Because…"

"Bringing a *date* to a *wedding* is as indefensible as actively going for the bouquet."

"I hear that," he said. But only because it made getting the heck out of there easier. "Shall we?"

"Shall we what?" she asked, her hazy gaze dropping to his mouth before lifting to his eyes. And his discomfort became…creative and focused.

"Shall we…blow this joint?"

The haze cleared, pushed aside by indignation. The woman was a veritable pot luck of reactions and it was mighty entertaining.

"I'm not 'blowing' anything with you, Holden Roarke," she said, using liberal air quotes. "Or doing you any more 'favours' for that matter. I mean, the guy shrugs his big, manly shoulders, and flashes his fetching eye crinkles, and thinks he can get away with anything."

"Can't believe I'm about to say this… Fetching eye crinkles?"

Emmy blinked.

Holden smiled. "Take care you don't reveal your secret crush. Or your banking password—"

"Kevin Costner," she shot back.

"Crush, or password?"

She ignored him, her pupils growing dense, her expression dreamy. "*Field of Dreams. Bull Dur-*

ham. Hidden Figures. Sigh… How about you, Holden Roarke? Ever had a secret crush?"

When her eyes moved back to his they were so dark, so deep, he felt the ground beneath his feet shift. Just a smidge.

"Crush, sure. Secret, no. Now, Emerson Adler, do you call everyone by both names, or should I feel special?"

Emmy shot him a look.

"Special," he muttered. "Well, that's nice, then. I'm still not giving you my passwords, so don't ask."

Her indignation cracked and she glimmered. There was no other word for it. Her eyes filled with light, and that dress—all those bronze sparkles wrapped about her as if she'd been sewn into the thing—reflected any and all atmospheric light that remained in the semi-darkness.

Holden breathed in. Emmy breathed out. And the night seemed to spin out around them.

Till Holden remembered himself, held out an arm, and gently shepherded her towards the exit.

Stepping over linen napkins, bruised flowers, a dropped fork, they made their way outside, where the forest was dark, the trees tall. And up above, the stars twinkled like sugar spilled across a black velvet rug.

Emmy stopped, looked up, rubbing her bare arms as a breeze swept off the nearby bay. "Don't move," she said, shifting a little closer. "You're warm. Like you have your own personal furnace."

Holden didn't move a muscle.

"I understand why people see stars as pretty," she said, "but they've always felt more poignant to me."

"And why's that?" he asked, tucking his hands into the pockets of his suit as he looked up at the night sky.

"I can never tell if they are happy or sad."

"I find the most beautiful things are often both."

After a few quiet moments he glanced down to find her eyes were on him. They were huge, sparkling in the starlight. A curl of dark hair dangled beside one eye. And when she smiled, she appeared completely lucid. "Holden Roarke, aren't you a surprise and a half?"

Right back at you.

Then she frowned, and shook, as if the cold night air had snapped her decision-making faculties back online. "I think it's time to go."

Holden couldn't agree more. "Where are you staying?"

"The Bay Inn with everyone else," she said, pulling her room key out of her bag. "Don't panic. I'm not about to stuff it into your pocket."

The edge of his mouth flickered. "I appreciate it. Come on, I'll drop you off before I head home."

"You're not at the inn?"

"Coming tonight was a...last-minute decision."

Funny. If she'd asked him why, with the forest shifting gently around them, and all that starlight pouring into her big, dark, attentive eyes, he might even have told her.

Instead, her eyes squeezed shut as she let go of the world's biggest yawn. Then she slipped on her shoes, one at a time, and went delving into her tiny bag for her phone as she said, "Thank you, I will accept a lift to my hotel. Though, since I do barely know you, I will send Camille a message to let her know you have me. That sounded wrong. That you're taking me— Nope. That's not right either."

Holden huffed out a ragged laugh.

"Just come here." Emmy grabbed him by the arm and hauled him close. Her cheek hovering near his own, she held up her phone. She frowned so hard he grinned, right as she touched the screen.

While she tapped at her phone, Holden ushered her to his rental sedan. Once he had her settled in the front seat, her eyes drifted closed. As if she was unable to hold them open a single second longer. As if—despite her protestations— she knew him enough to trust he'd do right by her. Which brought on a rush of affection he hadn't seen coming.

Keying the Bay Inn into his GPS, Holden took off down the coast road. Soon the gentle growl of the engine and the repetitive flash of the cat's eyes set the pace for his flickering thoughts.

Dazzling fairy lights above. The hum of the

sound system at his back. Emmy, exquisitely still, at the edge of the bouquet toss. That moment, right when he'd started to enjoy her rebellion, for its own sake, when she'd turned, a slow, sensuous, bolshie upward tilt of her lips as she'd lifted her glass in salute to the laughing bride, before disappearing into the crowd.

That moment he'd found himself stuck. Literally unable to move. Till she'd swept by him. And someone had called her name.

Slowing as the road curved with the coastline, Holden spared a glance sideways. Head tipped towards the glass, her face in the reflection of the window was soft with sleep. The moonlight shimmered over the coppery sparkles on Emmy's dress. Her hands—nails short and painted almost black—lightly clutched her bag, as if even in sleep she was on guard.

Who was this woman? Spectral and defiant as she had been on the dance floor? Wary and witty as she'd been in the bar? Or delightfully candid as she was at the end of what must have been a very long, very emotional day?

Not that he'd get the chance to find out. For he'd drop her at her hotel, drive back to his apartment in the city, attend the event he'd come home to attend, then get on a plane and end up someplace far, far away from here.

CHAPTER THREE

EMERSON SLUNK INTO work early Monday morning.

She'd made it home from the peninsula around lunchtime the day before, only to be met with a load of washing still in the machine, a note under her door from a grumpy neighbour about her mum's lemon tree dropping lemons over the fence, and a "gift" from Pumpkin on the kitchen floor.

Her planned recovery day on the couch listening to true crime podcasts had not eventuated. And it showed.

Strong takeaway coffee in hand, Pumpkin plodding sweetly beside her, the entire place quiet and empty that early in the morning, she—

"Happy Monday, Emerson!"

Emerson flinched and came to a halt, as Freya, her enthusiastic and highly dedicated assistant, appeared out of nowhere looking perky and fresh and wide awake. Pumpkin plonked his backside on the floor with a huff.

Freya crouched to give Pumpkin a little treat from the bag she kept on her person for the days he came into the office, then popped back up like a Jack in the box. Her eyes widened as she said, "Did you know you're still wearing your sunglasses?"

Emerson hitched her handbag on her elbow, the move making her brain hurt, and slowly lifted her hand to her face to find, yes, her Jackie O sunglasses were still perched on the end of her nose.

The thing she'd loved most about the top-floor warehouse conversion for which Pitch Perfect had been paying eye-watering rent for the past couple of years, was the light. The double-storey outer walls were mostly window—lots of tiny panels, ancient and all but impossible to clean—and the soaring ceilings boasted big, new, storm-resistant skylights.

She braced herself before sliding her sunglasses free.

"Whoa," Freya intoned. "You look wrecked. Big weekend?"

Emerson coughed out a laugh, a gentle one that didn't shake her skull too much. Yes, Freya was a natural wonder when it came to keeping Emerson's intricate schedule balanced, but she was also as blunt as a well-used pencil.

"Camille's wedding," Emerson reminded Freya.

"Of course! Saw pics on Insta. Looked amazing."

Freya, talking through the day's schedule, took Pumpkin's lead and gave it a gentle tug, then led the way past the currently uninhabited open-plan desks of the rest of the staff, towards Emerson's office at the very rear of the space.

Leaving Emerson an extra hand to check her

email on her phone, only to find her photo gallery open. More precisely, a selfie of her and Holden. Her likeness was frowning, eye makeup smudged, expression bolshie. While she'd caught Holden at the apex of an utterly heartache-inducing smile.

She'd never ended up sending it to Camille, hardly the kind of thing she needed to worry about on her wedding night, but she'd kept it all the same.

"Who's *he*?" said Freya.

Emerson slapped her phone to her chest and gave her assistant a look.

Freya backed up an inch. "Sorry."

"No, you're not."

Freya shot Emerson a grin. "You're right. I'm not. Come on, spill. Who's the guy?"

"He's nobody." Emerson gave her screen a deliberate swipe, before tossing her phone into her bag. "Can you eke me out a little time this morning?"

"Of course," said Freya, hooking the lead over her elbow, lifting her tablet, and hovering her finger over the keyboard. Assistant Extraordinaire Mode: Activated.

"No calls till…ten. I have some work—" aka mainlining coffee and napping with her eyes open "—to catch up on."

"Done." Freya tapped the note into her calendar, before passing the lead to Emerson and angling her way to her own floating desk outside the smoky glass wall of Emerson's office.

Emerson took the opportunity to close her glass door with a soft snick. The moment she was one with her office she breathed easier. With its delicately canted rear wall, aesthetic of cream furnishings, pale wood and caramel leather accents, its aseptic beauty was like a splash of cold water to the face. In the best way.

She picked Pumpkin up, so that he didn't have to navigate the gargantuan rug covering the pale wood floor, and popped him into his bed under her desk. Then sat in the chair behind her desk, kicked off her heels, and let her face sink into her hands.

With half an ear she heard her teams starting to arrive. The Temp Team chatting about their weekends, while readying to shore up employment contracts for the regulars who kept the business ticking over. While the Head Hunters made Monday morning plans to land a whale—the kind of client who could pay someone's yearly salary with one perfect placement.

After filling a spate of high-end corporate positions in the past few months, Pitch Perfect was generating some real buzz. Another one or two and Emerson could relax for a stretch. Or maybe even put in place the expansion dreams she harboured.

That was usually where her mind went, and

stayed, when she daydreamed. But that morning her mind kept turning to the wedding.

Phillip attempting to do the dolphin and doing himself a damage instead, the kind that would not have helped his wedding night. Bernadette showing the bouquet to many a wide-eyed male guest. Camille, panda eyes filled with tears, blowing Emerson a kiss before their Mustang rumbled off into the night.

And then there was the veritable slideshow of memorable moments featuring Holden Roarke. His hands on her ankle as he'd helped her with her shoe. His body heat as they'd stood side by side, looking at the stars. The rather large *oomph* sound he'd made as he'd swept her into his arms outside the door to her hotel room, then carried her inside, like *The Bodyguard* poster—

Emerson's eyes popped open. Oh, no. That had happened. And not in some romantic, over-the-threshold movie moment. Not even slightly.

She'd woken in his car. Edit. Holden had had to *wake* her after she'd fallen asleep in his car, the muffled sound in the back of her head the echo of her snoring.

She next remembered leaning. In the lift? Yes, there. And again, in the hall. There had been a cool brush of wallpaper against her shoulder as she slumped against the wall in order to kick off a shoe. Around which time he'd taken her by the hand, slipped an arm beneath her knees, then hoisted her into his arms.

The next bit was a little fuzzy—due to bubbly, or a self-protective brain snap—but she felt sure she'd said something, maybe even something risqué, as his eyes had gone dark, even as he'd laughed—a rough, raw, deep sound that had scraped perilously against her insides.

Then he'd let her slide to the floor, her hand running down his hard chest. His throat bobbing when she'd stayed there, bodily against him. Her nails scraping against expensive cotton as she'd curled her fingers into his shirt.

Yep, that had happened too. And he'd been nothing but a gentleman, extricating himself from her clutches and backing slowly out of the door. Then, finally, his deep voice on the other side of the door, telling her he wasn't leaving till he heard the click of the lock.

"Emerson?"

Emerson opened her eyes to find the room had changed colour, losing the sharp cool of the early hours and filling with the buttery warmth of mid-morning. She felt lost in the loose, soft warmth that came from a dream that wasn't entirely a dream.

Emerson cleared her throat. "Come on in."

Freya hustled into the room, bearing a tall, steaming glass of black coffee and a pretty plate bearing a mix of pastel macaroons.

Emerson felt Pumpkin's tail thump slowly under her desk at the scent of sugar on the air.

Freya said, "I managed to hold back the flood but it's half past ten. Perfect time for Pumpkin to have his outside time while you take your first call. Charming, but insistent this one."

"Right. Thanks. Give me thirty seconds then send it through."

Freya nodded, gathered a soft and sleepy Pumpkin, then hustled off to sprinkle whatever dark magic she practised to keep Pitch Perfect running like clockwork.

After running her fingers through her hair, Emerson reached out for the sparkly pink paperweight that sat incongruously on her spartan desk.

Before her mum passed a couple of years back—the cancer quick and ferocious, the heartache worse than the rest of them combined—she had collected paperweights, the clear kind with swirls of resin, or glitter, or flowers suspended within. When cleaning out the childhood home her mum had left to her, Emerson had kept just the one, only for it to become a touchstone. A means of infusing her with her mother's chin-up attitude, her determination to rise after every fall.

Giving the subtle dint in the paperweight one last swipe with her thumb, she put it back in place, then pressed the answer button on her speakerphone. "Emerson Adler."

"Emerson," a deep voice intoned. "It's Holden."

Emerson bumped her coffee, sending a splash over her desk. She quickly mopped up the spill with a bunch of tissues.

Then the voice returned, saying, "Holden *Roarke*," as if that might jog her memory.

And it did. She pictured the smile in his eyes as he noted her habit of calling him by both names. Then, for a second, she pictured him querying her about the List. But that couldn't possibly have happened. Meaning, maybe, other memories of the night were false too.

Awash with relief, she said, "Holden." Then, "How on earth did you get my number?"

"You gave it to me."

Her relief dissipated in a flash. "I did?"

"Work, mobile, home, email, social media. You were extremely thorough."

"That does not sound like me at all."

"Bolshie brunette? Sparkly dress? Maid of Dishonour? Before I left you to your beauty sleep, you clicked your fingers in my face till I passed my phone over. Humming a Neil Diamond medley under your breath, rather out of tune, I'm afraid to say. Then you added all your contact details, using the picture of the two of us you'd taken to send to Camille, and—"

"Yep. Okay." The clicking did sound like her. And the picture was real. Emerson slapped her hand across her eyes. "Well, this is mortifying."

His laughter rumbled down the line. "Not at all.

It was, all in all, an unexpectedly fun night. Illuminating." Then, "Whoa! All good!"

"Pardon?"

"Sorry. That wasn't for you. Almost had a collision with a Great Dane. I'm in Albert Park. Running."

"Oh," she said, leaning in towards the phone, as if she might hear the slap of his feet on the path, or any kind of stress in his breath.

Then, from nowhere, she remembered him running track in high school. Remembered taking her lunch on the hillside overlooking the oval, slowly eating her warm Vegemite sandwich as she watched his long, loping stride, and the sweat patches growing down the sides of his T-shirt with each lap—

Tossing her coffee-soaked tissue in the bin, Emerson righted herself and said, "Look, I'm glad you called, actually."

"I'm glad you're glad."

"Calm down. I'm *mildly* glad, at most."

"I'll take it," he said, his voice a rough burr that made her insides go all squidgy.

"I need to thank you. For your…consideration. After the wedding."

Carrying me over the threshold, not taking it the wrong way when I clutched at your shirt, or when I gave you goo-goo eyes. The way you stayed until I locked the door.

"I'm sure any of Phillip's friends would have done the same."

"Yes. That's true. He is a collector of good people." Emerson also knew that she'd never felt light-headed talking to any of Phillip's friends. She cleared her throat. "That said, I was feeling a little tender, which, again, is unlike me. I'm not at all sentimental—"

Her eyes slid to the paperweight and away again.

"By the end of the night I wasn't handling the…" Emerson waved her hand, trying to find a word that did not stray too close to anything "heart" or "ache" related. "Anyway, I was not exactly at my best, so, thank you for seeing me through it."

"You're welcome."

Emerson squeezed the bridge of her nose, her neck feeling warm as she worked herself up to say, "Now, as to the phone number thing. Despite what that might imply, I'm actually not in the market for a…phone number."

After a spell, Holden said, "As it turns out, I'm not in the market for…a phone number, either."

"Great," she said, slumping down in her chair, her eyes rolling towards the ceiling. "That's just…"

"Great?" he offered up.

"Yes. Now, can we please wipe Saturday night

from our minds? Pretend none of it ever happened?"

"Mmm. Not sure I can. Your rejection of the bouquet toss might be one of the greatest wedding moments of all time. And then there's the fact you told me I had big, manly shoulders and...what was it? Fetching eye crinkles—"

"Holden," Emerson declared, her fingers now rubbing her temples.

"Yes, Emmy."

She thought about correcting him, but the truth was, the implied intimacy of Holden calling her Emmy was the least of her worries. "Wipe it," she said. "Wipe it from your mind."

Holden laughed, all rough and raw. For a man who wasn't in the market for her *phone number*, he sure did phone call well.

Emerson rocked her chair side to side. "Now, what can I do for you, Holden?" See, she could say his name. Singularly. Not special at all.

"Right. Yes. I have a favour to ask."

"Another favour."

"Mmm?"

"Do me a favour. Protect me from the sweet young woman wielding the evil bouquet," said Emerson, her voice as deep and rough as she could manage.

Holden laughed. Something in the sound making her picture him slowing to a walk, a drip of sweat making a slow trail down the sculpted edge of his jaw.

Then suddenly she remembered what she'd said to Holden when he'd carried her into the hotel room. *Do me a favour. Don't leave, this time, without saying goodbye.*

So very glad this was a phone call not a video call, Emerson let her head fall to her desk. And there she stayed as Holden's voice said, "I'd rather think tucking you up in bed, and wishing you sweet dreams, would put me one favour up."

"You did *not* tuck me into bed." Of that she was nearly absolutely sure.

"Consider that artistic licence. Look. I truly do need a favour, Emmy. I have no problem taking no for an answer. But if you do this one thing for me, then…then we would not be even. Not even close. I would owe you, big time."

Emerson lifted her head and stared at her speak-erphone.

Yes, bumping into him had been nowhere near as horrible as she'd imagined it might be. Yes, the ache she'd once felt any time she even thought his name was long gone. But pushing it any further was tempting fate.

Unless…

Unless this was actually an opportunity. A chance to be absolutely sure that the Heartache List had done its job. That, due to the foundation built upon its lessons, no matter what life threw at her she would be okay.

"No promises," she said, "but give me the gist."

"Can do. I need you to be my date on Friday night."

Emerson may have snorted. And coughed. At the same time. Leading to a rather unladylike choking noise.

"Actually, strike that," Holden said. "*Not* a date, a plus one. Not to a wedding, for that would wipe out all the points I'd earned at the last one. The wedding I have now forgotten completely."

He stopped talking. Took a breath. Said, "What I am truly in need of is someone to accompany me to an upcoming dinner. And I was hoping you might be the one."

"A date," Emerson responded, the words flat, as if she didn't like the taste.

"But *not* a date," Holden reiterated, smiling briefly at another runner as he moved off the path and into the speckled shade of a gum tree, pacing so that the lactic acid wouldn't start to itch. "A seat at a table, on which there will be food and drink for you to enjoy. At a place. With great people who love a chance to dress up. And have a laugh. And eat together."

Holden pressed his earbud deeper into his ear and was reminded how it had been the other night, standing danger close, their voices low and intimate, the star-spangled sky hovering silently above. He wiped his hand down the side of his shorts, actually sweating as he waited for her response.

Which was, "So long as that's clear."

They'd spent a grand total of an hour together, at most, during and after the wedding, and yet he could picture, with clarity, Emmy's expression as she deadpanned him. Gaze direct, a slight lift of her right eyebrow, her mouth twisted to the left, a healthy amount of reticence apparent on her lovely face.

"Thought you'd appreciate the delineation," he said. "Considering your aversion to phone numbers."

She laughed at that. Or maybe it was a sigh. Either way, he pictured a squint to those striking, moss-green eyes. Impossibly long lashes creating shadows over elegant cheekbones. A brief flash of teeth, the front two slightly too long, slightly too big, adding whimsy to the list of things about her that he'd found stunning.

Dappled shade fluttering over his face, Holden pressed the bud deeper into his ear again, and looked to the jut of the Melbourne city skyline, a smear of grey on the horizon.

Yes, she was stunning. Empirically. Objectively. And yes, there had been a spark, one which he'd bet quite a bit went both ways. But he was in town for a blink. A fraught blink, at that. So that wasn't what this was about.

He was asking her to accompany him because he knew she'd be able to handle herself with the dinner crowd. And when he was with her, for whatever reason, she drew his focus and kept it. Add her stated lack of interest in his "phone number" and she was perfect. The perfect non-date date.

"Look," he said, "the entire reason I am here, in Melbourne, is to catch up with some people I haven't seen in some time. There is history between us. Complicated history. And I feel that it all might go more smoothly if I bring..." *a distraction, a foil, someone shiny and lovely and bright* "...a friend."

A definite sigh that time. "And you want me for this."

"I do want you. For this," he added belatedly enough he feared he might have shot himself in the foot.

Not quite, as she said, "Surely you could get an easy yes from anyone else."

Pacing no longer cutting it, he waited for a gap, then jogged back out onto the track. "As a single man, of good fortune, 'tis true, I am hugely popular."

"Good grief," she muttered.

"Thing is, Emmy, I trust that you are savvy enough to see this for what it is, a favour done, giving you a favour in hand, should you ever need it. Nothing more."

"Let me get this straight," she said. "You're asking me to join you for some complicated mystery dinner, because you believe I won't mistake a favour date for a *date-date* and what? Accidentally fall in love with you?"

Holden grinned, as he eased around a little old lady out walking her tiny dog. "Not accidentally falling in love with me is absolutely imperative. So, if that's going to be a problem…"

"The man's ego knows no bounds."

"So?"

"Just…give me a minute."

Emmy breathed out hard, and when Holden next swallowed he had the sense memory of lime on the back of his tongue.

He picked up his pace and looked out across the acres of parkland. Parents speed-walked, prams bumped over every tiny crack in the path, shuffle runners shuffled, and bike riders wove.

To think this was the same city in which he'd grown up.

His childhood had not been so green, or nearly so free. Controlled, it had been, by a man who'd taken every chance to assure him that being a smart arse would get him nowhere.

The very best thing about finding himself in a position to retire at such a young age had been the autonomy. He could go anywhere, stay as long as he liked, leave on a whim. He could work hard, or do nothing at all. There was no overriding force holding him to any one place, holding him back.

Which meant waiting on someone to decide his fate was now rare.

"What are you worried about?" he asked when he could no longer hold his tongue.

"I'm not worried."

"Great, because I've seen you in action. You're a force to be reckoned with when…sensical."

"Sensical?"

"The opposite of—"

"Nonsensical," she finished for him, the word dripping with irony.

"Don't get me wrong, when nonsensical you're an absolute delight. But I'd be far too worried that you'd hand over your phone number, and passwords, and your address, and your mother's maiden name and—"

"Yes, thank you. I get it."

"Great. So?"

"I think I'm going to regret this. But fine, I will be your platonic, non-date, favour mandated plus one."

Holden punched the air, scaring a golden retriever. He held out a placating hand in apology to the owner, a young woman in head-to-toe pink, who smiled and tugged on her ponytail.

"I honestly can't believe I've agreed to this." Emmy's voice came through his earbuds, husky and rich, yet grounding somehow. A tether, to some point in the past. Or perhaps it was the affinity he'd felt tug between them, as she'd stood on the outside of the crowd looking in.

"You hungry?" he asked.

"Often."

"I mean now. I'm ravenous all of a sudden. Let's have lunch."

"I can't have lunch with you, Holden."

"Sure, you can." A beat, then, "Not a lunch *date*."

"Holden," she said, her voice the very height of *sensical*.

"Yes, Emmy."

"I'll go to this dinner of yours. As a *favour*. Which you will then owe me. And I will call you on that favour any time I wish, for any reason that I see fit. Unless it's illegal, or impossible, you cannot refuse me. Those are the parameters of the deal."

Parameters, discreet edges, a neat and tidy package of an agreement. Actually, that sounded entirely sensical. Especially considering what had been the perilous lack of parameters the last time he'd spent time with the family.

"Deal," he said, picturing an imaginary shaking of hands. She with her short dark nails. The same ones that had gripped his shirt in her hotel room as she'd looked up at him, her eyes swimming with champagne and invitation.

"Friday," said Emmy, all business.

"Friday," he said, mirroring her tone. "I'll pick you up. Office or home?"

"Home." She gave him an address in Kew, not far from their old school. "I'll need to change."

"Nah," he said. "Don't change a thing."

"Smooth."

"I try."

"Stop trying. With me there is no need. For we are…friendly…and do favours…and have clear parameters. Till Friday." With that she rang off.

Holden punched the air again, a subtle, hip-high jab, before yanking the bud from his ear and shoving it in his pocket.

His return to Melbourne, for the first time in years, had been far easier than he'd imagined. Old friends were calling. Even the infamously changeable weather had been spectacular. As if wounds really might heal over, after enough time.

But he knew it wasn't that simple. Some wounds were so deep, they never fully healed. The scar tissue became formative, a reminder to stay frosty, and alert.

The dinner party would be his reckoning. Payment for his soft landing.

Whether it was right or wrong to rope in Emmy Adler would be something he'd face once it was all said and done.

CHAPTER FOUR

FRIDAY AFTERNOON, EMERSON slid into the back seat of her ride share, mentally spent after a Women in Business lunch at which she'd hobnobbed and networked like there was no tomorrow.

Freya hopped in after her, brimming with energy and enthusiasm, talking a mile a minute about the contacts they'd made.

When Emerson's phone buzzed and she held up a "just a second" finger, Freya turned to the driver to regale him with her stories. While Emerson's heart bucked when she saw Holden's message.

All good for tonight?

Her thumb hovered over the screen. If she wanted to beg off, bone-deep weariness after a long week was a fair excuse. In the end, she typed:

All good.

Brilliant. Quick question: I'm prepping the contract, for our exchange of favours. Would you prefer it typed out in triplicate? Or should we trust we are as good as our word?

Emerson twisted in her seat, tilting her phone so that Freya—who really couldn't help herself—didn't read over her shoulder as she typed:

I have no clue how trustworthy you are. We met outside the guidance counsellor's office, after all.

Holden's reply:

Pot, meet kettle.

Excuse me. My reasons for being there were innocent and good, bordering on angelic. You?

Fair call. So, written in blood. Got it.

Emerson realised she was smiling. She told her face to calm down. Then looked out of the window, watching the cityscape flicker by, before her gaze went back to her phone. She typed:

Look, as far as I could tell, you didn't steal any money from my purse when you saw me to my room, so let's go with our word.

I thought we were never to speak of that night again.

You are not to speak of it. I am under no such gag order.

Freya glanced at Emerson, and the phone she was cradling close to her chest, curiosity written all over her face. Emerson offered up a beatific smile, and Freya lost interest, leaning forward to ask the driver to take a particular route.

Emerson glanced back at her phone. Holden had written:

If I agree to never speak of the drool you left on my car seat, can we take that as the favour returned? Partially at least.

Negative.

Then I make no promises. See you tonight.

Emerson barked out a laugh, the sound echoing in the confined space.

"You're not going to tell me what that was all about, are you?" Freya asked, curiosity leaching so patently from her skin she vibrated.

"Nope," said Emerson, sliding her phone into her bag.

"I know your phone password."

"Ha! I have no doubt. And yet I know you'd never look at my phone without asking because you are the most wonderful, dedicated, loyal assistant in the whole wide world."

"Also true."

With that, Emerson settled into the car, closed

her eyes, and gave in to the rocking sensation as
they trundled back to work.

Emmy sat slumped in the red plastic chair in the
hallway outside Miss Kemp's office, holding her
unicorn backpack to her chest, bouncing the heels
of her school shoes against the linoleum floor. A
loud squeak had her peeking her head around her
bag to find she'd left a mark.

After a quick glance to the front desk to make
sure ancient Mrs Carmichael hadn't noticed, she
licked her thumb, bent at the waist, and rubbed
frantically at the stain.

The door banged—the way it always did before
opening—and she sat up so fast her head swam.

The sound of laughter, and a deep, warm voice,
wafted out into the hall—neither of which meshed
with her experiences with the earnest guidance
counsellor her mum insisted she see after she told
her mum, at dinner one night, that she hated her
dad and always would.

Then, through the doorway, came a boy. A boy
she'd never seen before. She'd have remembered
those smoky blue eyes. Those shoulders—like
a man's shoulders. The way he stood, as if he
wasn't hyper-aware of himself every moment of
the day.

That might be, she thought, *the most beautiful
boy to have ever walked planet earth.*

The guidance counsellor leaned in the doorway,

her face etched with concern, the way it had been on Emerson's first visit. Her voice low, private, and possibly muffled by the fluffy white clouds that had wafted into Emmy's head.

Then the boy started moving Emmy's way.

In slow motion, no less, his shoulder turning first, then hips, then feet. His head moved last, his hair swishing slightly, flicking across his face before landing in the most perfect spot for his face. Then he started to walk, slow, easy, chest out, all constrained power and vitality as he swung his near empty black backpack onto his shoulder.

Then, right when she was staring at him the very most, his eyes met hers.

Her heart stopped. Literally. *Ba-dum, ba-dum, ba-dum*...then nothing.

A smile kicked at the corner of his mouth. "Hey," he said, lifting his chin.

Emmy gulped. Eyes burning from not having blinked since the moment he'd appeared.

Then his smile grew, widening, showing actual teeth, as if he knew exactly why she sat there, unmoving. Dumbstruck. Completely and utterly crushing on him.

"I've warmed her up for you," he said, to her, in a voice that spread through her body like liquid heat.

The tip of his finger touched his brow in salute, and then he was gone.

And the guidance counsellor was calling her name as if she'd been calling it for some time.

"Emmy? *Emerson?*"

"Emerson. We're here."

Emerson blinked to find herself in the back of the ride share.

Freya slid out of the car, and Emerson went to follow before staying put.

"Are you free to take me to Kew?" she asked the driver.

He poked something into his machine and said, "You bet."

"Super. Freya, I'm clocking out. I have an... event to prepare for."

"Tonight?" Freya frowned at her trusty tablet. "It's not on the calendar."

"A private event."

"Ooh," said Freya, eyebrows waggling. "Exciting."

"No. Not like that."

"Oh," said Freya, her enthusiasm turning to disappointment on a dime.

"Can I leave it to you to make sure everyone leaves on time so they can enjoy their weekend? Can you remind the temp crew we have a meeting ten a.m. Monday? And—"

"I've got it." Freya tapped at her tablet. "I'm up to the task."

"Yes, you are."

Emerson closed the door, gave the driver her address.

With the memory of the first time she'd laid eyes on Holden Roarke still swimming in her subconscious, she made her way home to get ready for a non-date date with the guy.

Figuring a little extra time to put on a little extra armour couldn't hurt.

Emerson paced the entrance hall of her small, but lovingly refurbished childhood home, stepping from floorboard to floorboard in a repetitive pattern as the seconds slipped away till Holden was due to arrive at her door.

Pumpkin, no doubt picking up on her heightened energy, had found enough latent energy of his own in his dear old legs to leave his big, soft bed, his rheumy eyes following her as she paced.

"I'm not nervous," she said, bending to give her beautiful boy a gentle scruff behind his soft ears.

Pumpkin sniffed out a breath that appeared to be a doggy version of an eye roll.

"I'm not! I can hold up my end in *any* conversation. I spend my days going head-to-head with captains of industry. With entrenched politicians. I'm a boss, don't you know? No room in my life for nerves."

Yet as a shadow appeared at the frosted window in her front door just before a knock sounded, her heart *ba-da-boomed* in her chest.

She turned Pumpkin, gave his tail end a light nudge to send him walking back towards his bed for the evening. Then she grabbed her clutch bag, straightened her shoulders, ran a quick hand over her freshly washed and styled hair, another down the hip of her dress, and opened the door.

Only to have her mouth dry up at the sight of Holden Roarke standing on her porch, hands in pockets, smile hooking the corners of his mouth as his eyes roved over her porch swing, the bougainvillea spilling from her hanging pots, and the vintage brass lamps lit up warmly either side of her door.

It had been a little under a week since the wedding, at which time she'd seen him all dolled up. He'd even swept her off her feet that night, literally. But somehow in the days in between her subconscious had worked overtime to mitigate his impact.

Feeling an echo of that first time she'd seen him leaving the guidance counsellor's office, she swallowed at the sight of those shoulders. Those eyes. That mouth—full and relaxed, with the hint of a crescent in one cheek, as if prepared to smile at any time.

"This is not at all what I expected," said Holden, sounding utterly relaxed. While she vibrated like a freshly plucked guitar.

"Meaning?"

"I imagined something cool, modern, sleek.

Scandinavian aesthetic. Slightly intimidating. But this might well be the cutest house I have ever seen."

A mite agitated by the fact he'd described her workplace to a T and feeling more than a mite exposed by having this man at her home, she murmured, "I inherited it. From my mum. I grew up here."

"And you live here still? Aw... I'm adjusting my opinion of you accordingly."

"Super."

With that, Holden's eyes finally moved to her, and the open-mouthed delight dropped from his face. A single blink and he'd taken her measure— the gunmetal-grey silk of her dress, tucked and wrapped about her like a sexy toga, the thigh split, the sweep of her hair, left down. Something dark, rich, and devouring overcame his face as he took her in. *Drank her in*, more like. In a great, heady gulp that left her swaying on her heels.

Beyond the hum of cicadas and distant traffic, she could feel the energy trapped behind his loose, cool façade. Electricity barely contained. The man was permanently lying in wait.

"Emerson Adler," he all but growled. "When you do a guy a favour, you do a guy a favour."

Fine. So she'd wanted to look good. No, she'd wanted to look *smoking*. A little bit of a *screw you* to the guy not asking her to accompany him anywhere, not even on a non-date, back when she was a sweet, gawky, smart, interesting, totally worth-it fourteen-year-old.

"You said your friends dress up for dinner," she murmured.

"And I will, from this day forth, be grateful that I did. Now, your turn."

"To?"

"Compliment me on the effort I put into looking nice for you."

"Oh, this," she said, waving a hand down her side, "is not for you."

"Is that so?"

"The more effort I put into this favour, the more effort I'll expect when I call yours in."

"Right. Well, just so we're clear, this," he said, rocking side to side, flapping his jacket open, looking utterly scrumptious while doing so, "was all for you."

Emerson rolled her eyes. "You're not giving up, are you? Fine, you look very nice."

"I try."

"Stop trying!" She shooed him backwards so that she could lock her door.

Only he ignored her and unexpectedly dropped to a crouch.

"And who is this?" Holden asked, reaching out a hand.

Emerson looked down at her feet to find Pumpkin at the door.

Oh, honey, she thought, her heart squeezing at

the sight of her old boy, his whole body slowly shaking side to side as he attempted to wag his tail.

"This," said Emerson, her voice softening, "is Pumpkin. Pumpkin, meet Holden Roarke."

Holden ran a gentle hand over Pumpkin's crown, as if he knew he was fragile. "He's a gorgeous thing. Aren't you, mate?"

That he was, Emerson thought, her breath tightening, just a little. Only when seeing him through the eyes of someone new did she notice that his lustrous caramel fur was a little patchy these days, his gait a little wonky. But he was sweet and loving, and—her vet assured her—doing miraculously well for his age. And as precious to her today as when she'd first held him in her arms.

"Into bed," she said.

Holden's dark and stormy eyes lifted to hers.

"The dog," she deadpanned.

She waggled her fingers between them, motioning for Holden to move, then placed her hand under Pumpkin's chin and said, "Bed time."

With a snuffle the old dog gave her his best sad eyes, before he turned and padded back up the hall.

Emerson stood, only to find herself all but flush against her guest, her hand lifted to steady herself, flashing her back to the hotel room, when she'd gripped his shirt.

When her eyes lifted to his, she was certain he knew exactly where her mind had gone.

"Scoot," she said. "I can't shut the door with you standing in the way."

"You're in an all-fire rush," he said, before turning and ambling onto the porch, the view from behind as good as the view from the front.

She locked up. "The sooner we get there, the sooner it will be over."

"Not sure that's how dinner parties work, but hey, happy to be proven wrong."

"Why?" she said, noting a shift in tone beneath his easy words. "Do you not *want* to go?"

Holden shot her a look, as if he hadn't meant for her to take it that way. Or hadn't expected her to pick up on it. Then he jogged down her front steps and backed down her path, a hand pressed against the stark white of his button-down shirt. "Can it not be that I am simply looking forward to being in your incandescent company for as long as I can?"

He was prevaricating. But by that stage he'd reached a sleek black sedan, different from the one he'd taken to the wedding, she was sure.

He held open the car door, smiling into her eyes as he said, "If you feel the need to fall asleep, again, I'm good with that."

"So kind of you," she gritted out, his deep, warm waves of laughter rolling through her as she closed the door.

By the time Holden pulled up by a guarded gate between a wall of long box hedges, Emerson felt faint from holding her breath so as not to drown in his delicious scent. Some magical mix of chopped wood, sea air, and clean skin.

When he slid down his window, she breathed so deeply of the fresh air she nearly choked on it.

A woman in a security uniform popped her head out of the box. "Mr Roarke! It's been—"

"It has been some while." Holden smiled.

"Saw your name on the guest list. Thought it must have been an error."

"No error," said Holden easily. "Should be down for two. This is my friend Emerson Adler. Emerson, this is Sandra."

The guard leaned down. Saw Emerson. Blinked once. "Well. Ain't it the night for surprises?"

With that, the guard moved back inside her booth, and pressed a button that set big wrought-iron gates to opening.

"Good to see you again, Sandra," said Holden.

To which the guard said, "Good luck."

Curiosity spiking in a dozen different directions, Emerson was still deciding which question to ask first when the house came into view. It was like something out of *The Great Gatsby*, three storeys, with wings, and gables and what looked like a forest sprawled out behind it.

"Holy moly," she whispered, leaning so far forward her hands gripped the dashboard.

"Careful," Holden murmured as he curved onto

the huge circular drive, "you're starting to drool. Again."

Emerson shot him a look. The humour lighting the storm-cloud blue of his eyes made the backs of her knees tingle, as if he had a direct line to certain nerve clusters in her body and all he had to do was tug.

"Whose house *is* this?" she asked.

She felt rather than heard the slightest hesitation before he said, "Bettina and Chuck Sanderson."

"As in the *Sanderson Group* Sandersons?"

"The very ones."

While her work put her in the path of influential people with impressive staffing needs, the Sanderson real estate family was a whole other level.

This was not merely a favour any more, or the chance to exorcise her Heartache List demons for good. It was a huge opportunity. Perhaps even the opportunity of a lifetime.

Holden pulled the car to a stop in front of the house, its engine softening to a throaty rumble. "You need a moment?"

"Nope. I'm fine."

"Just so you know, I can practically hear the wheels cranking behind those big green eyes of yours."

Emerson looked to her lap, before shooting him a smile. "Perhaps that's the engine whimpering. You ride the clutch, you know."

A liveried gentleman opened her door right at

the perfect moment, so that she could decamp the car, rather than face Holden's burst of laughter.

Only to find she had to twist and contort herself, to navigate the split in her madly dressy dress. If only she'd asked more questions she might have dressed like an enterprising HR guru rather than an awards-show presenter.

"Shall we?" Holden asked, ambling around the front of the car, hand palm-up.

Emerson gripped tighter to her clutch bag.

He noticed, the edge of his mouth kicking up. As if he was playing with her. Testing her parameters. But he didn't press her.

With a tilt of his head, he motioned for her to join him on the walk up the wide front steps.

As they neared the front door—as wide as it was tall, and taller than her by double—Emerson felt Holden hesitate. Felt the energy coiled inside him expand, felt him lock it down hard, as if in preparation for something big.

And all her wild thoughts of using this night to sell herself to the Sandersons blew away like so much dust.

Holden had asked her to accompany him for a reason. This hulking, self-sufficient, charming genius felt as if he needed someone on his side. Maybe it was time to stop thinking about her own part in this, and give the guy a break.

"Hold up for a second," she said, moving in closer and sliding her hand into the crook of his arm. Ignoring, as best she could, the warmth of his skin seeping through the fabric, the hard strength against her palm. "What's our game plan?"

"Game plan?" he asked, the clouds sweeping from his eyes as he looked down into hers.

"What have you told them about me? Do we have a backstory? Are they aware this is not a date-date? Please tell me you don't expect me to act as if I'm madly in love with you. You're right, I'm good on my feet, but that might be beyond me."

"Might?" he asked, and that smile—the one that spread across his face in a slow, easy, sensuous sweep of warmth and deliciousness—came out to play. "No pretending required. You're you. I'm me. We came together. That simple."

"Okay, then," said Emerson, even while she was becoming more and more sure that it was far more complicated than he'd let on.

She realised then that, for all that he had occupied such an important place in *her* backstory, she knew very little about him. Apparently, he made apps and lived overseas. He definitely smelled great, and was devastatingly good-looking, and knew how to wear a suit. The rest was a puzzle that had been tipped out of the box at her feet.

"Ready?" she asked.

"As I'll ever be." With a deep breath, Holden opened the door without knocking, then waited for Emerson to precede him inside.

She barely had time to take in the soaring ceil-

ings, the sweeping staircase, the vases of hydran-
geas covering every surface, the art on the walls,
when a handsome silver-haired gentleman in a
wheelchair descended upon them, pulling to a stop
and opening his arms wide.

"Holden, my boy!"

"Chuck," said Holden, his arm hardening beneath Emerson's hand, before he let her hand fall,
and opened his arms just as wide.

Emerson held back, clutching her bag, as
Holden Roarke and one of the richest men in Australia indulged in a long hug.

"So, when are you coming out of this ridiculous
'retirement' of yours to come back and work for
me?" Chuck asked as Holden pulled away.

Holden laughed as he moved back to Emerson's side, putting her hand back into the crook
of his arm. She tucked his arm close, aware that
his laughter didn't have the same sense of release
as when he laughed at her.

"I like retirement," Holden said. "It's only
slightly ridiculous. Gives me the means to be a
man of the modern zeitgeist, following my bliss."

Chuck's eyes narrowed, as if he didn't believe
the spin. "Don't tell my wife you said that. She's
constantly telling me it's time to wind back. Take
up painting. Meditate. Can't imagine anything
worse."

"I heard that," said an attractive ice blonde
who'd ambled up behind him. Bettina Sander-

son leaned to place a kiss on her husband's cheek before standing and eyeballing Holden. "Why, hello there, stranger."

"Bettina," Holden returned, his voice lit with a level of affection Emerson wasn't expecting, considering how edgy he'd seemed outside.

"One day," said Bettina, "all that rolling stone rubbish will become tiresome and someone will make you an offer you can't refuse. Mark my words."

Chuck's gaze seemed to take in Emerson for the first time, as if he'd been blinded by the man at her side, surprise flickering behind his eyes before he blinked, his face a mask of amiability.

"Well, well, well," said Chuck. "Bettina mentioned you were bringing a friend."

Holden looked to Emerson, bathing her in a smile that sent goosebumps up and down her arms. "Chuck, Bettina, this is my friend Emerson Adler. Emerson, I give you Chuck and Bettina Sanderson."

Bettina moved out from behind her husband's wheelchair, took Emerson by the hands and looked her over as if trying to commit her to memory. "We are so pleased to meet you, Emerson."

"Likewise, I assure you."

"My turn," said Chuck, rolling his chair towards her.

Emerson readied to shake, only to find herself pulled down into her own warm, solid hug.

"Oh," she said, one hand fluttering against the man's beefy shoulder, the other still gripping her clutch bag. She truly hoped she didn't look as awkward as she felt.

Until she glanced to the side to find Holden being summarily hugged by Bettina, and he hugging her back. Something about the shape of them, the hunched shoulders, the closed eyes, the tight mouths, made her heart thud against her ribs. Made her look away, as if she'd accidentally witnessed something private.

"So, what do you do, Emerson? What's your *bliss*?" said Chuck, gathering her attention, a hand still holding hers.

"My bliss? Much like you, I fear, my bliss is my work. I run my own HR firm, Pitch Perfect. We wield a small, exclusive pool of highly experienced temps, but at our core we consult, source, scout, and place quality applicants into significant positions in corporate, charitable and political environments. And…that sounded like it came straight from our website. I'm so sorry. I was at the Women in Business lunch today and must have said those exact words a hundred times."

Chuck's eyes sharpened, the infamous businessman showing beneath the mask of gracious host. "You're a head hunter."

"I am. And a damned fine one at that."

Chuck chuckled as his wife came back to his side. "We're going to have to watch out for this one."

"Then we shall." Bettina's smile was kind and warm. "You're the last here—let's head in."

Emerson nodded, so starstruck she didn't realise how quiet Holden had been since that moment with Bettina until it was just the two of them, trailing behind their hosts as they made their way through the house.

Emerson slowed with him, lifting an eyebrow in question.

Everything okay?

His response, a flicker below one eye, and a shake of the head.

All good.

But he wasn't. Which was why she slowed further, till they walked side by side.

"Are you really retired? Like, actually?"

"Since I was in my mid-twenties. Though I'm dragged out of it on occasion, usually when finding myself frustrated by the lack of an app that I can't believe is yet to exist, and so have to build it myself."

She shook her head. Unable to imagine what it might feel like not to chase, not to grind, not to keep a sharp, narrow focus on one's life plan. Not to need that kind of control.

"What *have* you dragged me into, Roarke?" she asked, looking up as they passed under yet another chandelier. "Is it Stepford or Virginia Woolf?"

Holden's face broke into a quick, delighted grin, before it faded to a humourless smile. His spare hand ran the back of his neck, pinching hard. "Long story."

"Too long to tell me before dinner?"

"Much."

"I see."

He paused, forcing her to stop. "Emmy, if this is too much, if you'd prefer to leave, I will take you home. No judgement. No questions asked. Favour still owed to you in full."

She looked at him then, really looked at him. This real-life, flesh-and-blood man who needed her.

Before she could second guess herself, she held out her hand. A question flickered behind his eyes, before his long fingers closed around hers. Then they walked shoulder to shoulder, hip to hip, the fabric of his suit creating soft, rhythmic, enthralling friction all down her side.

When he leaned towards her, his mouth near her ear, and murmured, "Why do I get the feeling you've just amped up the kind of favour you plan to ask in return?" it took everything in her power not to shiver.

"Favour is such a small word for what I have in mind for you, Holden."

"Lucky me."

CHAPTER FIVE

HOLDEN'S JACKET HUNG over the back of the gilt dining chair, his shirtsleeves now rolled to his elbows. His right leg shook up and down beneath the table, dissipating the lashings of excess energy he could not hope to contain.

For the laughter, the heads tilted together in deep conversation, the random hands passing food across the table… It was years since he'd been a regular at such gatherings in this house, and yet it was so familiar to him it stung.

When he realised that he was rubbing the heel of his palm over his chest Holden dropped his hand to the table. Stretching out tight fingers. Rolling a tense shoulder till it cracked. He glanced down the table to find Emmy watching him over the top of her glass of wine.

She sat near enough that he could see the curiosity in her eyes. Too far away for his liking.

For, he was discovering, he liked having her close.

When he'd called, asking for her to join him, he hadn't exactly thought it through. It had been instinct, more than anything. An idea that, knowing she'd be there, he'd actually show up.

But the bigger truth was, he liked Emerson Adler. He found her lovely, and surprising, and hugely entertaining. Then there was the way she walked, as if a big band with a heavy bass drum played her into every room. And the way she smelled, like lime and spring time—

Holden blinked and looked deliberately about the table, to the walls, the ostentatious fresco on the ceiling, before finding Emmy's eyes again, unsurprised to find her watching him still.

So he offered up a slow smile. Intimate. Playful. Chancy, considering the company. But everything about the night was precarious; what was one more layer of exposure?

Nice digs, huh? he said with his eyes.

Emmy's glass twirled in response, the stem twisting between her fingers, catching the light which glinted and shifted across her lovely face. Then she lifted a shoulder in a shrug, the shoulder covered in the silken dark hair swept to one side like some forties siren.

Sure. Whatever.

He laughed out loud.

"Holden?"

He flinched. Then turned to Bettina, who sat to his left, at the end of the table. "Sorry. I was a million miles away."

Her chin tilted towards the other end of the table. "Not so very far as that."

His leg started jiggling once again.

"I only hope, now you're back, that you'll stay. For a while at least. All that rushing about isn't good for a person's health." Her gaze went to her husband.

Her comment, for all its sincerity, made his gut curl in on itself, like self-perpetuating quicksand. For there was enough water under that bridge to drown a man in minutes.

They were all there, ostensibly, to celebrate Chuck's seventieth birthday. But this month was ripe with unspoken anniversaries for this family. Five years since the accident that had put Chuck in that wheelchair, since Marnie had run off, Holden too.

And seven years since…since the horror that had tied them inexorably together in the first place.

Bettina looked at him and smiled. As if it had all been forgiven in five minutes. Then she asked, "Have you spoken to my daughter?"

"On occasion," Holden admitted, reaching for his iced water.

Marnie. Bettina and Chuck's daughter, who'd run off to America with the gardener. While still engaged to Holden. She now lived happily ever after in Maine with their two young kids.

"I thought she might be here."

Bettina's smile was soft. "She's always gone her own way, as you well know. But I am glad you two have kept in touch. You were always friends above all else." A sip of wine, then, "I knew she'd bounce back, she's a tough cookie. But I worried that what we did to you… I worried that whole thing might have given you all the ammunition you needed to go into your cave and stay there."

"What you did to me?" Holden reiterated, honestly stunned to hear her put it that way. "Taking me on, taking me in? Monsters, the lot of you."

She cocked her head. And waited.

"I'm fine," he assured her.

Bettina took his words at face value. Then leaned back in her chair. "I like her."

"Your daughter? I hope so."

Bettina slapped him lightly on the hand. And nodded once again towards Emmy. "I wasn't expecting to. In fact, I was ready to pretend like crazy. But she's wonderful."

"She's all right, I guess, if you can get past the toenail collection and raging kleptomania."

"Don't do that. She's *wonderful*, Holden. Stunning, which is no surprise. But that's only the half of it. She's substantial, and shrewd, with just a touch of wild. The two of you, together? Watch out, world."

Holden's chest grew tight, the muscles contracting as if weary of trying to hold all the parts of him together. "She's just a friend, Bettina. Newly minted. We knew one another for a short time a long time ago, met again at a wedding a week or so ago, and I invited her here in a fit of panic."

Bettina huffed out a small laugh. "You are the only young man I know who would do such a thing, and still end up with the gem of the ball. I've missed that. Missed you. Not just for Marnie's sake. Or Chuck's. Or Saul's."

Bettina blinked, a shimmer in her eyes that disappeared almost instantly, before she tipped her chin towards the other end of the table. "But since she is merely a friend, as you attest, then you won't mind if young Kris over there makes a play."

Though he knew he was being baited, Holden glanced down the table to find "young Kris" leaning into Emmy, resting his arm across the back of her chair.

A spike of possessiveness, for which he was not prepared or particularly proud, shot down his spine. Until Emmy turned to "young Kris", glanced pointedly at his arm, and watched as it was removed.

Feeling much better about things, Holden turned his back on the scene. "How is Chuck?"

"Retiring."

"You're kidding."

Bettina waved a placating hand. "It's time. I want him with me. By my side. As much as I can have him. I have him ninety-nine per cent convinced."

It was a night for surprises.

"On that note…" Bettina surged to her feet, tapping a spoon against her wine glass, and the conversation fizzled to a halt. "I want to thank you all for coming tonight to help us celebrate our beloved Chuck, on his birthday. Five years ago this very week we imagined this day might not come. And two years before that…" She stopped. Swallowed. "We couldn't imagine much in the way of happiness at all. Yet here we are. With our favourite people, celebrating the good that rises. If you would all be so kind, if you have any booze left in your glasses, I'd ask you all to raise them."

Shuffle of chairs and quick pours, the clink of glass against silverware and a couple of dozen glasses lifted into the air.

"To Chuck," she said.

"And my next seventy years," Chuck added from the other end of the table.

Much laughter followed, amid *hear hears.*

Until Bettina kept her own glass raised. "And to those who could not be with us today. Our beloved Marnie, and her beautiful family, all the way over in Maine. And to our most precious boy, Saul." The shimmer no longer held as it slid over her cheeks in a silvery waterfall. "We love him. We miss him. Oh, that he was here with us still."

"To Saul," said Chuck and the rest of the table followed suit.

After dinner, nobody seemed in any way inclined to leave, moving into the library, the pool room, the halls, despite the hotbed of emotion underpinning the evening, the very air overflowing with the taste of it, the temperature, the weight.

Only half understanding the stories whispered around her, Emerson's smiles and pep had begun to wane. So she made her way around the ground floor in search of her ride home.

Bettina was talking to Kris, the super-chatty guy who'd been hitting on her all through dinner. When she caught Emerson's eye, the older woman waved a hand towards the terrace.

A quick smile of thanks then Emerson made her way outside, but not before noting Bettina grabbing Kris by the elbow and hauling him back.

Emerson made her way down the back stairs, past heavily scented gardenia bushes growing lushly by the garden walls leading down to the lawn, small fountains, tall stone statues. Music and chatter spilled from inside, creating a kind of Renaissance Eden.

The stars were out again that night but the deeper she went into the garden, the less ground the house lights touched, creating patches of velvety darkness. Then she rounded a copse of conifers to find Holden, sitting on a bench, alone, elbows on knees, back hunched, eyes closed.

He seemed to stir at her approach, as if he'd felt a shift in the air, before he opened his eyes and turned to find her. And his eyes... They were savage. Pained. Punished.

And any discomfort she felt at not being in

the know fluttered off into the night like ash on the wind.

"Sorry," he said, making to stand. "I only meant to come out for a minute. What time is it?"

"Stay," she said, with a staying hand to match. For he looked far more exhausted than she felt.

Her heels sinking gently into the turf, she sat on the bench beside him, her hands curling around the cool stone.

"So," she said.

"So," he returned.

"I have questions."

He coughed out a rough laugh. "I bet you do. Do you want the long story or the short?"

"The short version is fine."

When she shivered, the cool of the night sending goosebumps down her arms, Holden lifted his jacket from the bench and moved closer to place it over her shoulders. She thanked him with a half-smile. Breathed deep, drinking in the scent of him. She could chastise herself for it later.

Holden went back to leaning forearms on his thighs, one hand rubbing over his chin, his body taut beside hers. "I must have been seventeen the first time I ate at that table, invited over by a new friend I'd made at my last high school. The one I went to after leaving East Kew, in fact. He was this towering, life-is-there-for-the-taking smile of a guy named Saul Sanderson."

We love him. We miss him. Oh, that he was here with us still.

"Chuck and Bettina's son?"

He nodded. "I went to so many dinners here after that. Spent entire school holidays. I'd been shuffling between couches of distant cousins at the time, none of whom particularly wanted me there; in comparison, this place was like a dream."

"You were a teenager. Why were you living with cousins?"

Holden glanced up, as if he'd almost forgotten she was there. Which was half the reason she'd spoken—she wanted him to remember who he was talking to.

He sat up, his hand gripping the concrete beside hers. "I grew up with my dad, though 'dad' might be too warm and fuzzy a term to describe the guy."

"How so?" she asked.

"The girl with all the questions," he said, his voice sounding far away. Then, "My father drank, he fought, he got into trouble, he pretended to look for work, he had a reputation, he owed money, and he took out all of life's frustrations on me."

Emmy thought of Chuck's open arms. Those big hugs that had stirred up all kinds of parental issues for her too. What a lure that must have been.

Emerson looked out into the night. Confronting the uncomfortable fact that when she'd been crushing on Holden Roarke, imagining him a happy, popular, easy-going hunk, she'd never once considered why a guy like that might need to see a guidance counsellor.

"Tell me about Saul," she said.

A muscle worked in his cheek. "We were like brothers. Even when we went to different universities we kept in touch, caught up every holiday. And then I wrote my app. The interest in the thing was insane, from right at the start. The early offers staggering for a twenty-year-old kid. Infamy ensued. Partying, travel, free hotels, more money than I knew what to do with. I lost touch with pretty much everyone who'd been a part of life in the 'before'. Including Saul."

A shadow passed over his face.

"A couple of years later I was in Amsterdam, prepping to speak at some future symposium, when there was a phone call, deep into the night. Saul was gone. Could I come home?"

"How did it happen?" she asked, her voice soft, yet it carried in the dark of the night.

"Car accident. Wet roads. Late night. Speed. Thankfully no one else was hurt."

That wasn't true. Every person inside that house at dinner had been hurt by what had happened to Saul Sanderson, and despite the festivities, and the birthday cheer, many were clearly hurting still.

"Come home, they said?" she nudged.

"So, I came home," Holden went on. "I was pall

bearer. I spoke at the funeral. It was so damned sad. Yet, I seemed to make them feel as if there was still a small connection to their boy. They asked me to stick around afterwards. What could I say?"

"So you stayed."

"I stayed. And, feeling utterly useless in the face of what those good people were all going through, I wrote an app. For Chuck. As if that might somehow make up for my prior absence. And Saul's. It was twisty stuff."

"What was the app?"

"It was called Real Time. Tracked movement in the real estate market, finding patterns in house sales with regards to suburbs, streets, pockets. I'd quietly imagined it a parting gift, before running away to Bermuda. Instead, Chuck convinced me to stay on, ostensibly to teach his staff how to wield it. And then he promoted me, again and again. Even after my father showed up in Chuck's office one day, asking for money, as he was wont to do now that I'd turned out not to be so useless after all. Then there was Marnie."

She'd heard the name bandied about through the night, with both censure and delight, as if she was a polarising character in the Sandersons' story, and yet she hadn't felt the dull pain in her belly as she did when Holden said the name.

"Marnie is Saul's older sister and she did not think it was healthy for Chuck to keep me around.

Her bluntness was a relief. Both hurting, and angry, we soon became a thing. Got engaged, really quickly. Chuck and Bettina wholeheartedly approved. But Marnie didn't love me. She was working through her own pain, and I had become the family conduit."

"Holden," Emerson whispered. Or maybe it was an internal thing—the echo of the ache she felt for him, now flowing freely through her.

"She snapped out of it. Started seeing the gardener. Did fall in love. Fell pregnant. And fled. Chuck was devastated. Accused her of spoiling Saul's memory by hurting me. Watching them fall apart was the final straw. I took the blame. Insisted she'd only left after realising I wasn't in love with her. Excruciating. But, at least, it was true."

Holden ran both hands over his face, kept his head tipped down, his hair falling over his forehead. "Then I quit. Announced, in a press release no less, that I was retiring. Moving to a beach somewhere. I knew it would send interest in Chuck's new app through the roof, which it did, as if that might mitigate the mess I'd let unfold. Then I got on a plane and left.

"And while I was in the air, Chuck had a heart attack, fell down some stairs and—"

"The wheelchair," Emmy whispered.

"The wheelchair."

"Good grief, Holden. That's…a lot." A lot for him to walk back through that door tonight. A lot for them to invite him to do the same. All those good people trying their best under truly trying circumstances. No wonder he'd needed her.

"It sounds like something out of a soap opera."

He looked to her then, a glint in his dark eyes, his laughter sudden and rough.

Emerson slapped a hand over her mouth. "That sounded so callous. I am so sorry."

"You're spot on. Imagine how it felt being caught up in the middle of it. It felt big and important and hyperreal. I never should have stayed. I never should have let it get that far. It took me far too long to remember that I was still the outsider, looking in."

Outliers in arms. She'd thought he was being flirty when he'd said those words at the wedding; now she understood what that had meant. That it was meaningful to him.

Emerson placed her hand gently over Holden's. "They were so happy to see you tonight. You might not be their son, but they do adore you. You were not an outsider then, and neither are you now. Not to them."

A muscle worked in Holden's cheek. He turned his hand beneath hers, till he cradled hers in his own. Then he slowly, *slowly* lifted it and placed a soft, sweet kiss upon her palm.

When his face turned to hers his eyes were deep and dark, unreadable, his jaw hard. Her hand remained tucked in his. "Thank you."

"For what?" she asked, her voice a husky whisper, her body now trembling despite the warmth of his jacket, of his body heat beside her.

His eyes roved between hers. "For saying yes when I asked."

Moonlight shone on half his face, leaving the other half in shadow. All angles and character and depth and dark male beauty. His thumb began tracing the inside of her palm, spreading warmth from the place he'd kissed up her arm and into her chest.

With some effort on her part, she took back her hand, ostensibly to adjust the jacket on her shoulders, mostly so that he didn't see how his touch affected her. "It was a hell of an evening. One I won't soon forget."

"I'll bet."

Emerson felt herself whipped back to the night of the wedding, when she'd said she wasn't sure if stars were happy or sad. What had Holden said? *The most beautiful things are often both.*

A few long, quiet moments later, Emerson said, "What happened to Chuck—it's not your fault."

Holden stilled. "I know that."

Did he? Emerson wasn't sure. The "ran away to Bermuda" slip made her think otherwise. Perhaps his lifestyle had less to do with having the means, and more to do with a need to keep moving. Not just around a park, and not just in the middle of a school term without stopping to say goodbye.

The revelation pressed against an ancient bruise that lived deep inside her. He was a runner, like her dad. No wonder that particular heartache had hit so hard.

Yet she kept her gaze direct, unflinching. While Holden did the same, his body wound tight, as if breathing too deep might unravel some long-held knot behind his ribs. But the longer he looked into her eyes, the more he seemed to loosen, his face easing, his eyes softening.

And that bruised place deep inside her began to pulse.

Emerson pressed herself to standing, Holden's jacket falling off her shoulder. He caught it, stood, and placed it back on her shoulders. Adjusting it, turning her gently to tug at the lapels, and not letting go as he looked into her eyes.

"Wanna get out of here?" she said, feigning a cool she did not feel.

He smiled. "And I thought I was hiding it so well."

She turned away from him then, releasing herself from the gravity in his eyes, hooking her hand through his arm, and said, "Last to arrive, first to leave. This might just be the perfect non-date date after all."

Holden kept hold of Emmy's hand as they said their goodbyes, finding her touch a comfort. An anchor. The shape of something he couldn't define but couldn't deny.

Chuck placed his hand over theirs, as if in some kind of benediction, while Bettina drew each into a long hug. And it all felt a zillion times lighter, easier, better than it had when they'd first arrived.

Then they were back in his car, heading through town, and pulling up outside her place far too soon.

As the engine cut, their breaths were loud in the sudden quiet. Moonlight fell on Emerson's quicksilver dress, her hands in her lap, her face remaining in darkness.

While Holden gripped the steering wheel, like a nervy teenager dropping off a pretty girl after the football game. If she lingered in the car, did it mean something? Would it be an invitation to tuck a hand into the heavy sweep of her hair and kiss her?

Or was it just that he *wanted* to kiss her? And had done since he'd seen her lift that glass of champagne in salute, not following anyone's rules but her own?

He'd imagined kissing her gently at first, getting a sense of her temperature, her texture, her taste. Taking his sweet time till his heart felt sluggish and thunderous all at once.

True, he'd also imagined hauling her into his lap and kissing her till he was wearing her lipstick and she was wearing none.

Either way, he might not be any good at spinning a line, but his moves were just fine.

The decision was taken out of his hands when she all but leapt from the car.

"Don't get out," she insisted, leaning back into the window. "It's been a big night, and I'm sure you want to get home."

Home? By that she must have meant the apartment he was staying in, a modern penthouse he'd bought off plan years back and had decorated by a friend of a friend when he'd heard his dad was sick. Made plans to come home, because that was what good sons did, if you could be a good son when you hadn't seen your father in years. Only to find out his father had died earlier that month and the funeral had gone ahead without him.

The walls were blinding white, the kitchen tiles and cupboards bright red, the dining chairs a mismatched array of rainbow colours—perfect for a hyperactive kindergarten teacher. And it made him think of his father. He was seriously considering selling it when he left.

He looked over Emerson's shoulder to her white picket fence, flowers spilling abundantly over the top, her quaint cottage, the porch light glowing warmly. Invitingly.

That was a home.

"What if there's a robber?" he said.

She reached down and took off a shoe with a mighty long heel. "I'll smack them with this."

She probably would too.

"And yet," he said, pausing till he'd hopped out

of the car and shut the door, "I'm seeing you to your door. You would be just as gallant if you were dropping me home."

Her hand gripped her shoe as she watched him round the car. "I can't see that happening. Me dropping you home any time. Since this was a favour, and not a date."

"True," said Holden, even while it hadn't felt that way to him. In fact, he could have kicked himself for ever suggesting it.

Then it hit him—she was right. It was unlikely they'd even see one another again, now that his reason for being in Melbourne was done. Which felt...unacceptable.

They got on. They were attracted to one another. He remembered the way her hand had trembled when he'd brought it to his lips, remembered the sweet taste of her skin, and the shards of heat that had spread throughout his body.

Date or not, asking her to dinner had felt like one of the top five decisions of his life. And he wasn't ready for it to end.

"Then consider this," he said, following her as she limped her way up her front path, shoe weapon still in hand, "me walking you to your door, at the ready to take down prowlers and peeping toms, that can be my favour returned."

"Ha," she said, shooting him a grin over her shoulder—a flash of white teeth, mischief in her eyes—as she hobbled up her front steps. "Not on your life. I am keeping that up my sleeve for when I need something huge."

"Aah. I get it." Holden stopped at the bottom of the stairs and rocked back on his heels. "You're not ready to be rid of me yet."

Something else glinted in her eyes then. A sense that she had been found out. Further proof he was *not* alone in this…curiosity.

As if she knew exactly what she'd just given away, she rolled her eyes and said, "Oh, shut up."

Holden laughed with the unexpectedness of her admission. And with that knowledge came another incremental shift in the ground beneath them both.

They weren't done here. Meaning he wasn't going anywhere. Not yet.

She shook her head side to side, as if she wasn't sure what she was going to do with him. If she'd asked, he'd have told her she could do *anything she liked*.

But she did not ask. She slid her other shoe from her foot, lowering her leg slowly to the ground, and said, "Don't go thinking I'd cry myself to sleep at the thought of never seeing you again, Holden Roarke."

Though far too late for it to have the impact it might if he didn't know she'd be thinking of him all the same.

"I survived you leaving once, I can do it again.

I'm holding on to my favour. For as long as it takes to find the perfect response."

With that she turned away from him, opened her front door and took a step inside.

"Thank you for walking me to my door," she said, innate politeness coming to the fore.

"Thank you for accompanying me to dinner," he said, gripping his hands behind him and bowing at the waist.

He thought about asking if he might, in fact, make a plan to see her again. That if she said yes he could stay in town another day or two.

Then he remembered, he owed her.

She'd be in touch. When she was ready. Meaning he might have to stick around just a little longer. At least until the ledger was square.

"Goodnight, Emmy."

"Goodnight, Holden," she said, surprise and maybe even disappointment flashing across her face, before she stepped inside and closed her door.

So much for his moves.

After a few moments the front lights turned off, and a light inside turned on. He heard a soft woof, a welcome home from her lovely old dog, and he felt a sharp twist of pain deep behind his solar plexus.

Once again he found himself back where he always seemed to end up—on the outside, looking in.

CHAPTER SIX

A HANDFUL OF days later Emerson, Camille and Phillip met up for the first time since the wedding at their favourite hang-out: a rustic little hole-in-the-wall café with moth-eaten velvet couches, and mismatched wooden chairs that was funky enough to boast "atmosphere" but not so busy they couldn't hear one another talk.

"It wasn't a load-bearing wall. I'm almost certain," said Phillip at the end of a long and rambling story about their first couple of weeks of home renovations.

Avoiding the spring that poked out at the back of her couch, Emerson took a hearty gulp of her super-strong double espresso. "Did you think to, you know, maybe, check? Before going at it with a mallet?"

"Turns out we're going with a more holistic, gut-based approach." Phillip glanced towards Camille, who was, if her dramatic hand movements were anything to go by, quite possibly telling the same story to the barista behind the counter.

"Enough about us," said Phillip. "Fill me in on the goings on in the life of Emmy Adler since the wedding. From what I heard, you and a certain gentleman rather hit it off that night." He waggled his eyebrows. "By that I mean Holden Roarke."

"Did you, now?"

"Ran into him yesterday, which was nice, because I was sure he'd planned to be long gone by now. Well, not so much *ran into*, as he called to thank me for the invitation, and then we met for a drink. And he had a lot of nice things to say about—"

"Phew! I'm famished!" Camille lolloped onto the couch beside her husband.

Leaving Emmy to wonder, *A lot of nice things to say about what? Or who?* Not that it mattered. Not a jot. For it was unlikely she'd ever see him again. Yes, he owed her a favour, but she'd never had any real sense it would happen. The man didn't even live in the same country she did, so she'd quietly planned to be magnanimous and let it go.

Only, now that he was unexpectedly still in town… Maybe she *could* call it in. Should she use his IT knowledge? Too easy. Could he build her a shed? A shed would be handy for storing gardening gear, in case she one day took up gardening. And the thought of him in her back yard, using a hammer, sweat dripping down his brow—

"Did he tell you about the water damage?" said Camille around the paper straw in her huge glass of Diet Coke.

"Not yet," said Phillip. "We were talking about the wedding night."

"Hey," said Camille, slapping him on the arm

with the back of her hand. "She's my best friend. That's my story to tell!"

"Not *the* wedding night," Phillip muttered. "We were talking about Holden Roarke."

Camille's gaze snapped to Emerson's. "Yeah, so my husband and your Holden had drinks yesterday, did he tell you? Mere days into our honeymoon and he's already fleeing at the first chance to meet up with another man."

"I wasn't fleeing you," said Phillip, leaving Emerson to shift on her seat at Camille's casual use of "your Holden". "I needed a little space from the *house*, in order to see things from a different perspective. And he's such an interesting guy. Well-travelled. And the success he's had. At his age. Puts our efforts to shame."

"Speak for yourself," Emmy and Camille said at the same time, before leaning in for a high five.

"Anyway," said Phillip, "it seems our Emmy has a fan."

"Oh, really?" said Camille. "Who?"

Phillip blinked at her. "Holden."

Camille's gaze snapped to Emmy's again before her face broke into a grin. "Really?"

Emmy rolled her eyes. "Calm down. We chatted at the wedding, which you know. And a little more, again, after you left. And—"

"And he dropped her at her hotel that night," Phillip added, most helpfully, cutting off Emmy before she could try to explain about dinner with the Sandersons, and the favours.

Camille smacked Phillip on the arm. "First you invite *Heartache Number Four* to our wedding without checking with me, then you find out some truly excellent gossip, which my best friend was no doubt waiting to tell me in person, and you ruin it for her! Married five minutes and you've already forgotten the rules."

"It's a lot to remember," Phillip said. "I never did apologise, though, Em. About Holden and all."

"No," Emmy insisted. "I know you didn't know. And it was fine. He was fine. He was perfectly..." What was the word he'd used? "Gallant."

Even though, several times, she'd had an inkling, a feminine rush of knowledge, that he might have been *thinking* less than gallant thoughts. About her. Good chance she was projecting, for she'd definitely been guilty of thinking less than gallant thoughts about him.

"Doth the lady protest too much?" Camille asked, wide eyes now sparkling with patent interest.

"She does not," said Emmy. "Every encounter we've had has been totally PG."

"She rated it," Camille murmured, looking at Emmy as if she was seeing a whole new side of her.

"I heard," Phillip murmured back.

Emmy breathed deep, gathering her strength.

During which time Camille said to her husband, "Before you and Holden join a bowling league, don't forget Emmy was once utterly besotted with the guy. In fact, the List came about only after *he* broke her fertile, fecund fourteen-year-old heart."

Phillip winced. Then braced himself before saying, "I am glad he came, though. It's been nice getting to know him again. He'd never talk it up, but I know he didn't charge the uni for speaking the night I bumped into him. And he's helped out a few friends, on the quiet, over the years, when they've got themselves into trouble. He acts like he's this loose, jet-setting, I-am-an-island type, but at heart he's really a good guy."

"Maybe now," Camille interjected, glancing at Emmy, her best-friend-for-ever skills right up there with the best. "But back then..."

"He was a good guy back then too," Emmy assured them. Having found a couple of the corner pieces of the Holden Roarke puzzle, she knew a little more of who he was, and what he'd been going through.

His leaving in the middle of the night back then had felt...specific. And, yes, heartbreaking. But it hadn't been his fault. And if he hadn't been a good guy back then, Emmy wouldn't have liked him so much.

He just…hadn't liked her back.

Emmy came back around to find Camille playing with one of Phillip's shirt buttons and smiling into his eyes. And felt an overwhelming sense that she had her nose pressed up against the window, as she witnessed something private.

How had Holden described it? Like an outsider, looking in.

Emmy slowly rose from her chair. "Guys, it's been fab, but I really have to scoot."

"Aw," said Camille. "Housewarming, next week. Yes?"

"Of course. Let me know if you need any help leading up."

"Will do."

Hugs all round, then Emerson left.

Standing outside the café, she looked left, then right, not, in fact, having anywhere in particular to scoot to.

But with the messy mix of thoughts nipping at her heels—the realisation she hadn't told her best friend that she'd been to dinner with Holden, and that she was pretty sure she wanted to kiss the man, along with that bittersweet feeling of disconnection that had hit her so hard at the wedding—she went there fast.

Keys in the door of the apartment, Holden looked to his phone as it buzzed in his hand, hoping it might be a certain green-eyed brunette.

Instead, it was a blue-eyed blonde he'd been avoiding for days.

"Joel," Holden answered, holding the phone a smidge further from his ear in preparation for his business manager's voice to come booming down the line.

"Mate!" Joel replied, his attempt at an Australian accent less than convincing.

Holden threw his keys on the frog-green kidney-shaped hall table. When he perched on a canary-yellow kitchen stool, he was forced to move as the sun slanted right in his eyes. Not that sitting anywhere else in the crazy place felt much better.

"I was expecting you to land on my doorstep a week ago," said Joel. "Jenny even had the linen washed and ready, just in case."

Yes, he could stay anywhere in the world, but he still found himself sleeping on people's couches on occasion. An old habit, a safety net from his childhood, that he just couldn't break.

Holden looked around the apartment. While he knew he couldn't spend another night in this place, he was not yet ready to get on a plane. Not while Emmy, and her favour, were out there.

"Decided to stay on for a bit," Holden said.

"Clearly. Word is out. I'm fielding offers."

"What kind of offers?"

"Teaching engagements, speaking, consultancy, investments, product spokesmanship…"

Joel paused, as if he'd run out of breath. As if he'd been waiting for Holden to cut him off far sooner. "Will you be home long enough to take something on?"

Home. There was that word again. Holden flopped back on the hard yellow leather couch and threw his arm over his eyes so that the colour didn't permanently burn his retinas.

"My youngest wants to start horse-riding lessons," Joel beseeched. "Do you know how expensive they are?"

Holden laughed despite himself. "I pay you a packet whether I take on any events or not."

"Yes, you do. For which my children are eternally grateful." A pause, then, "While the kids are hankering for some Uncle Holden time, I'm glad you've stuck it out a little longer. Make new memories. And while you're at it, make some local schools, or struggling businesspeople, or young entrepreneurs super-happy and talk to them. For money. It'll do you the world of good."

"Fine."

"Really? Brilliant! I'll swing the list over right away." With that, Joel rang off, sounding as if he couldn't believe his luck.

While Holden called up the app he'd built, the very one he'd gifted Chuck several iterations ago, and scrolled through a list of short-term rentals, focusing on places not too dissimilar from Emmy's cosy, comfortable, suburban spot.

* * *

Freya's cheeks were bright pink, her tablet in a death grip, as she swept into Emerson's office. "Phone call. Line one."

Freya could look like the sky was falling if someone was a minute late to work, so Emmy finished reading the contract page she was on before pressing the button to bring up the speakerphone, and said, "Emerson Adler."

"Emerson. Ah, that name of yours. It's like a song. Chuck Sanderson here."

Emerson flinched so hard the top few sheets of paper swept off her desk and landed on the floor.

Freya, as if expecting it, rushed in, her eyes preternaturally wide as she neatly plucked the pages off the floor and popped them back into order on the desk, before backing out of the room in a crouch and closing the door with a soft *snick*.

"Chuck! It was such an honour to meet you the other night."

Chuck laughed, entirely aware of his own power. "Well, you impressed me at dinner too. Even more importantly, you impressed my wife."

"That's so lovely," she said, sensing that Chuck Sanderson, CEO of the real estate and construction goliath the Sanderson Group, didn't make it a habit to call up house guests and personally thank them for attending a party. She picked up the sparkly paperweight on her desk, rubbed her thumb over the soft indent beneath, and said, "Is there something I can help you with today?"

"Well, Emerson, I find myself in need of some…key staff."

Emerson punched the air. Then reached for a notebook and pen so she didn't forget a word. "I thought I heard, at dinner the other night, that you were on the verge of retiring."

"Rumours. I'm as invigorated today as I've ever been. Now, human resources are your area of expertise, yes?"

"Very much. What are you after?"

"Temps. A few new bodies in middle management as we look towards expanding our development sector."

She jotted down a bullet list. "Temps. Middle management. Can do."

"I also have a very important position that needs filling. In the spirit of transparency, I have another couple of mobs on the case already, but they've yet to produce the goods, so I'd like you to have a go as well."

Normal business practice, at his level. "What position is that?"

"COO."

Chief Operating Officer for the Sanderson Group. A multimillion-dollar package, no doubt. With the kind of finder's fee that would pay her staff, her rent, and then some for some time. "My team and I are absolutely up to the task."

"So, you have someone in mind, then?"

She paused, mind ticking over several women and men she'd made relationships with over the years who would be ready and raring. "I just might."

"I can't tell you how glad I am to hear it. He's a stubborn fellow, but if anyone can swing him around to taking on the gig, you can."

And just like that Emerson's happy bubble popped.

Chuck Sanderson hadn't called because he'd been impressed with her. Not solely. He'd called because he thought she might be able to bring Holden on as COO of the Sanderson Group.

Emerson nibbled on the end of her pencil and thought it through.

Her own history with the guy aside, his relationship with the Sanderson family was staggeringly complicated. And he was very clearly *not* in need of a job, or looking for work, much less a high-pressure, high-investment, settle-in-one-place gig.

He was also, as far as she knew, still intending to fly off into the sunset whenever the urge took him. Because that was the kind of person he was. A man who walked into a room as easily as he left it.

And yet...

He *was* still in town, which went against his original plan. She knew because he'd begun texting her every day or so, asking if she wanted lunch. Asking after Pumpkin. Asking if she wanted help choosing her favour.

And he *had* worked for the company. He was beloved by the boss. They were all most definitely in a better place with one another than they had been before, thanks to that dinner.

If she was able to land Holden—even as a *candidate*—she had zero doubt the commission would be hers.

And Holden *did* owe her that huge favour.

No. *No.* She couldn't. She wouldn't. She didn't know the man that well, but, having heard his story, in his own words, in the silvery darkness in the Sandersons' own garden, she knew enough to know she would never ask it of him. Ever.

Holden may have given her the in, but he was not the answer.

"Chuck," she said, putting on her best I-am-the-expert-here-so-it-would-behove-you-to-listen voice, "in line with our spirit of transparency, I do not believe Holden is the right person for the job. He's brilliant, yes. He knows the business, yes. He adores you. He's in town. But as he said the other night, he's not keen on being tied down. And…"

Always better to be honest. Allowing someone to get their hopes up, knowing they'd be dashed, was, to Emerson, the cruellest thing in the world.

"I honestly believe your history together would make a partnership problematic." She paused. Let that sit. Then said, "There *is* someone else out there who is suited to the job. Someone just as brilliant, just as talented, just as charismatic—but keen. Eager. Excited by the prospect. And I am going to be the one to find them."

She would. She had to. For it would cement her position in the world of corporate HR like nothing else could.

She waited for Chuck to say something, hoping she hadn't just shot herself in the foot, but also knowing there was no way forward if he wanted her to be some kind of pawn in his get Holden game.

The man cleared his throat, and said, "I'll have my people contact your people to put the staffing contract in place. And I look forward to seeing these fantastic candidates you assure me are out there. Good day, Emerson."

"Good day—" she said, but he'd already hung up.

She stared into the middle distance, her mind whirring.

The Sanderson Group. *The Sanderson Group.*

As it truly sank in, she leaned back in her chair and let out a great, "Whoop!"

Emerson turned out the lights in her office late that same evening. Moonlight spilled through the huge windows, and the only sound was the hum of the exit signs.

Still buzzing with energy as she headed down in the lift, after hours spent with her teams working through the Sanderson Group portfolio, she pulled out her phone, thumb hovering over her contacts.

It was a Tuesday, so Camille would be at bingo with her dad. Phillip—if not painting something or ripping something up—would happily chat, and he'd make all the right noises, but it wasn't quite the same.

Strangely, though, neither was the "someone" she wanted to tell.

When the lift doors opened, she pressed call before she could change her mind.

"Emerson." Holden's voice came through the phone right as she pressed the door to let her out of the building. The night air was an icy rush against her body; in contrast, with the phone to her ear, his voice was warm and welcoming.

"Holden. Um, hi."

"Um, hi, right on back. What's up? What do you need from me? Shall I rush out the door this instant, ready and raring to do your bidding?"

"There is nothing I need from you," she said, heels tapping on the footpath as she ducked around a group of young women heading out for a night on the town.

"I'm sure I could think of something."

She bet he could. "I called as I have news."

"And you thought of me. That's nice." No humour in his voice that time. Just easy acceptance. She imagined him saying so while lying back on a couch, head resting on his bent arm, bare feet on the opposite arm rest. He might have been wearing a shirt, he might not.

"The *only* reason I thought of you is because I have you to thank for said news. In a small, teeny-tiny, miniscule way."

"Now I'm really intrigued."

She reached the door leading to the car park and pulled out her key card. But held off, knowing the reception was patchy when she went underground.

There was no way she could hide her smile as she said, "I received a call from Chuck Sanderson this afternoon. Pitch Perfect is to be the Sanderson Group's new temp staffing *and* management recruitment firm."

In the beat that followed, the silence felt so loaded, she wondered if calling him had been the right thing to do at all. If she might be pressing on that ancient bruise of his after all. She opened her mouth to apologise, or take it back, or change the subject, when his voice tumbled into her ear.

"Why, Emerson Francesca Adler, that's damn fantastic news."

Emerson looked up at the dark sky and beamed, fizzy joy settling over her. "I know, right?"

Holden chuckled, enjoying her enjoyment. Which was nice. For all that the news was amazing, sharing it, with someone who understood, made it feel more real. While the sound of his laughter—deep and intimate—skittered down her arms, the sides of her torso, along her ticklish spots just above her hip bones.

"Hold up. How do you know my middle name?"

A beat. "Has it come up?"

"It has not."

"I can see it written down. Emerson Francesca Adler." His voice sounded a little faraway, as if he was tracing her name in the air. "I remember thinking it sounded like a character from an old movie. But when? It'll come to me." A moment, then, "Do you remember those mornings we both found ourselves stuck in the hall outside the guidance counsellor's office?"

Did she remember? Ha. Ha-ha-ha-ha-ha.

"Ancient Mrs Carmichael, on the front desk, had us check our medical histories constantly. One time she accidentally gave me yours."

Emerson remembered. She could feel the heat rushing into her cheeks as he'd leaned towards her, holding out the page, holding eye contact, with that gorgeous smile on his gorgeous face, as if it was happening in real time.

"I handed it straight over…after reading the first few lines," said Holden, when Emerson remained unable to say words. "The big question is, did you do the same? Or did you take the chance to read about all my many stupid feats that led to many broken bones?"

"Of course not."

"Ah. So you were a good girl," he extrapolated.

Nope. She'd simply realised all too late what she'd held in her hand.

"I was always more curious than I was careful," Holden said. "Got me into trouble. But served me when it needed to. On that note, I'm taking you to dinner. News such as yours requires celebration."

Emerson's mouth popped open but no sounds came out. She'd avoided his lunch requests, blowing them off as a bit of a running joke. But dinner? Dinner leaned precariously close to a date-type encounter.

Maybe she could look at it as a business meeting. Maybe she could drill him for info. He had worked for the Sanderson family before, after all... No. She couldn't. *Wouldn't* ask it of him. Not even that little.

"You okay over there?" he asked, a smile in his voice. "I can hear the wheels cranking again. If you're concerned this is my way of chipping away at my favour owed, it's not. Heck, you can even pay if you'd like, just so you can be sure."

She couldn't help but laugh. "Magnanimous of you."

"Mmm. The celebration is a handy excuse, for the truth is, I would like to take you to dinner. I'd really like to see you again."

"Oh," she said on a sigh, then bit her lip to stop any more telling sounds from slipping out.

Holden Roarke wanted to see her again. And she wanted to see him too. Texting had given her a fix, but it wasn't enough. She'd started to miss that face. Miss how he looked at her, as if he liked what he saw. So much the thought of seeing him again made her feel light-headed.

Pumpkin had spent the day at home as the neighbour's university-aged daughter, Kerri, was using Emmy's sunny back sitting room to study. Kerri—who had grown up next door to Pumpkin, and house-sat if Emerson was away—had sent her usual babysitting proof-of-life picture, so Emerson didn't need to rush home.

But this couldn't be about convenience. What if she was wrong about Holden? Again? What if he was a flirty, enthusiastic, bored guy who enjoyed hanging out with her, but that was it? What if she was reliving the exact same arc as before?

Frantically swiping her card over the sensor and pulling the door open when she heard the latch unlock, she thought, *This is different*. But the only thing she could be sure of was that when he left this time, he'd say goodbye first.

"Emmy?"

"Thank you for the offer. But my mind is still spinning with ideas, and I want to get them all down before they fly off into the ether."

His outshot of breath made her wonder if his disappointment matched her own. "You've got this, Emmy. Remember, you're not the only one who's just made an excellent alliance. Chuck has too."

Emmy closed her eyes as she leaned her forehead on the cold metal door. "I'm at my parking garage and am about to lose reception, so... I'd better go."

She stepped through the door and into the dark. And just before the sensor lights flickered on, and she lost reception, Holden's voice washed over her, "Goodnight, Emmy."

She walked up the ramp to her car, their conversation playing over and over in her head. Until something he'd said snagged on something.

More careful than curious. That was how he'd described her, after a fashion.

When it came to clients, she was gung-ho, asking questions until she knew more about them—their motivations, their goals, their fears—than they did about themselves.

But when it came to her personal life she did hold back, having built big, strong firewalls around herself, and only giving a select few the password.

She pressed the remote to unlock her car as a flutter of melancholy overcame her. Somewhere along the way the young woman who had been hungry enough to start her own company had become so personally risk adverse she couldn't even allow herself to have dinner with a man she liked, just in case.

In case what? In case he didn't like her? In case he did? In case he stayed, and stuck by her, and she grew truly used to having him in her life, and *then* something bad happened? Because, according to the Heartache List, something bad always happened.

But if Holden didn't deserve his place on that list, after all, then his name wasn't a threat to that terrifying *Heartache Number Nine* slot that she so adamantly refused to fill.

The only person holding her back these days, was her.

CHAPTER SEVEN

THE NEXT MORNING, the second Emmy's eyes popped open she felt wide awake. Cleansed. Refreshed. As if she'd broken through some mental barrier.

This whole time she'd been telling herself that spending *any* time with Holden proved how much she'd grown beyond the Heartache List. For hadn't she survived a dinner, and a few cheeky texts, without a) accidentally falling in love with him, and b) having her heart broken?

So what? What did that prove? Only that *she was being too careful.*

She'd been half-hearted. If she really wanted to see where she stood, she needed to use her whole heart. So to speak.

Once at work, she waited till her teams were busy with the Sanderson brief, then, feeling tremendously determined while also slightly sick to the stomach, she punched Holden's number into her work phone and put it on speaker.

He answered, short of breath, "Hey."

"You're running," she said.

"That I am."

He's a runner, remember? Abort! Abort!

"Should I call back?" she asked.

"You can call me anytime you want. But I'm

okay to talk now, so long as you don't mind me huffing and puffing in your ear."

Emerson lifted a finger to her mouth and nibbled on the end of her fingernail as she dealt with the image that put in her head. "Something you said last night has been playing on my mind."

"Which part?"

I really want to see you again. No, *not* that. Though it had been playing on her mind. On a loop. So much so she might have even considered going for a run herself so as to shake it off, till she remembered she didn't own running shoes.

"First things first, do you know how much longer you'll be in town?"

"I do not." A beat, then, "But I have no imminent plans to leave just yet."

"Great."

"I'm glad you think so."

Warmth fluttered in her belly, reminding her that she was dealing with a guy who didn't go for lines, or games. *No pretending required.* "What does your calendar look like at the moment?"

"Is that your way of asking *me* to dinner?"

"It's my way of finding out your movements before seeing if we might implement the next phase of our...deal."

"There's a next phase?"

"There could be."

"Intriguing. Sending it to you now."

Her phone pinged, with an invitation to add

Holden Roarke's calendar to her own. A shimmer shot through her at the intimacy that suggested. The trust.

Rather than battening down the hatches, she followed her newly unleashed curiosity, opened his calendar, and found herself surprised to see that it was rather impressive. Especially for a guy who considered himself "retired". "Is this for real?"

He laughed. "Turns out I'm not just a pretty face. I have skills and people are keen to hear about those skills. And, since I am a generous soul, I am willing to share those skills, for the right price."

"So, you're a mercenary," she asked as she continued scrolling through his calendar, some in bold—booked—many more in italics—possibilities. Her heart stuttered when she saw their old school listed as a possibility. And she remembered Phillip's assertion that he picked and chose who he charged.

"East Kew High School is willing to pay you the big bucks to give a talk on… Youth Entrepreneurship?" she said.

"So many bucks."

Emmy sat back in her chair, distracted from her original plan. Something Holden was extremely adept at making happen. "I don't believe you."

"That's your prerogative."

"Does it bother you that people write you off as some sort of rich, easy-going, playboy type?"

"What people? Have you been reading up on me, Ms Adler?"

"I took a photo of you in case I went missing. I've introduced you to my dog. Yes, I've read up on you. It was the only safe thing to do."

He hummed into her ear, the sound doing things to her the huffing and puffing had not. "Good for you. As to your query, people hear 'retired in his twenties' and think I spend most of my days living on a beach somewhere being served pina coladas by nubile young women in bikinis."

She looked again at the list of groups he was speaking with, mostly small groups rather than corporate gigs. As if he really was an honestly generous soul. "Why don't you? No judgement, it sounds pretty fabulous."

"You are brimming with judgement, Emerson Adler."

Emerson rolled her neck. "A little bit."

"I imagine," Holden went on, "that when you go on a beach holiday, you book tours and naps and food stops down to the minute."

"That's what you imagine when you picture me on a beach holiday?" A slight pause, to let that sink in. Then, "I'm disappointed in you, Holden. I'd have thought you more imaginative."

She felt a wind of change, as if it swept over them both.

"I'm disappointed in myself," he said, his voice

low, confidential. "You said something I said has been playing on your mind?"

She had? "I did. Here's my thinking. Since you are sticking around a little longer than expected, and the chances of me coming up with a favour as huge, as mighty, as worthy as the one I did for you are slim, how do you feel about chipping away at it instead? A series of…mini favours, if you like?"

"Such as?"

"Nothing comes to mind, just yet. But it will."

"And if I have a small favour I need to add to the tally?"

It might take longer to redress the imbalance. "Bring it. Only fair."

"I'm liking the sound of this. And when the tally is finally even? What then? Phase Three?" Holden suggested.

"Sure. Let's go with that."

"Okay then. I await your next call with bated breath."

"Super. Enjoy your run, Holden."

Emerson reached out and pressed the button to end the call, her hands moving to cover her mouth. Then she started to laugh.

This was going to be fun. Or terrible. It was going to be something, which, after years of living within a very tight bandwidth, felt as if the lid had just opened on a box she hadn't known she'd been living in, letting in fresh air and sunshine.

And possibility.

* * *

"I need to get to work but I'm parked in," Emerson blurted, while standing by her car one morning to find a moving truck had parked halfway across her skinny driveway.

"Give me ten," Holden said, arriving in eight in a black convertible. With track pants and running top doing a terrible job of hiding a killer body beneath.

"What's with the new car?" she asked, trying not to stare at his arms. And the veins roping towards his wrists.

"I might take a run down the coast later. Better this than a sedan. Get in."

She did. Twisting like a pretzel in order to deal with the confined space.

Biting her tongue when Holden rested his hand on the gearstick, his little finger mere millimetres from the bare thigh showing beneath her pencil skirt.

Holding her breath when she glanced sideways right when he did the same, catching his eye, sharing smiles that seemed filled with some illicit promise. As if this was the beginning of something.

"Free for lunch?" he asked when he dropped her off, the engine still running while she slid from the car.

"I thought you were going for a drive down the coast."

He levelled her with a look. "Changed my mind. Lunch?"

"Sure," she said, feeling a sweeping sense of inevitability rock through her. "The place across the road. One o'clock. You're paying."

"You're on." He grinned and she felt it, like little spot fires all over her body.

Freya asked if she was feeling okay when she hopped out of the lift, ten minutes late, her cheeks still warm, the scent of him lingering on her clothes. "You look flushed. Feverish. Should I call a doctor?"

"I'm fine," Emerson said, laughing. Before hotfooting it to her office, where she slumped in her chair and fanned herself with a stapler.

"I need a tie," Holden said.

When Emerson showed up at his new digs—a town house not all that far from her place—it was to find him getting dressed for a keynote speech he was giving that night. Dark grey suit pants, beautifully cut, hugged his legs, his feet were bare and he was yet to put on a shirt.

"Really?" she said, trying to look anywhere bar the sculpted wonder that was his chest.

"What?"

She lifted the bag in her hand to cover the view.

Holden looked down and his abs flexed. "Please. You'd see more of me at the beach."

The thought of seeing more of him had her swallowing. Hard.

He noticed. His grin widened.

Emerson chose to pretend it hadn't happened, and said, "I think we've established I'm not a beach person. More a laze-on-a-chair-by-the-pool person, while slathered in sunscreen, and wearing a big hat, under a huge umbrella."

"I'll remember that. If we ever find ourselves, at a beach, together." He said it as if it was a throwaway comment. But somehow it also felt like a promise. Like a plan. As if this wasn't some temporary deal they were seeing through before he went back to his real life.

"Hurry up," she said, shooing him away. "Put your shirt on, or you'll be late."

Trying not to stare at his gorgeous back, all muscle and warm skin and, *Oh, Mama*, she followed him down the hall. Then found herself in his bedroom. Where he kept his bed.

Expensive-looking sheets—no shock there—in shades of caramel and cream, lay tousled on the huge mattress. No blanket or comforter, for the man ran hot. A pair of pillows lay at one end, smushed and askew. As if he slept on one and hugged the other.

"What do you think?" he asked.

Emerson dragged her eyes from the bed, and the endearing yet aphrodisiacal story it told, to find him standing in front of a mirror holding up different shirts. Both snow-white.

She found the three ties she'd picked up at the boutique near work on her way over. Red, blue to match his eyes, and silver.

He chose the silver.

She rolled her eyes as she sat. "No ability to spin a line, and no sense of colour. Sigh."

He met her eyes in the mirror as he slowly did up the buttons on his shirt. Smiling eyes. Eyes that liked the fact that she was perched on the end of his bed. She popped up like a Jack in the box.

"Wanna come see me talk tonight?" he asked.

"I can see you talk anytime. Look at us now. Talking."

"'Tis true. But this is different. This will be me being erudite. And lauded. There may even be clapping afterwards. You never clap after I speak. It's quite the thing."

"Then, sure. That I have to see."

So she went to watch him speak to a room filled with IT types, after he made sure to snag her a seat at a table with friendly people. And he was brilliant and articulate, but also charming and warm, exactly the same man that he was when it was just the two of them.

No surprise, then, that, while a fair bit went over Emerson's head, the crowd lapped it up. She joined them in the standing ovation. And somehow, in the dark of the crowd, his eyes found hers.

And he smiled. Smiled as he breathed out, a long, slow breath.

Oh, no, a voice inside her intoned, as the sense of sweeping that had been buffeting her for days swept over her so hard, so fast, it was a miracle she managed to keep her feet.

But by then, it was too late.

The next time Emmy had plans to see Camille, Holden finally took that drive down the coast road.

It was something he liked to do on occasion, just get in the car and go. Top of the car down, the wind in his hair, the engine rumbling beneath him. It satisfied the primal need to escape he'd never quite outgrown.

He'd been driving this very road when he'd had the idea for the app that had started it all. A virtual study app. Uni friends, Phillip included, had been his beta testers, before universities the world over had got wind of it and bought the app, making him a fortune. Ironic that its success had seen him never finish his degree, and not see those guys again for years.

He remembered the moment he'd realised that app might be something special. A magic trick that could yank him out of the state of impoverishment in which he'd grown up. He'd pictured himself finally having access to everything he'd wished he'd had as a kid—shelter, money, ease. And he'd been right.

What he'd not expected was the number of people who came begging, acquaintances, distant relatives, complete strangers—all after a handout, a leg-up, a crumb. The shine had worn off pretty quick, as soon he'd grown wary. His life was now littered with the detritus of those who'd pretended to be on his side, only to expect something in return.

Malaise set in. Loneliness. So he kept on moving, finding more out-of-the-way places, ends of the earth, depths of nowhere, as if standing still would be spitting in the face of his good fortune.

Until he built the next app. New levels of mania ensued. Bidding wars for his next app, unseen, undreamt. So was his new pattern. Build it up, then leave it behind. All the while chasing that feeling he'd felt while driving this road—dreaming what it might be like to get everything he'd ever wished for.

Till the day he'd woken up in Amsterdam, to a middle-of-the-night phone call, and realised he'd been chasing something that wasn't real. Something that would never satisfy him, even if it was.

An app functioned, or it didn't. It served a purpose, or it didn't. Success, on that score, was clearcut. After the Sanderson debacle, he pared back, stopped wanting what it was clear he'd never have. And soon found balance that suited him.

Noisy Work—launching the occasional new app to applause and accolades and loud congratulations—which drowned out any interest in his Quiet Work—behind the scenes, sometimes anonymous, helping create frameworks for medical research, education reform, universal health care.

In order to protect that balance, his friendship groups, the people he trusted, had become restricted, or short-lived.

While unrecognisable from the life he'd dreamt of, the one people ironically thought he enjoyed, and the gruelling life he'd once known, he'd found it perfectly fulfilling.

Until Emerson Adler had come along and any feelings of fulfilment had gone out the window.

The woman confused the heck out of him.

She'd made it all too clear she wanted nothing from him, which was unbelievably refreshing. Except those times she was outright demanding something of him. Where he'd found most people obscure to a fault, she was black and white. That he had to respect.

Then there was the attraction, a living, breathing thing that was becoming harder to contain. He could have kissed her a thousand times. And he knew, if he had, it wouldn't be the end of it. He'd still want to kiss her a thousand times more.

If Joel, his business manager, who knew enough about where he'd come from, had a single clue that he was here because of a woman, he'd have laughed till he split his spleen. His wife, Jenny, would likely burst into happy tears.

Infamously impervious Holden Roarke taken down by a bolshie brunette with a penchant for asking hard questions and sweet old dogs. And he had been taken down. Brought to his knees.

He wasn't sleeping. He had little room for ideas in his head that didn't involve ways to invent a favour he might ask or perform. And he had left behind a perfectly liveable penthouse so that he could rent a place, short-term, in the suburbs.

All so that he might be near to her.

Treading lightly all the while. His instincts assured him that was necessary. For all her big talk, there was something wildly delicate about Emerson Adler. Uncertain. Skittish.

Which was the only way he was able to stop himself from telling her how much he wanted to touch her, to hold her, to kiss her, to make love to her, to wake up beside her and do it all over again. This was the one time in his life where he had to be more careful than he was curious.

And so, rather than enjoying a delicious, torrid affair with a woman he found utterly captivating, before heading back to Stockholm or the Seychelles, or wherever the first plane he found might take him, he'd found himself in the midst of an old-fashioned courting.

And he couldn't get enough of it.

Yep. The woman confused the heck out of him.

Holden hung a left, leaving the beach huts behind and spinning up into the hills.

This he could measure. This he could enjoy without censure or self-recrimination. To be out here, midweek, while others plugged away at their office jobs, he knew himself to be a very lucky man.

He would relish these spoils of his success, before the rubber band wrapped around his heart no doubt sent him thwacking all the way back to her.

At the same time, back in Melbourne, Emerson found Camille in the succulent section of Wild Willow Plant Nursery.

"Sorry I'm late!" said Emmy. "Heck of a morning. The family next door used their new barbecue and set off my smoke alarms. And you know how Pumpkin gets with smoke alarms. Then, would you believe I had a flat tyre?"

Camille looked at Emerson's white-on-white ensemble. "Not even slightly. You should have called me. Turns out I'm now amazing with a wrench!"

"Good to know," she said. "Anyway, I called Holden, but he's off on some joy ride, so I got onto the auto club, and here I am!"

Camille's eyes widened comically. "Back up. You called *Holden*? As in Holden Roarke? As in *Heartache Number Four*?"

Emerson blinked. "Um—"

"No," said Camille, turning away, holding up a dramatic shushing hand. "I get it. I've been replaced."

"What? No!" Emerson insisted, even while she felt prickly heat swoosh into her cheeks. "Holden is... Well, we've been doing these favours for one another, you see."

When Camille clearly didn't see, Emerson gave her a quick, awkward rundown of the past few weeks. Then added, "Serendipitous timing, really, as I can't keep relying on you because you're busy, you're on your homey-moon, Phillip is your person now—"

Camille reached out and took Emerson's hands. "Stop. Breathe. I get it. It's been weird, right? This new normal?"

Emerson nodded, and smiled, relieved to be talking this out rather than shoving it down deep inside. "But getting less weird. Don't you think?"

Camille nodded, eyes a little bright. Then pointed towards the outdoor plant section before ambling that way. "So, these favours of yours. You do realise this is basically how being a couple works. You drive him somewhere, he picks up your laundry. It's a relationship without the sex. Unless... Unless this is some long-term, stretch-things-out-until-you-feel-you-might-die mode of foreplay."

Emerson, who was sniffing the leaves of a velvety plant, stilled. A lightbulb, then a thousand more, like wild, out-of-control fairy lights, were springing to life inside her head. "Oh, my."

"I knew it!" Camille spun on the spot.

"Unless—"

"Here we go."

"Unless I'm right back where I was all those years ago, feeling all these feelings and he just thinks I'm his cute little hallway friend."

"You're not cute."

"That's what you took from that?"

"Honeybun, you're *va-va-voom*. So maybe he thinks of you as his *va-va-voom* little hallway friend."

Emerson shot Camille a look. "Not helping."

"Then *ask* him! Or better yet, jump him. Either way it's gotta be better than being wound so tight."

"I'm not wound tight."

"You know what? You actually don't look it, either. What's with that?"

"I have endeavoured to make sure I don't implode with all the pent-up, built-up, you know… Let's just say Holden Roarke is mighty good fantasy material."

Camille held up a hand for a high five, which Emerson duly gave up.

"Wow. This is some huge progress you've made. Like day-one-in-therapy-then-fast-forward-to-graduation-level progress."

Emerson agreed. This was *exactly* what she'd

been hoping for when she'd allowed herself to enjoy being with Holden, rather than constantly waiting for the other shoe to drop. "I do feel like a stronger, more evolved version of myself. More... open to possibility."

"By possibility do you mean giving your vibrator a night off, dragging Holden Roarke into your bed for some good old-fashioned rumpy-pumpy?"

Emerson smiled at the grey-haired couple who gawped at them as they meandered by. "Maybe. Though without the old-fashioned bit."

Camille stopped in the middle of the aisle, sunlight dappling her face through the leaves of a row of potted palms. "Just so long as you don't forget, this is Holden Roarke."

"Meaning?"

"From what Phillip has told me—and he's told me a lot, because he is semi in love with the guy—Holden is not a stay-at-home-and-watch-true-crime-documentaries kind of man. He's a big deal. So, for all that you're having fun now, there's a really good chance he'll be heading back to his real life soon. And you... Well, you do know that people leaving you is your kryptonite. It's kind of a running theme in the... You Know List."

"I know," said Emerson.

And she did. She really did.

She still had his calendar linked to hers. Saw the eye-popping lists of people his business manager, an excitable-sounding guy named Joel, added to his "maybe" calendar—the majority of them overseas, in places like Geneva and Washington and Dubai. All of which had been crossed through, because Holden was here.

Still, hearing Camille say it sent little impacts all over her body. Like buckshot—not enough to take her down, but enough for it to sting.

Then Camille clicked her fingers. "Unless… Unless you're doing this because you *know* he'll leave. You're fooling around with him *because* there's an end point. That's genius!"

Emerson moved on, towards the fern section, Camille's theory running through her head. Maybe there was something to that too. A safety net to her experiment. Was that such a bad thing? "You make me sound so mercenary."

Camille shrugged. "You do you, boo. And, hey, when he does vamoose, after unlocking the wanton, voracious, cavalier side we all know is lurking beneath your pristine façade, I still have that list of Phillip's friends, who would ask you out in a heartbeat if only they weren't terrified of you."

"I'll keep that in mind," Emerson deadpanned. "So…plants!"

"Plants!"

While Camille talked up her idea of a wall of hanging plants in her tiny lounge, as inspired by some random Instagrammer with a much bigger house, Emmy nodded along, and tried not to think about Holden leaving, in actuality, and what that might feel like. Not having him at the end of the phone. Not being able to see him whenever the fancy took her.

And those thoughts set some small, dangerous thing alight deep inside her.

Not an ache. Nothing quite so blunt. More the sharp, painful constancy of an accidental burn.

That was the thing about burns, the small ones that travelled slowly through dry scrub. If not doused soon, a wind might whip up and soon the whole forest would burn to the ground.

"That's an A380." One eye open, Holden held his finger to the sky, tracing the underbelly of the plane as it lifted into the darkening dusk over their heads, heading to destinations unknown.

"How can you tell?" Emerson asked, while busy poking and prodding at the pile of soft blankets and cushions Holden had thrown in the back of the ute after trading it for his rental convertible.

"I know my planes," he said.

Giving up on perfection, she leaned back on her elbows, and squinted up at the plane as it lifted higher into the sky. "A man of hidden skills."

"Not so hidden, I hope. In fact, perhaps I ought to write them all down on a list, carry them on my person, so that any time people are in need of one of my many skills I can whip it out."

"Lists can be helpful." Her mouth twitched before her head turned his way. The dying rays of sunlight spilled over the dark waves of her hair, the delicate edge of her face, her shoulder. "Whip it out, you say?"

"At any time," he offered. "For the benefit of the community."

"For an ideas man, some of your ideas are whackadoo."

"The download numbers of my apps tell a different story."

"Over-confidence is not an attractive trait."

Holden's grin hit his face before he even felt it coming. "Not in my experience."

Emerson scoffed, but didn't argue the fact. Instead, she once more became preoccupied with getting comfortable.

For all that watching her wriggle about in a bed of blankets and cushions may not have been the smartest idea for a man who was struggling not to spook her by hauling her into his arms and kissing her senseless, he felt rather good about his decision to bring her.

Their arrival at their current location—an aircraft viewing spot in Greenvale—had come about due to his latest favour request.

Andy, another friend from uni, worked for Australian air traffic control. Nearing the end of a major software update, they were keen to get his input on how to make the interface less spartan, and more user-friendly.

Emerson had called the night before, asking

for a favour. One of her staff, an older, rather sophisticated gent, was having a birthday and could Holden recommend a unique gift? He'd agreed to pick something up—a signed Graham Greene book he'd spotted in a vintage store near hers— if she'd come along to a meeting as a second pair of eyes.

Partly because he had learned that spending time with her was better than not, and partly because the thought of spending any time in the bowels of the airport where his father had worked on and off his whole childhood did not entice.

Now—wriggling as if she had ants in the pants of the classy, black, all-in-one get-up that she had going on—she got her high heels caught in a blanket and it took her a good ten seconds to get free. Then she flapped a wild hand at some bug—real or imagined—that had wafted too close to her face. And huffed. Loudly.

"We can go," said Holden, not minding what they did, so long as he got to watch her do it. "If this isn't your thing."

"No! This is lovely. Really. It's…"

She looked at him a moment, her gaze a little hot, colour sweeping into her cheeks, and he felt the word *romantic* whisper on the breeze.

In the end, she went with, "Fine. If I wasn't here, I'd probably have taken Pumpkin into the office, as there is so much work to do on the Sanderson job, which is brilliant, but also a lot. My assistant, Freya—you'd have spoken to her on the phone a couple of times in the early days—sends me memes daily about ways to relax. If I tell her I lie out under the stars, on a pile of blankets, in the middle of nowhere, she'll be beside herself."

"Well, so long as you're excited to be here…"

Her grin was quick and intoxicating. The urge to stroke his thumb over that full bottom lip, to watch her eyes flash with surprise, then turn dark with longing, was a strong one. The certainty that it would change everything between them hovered on the air. Ripe and sweet.

The way her chest lifted and fell, he was sure she could feel it too. But then she lay back, and placed her hands over her chest like some kind of beatific painting. It was so damned endearing his chest hurt.

He was a goner. Truly.

With no planes in the sky, the great dome above having quickly turned dark, they watched in companionable silence as wispy clouds wafted by, blocking out the crescent moon, before wafting on again.

Emerson sighed, the sound warmed by a kind of contentment that Holden felt in his bones. "I've lived in Melbourne all my life and I never knew this was a thing."

"It's a favourite haunt of mine."

"You came here as a kid?"

"Mmm," he said. It hadn't been a thing to do,

it had been a safe space, a lifesaver. "I grew up out this way."

"Really?" She lifted back to her elbows, and glanced around, taking in the great tracts of farmland. "It's lovely."

"This is. Where we were was near enough to the airport for the plane noise to be a daily grind, not near enough to live on more than a postage stamp of land in dilapidated council housing."

"You and your dad?"

"Mmm. See that farm over there," he said, pointing over her shoulder to an undulating patch of shadowy forest green across the way. "It's a retirement home for ex-racehorses, including a few Melbourne Cup winners."

He knew she hadn't been fooled by his clumsy distraction. He only liked her more when she went with it. "Oh! That's wonderful. They get to live out their days frolicking through acres of lush pastures. Far better than the alternative."

"When they 'go to the farm', they actually go to the farm."

"Groan."

When he laughed, she lay back and smiled up into the sky. Now he wanted to trace the line of her nose, her chin, her collarbone. What was happening to him? It was like he was sixteen again, seeing a girl, liking a girl, not knowing what to do with a girl.

"So, if you grew up out this way, how did you

end up in high school in Kew? And for such a brief stint?"

"You noticed that, did you?"

Her mouth twisted. "We had matching guidance counsellor sessions every single week. When you didn't show up one week, or ever again, I noticed."

Holden squinted up into the sky. "Why don't you tell me more about the memes this assistant of yours sends—are they the types you find on inspirational calendars, all bordered in flowers? Or more along the black and white dirge line?"

She turned fully on her side, her hands tucked under her head. And said nothing. He knew it cost her—the girl with all the questions—but she held her tongue.

Holden breathed out hard. "I'd call you pushy, in the hopes of sending you spiralling off in another direction, but I get the feeling you'd take it as a compliment."

He tipped his head, and found himself looking into Emerson's curious eyes. Her lovely face, her warm body all curled up beside his. Happy to listen if he wanted to talk, or to simply be with him if he didn't. As if she wanted nothing from him bar what he was willing to give.

It cost her nothing to be that way, yet it didn't feel like nothing. In fact, it felt closer to a continental shift. If he hadn't been lying down, he might have had to reach out for something to grip.

"Change of subject," she said. "Your airport friend's proposal. It's a huge project. My advice? Don't say yes unless you see yourself surrendering to it for the next eighteen months to two years. Can you? Can you see yourself sticking to one thing for that long?"

The question was simple. And yet… That was the second time she'd asked him how long he was sticking around. Which was not an accident. Did it indicate she had a vested interest in his answer?

The continental shift cracked open a fraction wider.

When he didn't answer she huffed out a breath. Of frustration? Then she reached out blindly, grabbed a fluffy cushion and brought it to her chest. "Where on earth did you find all this stuff?"

Finally, a question he could answer. "I may have called Camille last night to ask where I might find such frippery at short notice. After two of the longest minutes of my life, in which I was asked a barrage of questions far more brazen than even you dare ask, she sent me to some frou-frou boutique. Apparently 'the plan' is that she's happy to take it all off my hands for the new house when we're done here tonight."

"She is industrious," Emmy said, with a quick smile. Then he could feel her mulling over her next words. "So, you called Camille before I called you. Meaning you were already planning this before I agreed to come. I can either assume you always liked being surrounded by pretty cushions when watching planes, or—" She breathed in, breathed out, and said, "Or you did all this for me. Knowing, somehow, how very much I needed a break."

"Sprung," he said. He smiled, she smiled back, and he felt it like an arrow in his chest fired at close range. "When I was working on my first app, I turned into a madman, locked away in my dark tower, hunched over my work, squinting if I ever accidentally stumbled into the light."

"Like Quasimodo?"

"Ah, I think you mean Batman."

"He has a cave, not a tower."

"Can't you let a man dream?"

She lifted her fingers in submission. "Dream away."

Then she turned to face the sky as a plane began its descent up high over their heads, her eyes tracking the slow movement of the big, metallic beast.

While Holden's fingertips pressed into his chest.

Dream away, she'd said. When his wish was to reach out, and cup her cheek. Or sweep that rogue lock of hair behind her ear. Or tell her that if he didn't kiss her, soon, he might literally expire, and his disappearance would be on her hands.

Unfortunately, his talk of not being able to spin

a line had not been a line. Meaning all he could do was tell her the truth.

"First time I came here I was fifteen," he said. "Too young for a licence, I stole my father's car. He'd just finished telling me how worthless I was, and passed out drunk. I drove and drove, with no destination in mind, only slowing when I saw a dozen-odd cars lined up in the field here, right as a plane flew low overhead. I pulled onto the hard shoulder, the noise of the thing filling my head. My panic slowly abated, as plane after plane headed off into the wild blue yonder. My dream, as it was, from that day on, was to one day be up there, heading far, far away from here."

He squinted at the first stars hovering above the horizon.

"A few weeks later, next time my dad passed out drunk, I packed up my stuff and left. My great-aunt lived in Kew—she let me stay with her so long as I kept going to school. Counselling meant I could attend without guardian approval. Then one day my dad turned up at his aunt's place with a cricket bat and a slur. I've been on the move pretty much ever since."

She was quiet for a few long beats, before she said, "Why do you think he was like that?"

"According to him, everything that went wrong in his life began the moment I was born. My mother died in childbirth, so there was some truth to it. Made it hard to disassociate that from his drinking, his anger, his self-pity."

"How does a man like that end up with a son like you?"

His chest squeezed, the hollowness that had lived behind his ribs for so long pressed so tight it nearly popped. "So, you're saying I'm *not* worthless," he said, turning his head and adding a smile to soften the joke.

She lay back on her side, watching him, her brow furrowed. As if, if the man was still alive today she'd take a swing.

He adored her for it. This beautiful, challenging, skittish, intense creature who made him work for every smile, every laugh, every drop of trust. Made him dig deep. And speak truth.

He *adored* her.

It was the only thing that made any sense. For the way he felt, had been feeling these past weeks, was nothing he'd ever felt before. It was as wholesome as it was raw. As comforting and gentle as it was a roar in the back of his head, thunder behind his ribs, a pressing and constant need that lived and roiled at his centre, all of which was held back by the barest thread of civility.

This woman he'd never even kissed.

It was past time he did something about that.

"Emmy," he said. "Emerson." Then he reached out for her. Slowly. So she knew what was coming. As if she couldn't hear it in the raw scrape of his voice. The clawing need.

Giving her time to make it clear if this wasn't what she wanted. But, gods, he hoped it was. Hoped more than he remembered hoping for anything since he'd last been here, hoping something up there might be the answer to making his life better down here.

His fingers slid through her hair, the strands falling over his hands like heavy silk. He exhaled with relief, as it felt as if he'd been waiting for this exact moment all his life.

He cradled her gently, his thumb tracing her cheekbone, as he moved in. Caught by the heat in her eyes. By the soft catch in her breath.

When he was close enough for their lips to almost touch, he paused. Took a moment to sink into the anticipation, grateful it was finally at an end. Or was this the beginning?

And then he kissed her.

When their lips met, she sighed, as if she'd been imagining this moment as long as he had. As if she too had been holding on for dear life and could finally let go.

When he tilted her face, so he could deepen the kiss, she opened to him, swept her tongue against his, and he was lost.

Lost to heat and need. And regret. Regret that they'd waited. And joy. Joy that they'd waited. That this moment had finally come, with the starlight raining down upon her face, as she scooted closer and wrapped herself around him, and met his kisses with her own, in this bed of blankets he'd built for her.

"Holden," she said, coming up for air. Looking into his eyes, searching.

Whatever she saw there, things soon turned frantic, desperate. As if they were trying to find a way into one another's skin.

She rolled on top of him, kissing him madly, even as her hands reached for his shirt, tugging it free of his jeans. When her hands found skin they slowed, tracing his sides with deliberation and pace, sending the painful prick of a million goosebumps racing all over his body. And it was a miracle it wasn't all over for him, then and there.

When his hands mirrored her pace, sliding slowly up her thighs, her whole body seemed to sing.

She rocked against him, setting off explosions behind his eyes, as she plied him with drugging kisses—

A car door slammed. And Holden remembered where they were.

"Emmy," he said, the word playing against her mouth.

She hummed, and rolled against him again.

With supernatural strength Holden rolled her over, till he was on top, his thigh between hers. He pressed down. Her eyes rolled back in her head, her front teeth bearing down on her bottom lip.

He gritted out, "We have company."

Her eyes flew open, her hands gripping his messed-up shirt as she lifted her head to look over his shoulder.

Glancing back, he saw a dad and three young kids pile out of a station wagon, holding apples and juice boxes, before piling into the boot when the dad opened the rear door, clearly about to set up for an evening of plane-watching at the popular spot.

Holden quickly sat up, fixed his shirt, tossed a blanket over his junk. The dad gave him a quick nod, and a wave, as if he remembered how it felt to be young and so caught up in another you forgot who you were.

Not *who* you were, where you were.

Holden was very aware of who he was—a guy whose dad would never have taken him on an "outing" such as this. Never packed him a juice box. Or told him to eat an apple. He'd offered cigarettes, drink, a kick in the backside as he shoved him out the door of a morning, telling him not to come back unless he had money in his pocket.

"Oh, my God," said Emerson, her hand flopping over her eyes. "Can you imagine if they'd been a few minutes later?"

"Whatever do you mean?" he asked, moving

gently, so as not to damage himself, even as his mind spun. "Explain it to me. In lurid detail."

She laughed, the sound bright and light. And gorgeous. A sound he could listen to for ever and never tire of it.

His earlier musings lurked, like a virus—who was he to think of forever? His first real attempt at such a life with the Sandersons had been disastrous. All these years later he still hadn't learned how to settle into a life that required a fixed address. He had no clue what *home* even meant.

"Why did it take us so damn long to do that?" Emerson asked.

"You tell me."

She tipped her head to face him, so utterly gorgeous it hurt. "Should I be asking you to forget that too? It was miles outside the boundaries of our agreement after all."

Holden's jaw twitched hard enough to crack a tooth. He said, "You can ask. But then, you'd also have to ask me to forget about how much you wanted to kiss me when I dropped you to your hotel room after the wedding."

Her mouth fell open.

"Or how much I wanted to kiss you on the garden bench after dinner at the Sandersons'. Then again when I dropped you home that night. And when you brought me those ties. I can go on."

"Mmm," she said, stretching like a cat who'd got the cream.

That was neither a yes nor a no, which, as far as Holden could see, was progress. Progressing towards what, he had no idea. All he knew was that it was going in a direction that felt right.

Then she shivered. For the night had turned cold.

"Come on," he said, climbing off the back of the tray, and holding out a hand. "Let's get you home."

Home he took her. And at home he left her. After a chaste kiss at her door. A press of his lips on hers that lasted a breath or two. A kiss that left her looking dreamy and soft as she floated inside her house, her voice already calling for her dog, as if she had a story to tell.

While Holden took the throws and cushions back to the town house he was renting.

He'd buy Camille a voucher to get her own.

CHAPTER EIGHT

EMERSON HOPPED OUT of her ride share, juggling a large gift bag, a bottle of wine, and her phone. And looked, in marvel, at the changes her friends had made to their new home.

The garden bed was new, lined with little stones and boasting a string of tiny plants poking out of mounds of bark, much of which must have been done earlier that day by the team of friends and colleagues who'd turned up early for the Working Bee, Beer, and Barbecue extravaganza.

Emmy had been invited, of course, but Camille had followed up with:

do not show up before the after-party begins the rest of the day will be backbreaking love you!

With the new fence and Camille's beloved fairy lights strung along the front porch, it all looked so pretty. So very much theirs. Those bittersweet pickled feelings threatened to rise up inside Emmy again, only this time she was able to still them. For it was all okay. She was okay. They'd all be okay.

"Emmy!" cried Bernadette, Camille's lovely young cousin, when she opened the door. Dust in her hair, a scratch on her cheek, she wiped a

hand down her old overalls before pulling Emmy
in for a hug.

"Emmy's here!" she cried.

The crowd turned as one and called out,
"Emmy!" before going back to their conversations, while Bernie took the gift bag from Emmy
and popped it with the pile in the corner of the
lounge.

"Did you hear?" Bernie asked, before flashing
her left hand and showing off a tiny diamond on
a band of gold.

"Oh. Wow! When?" *Who?*

"Barry," said Bernie, with a sigh. "We were
high school sweethearts, you know. Fell apart,
as you do at that age. Then reconnected at Camille and Phillip's wedding. It seems the bouquet
worked after all."

Emmy's delighted laughter was genuine. "It
seems so."

She wondered if Bernadette remembered trying
to slip her room key into Holden's pocket. Then
figured, by the lovestruck look in Bernie's eyes
as she waved to Barry across the room, that she
did not. Emmy decided then and there that it had
never happened.

"Camille?" Emmy asked.

As if hearing her name, Camille appeared out
of nowhere, looking glorious in a long green dress,
her curls piled up on top of her head, making it

clear she'd also managed to avoid the Working Bee part of the party.

Camille placed a glass of bubbly in Emmy's hand then gave her a quick tour. The place was still a mess, most rooms unfinished. But the pantry was huge, the light in the bedrooms gorgeous. It was on its way to being perfect.

"Do you love it?" Camille asked, as they ended up in the lounge.

"More than life itself."

"Good. Turns out we need a kettle. And a toaster. Remember we didn't put them on the wedding gift list?"

"Too bourgeois, I believe you said."

"Bit us on the backside, that did."

Emmy pointed to her gift bag. "Cream wrapping, rose-gold ribbon."

"I knew I loved you."

"These are great," said Emmy, running her fingers over the spring greens and dusty pinks of the cushions and throws draped over the couches in the lounge. Not at all like the greys and creams of the furnishings Holden had used in the ute the other night. She could still feel them under her head when he'd kissed her. Under her knees when she'd straddled him.

"New?" she asked, before clearing her throat.

"Yep! Holden gave us a very generous tab at a local boutique as a house-warming gift, so I went a little crazy."

"You came!"

Camille and Emmy both looked up at Phillip's enthusiastic outburst, only to find him looking to the front door. To Holden, standing there, holding a huge potted cactus.

Emmy's heart smacked against her ribs with such force she actually tripped forward.

They hadn't seen one another in person since the plane-watching night. They'd texted. They'd talked, sometimes late into the night. He'd called to ask for advice on a good house-warming present. Not a favour, *advice*. She'd gone with, "Something Camille can't kill." The promise of *next time* building between them like a dormant volcano.

Holden's smile when his eyes found hers was scorching. Emerson hid her own goofy smile behind her drink.

Then her view was blocked as a bunch of Phillip's friends saw who'd arrived and descended upon Holden with questions, app ideas, requests, before the guy had even made it over the threshold.

"Sit," said Camille, pressing Emmy into her old couch, when all she wanted to do was go to him, hold out a hand and tell everyone to back the hell away.

Knowing how crazy that was, Emmy sat with a whoosh of expelled air.

"Holden!" said Camille. "Lovely to see you. Drink?"

Emmy's heart thundered in her throat as she looked up to find he'd pushed his way through the crowd just fine. He'd done so to see her. "Iced water, please. With lime if you have it."

"Do I have lime? he asks. I'll be back." Camille left.

And Holden continued smiling down at Emmy, the heat in his eyes making her wonder which part of their recent kiss *he* was reliving. She was up to the part when his tongue had traced the edges of her top teeth, sending sparks rocketing through her entire body, as if she'd been hit by lightning.

She motioned for him to sit.

And he did. Close beside her. So close that, when he pressed his hand into the seat to make himself comfortable, his little finger stroked against hers.

Phillip plonked down on the tub chair near the couch, his cheeks pink from happiness. And beer.

Holden shifted so that his arm rubbed against hers.

Emmy may have shivered from top to toe, and Holden may have noticed.

Camille reappeared, handing Holden his drink before sitting on her husband's lap, bubbly sloshing over the edge of her glass, and looking as contented as Emmy had ever seen her. She waited for a flicker of the bittersweets, only this time it didn't come. No twinge, not even an echo, too

;wamped with happiness was she at seeing her
riends so content.

"Look at us," said Phillip, beaming. "Camille
ınd I, all grown up in our amazing new house.
Then there's Holden with his apps and his world
renown."

Holden laughed, rubbing a hand up the back of
ıis head. And was that a little flush creeping up
ıis neck? Emmy shifted so that her knee bumped
ıis. The look he shot her was quick, but sizzling,
ınd she tucked her knees together so as to hold
ıerself in one piece.

"And then there's our Emmy," said Phillip, "the
Heartache List now so far in her rear-view mirror
she'd have to squint to see it."

"What's the Heartache List?" Holden asked.

Camille smacked Phillip on the arm.

"What?" Phillip asked. Then, "God, Emmy.
I'm so sorry. It just slipped out. I figured he knew,
considering…" Phillip waved a hand at them, motioning to how close they were sitting.

"Why do I get the sense Phillip just put his foot
in it?" Holden asked, leaning into Emmy's side.

"It's nothing. Don't worry about it."

His hand moved to her knee, his eyes searching
ıers. "I'm not worried about it. What with all the
stage-whispering and arm-hitting and the panic
in your eyes, I am a little intrigued. And now that
I think about it, you mentioned something about
the List the night of the wedding."

"Do you forget nothing?"

"Big brain," he said, tapping the side of his head.

Emmy sucked her lips between her teeth, and glanced around the room, looking for an escape. Till Camille caught her eye and mouthed, *Tell him*.

Careful Emmy would never have considered giving up that part of herself to Holden Roarke. The evolved Emmy, the bold, brave, curious Emmy, pulled herself to standing. And motioned for Holden to follow.

Follow he did, through the lounge, the dining room, the den. But everywhere they went there were people. Eventually they ended up in the kitchen.

The pantry! Grabbing Holden by the hand, Emmy dragged him into the huge walk-in cupboard. A light flickered on as the door opened, then off again after the door closed.

In the semi-darkness, lit only by a sliver of light coming under the door, she could feel Holden's warmth. Hear the shift of his clothes, the huff of his breath.

"It looked bigger from the outside," she muttered.

"Emerson."

"Hmm?"

"Was there a reason you brought me in here?"

Darkness was nice, but as her other senses heightened, forcing her to focus on his gorgeous scent, she started to feel a little woozy. She found her phone, switched on the light, and placed it on a shelf beside a bag of pasta.

The shaft of overbright light shone on one side of Holden's face, creating shadows and valleys in the most beautiful shapes.

The slide of his hands into the pockets of his jeans were the only sign he was holding his patience in check.

"Okay," she said. "I'm going to tell you something, but you have to promise not to freak out."

"Do I seem like someone prone to freaking out?"

"Fair enough. For a number of years, I kept a notebook in which I detailed the times I'd had my heart broken."

"The Heartache List."

"The very one. I only documented the big hurts. The ones I felt sure I would never get over. My third-grade teacher leaving mid-term, the rock star whose posters covered my walls marrying some other woman."

"Those were your big hurts?"

"They were big. To me."

"Of course," he said, his expression chagrined. "Go on."

"Yes, I had other knocks, disappointments, frustrations, and sorrows that did not end up on the list. Such as when a school friend 'washed' my favourite Barbie doll's hair in the toilet. When I

missed making the Dean's List at university while
the kid who never showed up to lectures who also
had the same name as one of the college librar-
ies made it." She paused. "Though, to be fair, I
looked up that old Barbie when it came up in one
of those 'you are this old if you remember this
toy' things on social media. In pristine condition
they're now worth a packet."

"Emmy, I am loving this insight into what
makes you *you*, but I'm not sure you needed to
drag me into a cupboard to tell me about it."

"Okay. Yes. Here goes. And I can't believe I'm
about to say this out loud, but maybe it's all part
of the great Heartache List therapy session I'm in
the midst of—I had a crush on you. Back then.
At school."

In the quiet that followed, the white noise of
the party permeated, but it was a blur beneath
the thumping rush of blood behind Emmy's ears.

"Yeah," Holden eventually said. "I kind of figured."

Emerson stared at him. Gobsmacked. "You
kind of *figured*?"

"Well, you're not exactly the most subtle person
on the planet," he said, reaching out to her as if
he might cup her cheek before curling his fingers
into his palm. "Back then, you'd look at me with
those big eyes of yours and kind of…"

"Kind of what?"

"Sigh."

Kill her now.

"Hang on a second," he said, as he came full circle. "Are you suggesting I was on your Heartbreak List?"

"Heartache."

"Oh, good. I'd hate to think I'd broken you as opposed to making you ache."

His words, while flippant, hit deep. Aching, feeling broken, these were feelings she'd worked hard to keep out of her life. Something she still hoped to do, no matter how this "therapy" worked out.

"It wasn't your fault," she said. "You did nothing wrong." She knew that now.

"Then why—?"

"It all started with my dad." Emerson leaned back, needing space, only to rattle up against a shelf that was yet to be bolted to the wall.

Holden reached out, steadied her, and said, "Your dad."

"He left when I was ten. We… I…never saw it coming. And I… I don't think I've ever really got over it. My mum tried to help me understand, that marriage can be hard work, and some people aren't built for it, but the fact he could leave *me*, and never even get in touch… It broke my heart."

Yes, broke. Every other slight after that had been like pressing into a deep wound.

"During our sojourns in the hall outside Miss Kemp's office, you were so sweet to me. During a time when life felt sour. And when you left, and I didn't see it coming, again, it brought up things I'd been trying to pretend hadn't affected me as much as they had."

"Fathers, eh?" Holden said, moving in a little closer, his thumbs moving up and down her arms.

"Camille's dad is a gem. Phillip's too. And, from what you told me, Chuck was a pretty amazing stand-in."

"So, genetically we lucked out?" he asked, a dash of irony lighting his voice, even while it remained warm and kind and understanding.

"Ha. I guess we did."

Emerson looked up into Holden's eyes, and felt that flicker of familiarity he'd said he felt when he'd spotted her on the dance floor. Outsiders looking in. Only, here in this tight space, his hands on her, she didn't feel like an outsider. She felt as if she was inside something bigger than herself. Something magical.

Refusing to think, or overthink, or mentally play out any scenarios to their possible end games, she lifted onto her toes and kissed him.

His lips were cool and smooth, the taste of lime and ice sending a beautiful chill right through her. Already holding her, keeping her steady, Holden pulled her a little higher and kissed her back.

And while their first kiss—*their first kiss!*— in the back of the ute had been scorching hot—

decades of pent-up frustration hot—a dam bursting—this...

This kiss was sweet. Slow. Lingering.

Tasting, testing, learning one another's shape and feel.

The whole thing felt as if it was happening in slow motion.

Pressed as high as she could go, Emerson slid her hands up Holden's chest, and around his neck, her fingers tingling at the touch of his hair. His hands slid slowly down her arms to circle her waist, pulling her close.

This beautiful man. This good, generous, gorgeous hulk of a man who knew what it was to hurt. To move beyond it. And to thrive.

Her limbs began to tremble as the kiss deepened. Incrementally. Unceasingly. Settling in her limbs like warm honey. Hands now roving. Touching, caressing. Finding tender spots. Finding skin.

Small sounds of pleasure backed up in her throat, keeping her breathless. Heat pooled in her centre, till her head spun. Until she was a molten puddle of gooey pleasure.

Aeons later, Emmy pulled back, needing breath. Needing to feel the ground beneath her feet.

She dropped slowly back to her heels. Rested her head against Holden's chest, her eyes filling when he wrapped his arms even tighter about her and dropped a kiss on the top of her head.

As her pulse thudded sluggishly through her

body, she mused that until that moment it was entirely possible she hadn't known what heart-ache was.

For, like a foot that had fallen asleep, it seemed that her heart had been slumbering. And now, as it filled with blood, and warmth, and life, like pins and needles in her chest the pain was real.

This was no crush. A crush was tender, and warm. Distant.

The feelings rushing through her, the knowl-edge of how much she felt for this man, was wild, and raw, and out of control.

She felt as if she'd been sliced open, exposed.

His hands began sweeping over her back, calm-ing her heart rate. Calming them both.

There was no chance he couldn't feel the thump of her heart, the tremble in her chest. No chance he didn't have some inkling that these feelings were overwhelming her. That this was not a test. That there was no going back.

"So, this Heartache List—"

"Forget about it. I have. Or, to be fair, I'm work-ing on it."

"With the…great Heartache List therapy ses-sion that you're in the midst of."

"Mm-hmm."

"Am I a part of that?"

Emerson twisted to lay her cheek over his heart and said nothing. Not sure how he'd handle know-ing he was all of that.

He lifted a hand to cradle her face, to turn it to him. "So long as you know that there is no point in asking me to forget about that kiss. It happened. And it's going to happen again."

He leaned down and kissed her once more. Pulled back to say, "And again."

Another kiss, this one rich with longing, turning her knees to jelly and her brain to mush.

He pulled back again just enough to hold eye contact as he said, "I'm done pretending this isn't happening, Emerson. I'm more than okay with you and me, if you are too."

She sucked in a slow breath, enough to gather her thoughts. "I'm more than okay with that, too." Adding, "For as long as you're in town."

His gaze intense, solid, true, he said, "I'm not going anywhere."

Then, before she could brace herself against the fresh onslaught of feelings *that* brought on, he took her by the hand and twirled her under his arm till she was tucked up against his side. With his spare hand he passed her her phone, and waited for her to turn off the light.

"Shall we?" he asked, his voice a rumble in the darkness.

She held his hand in place. And nodded.

With his arm around her he led her out into the fray.

A few wide-eyed looks from Phillip's friends, a few side-eyes from people who'd never have

put "Emerson" and "public display of affection"
in the same sentence. When Camille spied them
her mouth dropped open, before she clapped her
hands effusively, forcing everyone to look her
way. "Everyone out back. Time for Strip Charades!"

Laughter and murmurs of dissent abounded
before she said, "Fine. Normal charades."

Thus having provided the perfect distraction,
Camille gave Emmy a quick wink and shuffled everyone outside. She gave Holden the two-fingered
I'm watching you move. Then the party went on
as if nothing had changed.

When, to Emerson's mind, it would never be
the same again.

"I need a favour," Emerson blurted the moment
the phone was answered. Then, "Aargh, I forgot
to check your calendar. If you're busy—"

"Shoot," Holden said, no hesitation.

Emerson breathed out in relief. "It's Pumpkin."

"Is he okay?" Holden asked, his voice tight, as
if he wasn't merely asking. As if he truly cared
about her patchy old pup.

Emerson had no hope of muffling the warm
fuzzies that crept up her insides as she said, "Yes.
Yes, he's fine. I left him home today as he was
super-cute and sleepy this morning. It's just, I
remembered he's run out of his special food. I

usually pre-order it from the vet but they were changing brands last time we visited. I ran out this morning, the vet closes really early today, in about twenty minutes, and I have a pre-interview with an amazing Sanderson Group COO candidate in ten minutes, and Chuck is being very stubborn and I'm finding it harder and harder to even find anyone to talk to about the position much less suggest, so I won't make it in time, and I usually use Kerri, next door, who I pay to look after Pumpkin when I can't, but she's at uni this arvo, and—"

"Text me the details."

"Are you sure?"

"Emmy, I'm the one you call."

"Thank you."

"My pleasure," he said, in that voice of his that made her believe it really was. His pleasure. "Where's his bowl?"

"Don't worry about that. Kerri can feed him when she gets home."

"Emmy, just tell me where his bowl is?"

"If you're sure…" *Two favours to tick off the tally*, she thought. Then thought again. *Did any of that matter any more, now that things had shifted so considerably between them? And honestly, looking back, had it ever?* "Pumpkin's bowl is just inside the doggy door round the back, so if you reach a hand in you'll find it."

"Do I need a key?"

"For?"

"The side gate."

"No lock, so no key. It has been a while since you've lived here, hasn't it? His hearing isn't great but his sense of smell is top notch, so he'll come once you pour the food. And…thank you."

"You said that already."

"Well, I mean it."

"I appreciate the fact that you mean it."

To think, this man, this experiment to prove to herself she'd put the Heartache List to bed once and for all, had become top of her contacts list. He was the person she called.

When Emerson realised that she was leaning her elbow on her desk, head resting in her palm, thumb rubbing the paperweight, gaze looking dreamily into the middle distance while imagining what Holden might be doing, or wearing, or not wearing, she sat bolt upright, knocking over a pen caddy.

"I owe you one," she said.

He laughed, as if he too had been mulling over the fact that they'd moved way beyond favours into…something rather wonderful. "Don't mention it."

"I'm hanging up now. So I can call the vet."

"After you," he said. And waited for her to end the call, as if he believed she might not want to.

And he was right.

* * *

Emerson came home to find Holden's rental car—now a big, black, hulking all-wheel drive—outside her house.

Using the side gate, she followed the stepping stones around to the back of the house, past her mum's beloved lemon tree, to find the man himself sitting on her back porch. Fast asleep.

Emerson slowly made her way up the wide wooden back steps, to find Holden had taken a couple of cushions from her outdoor setting, sat on one and propped another behind his back. His left knee was cocked, his hand was resting on Pumpkin's sleeping back as the dog's head lay across the man's right leg.

Emerson crouched down, reaching out a hand to touch Holden's shoulder, to gently wake him. Only her hand stopped at the last second, and she took her chance to soak him in.

The sweep of tangled lashes against his cheek, the five o'clock shadow covering his sharp jaw, the smudges under his eyes as he'd spent the week working long hours with his friend Andy, at the airport, after all. The way his hair was mussed, as if he'd run a hand through it one too many times. The strength of his collarbone, the column of his throat, the veins that roped down his beautiful forearms…

Despite his "I'm not going anywhere" line at the house-warming, convincing herself she'd be fine when he went back to his real life had become a daily mantra. And yet, seeing him in her space felt really good. It felt so right. It felt like a level of want she wasn't sure she was equipped to handle.

Pumpkin whimpered, having sensed her and woken.

Holden's eyes opened next, training instantly on hers.

Emerson stilled, like a hunter sighted by a deer, too slow, too helpless to shut down the thoughts that must be written all over her face.

"Hi," he said, his voice rough.

"Hi," she said, her voice barely a breath.

His smile was slow, and warm, and all too knowing.

But then he winced as some part of him that had been stuck in place too long pushed back.

Freed from the gravity of his gaze, Emerson quickly pressed herself to standing.

Then she clicked her fingers in front of Pumpkin's face, till the old dog groaned and eased himself away from Holden's lap to totter over to her hand for a pat. "Hey, boy, you like your new food?"

"Gobbled it down," said Holden, stretching out his long legs.

"You didn't have to stay," she said.

"Every time I tried to leave, he looked at me."

"Looked at you?"

"With sad eyes."

"Holden, he's a spaniel. Sad eyes are their superpower."

"Right." He ran a hand up the back of his neck. Boy, she loved it when he did that. "Either way, I figured it was best to settle him before I headed off."

"He looked plenty settled when I arrived."

Holden hauled his tall frame to standing. "I bet he did."

He wore old jeans, worn in all the best places, and an olive Henley T-shirt that had ridden up a fraction, revealing a flat stomach, more than one ab, and an arrow of dark hair pointing south. Not sure if she was allowed to look her fill now that they weren't "forgetting" about the attraction they both felt, she couldn't have looked away for all the world.

"Are you free now?" she asked.

He caught her eye. "As a bird."

"Do you want to come in?"

"Yes," he said, without equivocation. "I do."

"Great." She used the key to open the back door, hustled Pumpkin inside the kitchen, and watched till he found his way to his bed in the hall.

Then turned to find Holden right behind her. A wall of warmth. Of spice and cotton and fresh air. And a little bit like warm dog, which, when she imagined him sitting on her patio, his hand on Pumpkin's back, made for a very dangerous scent.

"You hungry?" she asked, then regretted it when his gaze dropped to her mouth.

"I'd love to wash up first. I feel like I'm sporting a layer of drool."

Emerson very deliberately did not offer to smell him to make sure, knowing that kind of thing seemed to send her down mental rabbit holes she was finding it harder and harder to find her way out of.

She pointed the way to the guest bathroom, and watched him walk away. Allowing herself a quiet whistle of appreciation before she shook it off and quickly fixed herself.

Jacket off, bag away. Quick swipe of toothpaste from the spare tube in the kitchen. No particular reason—it had been a long day and it seemed rude to smell like the coffee she'd tossed back an hour before.

"So," she said, when Holden ambled back into the kitchen, stopping to lean in the doorway. All lanky legs and crossed arms, as if he was holding up the entire house by the sheer force of his presence. "Dinner."

She opened the freezer to find it fairly bare. Her fridge looked little better.

"Takeaway?" she asked, looking over her shoulder to find him watching her with a small smile on his face, heat flickering behind his eyes.

Holden pushed away from the doorframe, his pace unhurried, his gaze focused, stopping only when he was inside her personal space. Then he slowly swept her hair behind one ear, then the other, till his palms rested on her cheeks, his gaze coming to settle on hers.

"Is that a yes to takeaway?" she said.

"Thank you for inviting me in, Emmy."

His words seemed straightforward, but she couldn't help imagining he meant something deeper. Something big and wonderful and terrifying. It was the only excuse for her next words. "You sound like a vampire."

"Not a vampire. Vampires sparkle in sunlight, if I remember rightly."

Emerson snorted. "Not real vampires. They burn."

As she said the word, his fingers delved deeper into her hair, the band she'd used to loosely tie it off her face falling free.

Her nerves were so taut, her skin so sensitive, she shivered as her hair fell over her shoulders, skittering over her bare arms. While the heat from his body, so close to hers, seemed to infuse her, till she was the one in danger of burning.

"Either way," he said, his voice deepening, the colour disappearing from his eyes, "my blood is warm. My heart beats. And I'm not immortal. At least I don't think so. Only time will tell."

When he used his thumbs to tilt her chin, when she felt the sweep of his breath over her cheeks, her neck, her mouth, he could have been speaking

Martian for all she knew as her head filled with clouds, her body nothing but sensation.

Her hands had curled into the front of his shirt. Was she pulling him in or holding him at bay? When her body seemed to roll into him with her next breath, she got her answer.

Her brain, the last bastion of defence, flickered one final time. "I'm not..." she managed to eke out.

"Not what?" he asked.

She licked her lips, and wild storm clouds overwhelmed the last of the deep blue in his eyes. "I know how much you've put your life on hold these past weeks. And I think... I think some of that is because of this, because of me. But I have no expectations."

"Isn't that meant to be my line?" he asked, his mouth lifting at one corner, his gaze sure and true.

"You don't do lines."

"You got me there." He breathed out through his nose. "I'm not asking for the world, Emmy. I'd just really like to kiss you again. And I think you'd really like to kiss me."

She opened her mouth to make some Smart Alec response when his thumb moved to the corner of her mouth, before bringing it into her eyeline. "Toothpaste? Was that for me?"

Sprung.

Hands already gripping his shirt, she gave him

a tug, tipped up onto her toes, and said, "Of course it was for you. So what are you waiting for?"

That, apparently. A wolfish grin lit up his face before his eyes grew so dark there was no telling what he was thinking. Or feeling. Only what he wanted.

And while, by this point, Emmy was a quivering bundle of nerves, Holden's cool held strong. And he took his sweet time.

Starting at the corner of her mouth, where toothpaste, of all things, had given her away—a kiss, then a lick.

A nudge of his lips, as close to hers as they could be without actually touching.

Then he moved to her ear, a waft of warm breath, a tug of teeth. Before he buried his nose in her neck, breathing deep as he pulled her liquefied body up against his.

"Holden," she breathed.

"Mmm," he murmured against her mouth, the tightness in his voice, the rough burr, the want spilling into his touch. Roving hands. Hardening body. Need, barely contained.

While she was melting, melting, *melting*. "Do me a favour and kiss me already."

She didn't need to ask a third time. And once his hot mouth met hers, everything changed. Her warmth became heat, her pliancy need. Her arms reaching around his neck, she lifted so high on her toes they creaked, and then, pressing herself to him, she got as close as she could, so that she might kiss him right on back.

Only this wasn't a kiss. This was an undoing. An unravelling. A revelation.

She found herself reaching for the hem of his shirt, hands frantic, desperate to find skin. When she did, it was so worth it. Warm skin, rough hair, hard muscle beneath.

His muscles twitched at the sweep of her hands. His words no more than a growl.

Relishing the fact she could cause such a re-action in such a man, she kissed him hard, deep, her hips rolling against his, her fingernails trailing down his belly. Tracing the edge of his jeans. Tugging at the button, snapping the thing free.

His moan, the hitch of his breath, the jerk of his body was like a drug. And she must have been high, as soon she was yanking his shirt up his body, her lips releasing his for a half second so she could whip the thing over his head.

Their eyes caught in that moment, their breathing rough and wild.

Her dress—black, frilly, with a deep V— was pulled off one shoulder, then the other, then tugged down her arms by strong, rough, sure hands, before it clung to her waist.

He stopped, breaths heaving in his big chest as his eyes roved over her. Her flushed skin. Her lace bra, her nipples pressing hard and painful against the fabric.

Eyes dropping, hungry eyes, he cupped her breast, his thumb sweeping over the peak.

Her head dropped back, her breath leaving her in a great long sigh.

"That's the sound," he said, his voice gruff. "That's how you used to sigh every time you saw me. I thought it was sweet. We were both too damn young to know what it meant."

Then he kissed her, his hands delving deep into her hair, before his arm tucked under her knees and she found herself lifted off the ground, literally swept off her feet. As he'd been doing to her since the beginning.

Not when they were kids. Not some foggy, long-ago era—aeons, ages, millennia before now—when she'd had no idea who she was, or what she wanted. When every turn, every decision, every comment slung her way had felt deeply personal. Deeply cutting.

Their true beginning was the moment he'd walked up to her, at that secluded bar, in that star-spangled marquee at her best friend's wedding, fairy lights dancing in his eyes, the most beautiful man she had ever seen, who had no clue how to spin a line.

She reached for him, holding his face between her hands, relishing the feel of his stubble against her sensitive palms, before she kissed him. Gently, deliciously, achingly.

"Where to?" he asked, when she pulled back to

rest her forehead against his, unwilling to break the connection.

She cocked her head towards her bedroom.

His nostrils flared, his eyes a winter storm, before he all but sprinted for the bedroom, forcing Emerson to hold on for dear life, her laughter scattering behind her like sparks from a firecracker.

In her bedroom, her most private space, Emerson slid down Holden's big, strong body, took him by the hand and led him to her bed.

Where they took their time undressing one another with care. And curiosity. In equal measure.

Before tumbling onto the bed with abandon. And there they found their rhythms, their touchstones, gentle affirmations and slippery heat.

He kissed his way down her body, taking his time, making it last, making it magic, while whirls and swirls of smoke rose inside her. She could taste the heat on her tongue, as he teased and tasted and tortured her till every thought, every fear, every last fragment of self-protection coalesced into a tiny sun bursting inside her.

And then she was lost. Dissolving, into a trillion tiny specks of light. When she came back into her body, slowly, she was all molten bones and trembling limbs.

And so it went on, savouring one another's bodies, one another's gasps, one another's sighs as the evening turned into night. And beyond.

As Emmy finally fell into a deep, boneless

sleep, her head tucked into Holden's shoulder, her hand resting over his heart, her mind cresting and settling, adrift on the rise and fall of his chest, she could barely remember why she'd been so adamant as to deny herself this pleasure. This sweetness. This moment.

Her last thought was that perhaps *this* had been the way to put the Heartache List behind her for good, after all.

Emerson woke in the pre-dawn, the birds not yet chirping, Pumpkin not yet up and about, banging into walls as he tried to find his way to the doggy door. And a man's arm was slung heavily across her chest.

It was Holden Roarke's arm. For Holden Roarke was in her bed.

He'd stayed with her patchy old dog because he'd been given the sad eyes.

He'd stayed when all she'd been able to offer him for dinner was Vegemite on toast.

He'd stayed.

"Hello, gorgeous."

She blinked to find his eyes on hers. No storm within, just a clear summer blue.

She lifted a hand to the bird's nest atop her head. "That might be your worst attempt at a line yet. I'm a wreck. And it's all your fault. You wrecked me."

He ran his thumb down her cheek. "You're a gorgeous wreck."

Eyes locked onto hers, Holden shifted to cover her with his body. While she shifted to accommodate him, her breath catching in her throat as she felt exactly what she'd be accommodating.

Settled, for now, he twirled a lock of her hair around his finger, then leaned down to press a soft, sweet, place-marking kiss upon her mouth. She waited for some flutter of resistance, of instinct, reminding her that this—while lovely, and unexpected, and therapeutic—was temporary.

No expectations.

But her instincts remained quiet. Less than quiet. It was as if he'd wrecked them too.

She tipped her head so that her mouth brushed the underside of his thumb. Then, having distracted him, she rolled till she straddled his thighs.

The flimsy tank top she'd slipped into during the night twisted around her body. His big hands spanned her waist, before gently tugging the top back into place, his thumbs sweeping over the exposed sides of her breasts.

While she told herself she was in the power position, the look in Holden's eyes made her feel as if her whole world might go dark without him holding her there in place.

As if to prove it, he sat up, his arms going around her, holding her close as he buried his nose in her neck, one hand gliding into her hair, the other lining up along her spine.

Her hand went to the back of his head, the other wrapped around his shoulder till they were pressed together close. Entwined. Just breathing one another in.

Holden's lips moved to her neck, pressing, suckling, biting. Tracing her collarbone. His fingertips slipped the strap of her top over her shoulder and followed the move with his mouth till her breast was free, his mouth taking over.

By the time she was ready for him, her skin on fire, her soul stripped bare, he made quick work with a condom, waited for her to line up, then eased her down, his hard heat sliding into her.

Deeper. Deepest. Friction building, heat burning, sensation, feelings, sweeping through her, too much.

"Do me a favour," he murmured into her ear, creating sparks amongst the light.

"What?" she breathed.

"Come."

And she did. Boy, oh, boy, oh, boy, she did.

CHAPTER NINE

STRIDING DOWN THE busy city footpath on the way back to the office, after a fabulous first meeting with an excellent candidate for the Sanderson Group COO, Emerson let her mind wander to thoughts of Holden as it was wont to do. His smile when she caught him unawares. The deep notes of his voice when he'd pick up the book on her bedside table and read it to her. The sweep of his broad hand down her back as she fell asleep in his arms.

She slowed in front of a café-slash-bookshop boasting a bountiful display of classics in their beautiful front window. Her gaze picking out *Persuasion*, she imagined lying with her cheek against Holden's warm, bare chest as he read aloud Wentworth's final letter to Anne. Then she had to stop imagining it lest she expire on the street.

She looked over the artfully teetering piles till she found—there! *The Catcher in the Rye*. Way back when, she'd bought that book for Holden as a gift, as the hero had his name. She could still feel the press of it into her fingers as she'd clutched it to her chest while sitting outside Miss Kemp's office.

Before their previous session, they'd been stuck

in the hallway a good half an hour, before Holden had turned to her, asking what her favourite movie was. He'd had to write a report in English and it had been so long since he'd seen a movie, he couldn't think of one.

"Field of Dreams," she'd blurted. "A movie about a guy who misses his dad, starring Kevin Costner? Come on!"

They'd moved onto favourite TV show, favourite breakfast, favourite song.

It had felt like fate, for favourites were *her* favourite. She kept copious lists of her favourite things, and always had—favourite actors, favourite cakes, favourite holidays. Hanging on tight to the things that brought her joy. And she and Holden had covered every topic, bar favourite books. Hence her gift.

That next week, Miss Kemp's door had bumped. Emmy had held the book tighter, her breath catching, her heart thundering in her ears.

But then some sullen grade twelve girl with long, greasy hair had left the counsellor's room before loping morosely by.

"Where's Holden?" Emmy had asked the counsellor as she'd approached the room, a sense of dread coming over her.

"He's gone, honey. To another school. Come on in and tell me about your week."

Emmy remembered nothing from that session, bar Miss Kemp telling her that Holden, the week before, had mentioned her love of lists. She'd told Emmy that writing things down could help some people and encouraged her to grab a notebook, start a journal, to see if it helped her let things go.

That afternoon, while Emmy had been laid out on her bed, awash with tears, Camille had arrived with notebook in hand. Sparkly cactus on the cover.

Only Emmy had never used her writings to let things go, only to hold on tight. How could letting things go be her intention when it was her actual nightmare? What Miss Kemp didn't know wouldn't hurt her.

Emmy blinked to find herself still in front of the bookshop.

In the window's reflection the sky looked ominous, meaning she should get back to the office. And yet she ducked inside, moving straight to the stationery section. No sparkles and cartoony motifs here, only high-end, leather-bound recycled paper. When she picked up a gorgeous cream notebook, with pages soft to the touch and thin black ribbon bookmarks attached, she felt a frisson of warmth run up her arm.

New notebook, and pen to match, in hand, Emmy ordered a double espresso and pointed to a table out the front. Once settled, she opened the notebook, the spine cracking just the way her Heartache List notebook had all those years ago. It too had started out clean and full of possibility, before it had become covered in her passionate scrawl, as a means to understanding why people disappointed her, why they left her behind.

The final entry?

Heartache Number Eight: twenty-five years old.

Losing Mum. That was all. No details. No questions. It had been enough. And too much.

She'd tossed that old notebook in the skip, along with so many memories from her childhood, before gutting the house and refurbishing it till it was unrecognisable. As if that put a great big underline beneath that part of her life.

All she'd kept was her mum's glass paperweight, the lovely old dog who'd marked time with her, and the façade of the house that quietly, secretly, she'd never changed in case her dad wanted to find his way home.

And, quite amazingly, since the day she'd thrown the Heartache List away, her life had been fine. Narrow, yes. Tightly controlled, sure. But *fine*.

Until Holden had strolled back in with his sexy smile, his quiet courtship, his constancy. And his favours.

Emmy popped the lid on her new pen, and the wind seemed to lift and bustle the leaves around her feet.

She let the pen hover over the page. Then, her penmanship not a lot better than it had been at fourteen, she wrote in bold capital letters atop the first page: THE FAVOURS LIST. Turning the page, she ruled a line down the centre. Put an "E" at the top of one column, an "H" at the top of the other.

Then, as if she'd been taken over by some external force, she set to noting down every single favour she and Holden had done for one another since Camille and Phillip's wedding. Starting with him helping her with her shoe, and her helping him let Bernadette down gently, and ending with his command, *Do me a favour. Come.* Before she'd fallen apart in his arms.

Her hand shook a little as she wrote those last words. The power of them. The command. Her effortless acquiescence. As if her world was no longer so very narrow, as if she no longer had control of it at all.

A frown now tightening her brow, she went back to the beginning. Some favours were bigger than others. Meaning they ought to be given ratings. Which also meant she couldn't leave out the teeny, tiny favours they'd done, those that had occurred without asking, or any expectation of return.

When done, the list was pages long. Unwieldy. And with its scrawls and doodles and notes, and arrows, it resembled the Heartache List far more than she'd intended.

A drop of water hit the page, blurring the ink. Then another.

It had started to rain.

"Emerson?"

"What's up?"

So drenched had she been by the time she made it back to work, she'd changed into jeans and a blousy top she kept in her office in case of long late-night sessions where comfort won out over *va-va-voom*, but she hadn't thought to keep a hair-dryer on hand. She added a note to her to-do list notebook on her desk and popped it under her mum's paperweight, along with her new Favour List notebook and an invitation to Bernadette's surprise wedding.

When Freya didn't answer, Emerson looked up to find her assistant in the doorway of her office, motioning over her shoulder with a pencil, to where Bettina Sanderson stood on the other side of Emerson's smoked windows, elegance personified in a drapey cream suit, hands gently clasped behind her back, gaze roving over the bright white office space beyond.

Emmy ran fingers through her damp hair, then under her eyes, hoping she didn't look like a crazed panda, as Bettina turned and caught her eye. She motioned for Bettina to come on in, moved around her desk, preparing for a hand-shake, but soon found herself enveloped in Bet-tina's warm hug.

"Thank you for seeing me at such short notice, Emerson."

"Of course. Sorry for the damp hug. I was out-doors when the rain bucketed down. In fact, I'd just had a wonderful meeting with a brilliant can-didate for the COO job, which I hope balances out the fact I must look like a drowned rat."

Bettina smiled. "Not at all. Can we sit? Talk?"

Emerson motioned to the soft couches by the large triangular window at the end of her office, and quickly twirled her hair into a knot at her nape while Bettina made a happy sound as she took in all the details of the space, before choosing a chair warmed by a patch of muted sunshine.

Emerson was halfway to sitting when Bettina said, "How is Holden?"

A vision of the last time she'd seen him popped into her head, his clothes a little rumpled, shoes in hand as he'd grabbed her and kissed her as if his life depended on it, before jogging down her front steps. "He's fine. I think."

"Mmm. I'd thought we might see him again, after the dinner, but alas. Though he did send a lovely note, and a beautiful bouquet of wild flow-ers, to thank us for having the both of you along. A truly decent man, that one."

He really was, thought Emerson. Decent and

wonderful. Solid and adventurous. Interested and interesting. A heartbreaker, yes, but only to those whose hearts were already damaged long before they'd given theirs to him.

"Now, enough about that," said Bettina. "I've come to ask a favour."

A bubble of laughter caught in Emerson's throat. Ah, the irony. She grabbed a pencil and notebook— she really did have a thing for notebooks—from the coffee table and settled them on her lap. "Tell me what you need."

"I need for you to convince Holden to consider the position of COO at the Sanderson Group."

The bubble burst, and with it came a wave of dread. "I'm sorry, Bettina. There must have been a misunderstanding. Firstly, I'm not sure anyone could convince Holden to do anything he does not wish to do. And secondly, as I told Chuck, I don't believe that would be in his best interests, or Holden's, considering their history—"

"I worked for the company—did you know that?"

Emerson blinked at Bettina's change of direction.

Bettina went on. "My name might not be on the letterhead, but the Sanderson Group is as much mine as it is Chuck's. I pulled back, a few years ago, when…family matters necessitated the move. Now that those family matters are no longer so pressing, I want my husband by my side for as long as I can have him. I'd all but convinced him, believing he might announce his retirement at his birthday dinner. Alas, seeing Holden sparked something inside him. And he's hanging on tight."

Something flashed behind Bettina's eyes—a mix of sorrow, and distress. As if, despite her elegant façade, it took an effort to be there. As if she knew what she was asking of Emmy was ill-advised, but she saw no other choice.

"I understand," said Emmy, leaning forward, her hand gripping the pencil as she madly tried to figure out a way around the request Bettina was about to reiterate. "Holden told me what you meant to one another. How you were so kind to him. How you took him in. About his wonderful friendship with Saul."

Bettina breathed out hard, her throat bobbing delicately, before she collected herself, pressing her shoulders back, lifting her chin. "Then you understand that my family has been through a lot. That I must do what I can to protect those I have left. My husband needs a reason to retire. Holden is it."

Emerson pressed her toes into her shoes, as she felt the ground tipping beneath her feet. "You are welcome to talk to Holden, Bettina, but I am certain he'll—in my opinion rightly—say no."

Bettina's smile was gentle, and painful, all at once. "I saw the way Holden deferred to you. I'd say you could convince that man of pretty much anything."

Emerson's world tipped just a little more, leaving her off kilter when Bettina steeled herself, and years of running a multimillion-dollar business came to the fore. "So here is what's going to happen. You will convince Holden to take the position, and the commission will be yours. In fact, I will double it. Personally."

Bettina's *favour* hung in the air between them. That kind of money, of prestige, was all that Emmy had dreamt of since the moment she'd opened Pitch Perfect's doors.

And yet Emerson desperately tried to come up with an alternative. Mind flitting over her best candidates, it landed on one she'd not yet considered. "Chuck clearly needs a little more time to transition into retirement. You want to spend more time with him. Maybe…maybe it's time your name did end up on the letterhead. Then, together, we can find the right team to take over when the time is right for both of you."

Bettina held up a hand and shook her head, her gaze pained, but also stubborn, as she gracefully unfolded herself from the chair. "My mind is made up."

Emerson somehow managed to get to her feet, even while her legs felt shaky, her feet numb.

"And if I can't?" Emerson asked, when what she meant was, *If I won't.*

Bettina's quick, sorry smile showed she knew it too. "You are a capable young woman with a bright future. I have every faith that together we can make this happen."

Bettina held out a hand, not to shake, but to enclose Emerson's in hers. As if she knew what she was asking was impossible, but that, as far as she saw things, she had no other choice.

And then she was gone. Leaving Emerson in the very rottenest possible position after all.

Emerson made it back to her desk and plonked herself in her chair. She slung an arm over her face, as if an answer might come to her in the darkness.

What was she to do?

Write a pro/con list? Yeah, no. A list would not help her this time.

Emerson dragged herself upright and slumped over her desk, her eye catching on the new notebook under her mum's paperweight.

She'd made it clear to Bettina, *and* to Chuck, that what they were asking was impossible. But the truth was, Bettina was right about one thing: all Emerson had to do was ask.

For, despite the many favours they had done for one another over the past weeks, officially Holden still owed her the Big One.

Could she actually do it? Would Holden understand? Was she making too big a deal of this? Holden and Chuck really did need to get in a room together and talk, so in instigating that she'd be doing him a favour!

And, a quiet yet hopeful voice piped up in the back of her head, *if, by some miracle, he accepted the job, even in the short term, he would have a reason to stay.*

He had told her, his voice earnest and deeply sexy, *I'm not going anywhere,* but he'd also swapped houses as if it was nothing and changed rental cars as though they were dirty socks.

Staying hadn't killed him so far. Staying so that they could continue their favour game. Staying as things had heated up between them. Staying, gifting her all the time she'd needed to get to know him, to trust him, to want him, to lean on him, to need him…

And to fall in love with him.

She had. She'd fallen in love with Holden Roarke. Utterly, hopelessly. Not with the shuttered gaze of a confused fourteen-year-old but the wide-open eyes of a woman who still never saw it coming.

And loving him meant she had her answer.

Asking him to go to that interview would be asking the man she loved to do something that would hurt *his* heart.

An end was coming either way. And endings, in her world, meant heartache.

Emmy picked up her phone with no plan in

mind, only to find a missed call from Kerri from next door.

She called her back. "Hey, Kerri, everything okay?"

"It's Pumpkin." Kerri sniffed, as if she'd been crying.

And all the worries in Emerson's head fled, every thought coagulating into one singular fear. Ice-cold. And infinite. Her beautiful boy, her one constant through it all.

"What about Pumpkin, honey?"

"He's not moving. I fed him earlier today, but his bowl is still full. I came by to see if he wanted to go for a walk, and I can see him through the doggy door, that he's in his bed, but he won't come when I call."

"You have a key, honey. You can go in any time, you know that."

"I know. I just… I'm not sure I can."

"I'm sure he's fine," said Emmy, as she madly grabbed her keys, her jacket, and for some reason the damp notebook, and shoved them in her bag. "He's nearly deaf, remember, so maybe he just can't hear you. Is your mum home?"

"At work."

"Right. Well, I'll give her a quick buzz and let her know you're worried, then I'll be right there. You head on home and leave Pumpkin to me. Okay?"

"Okay."

Emerson rang off, then shot out the door. "I'm off for the day," she called to Freya as she ran past.

Freya, wonder that she was, sent Emmy a salute.

Running on instinct, as the lift doors opened, Emmy made one more call.

"It's Pumpkin," she said, the moment Holden answered.

Whatever he heard in her voice, all he said was, "I'm on my way."

Emerson somehow kept to the speed limit, even while adrenalin had her slightly out of sync with the world.

Pumpkin.

Her beautiful boy. Half deaf, mostly blind, fully sweet. He'd beaten kidney infections, a snake bite, a broken leg, near record old age. He'd run away. That would have been *Heartache Number Four*, except he'd come back, covered in detritus and matted fur that had taken two baths, a short clip, and a lot of gentle tugging to remove, but panting happily after his adventure.

He'd put her through the wringer, but she'd still loved him with her whole heart, all the same. Pumpkin, with his soft, sweet doggy fur, absorbing her tears when she knew for sure her dad was not coming back. Her last link to her big, funny, huggy, sad, shadowy dad, who'd left her with the words, "Life ebbs and flows, kiddo. When it feels hard, remember it'll be okay. It always gets better."

As if that might help.

As if she wouldn't use his desertion as an excuse to keep people at bay. As if she could ever again feel as if the foundations beneath her feet were truly stable. Leaving her preparing for the worst, and being happily surprised when things worked out, then believing that was a good thing.

Emmy shook her head, and blinked the tears from her eyes. Angry tears. Worried tears. Tears for Holden too. For what she might yet have to ask of him. And how he might look at her from that moment on.

There were too many feelings. She really wasn't *sensical* when faced with too many feelings.

She pulled into her driveway, the bump of the car over the old gutter rocking her from side to side.

Her hands shook as she opened the front door, her heart lodged in her throat.

She banged her feet on the floor, the reverberations in the floorboards often enough to rouse him. But no skitters of doggy claws met her ears.

"Pumpkin?" she called, as loud as her tight voice would allow.

Still he didn't appear.

Kicking off her shoes, she dumped her things on the floor and padded up the hall, her chest squeezing when she saw his sweet foot poking out over the edge of his soft bed, along with the white tip of his caramel tail.

Dropping to her hands and knees, she made her way to him slowly. "Pumpkin? Buddy?" she called, knowing he couldn't hear her.

She placed her hand on his back, her breath hitching when she felt him move, his chest rising and falling, gently, slowly. Then his eye opened, and he tried to sit up.

"Hey, boy," she said, keeping her hand on him as she leaned down to press her cheek against his. As tears slid down her cheeks, she kept whispering that she was there, that he was a good boy, the best boy. She told him how deeply and incessantly she loved him, how grateful she was to have known him, to have known that he loved her back.

Then, several minutes later, a long, slow breath left his body. And his chest did not rise again.

Tears flowing freely now, Emmy lifted the old boy gently out of his bed, his frail body lighter than it had been in years, as if he'd been slowly leaving her for a while now, but she'd been holding on so tight she'd refused to notice.

She held him in her lap, where he'd used to sleep when he was half the size, and stroked him. Breathed in his doggy scent. Committed the exact feel of his fur to memory.

A knock at the door had her heart leaping into her throat.

The door nudged open—she'd forgotten to close it.

Holden's big, broad body created a shadow in the doorway as he let himself in, his form taking shape, and colour, strength, warmth, and vigour as he padded down the hall. Such gentleness in his big body, as if he knew that was all she could take.

She felt his approach, a waft of warmth and fresh laundry, a flutter of sensation up the back of her neck, before his hand landed on her shoulder and he reached around for her chin, tipping it back, so he could plant an upside-down kiss upon her forehead. Setting off feelings inside her that at fourteen she'd never have been able to imagine, much less handle. Heck, she could barely handle them now, her heart squeezing and kicking, bucking against the constraints under which it had been imprisoned for so long.

His hair was mussed, his cheeks a little pink from the wind that had followed the rain, the rush to get to her. This big, beautiful man who'd carved such inroads into her life. The man who had set so many things in motion. The man whose simple existence might yet tear it all apart.

The person she called when she needed to make a call.

Her person.

Her person.

He dropped to his knees, then slid in behind

her, wrapped his arms around her, and hauled her close.

Careful not to disrupt the bundle in her arms, he held her as she cried and cried and cried.

Emerson blinked up at the mottled grey sky above her house as she hopped out of the car. After what had felt like a lifetime at the vet's, her brain struggled to connect with the fact that it was still daylight.

She held Pumpkin's collar in her hand as she glanced up at the façade of her childhood home, the paintwork dull despite the wash of recent rain. The home her father had left, the home her mother had gifted her, the home Pumpkin had shared with her on and off her whole life.

To think she was about to walk in there, on her own, truly alone, for the first time in her life. Legs rocky, she leaned back against her car, the warm metal a surprise against her sensitive nerves.

Holden came around the front of the car, keys in hand, and stood by her. He looked as wretched as she felt, his care for her etched into the lines and hollows of his beautiful face.

Every single atom in her being ached to reach for him. To have him envelop her in his strong arms. To lean on him. To breathe him in. So that he might absorb some of her pain. Which he would do, without question, without being asked.

Not out of any favour nonsense, but just because it was who he was.

Yet when he reached out, she flinched. So thinly stretched did she feel. She'd not be surprised to look down and find herself translucent.

"Give me your house keys," he said, his voice gentle. "Let me take you inside."

It made sense. She could barely feel her feet.

But as she looked up at the house again, at the façade she'd never allowed her mum to change, even during the years she'd not lived at home, a kind of preternatural calm came over her. And she finally began to see things clearly.

"I've decided…" She swallowed against the dryness of her throat. "Decided what my favour will be."

"Favour?" Holden said, as if he'd forgotten that was ever a part of their story.

"The Big One. The one that you agreed that I could ask for any time I wished. So long as it wasn't illegal, or impossible, you could not refuse me. Remember?"

He cocked his head, the slightest smile easing across his lovely face. "You want to do this now?"

Did she? Not even slightly.

"Let's get you inside." Holden moved ever so slightly into the bubble of air surrounding her, his warmth like a balm. "I'll brew you a hot chocolate. Run you a bath. Make you dinner. And tuck you into bed, for real this time, then you can ask me any favour you want. As many as you want. As big as you want. For as long as you want."

He smiled, but his eyes were sad. Sad about Pumpkin. Sad for her. But also filled with tenderness, and steadiness, and truth. A decent man, he believed what he was promising. Even the "for as long as you want" bit. Only he had no idea that she wanted forever.

It was enough to give her a second wind, one last push of strength.

"Bettina came to see me yesterday." Or was it today?

"Did she, now?" he asked, his nostrils flaring, as if only now he sensed the fight in her and was grounding himself, ready to push back.

Emmy lifted her chin. "Chuck wants you for the COO position. He has done since the beginning. In fact, I'd go so far as to say that's why he took me on. Bettina came to my office to ask me to convince you of the same."

Time seemed to stretch and fold between them, before Holden said, "*That* is your favour? You are asking me to work for the man whose son I tried to replace, whose daughter left me, all of which put the same man into a wheelchair." He lifted his hand to the back of his neck and squeezed. "Why? For the commission? Chuck's respect? Hell, Emmy."

"No," Emerson said, her voice cracking. "That's not… I want you to refuse."

Holden's stormy blue eyes locked onto hers. "I'm not sure I understand."

"While I do think that it would do both you and Chuck the world of good to stop circling one another and actually talk, I want your authorisation to tell them no."

"My authorisation."

"Assuming that's your wish, of course. Say the word, and it's done. The Sandersons can move on and find the right person for the job. And you and I will owe one another no more favours. Decks cleared in one fell swoop."

Her declaration, such as it was, fell flat.

Especially when she saw the realisation wash across his face. For he knew her too well. He *saw* her. No wonder she'd accidentally fallen in love with him, after all.

He closed his eyes. Shook his head. "Sorry. It's been a rough afternoon, I know. Not the time to be jumping to conclusions. Just...talk to me. Tell me what's going on in your head right now."

She glanced at her feet, unable to deal with the dislocation in his gaze, the dawning understanding. "It's been a lot, these last few weeks. The wedding, the insane workload, Pumpkin." *Falling in love with the last man I'd ever have expected could sweep me off my feet.* "I feel as if I hopped on one of your planes, thinking I was heading to a particular destination, then, mid-air, I jumped.

And I've been free-falling ever since…weightless, and floaty, and still yet to land."

She glanced up to find him running a hand over his mouth, as if carefully considering his words.

"I hear that," he said. "I feel the same way."

If only…

Emmy breathed out hard. "The thing is, you're used to living like that. You feed off the adventure, the variety, the change of scenery." It was how he dealt with *his* past the same way she used lists to understand hers. "Me? I need to know I'm on solid ground. And with you… I don't. I never have."

His face, oh, his lovely face as he looked at her. As if he was the one who ached. "Emmy, I really thought—"

"You thought right," she said, not sure she'd be able to go through with this if he told her that he cared. And she knew he cared. Just as she knew that, eventually, it would no longer be enough to make him stay. "And it's been lovely. But I've seen your calendar. I know what you've given up to be here. This feels like the right time to… For us to…" She waved a hand between them.

"Say, it, Emmy. I need to hear you say the words."

Words. Like the words Miss Kemp had told her to write, so that she might let things go. When instead she'd used them to hold on tight.

The way she'd held on to dear old Pumpkin,

not even allowing herself to imagine what choices she might have to make if his health had begun to fail him.

The way she'd held tight to her best friends, suffering a physical shock to the system when it had finally hit her that they were married.

The way she'd held on to the exterior of her childhood house, just in case her dad needed to find his way home…eighteen years after he left.

The very best thing she could do for Holden, and for herself, was to let him go.

"Holden, it's time for you to go home."

His expression didn't change, as if he'd been braced, expecting it. But his voice—rough, low, and grave—gave him away. "That's what you really want?"

Emmy nodded. Just the once.

Then Holden asked, "What about what I want?"

By that point Emmy felt as if she was being held upright by a single fraught nerve. Empathy spent, softness depleted, she said, "You are retired, then not retired. You move more often than I change my sheets. You flit from car to car depending on your whims. You don't want to be here, yet you don't leave. I don't think you know what you want."

Holden took a step back. A literal step back. Then he turned and leaned his hands against the bonnet of her car, his entire body taut.

He ran a hand over his face, the skin dragging

at the last. As if he too was barely holding on. "If you weren't standing there, looking like a gust of wind might blow you over, I think I'd actually throw you over my shoulder, take you inside and demand you not to say another word till you'd eaten, drunk and slept."

In his eyes, the storm was real, confusion warring with the heat that simmered between them at all times. She squeezed the skin between her thumb and forefinger so as not to find herself swept up in him.

"This isn't about Pumpkin."

"Like hell it's not," he shot back. Energy no longer contained as it seemed to flicker about him, wild and wondrous. "I keep telling you I'm not going anywhere, even when I can see you don't believe me. Do you know how it feels, to be so easily dismissed? Hell, it's my father all over again."

The rush of emotion in his voice gave her strength. "Are you comparing me to your *father*?"

He threw his hands out to the side and paced away from the car. "I have absolutely no idea what I am doing. Clearly. In fact, I've been rudderless since I looked up and saw you standing on the edge of the dance floor. You were like this silent siren, grabbing me right through the middle and refusing to let go. I've been stuck here, stuck in this place that gave me such grief for such a long time, because you… Because you…"

He reached out, fingers stretched as if he wanted to shake her. Or grab her and kiss her. Or hold her and rock her until whatever had taken over her had passed.

She licked her suddenly dry lips. "Lucky for you, then, you don't have to feel stuck any more. I'm letting you go, Holden. No more favours. Go, find work that engages you, rather than that which falls into your lap. Go, before that impressive restlessness of yours makes you regret staying. Before I—"

"Before you what?" he asked.

She bit her lip. Let it go when his eyes dropped to her mouth and stayed.

He looked up again, deep into her eyes. Soul deep. "You think I needed *interesting work* in order to have a reason to stay?"

You, his gaze said, *you were all the reason I needed.*

He moved to her then, slowly, reaching out to hold her gently by the upper arms. Then he leaned in, slowly, till his forehead touched hers.

Emerson's eyes drifted closed. Now it was only the thousand butterflies beating against the inside of her skin that held her upright.

"This is what you really want?" he asked. "What you really need?"

"Yes," she said, "it is."

He dropped a hand over his heart, his fingers curling over his collarbone. Then he lifted his head and stepped away. Then he placed her keys on top of her car and headed towards the street.

Only to stop, turn, look at the house, then look back at her. "I heard you, Emmy. I did. But if you need company, if you don't want to go in there alone, I'll stay. Just say the word."

"I'll be fine." And she would. Eventually. She always was.

Holden nodded, every angle of his body tight and hard as he strode towards his rental car, folded his long body inside, gunned the engine, and was gone.

Emerson somehow made it up the front steps and inside her house, where she folded up like a puppet whose strings had been cut.

Sitting against the wall, she waited for panic to set in. For she'd killed the biggest deal of her life and pushed away the only man she'd ever loved.

But, like a cat with nine lives, nine heartaches were all she had. And she'd just given that ninth to the sweetest pup who'd ever lived.

She had nothing left to give.

CHAPTER TEN

A FEW DAYS LATER, Holden sat in the reception area on the twelfth floor of the Sanderson Group building, pressing at his cuticles with his thumbnails, and frowning so hard his forehead hurt.

Despite the low grey clouds blanketing the city, a shaft of sunlight slanted into his eyes. But he didn't change seats. It kept him sharp. The only possible reason why he'd ended up in such a mess was that this damnable city had blunted him. Softening his edges. Turning him to putty.

No more.

When he'd told Emmy he'd heard her, given her "authorisation" to refuse a role he'd never asked for, on his behalf, he'd never promised he'd not have words with Bettina and Chuck himself.

He wasn't exactly sure what those words would be, only that they had to be said. There had to be some sort of closure, on all of this, once and for all. Or else the hot, heavy feeling that had taken up residence behind his ribs the moment he'd seen Emmy sitting on the floor, her lovely old dog on her lap, the knowledge that her happiness meant more to him than anything ever had, would haunt him for ever.

"Holden?"

Looking up to find Bettina Sanderson heading

his way, Holden stood, wiped dry hands down the sides of his jacket, before leaning in to kiss her cheek.

"So lovely to see you, dear boy. I wish you'd called; I'd have put aside time for a coffee."

"I'm not here for coffee. I'm here to interview for the COO position."

He might have relished the shock on her face if he was actually there for some damn interview. But he was not. He was there to give Chuck— Bettina too, since fate seemed to have placed her there, right on time—a piece of his mind.

Lying in bed in the plush hotel room he'd moved to a couple of days back, right after leaving Emmy's for the last time, staring at a small crack in the ceiling, he'd come to the conclusion that there was no way around the fact Emmy's happiness had come to mean more to him than his own.

That alone meant he had to heed her wishes. What else could he do?

Yet, for all that Emmy had done his head in, and his heart, and most of his major organs if the ache inside him was anything to go by, and while he knew she could absolutely take care of herself, nobody messed with her on his watch.

He would walk away. Eventually. But not until he made sure she'd be okay.

"The COO position," said Bettina, her hands wringing, her expression riddled with guilt. Good.

It meant she had some semblance of an idea of the mess she had wrought. "Might I ask why?"

Holden slowly dipped his hands into the pockets of his suit pants, his throat tight, his voice a little above a growl. "If you're asking if Emerson sent me here, after your…conversation the other day, she did not. In fact, she made it clear, it was her preference that I refuse to even consider the notion."

"Oh?" Bettina blinked. Then, strangely, her shoulders dropped, and she broke out in a smile. "Well, good for her. Bright, capable, *and* formidable. I knew I liked that one."

Holden opened his mouth but found he did not have the words. What the heck was he missing?

Bettina must have seen it on his face, as she reached out and squeezed his arm. "I know. I do believe Chuck and I have not handled this whole thing as best we might. Seeing you again, while wonderful, stirred up dust we thought had been brushed away. And, while I can't speak for my stubborn husband, I do love him. Which is why I had to do whatever it took to make sure he is taken care of. I hope the both of you can understand our hearts were in the right place, even if our efforts were inelegant. I hope you can forgive us."

"Always," Holden said, as, for all that his insides were a tangled mess in no small part due to Bettina's influence, he believed her. Considering her words very much mirrored his own recent reflections, he found that he understood her too.

"Oh," said Bettina, "and the COO position has been filled."

"By whom?"

"By me." Bettina held out both arms with a flourish. "Chuck is not ready to retire. I wish to spend more time with him in our twilight years. Then it seems about time I finally have my own name on the letterhead. It was your Emerson who gave me the idea."

"She's not—" Not his Emerson. He couldn't say the words. For, despite recent events, it still felt as if she was. His Emmy.

"Did she truly insist you not apply for the position?"

Holden nodded.

"Even while fully aware that would put her relationship with the Sanderson Group at risk. Bright, capable, formidable...and staggeringly selfless. Where you are concerned, at least."

Selfless. Holden grabbed onto that thought. He wasn't here for him. He was here for Emerson. "Back up a moment," he said, pinning Bettina with a glance. "If Emerson was the one who suggested you for the role, the commission is hers. Correct?"

Bettina's eyes widened for the briefest flash, the only sign that she'd been stymied. "Correct. And serendipitous, to have you on her side."

"Serendipity has nothing to do with it."

"No," said Bettina, "I can see that it does not. Now, dear boy, I have work to do. Was there anything else?"

Yes, there was. A good deal, in fact. "Dinner one night this week? You, me and the big guy. How about we put that dust to rest?"

Bettina's eyes misted over. "We'd like that very much."

Holden gave Bettina a quick hug, congratulated her, wished *her* luck, then headed outside where the clouds lurked low overhead, threatening to spill at any moment.

He'd done what he'd gone there to do—make sure Emerson would be okay. Which should have put a line under his time in Melbourne.

And yet…

Now he had dinner plans. And Bettina's words echoing in the back of his mind: *Your Emerson… Staggeringly selfless… Serendipitous, to have you on her side.*

He still wasn't going anywhere. Not yet.

Only now, his reasons why were shifting. Or maybe, just maybe, they were the same as they had been all along.

Thoughts now spiralling in a thousand different directions, Holden chose a number from his contacts list, and after it answered was aware of the irony as he said, "Mate. Can I ask a favour?"

* * *

Camille opened her door, eyes widening at the sight of her friend.

"Oh, honey," Camille said. "A little wet out?"

Emmy pushed her dripping hair out of her eyes. "A little."

More like a lot. It had been raining, on and off, ever since Emmy had let Holden go. Pushed him away. Told him to leave. *Semantics.*

"Wait there." Camille ran inside and came back with towels, one for Emmy to wrap around her hair, another on which to wipe her feet. Smiling apologetically, she said, "New floors."

After setting Emmy up on another huge towel on the new couch, Camille quickly made coffees before pulling her friend in for a long hug. "I'm so sorry about Pumpkin, hon."

"Thank you."

Camille pulled back, eyes fierce. "I know some would never understand, but if you need a proper funeral for the old boy, you know we'll be there."

Emmy hiccupped. It was not a laugh. It was far too soon for all that. "No funeral. I will scatter his ashes, though, beneath Mum's lemon tree."

"Well, that's far better." A pat on the knee, then, "So, did you hear Bernie's getting married?"

"Got my invitation."

"Super. We can car pool. Bernie mentioned something about my being Matron of Honour, but intimated it's all very casual. Show up, carry flowers, sit at the big table. Though I'm considering asking for a name change. Babe of Honour, perhaps? I'm working on it. So, how are things otherwise?"

Emmy tipped forward to grab her drink, only for the towel on her head to slip over her face. Nerves a little tetchy, she quickly balled it up and hugged it to her chest.

"Super-well from the looks of things," Camille answered for her.

Emmy did laugh that time. Then reached inside her bag, pulled out the Favour List, and handed it over.

Camille—understanding the power of a good notebook—balanced it on her upturned palms. "May I?"

Emmy nodded.

Camille's eyes shifted from side to side as she read the title. "Ah. I didn't know you were still keeping track. I thought, perhaps, the two of you might have moved beyond that."

"I had. Until I hadn't."

"I see." Camille flicked through the pages. "The detail is impressive."

"Do you mean detective-impressive or the-psychopath-the-detective-is-investigating-impressive?"

"Oh, the latter, for sure." Then, "You really did all this for one another, in the past few weeks? This is more than Phillip and I would do for one another in a year. And we'd be all passive aggressive about it. Lots of huffing and puffing and muttering about being taken for granted. Does Holden mutter?"

"No muttering."

"Then the man is a saint. And clearly smitten." Camille's gaze hit a certain point in the notebook and her eyes grew wide. "Holy smokes. Did he really say that?"

"Which one?"

Camile turned the notebook and pointed, mouthing the word, *Come.*

Emmy nodded.

"That's…seriously. Wow. I mean… I'm feeling a little hot under the collar. And in need of my husband. But he's hiding in the bedroom." Camille shook herself so as to regain focus on the issue at hand. "Where is Mr Heartache, and why are you here rather than…" Camille's voice dropped an octave *"…doing one another favours?"*

Emmy held the balled-up towel closer to her chest. "He's gone."

"Gone where?"

"Gone, gone. Away. Elsewhere. Home."

Camille madly flicked to the last page, where Emmy had ruled a big angry line under the final favour. Adding squiggles. And crossing out all the space at the bottom of the page. Then, "Did he read the notebook?"

"No, he didn't read the notebook!"

"The bastard. I'll sic Phillip onto him. There's not much of him, but he's scrappy."

"No. It's fine. I'm fine."

It wasn't fine. *She* wasn't fine.

She couldn't sleep. She felt low, constantly. As if she had the flu. Yes, she'd lost her pup, and had screwed up her biggest contract to date, but she knew, *knew*, if she'd had Holden holding her through it all she'd be okay.

And yet…beneath the yuck was a sense of rightness in making sure Holden was no longer marking time. That he was out there flourishing.

"That's not what I get from this crazy manifesto of yours."

"Ignore the crazy manifesto. We had simply… run our course. Our favours finally balanced out, and that…" She stopped to take a breath, though it did sound more like a sigh even to her ears.

Camille narrowed her eyes and tapped at the Favour List. "You know that man did not stick around to pick up your laundry because he felt morally indentured to some list. That's *your* kink. The man stuck around for you."

Emmy let the towel drop into her lap. "Maybe. Yes. Of course, I know that. But it doesn't matter. Because he's gone. For ever."

For someone so okay with *nothing* lasting for ever, saying it out loud felt raw. And unbearable.

Camille watched her face, before lifting her shoulders in a shrug and handing the notebook back. "He is gone. He is dead to me. Now, we can check out Bernie's gift list later, so we can pick something wonderful and whacky, but first give me your feet. Everything feels better when you have sparkly toenails."

Emmy slid down deeper into the chair, the notebook in her hand, and propped the towel behind her head as she leaned back against the couch. Eyes closed, she toyed with the notebook ribbon.

She'd decided not to tell Camille about the texts Holden had sent since she'd sent him packing, the ones checking that she was okay. No point Camille staying attached to the guy.

Attachment only led to ache. Bone-deep ache. Soul-deep ache. She knew as she was living it. Despite all her best efforts for that not to happen, it had happened anyway. Meaning, if she'd waited any longer to end things, his leaving would surely have cleaved her neatly in half.

"Salut," said Phillip later that evening, raising his near empty beer.

Holden shuffled on the barstool and clinked the bottle with his iced water and lime. "Thanks for getting away."

"All good. Camille's at home. In the middle of what might be days of girl talk with…you know who. I'm meant to be hiding in the bedroom till they're done."

Holden laughed, despite himself.

"I'm not kidding," said Phillip, looking over his shoulder. "If she knew I was here, no sex for a week. The woman's stubbornness knows no bounds. So, did you call me because you wanted to talk about it too?"

"*It* being Emerson?"

Phillip winced. "Spill, whinge, get it all out. I'll say *There, there* and pretend to be on your side, even though that can never happen. Or we can say nothing at all. Talk about football. Or stock prices. Or life on Mars. Whatever you need."

"I need a drink."

Phillip breathed out. "Thank God. Two beers!"

"Light," Holden added, holding out his phone to pay.

"So, what did happen?" Phillip asked. "If you don't mind me asking. Last time I saw Emmy she was all sparkly-eyed, and floating off the ground. And Emmy does not float. She's the most pragmatic person I have ever met."

A muscle twitched under Holden's left eye. Emmy had mentioned the floating thing to him too, in an accusatory way. The way Phillip put it made it sound nice. The woman still confused the heck out of him, even in absentia.

The thing was, he liked it. He fed off it. She'd charged him with feeding off adventure and variety and change of scene, as if she wasn't all of them combined.

The same woman who wore her hair twisted

into a complicated mess at home, while eating peanut butter out of the jar, raged if a temp on her books was offered less than exemplary working conditions, and in the next breath listened, actively, intently, as he talked about the minutiae of his day.

She'd also accused him of playing house, when he hadn't played at anything when it came to her. Not for a single second.

He'd been all in from day dot.

Holding back, waiting for her to catch up, he'd had to keep reminding himself it might take her more time. Reminding himself she was softer than she thought she was. Trusted her own feelings tremulously. Determined, if she needed more time, to give her as much time as it took.

That was then. Before she'd told him to go home.

Phillip passed a beer to Holden and Holden took a slow sip. "You want to know what happened?"

"Sure."

"She told me not to take a job I didn't want."

"Right. Heartless of her. Terrible." Phillip paused. "I'm imagining, being Emmy, it was a really good job."

"COO of the Sanderson Group."

Phillip whistled long and high. "You really don't want it?"

"I really don't."

"Excellent. So, you're both on the same page.

Yet here you sit. Oozing misery, like a barfly waiting to happen."

Holden glanced at his *light* beer. Then said, "I thought we were on the same page. Then she skipped right to the end when I was still very much enjoying the start. She told me, outright, to go home."

"Home?"

Exactly. When the only place he'd ever thought of as *home* was any place she was. What he said was, "By which she meant away. Back to where I came from."

"Ouch. Harsh. Makes sense though. Considering."

"Considering?" Holden repeated, letting his drink drop to the bar, and slanting a hard look Phillip's way.

Phillip leaned back in his chair, hands up, conciliatory. "I mean, you know...the Heartache List."

"She said that was all in the past."

"Well, yeah. But that doesn't mean it can't ever affect the here and now. What's her big bad wolf?"

"Her—?"

"The thing that scares her the most."

Holden didn't have to think about it. *Fathers, right?* "Her dad leaving."

"Her dad. Her favourite teacher. Her childhood best friend. As you said, all in the past. Then you came along. A guy who's infamous for never staying in one place long." Phillip took a swig of his beer.

While Holden blinked. And blinked again. "She didn't much talk about her mum passing, but when she did…it nearly killed me. And then poor Pumpkin." Hell. "I'm her big bad wolf."

"Not you, *per se*, but you—someone who has loomed large in her life—leaving her? For sure."

Holden's fingers slipped off the glass to run through his hair.

How had he not seen it? She'd pushed him away before he could leave, because in her mind that was what happened to those she loved. She'd pushed him away because she believed she was holding him back.

Meaning…

"She loves me."

"Yup," said Phillip. "Hell of a thing."

He'd been so busy giving her space, giving her time, he'd not seen it when it was right in front of his eyes.

She'd refused to put his name up for the COO gig, knowing it would put her relationship with the Sanderson Group at risk. Knowing it would give him one less reason to stay. She'd protected him, and she'd faced her greatest fear, while torpedoing her own efforts in one fell swoop.

Because she loved him.

He'd felt so smacked by the "off you go" portion of her speech, as it had pressed into his own ancient wounds, he'd lost sight of the rest.

Phillip said, "If you don't want that job you mentioned, I'd take it. Do you think the renovation work we've done qualifies me for a gig in real estate?"

"Sorry, mate," said Holden, distractedly, his mind reeling. "It's already gone to someone else."

"Ah. Probably for the best. Camille wouldn't be keen on me working those kinds of hours."

Holden laughed despite himself. "Are you really as under the thumb as you make out?"

"Nah. And yeah, a bit. But I love her. She loves me. We have one another's backs no matter what. The rest we work out as we go along."

That, Holden was beginning to realise, might be the key to the whole thing.

There was no right way to be with a person, no balance sheet, or list you could tick off. No single set of qualities or interests or locations. A couple lived or died by how deeply they committed to whatever worked for them.

They both simply had to want it enough.

Later that same night, when Camille padded into the kitchen to swap coffee for wine, Emmy checked her phone to find a message from Freya.

Check the bank account!!!

The several smiley faces added to the end of the message took the edge off any concern as Emerson pulled up her bank details to see a staggering bump in the balance. Emmy typed:

What the heck?

It has to be the commission, for the COO position. Maybe one of your early suggestions impressed after all!

Maybe, thought Emmy. But surely the applicant would have let her know. The only other person it could possibly be…

"No," Emmy growled as she uncurled herself from the couch, her backside numbed from not having moved for hours. He couldn't have. He'd promised!

"Everything okay?" Camille called from the kitchen.

"Yep! Fine!" Emmy called, as she hobbled towards the bathroom. Door shut, she sat on the edge of the bath and stared at her phone. Knowing there was only one way to find out.

Yes, Holden had texted her. Several times. She'd answered him every time. But she'd yet to make the first move. She'd been the one to break things off, after all. Getting in contact, so that *she* might feel better for hearing from him, seemed cruel.

But this was different. This was insurrection!

This made a mockery of the Favour List! And to Emmy such a list was sacred.

She swore, rather vociferously, as she jabbed at her phone.

Tell me you didn't!

Holden's message came back so fast it was almost as if he was waiting for it.

Didn't do what?

Take that stupid job you promised me you wouldn't take. If you did, tear up the stupid contract right now!

A few long, painful beats slunk by.

Not necessary.

She could almost hear his voice as he typed. Picture a small smile tugging at the corner of his beautiful, kissable mouth. It was agony.

So much agony, she pressed the call button before she had a hope of stopping herself.

He answered, but before he had the chance to draw breath, she stage-whispered, "Holden Roarke, you listen up and you listen good. I will not let you take that job. I will call the bank now and have them return the commission. And if

Chuck or Bettina have a problem with that, they can go through me."

"You done?" he asked, the sound of glasses clinking and low-level chatter in the background of whatever fabulous faraway place he was enjoying fading as if he too was finding a quiet spot.

"So long as you do as I say."

"Ah, but that would be asking for a favour."

Emmy's heart was suddenly beating in her throat. A favour would mean they were no longer null and void. No. She couldn't keep doing this. She had to get over him.

"No. No favour."

"Right. Just wanted to make sure. After *the listen up and listen good* bit—"

At the tone of his voice, warm and intimate, a smile curled around her heart. She told it to calm down. The fact that she could sit here, talking to the man, missing him, aching for him, and smile—surely that was the kind of progress she'd have once believed she couldn't buy.

"For transparency's sake," he said, his voice low and lovely and just for her, "I did book in for an interview."

"Holden!"

"Only so that I could tell Chuck to back the hell off. You stood up to him, for me; I wanted to do the same for you. Not as a favour, so don't panic. It was something I had to do."

Wow. "And how did that go?"

"Bettina showed up instead. Turns out, she'd already taken the position herself. Said you'd given her the idea. Hence you get your commission."

"Oh, wow. Go, Bettina. But *boo* for putting us both through that." It was cutthroat stuff, playing with the big boys and girls.

Holden laughed, the sound of it spilling over her shoulders, and she held the phone tighter.

"We can hack it," he said, stressing the *we* in a way that had Emmy wriggling on the edge of the bath. "And she apologised, to us both. Explained that she was doing what she had to do to look after the person she loved."

"Right." Emmy closed her eyes tight and hoped her voice didn't sound as pained as it felt.

"Is Chuck okay, do you know?" she asked, showing her soft spot for the old guy. Even while what she really meant was, *Are you okay?*

"Well, we've made plans to have dinner. I took what you said on board. It's past time we cleared the air. Time I let go of all the old ghosts that kept me away, from here, from home, for far too long."

"Oh, that's…wonderful." It really was. "But hang on—how can you have dinner if—?" She swallowed her words, her hope.

"I'm far, far away? I'm still around, Emmy. Tying up loose ends. And I don't know if you remember, but I did promise you once that I wouldn't leave without saying goodbye."

Do me a favour, she'd said as he held her in his

arms at the hotel after the wedding. *Don't leave, this time, without saying goodbye.*

Emmy bit her lip and tipped forward to press her forehead against the cool of the sink. "I'm glad. About you and Chuck. You'll feel so much better for having let that go."

Like she did, having let Holden go? That was a laugh. But still, apart from the great, gaping hole that had taken up residence inside her chest, it worked out for everyone. She got her commission. Bettina and Chuck would be working side by side. Holden would be truly free to live his life however he saw fit.

"Look," she said, when her throat began to feel tight, "I'd better go."

"Right. Look, Emmy—"

When she realised her hand was clutching at her shirt, right over her heart, she said, "Good luck with your future endeavours."

She heard him say something, but her thumb was already pressing the button to cut the call.

When she came out of the bathroom, Camille was quickly hopping onto the couch.

Emmy said, "You were listening at the bathroom door, weren't you?"

"A little bit. I heard talking. Had to make sure you hadn't fallen and hit your head and started hallucinating."

"I was talking to Holden."

"Well, that's…whatever you think it is. I heard

mention of favours. Figured I'd better walk away before they turned into a certain kind. Of a sexual nature—"

"Yes, I get it. Thank you." As she tucked herself back into the couch, Emmy glanced at the Favour List notebook which sat innocently closed on the coffee table. "When we started the Heartache List, what did we imagine the end game might be?"

"For you to not get your heart broken." Camille looked at her through the glass of wine. "If your next question is: did it work? From where I sit, I'd say it failed pretty spectacularly."

"A little bit," Emmy admitted, the heel of her hand now rubbing the spot where it ached most. "Thing is, this one was entirely my fault. I broke my own heart. Pre-emptively. Before Holden had the chance."

"Might be worth rethinking the efficacy of such a move in future."

Camille lifted her wine glass and Emmy grabbed hers to tap it in agreement.

They settled in to watch some horrid reality TV show, knowing that whatever was happening in their own lives they'd never be as screwed up as the contestants. But Emmy's mind wandered.

Once upon a time Holden had said, the *only way to find out if someone you like likes you back is to be a little brave*. Choosing to protect Holden's interests over her own had been pretty brave.

Was it possible he'd known that was why she'd

done it, even before she'd known it? Was that why he was still messaging her? Why he'd stayed?

Emmy sat up, while Camille snorted before falling back to sleep.

Holden hadn't left. A man known for his inability to stay in one place for long, a man she'd accused of needing variety, adventure, and change of scene, more than he'd ever need her, Had Not Gone Anywhere.

He'd stood up for her against Chuck and Bettina, he'd looked out for her interests, he'd answered the phone the moment she'd called. As if nothing had changed at his end.

Was he trying to tell her something too?

Holden had stayed. Meaning, if she was very, very lucky, and the bravest she'd ever been, she might have one last chance to find out.

"Rain's meant to be good luck, right?" said Phillip, peering through the windscreen.

Raindrops slithered moodily down the car windows while Taylor Swift crooned softly through the speakers as they wound their way through the streets of east Melbourne.

It was the morning of Bernadette's wedding, and the perfect match for Emmy's mood, for, while she knew, in every bit of her banged-up heart, that aching for Holden while with him was far better than aching for him when not, she had no idea how to tell him. Or find him, for that matter.

She'd called Bettina, to thank her for the commission. Emmy had managed to leverage it into an even better deal for Pitch Perfect, but had not been able to trick the woman into giving away Holden's whereabouts.

She'd then bought a new notebook in which to write her "Find Holden and Tell Him How I Feel" ideas, but her list-building skills had deserted her right when she needed them most. She'd considered jotting down Phillip's idea—flashmob!—just to get things started.

Camille pulled down the sun visor to check her make-up and caught Emmy's eye. Emmy motioned for her to angle the mirror. Swiping a hand over the peacock-blue clip in her hair, then a finger along the edge of a red lip, she tried a smile on for size, only to be met with the faraway gaze of a woman who felt time slipping through her fingers.

"We're here!" Camille called as they pulled up a little way from Bernadette's parents' lovely house in Camberwell. "Look at that. Rain's stopped!"

When Emmy hopped out of the car, stepping up onto the verdant edge of the footpath, Phillip walked on tip toes to avoid the wet. While Emmy's heels sank into the wet grass. So deeply she couldn't move. Camille bit her lip before bursting into laughter.

Once Phillip and Camille had yanked Emmy

out of the mire, they each took an elbow, and, arm in arm, just as they had been for so many years before this one, they made their way up the path, following the sound of laughter, and music and voices, until—

"Oh, my," Emmy gasped.

A big, round, red-and-white-striped marquee, with a wilting roof and small red flags hanging limply from the gutters every few metres, sat plonked in the centre of the huge lawn.

"It's like a giant mushroom," Phillip said, awe tinging his voice.

"A giant circus mushroom," Camille added, clapping madly. "I love it so much I can barely blink."

"It's wonderful. It could not be more perfectly Bernadette," Emmy said, a true smile lighting her up for the first time in days.

"Now I have to go find the most easy-going bride that ever lived." Camille headed off towards the house, while Phillip led Emmy towards the opening at the back of the tent, where bunches of guests congregated, chatting happily, drinks already in hand.

Inside the circus theme continued, with flickering vintage circus videos playing across the walls of the tent like some magical dream. And up front, where the bride and groom would do their thing, a massive elephant statue looked over them all.

Emmy went to grab Phillip's sleeve to point out

the monkey doll climbing a ladder to the trapeze set, when she turned to stone.

For there, just off stage, chatting to the groom...

Holden. Holden was here!

Emmy hiked up her skirt, and darted through the tightly packed crowd, her heels catching in the grass, eyes locked onto the beautiful man in the dark suit.

She had no idea what she'd say, only that she had to get to him. For after months of near constant contact, this was the first time she'd seen his face in days, and she could barely hold herself together.

She'd made it to the end of the aisle, right as Elvis started singing *Can't Help Falling in Love*.

The crowd all turned, right as a spotlight swung to land on Emmy, dress hitched, heels half sunken into the ground, heat creeping up her neck.

Holden, after giving Barry a nudge up onto the stage, was the last to turn. He stilled the moment he saw her, his hands dropping slowly to his sides. Then a smile stretched across his face. A slow, warm, charming, beautiful smile.

What could she do but smile back? A real smile. Not the kind she'd practised in the mirror in the car. One that started in her heart and spread out to her extremities, till she felt bathed in light and warmth and hope.

"Emmy! Move it!"

Emmy turned to see Camille heading up the

aisle, a grinning Bernadette, giving her a thumbs-up, coming up behind. Camille spun Emmy to face the front and gave her a shove.

Emmy found the beat, and made her way up the aisle, ducking off to the side at the last second and finding a spot against the wall, which gave her the perfect view of Holden, who mirrored her position on the other side of the wedding party.

And there she spent the longest half an hour of her life staring into Holden's stormy blue eyes as Bernie and Barry promised to love, honour, and cherish one another for the rest of time.

Everything went a little wild after that, for the bride and groom were playing fast and loose with scheduling and had disappeared. The guests happily headed for the booze till they were told differently.

All bar Emmy, who'd lost track of Holden once the bridal party was swept away for photos, and began to worry that he had been a mirage.

After tables and chairs were brought in, and a huge dance floor set up by a swift staging team in red noses and clown wigs, Emmy found her seat. She kicked off her sodden shoes, tucked them under her chair, and stretched out her toes.

Then, adrenalin fading, she leaned forward, rested her chin on her hand, closed her eyes, and sighed.

When she opened her eyes again, it was to find

a pair of long, strong male legs decked out in a beautifully tailored suit and shiny black shoes walking slowly towards her. She knew those legs. She knew that walk. Knew that unhurried confidence.

Feeling a little trembly, Emmy pressed herself to standing, and lifted her chin to face the man head-on. Only to remember her lack of shoes. And that he was well over six feet tall.

And so she sat, plonking back into her chair, her toes madly reaching for her shoes.

Holden, having played this game before, crouched down till his eyes were in line with hers. Tired eyes. Eyes that had seen some late nights and long days since she'd last seen them. But smiling eyes, all the same. Stormy blue and lovely. With those unfairly long lashes, and those endearing crinkles. Oh, how she'd missed that face.

"Emerson Adler," he said. "Fancy meeting you here."

"Holden Roarke," she shot back, trying to sound all confident and fine, but even she heard the note of yearning. "What are you doing here?"

"Always with the questions."

"Just one. I know Bernie didn't invite you. She doesn't even remember having met you."

His gaze hooked onto hers, as if he never wanted to let go. "Your calendar, it's still synced to mine."

"Ha!" She leaned in when she felt heads turn

her way. Leaned in so close she could feel his warmth. "You totally crashed."

He leaned in a smidgeon himself, till their noses were mere inches from touching. "I don't look at it as 'crashing' so much as coming full circle. I feel somewhat involved in how those crazy kids came to fall madly in love."

Emmy shook her head. "How did you end up as Barry's leaning post?"

"Met him on the way in. Poor fellow looked ready to pass out. His best man didn't look much better. I offered my services until showtime. I can be pretty irresistible when I want to be."

"Oh, I know."

"You do?"

Emmy nodded. With no list to follow, she had to follow her gut. And it was telling her to be honest. To leave her heart wide open for once and trust it to do its thing. To trust this man to do his.

When she let out a great big sigh, filled with hope and relief, Holden reached out and swept his thumb across her cheek. Gently. So gently. The same way he went about everything, with honour and kindness and thoughtfulness and decency.

"Holden."

"Mm-hmm."

"I should never have asked you to leave."

"You didn't. You told me to go home." His gaze roved over her face, as if it had been far too long since he'd seen it last. "And here I am, doing just as you asked."

Emerson swallowed.

"It did take me a little longer to figure out *why* you said it. That and a little advice from some folks with smarter hearts than mine. You want to know what we came up with?"

"I do," Emmy said, certain she was going to like his answer.

His eyes stopped roving and landed on hers. "You did it because you love me."

A smile bloomed in her chest before landing on her face, the warmth of it like a bubble around them, keeping out the damp, the past, the people milling around them.

"But how could I?" she asked, her voice growing quiet, intimate, just for him. "We had a deal. *No* accidental falling in love."

"True," said Holden. "As I remember it, *you* promised not to fall for *me* while I made no such promise. So, while you failed miserably, I'm off the hook."

"You are?" she asked, her voice barely a whisper now. Enough that he dropped a knee, his suit fabric sinking into the squelch, so that he could be nearer her still.

"Completely and utterly," he said, his voice raw. "Deeply, shockingly, nauseatingly, incandescently. Off. The. Hook. In love, with you." He smiled a slow, easy smile at whatever he saw on her face. "You okay there?"

Emmy nodded. Then grinned as tears started flowing down her cheeks. Happy tears. Nauseatingly incandescent tears.

"Tell me," he said, his voice rough, as if he too was overwhelmed by emotion. "I want to hear you say the words. Tell me you knew how I felt about you, how I *feel*, all along. Because I can't stand the thought that a day went by when you didn't know that I am crazy about you."

Did she? Of course she did. How could she not? His love had filled up all the tender, yearning places inside her that had craved him, even before she'd found him.

She tucked her knees together, her bare feet crossed beneath her chair, and leaned forward till her forehead touched his. And she said, "I know it."

"Tell me you believe it."

She could feel the vibration of his voice through his hand at the back of her neck, through the point where their foreheads met. "I believe it."

"Tell me you feel it."

She slid off the chair until she was on her knees before him, her slinky peacock-blue dress meeting wet grass as she cupped his face and kissed him. A kiss that was half smile, half laugh, and half utter joy.

"Hey, folks," Phillip's voice boomed over the

sound system, "Bernie and Barry have returned from wherever it is they've been, and, since this is their day, and they are doing things on their timetable, I've been told it's time for the bouquet toss. So all the singletons, please gather on the dance floor!"

Emmy lifted her head, but moved no further.

Holden did the same, a single eyebrow raising in question. "What do you say?"

She mirrored his cocked eyebrow. "I'm fine right here, thank you very much. Nice and invisible."

His eyes crinkled a moment before one side of his mouth lifted into a sexy half-smile. Their faces stayed close enough she could see an eyelash that had fallen to his cheek.

This time she lifted her hand, gently gathered it with her index finger and held it up to his lips. "Make a wish."

"You don't believe in the bouquet toss, but you do believe in eyelash wishes. You are an interesting woman, Emerson Adler." He took a hold of her wrist, pulling her finger to his lips, and blew, sending the eyelash spinning off into the ether.

Emerson grinned as she watched the eyelash flutter and disappear, and with the shift in focus came the realisation that many, many people were watching her. And Holden. On their knees in the grass. So much for invisible.

"Up," she whispered. "Up, up, up."

"Okay, okay, okay," he muttered. Pressing himself to standing, he reached down and lifted her to her feet and pulled her against him. As if, now he'd found her again, he was not about to let her go. "Much better."

"Mmm," she said, curling her hand into the front of his shirt and rather marvelling at the fact that she could do so with clear intent.

"Want to know what I wished for?" Holden asked, smiling down into her eyes.

"What if that means it won't come true?"

He seemed to think about it for a second, his mouth twisting, one eye narrowing, before saying, "I reckon it's worth the risk. I wished for you to enter the bouquet toss."

"You did not." Emmy glanced towards the makeshift dance floor, expecting to find the usual seething horde of glittery guests, only to find it was empty bar the bride, who was grinning at her like a loon. "What's happening right now?"

With a roll of her eyes, the bride all but skipped over to their table, stopped, sighed, and held out the bouquet.

"Ahh…" Emmy's gaze moved to Holden for back-up, only to find him watching her, smiling, that face she loved so much full of questions.

Take the bouquet, or don't take the bouquet.

As if one's life really could hinge on a single moment.

The post-Heartache List Emmy would have

fought that notion, found it terrifying. While the *post*-post-Heartache List Emmy knew it could happen and that it could be wonderful.

Emmy accepted the bouquet.

Bernie took her in a tight hug. Then gave the same to Holden, holding on a fraction longer, as Holden whispered something in her ear, after which she nodded enthusiastically.

When the wedding crowd hollered and whistled, Emmy couldn't help but laugh. And curtsy. And offer up a little royal wave, the happiness rushing through her leaving her feeling as if she was floating an inch off the ground. In the best possible way.

At which point the bride headed to the dance floor, and her new husband, who met her there, right as the opening strains of *You Can Leave Your Hat On* burst from the speakers.

"Do me a favour."

Emmy turned back to Holden, her nose buried in the sweetest spray of wild jasmine. "Depends on the favour."

"I think it's high time we move on to Phase Three."

At the shift in Holden's voice—deep, husky and compelling—her gaze skewed to his. "What's Phase Three?"

"We never did thrash that out. So, I guess it's whatever we want it to be." He took her by the hand, looked around, his expression highly focused. Then he looked back at her. "Why are you so short?"

"Took off my shoes."

Muttering under his breath about falling head over heels for a woman who couldn't keep her heels on her feet, Holden leaned around her, gathered her shoes from under her chair, then slipped an arm beneath her knees and lifted her off the ground. "First step of Phase Three," he said. "We're getting the heck out of here."

"We can't!" she said, holding on tight and brimming with breathless laughter.

Holden, holding all the cards as well as herself, ignored her, edging around tables. "The bride insisted. Just now. Said she hoped it made up for the key incident."

Emmy looked over her shoulder in search of the bride, only to find her dancing up a storm. "She *did* remember."

"Oh, yeah. Now let's go." Holden picked up the pace, a man on a mission.

Then Emmy caught Camille's eye. She gave her best friend a finger wave. Camille pretended to burst into tears, her hands clutched over her heart, before Phillip dragged her onto the dance floor.

Emmy sighed as Holden tucked her tighter against his chest and strode from the tent, just like Kevin Costner and Whitney Houston in *The Bodyguard*. It was the single sexiest moment of her life. But, considering the intention in his stride as he made his way up the side of the house, she had a feeling it would soon be pipped.

Emmy lifted a hand to Holden's cheek. "How many points do I get for bagging a Back-Up Best Man Slash Wedding Crasher?"

He slowed, just a mite, as his gaze moved to hers. "Considering how rare a breed we are, it's gotta be up near seven hundred and fifty points. Maybe even a thousand."

"Wow," she said. "To think, I had no intention of playing the game, when it turns out I'm so very good at it."

With that, she reached up and grabbed her prize by the tie and dragged his mouth to hers. Or maybe she simply caught him on the way down.

Either way, if that kiss was anything to go by, Phase Three was going to be the very best of all.

EPILOGUE

EMMY FINISHED SMEARING Vegemite on her toast, tucked a corner between her teeth, and turned to find Holden ambling into the kitchen—suit pants unbuttoned, chest bare.

Her heart still kicked at the sight of him. "Nearly ready?"

Holden spun on the spot, arms out, showing off. "Thought I'd just go like this today."

"The investors will be thrilled."

He finished his spin, and moved in, his arm sliding around her waist before hauling her close. Then he tugged her a little closer still, till she was flush up against him, his smile growing when he felt her breath hitch.

Then he grabbed the slice of toast from her mouth, placed a slow, soft kiss upon her lips, followed by a quick swipe of his tongue that had her eyes all but rolling back in her head, before taking a bite of her toast and putting it back where he found it.

"Need a lift?" she asked, when he let her go, patting down her hair, tugging on her skirt, and generally trying to feel less discombobulated.

"No, but I'll take it. Lunch?"

"Not today. I can take off early if you want to try that new Italian place around the corner."

"Done."

"When do you head to Paris?" she asked. "This Thursday or next?"

Her hand went to her phone, to check their joint calendar, but his hand closed over hers, before spinning her back into his arms, then rocking her side to side, till they were slow dancing in the kitchen.

Dust motes fluttered through the shards of buttery sunlight pouring through her kitchen window. Her mother's lemon tree, nourished by Pumpkin's ashes, flourished just outside.

While Holden's eyes, gazing into hers, were such a sharp, clear blue in the morning light. No storm, no clouds, not any more. "I think you mean, when do *we* head to Paris?"

"We?"

"Why not? I *may* have had a sly chat to Freya, before confirming the dates, to make sure you could fit it in. Freya did consider coming with me to Paris, if you refused, but in the end she chose to stay behind, keep Pitch Perfect rolling along."

"A week in Paris," Emmy said out loud.

For this was the deal. A side effect of living with a man who was more curious than cautious, who had connections the world over, who *was*— it turned out—just as happy lazing on her couch watching her true crime documentaries, or building her a shed, as he was jet-setting all over the world to talk about his new app that people were already saying would lift the ability of small businesses to compete in the global space for ever.

Having been his wildly successful beta tester, Pitch Perfect could attest to the fact that business had never looked brighter.

"What do you say?"

"I say…yes. A week in Paris, with you, sounds perfect. Now, will you do me a favour?"

"Anything."

"When you finally decide to put some clothes on, wear the pale blue. Nobody will be able to say no to you in that shirt."

"Nobody says no to me anyway."

Emerson snorted. She sure had. For quite some time.

"Fine, I'll wear the shirt. And will you do me a favour?"

"Depends on the favour."

"Always so cautious," he said, a smile in his eyes as they roved over her face.

"Not always," she said, reaching around to run her hand over his backside, before pulling him a little closer.

"Fair enough. My request is that you go a little lighter on the Vegemite for our morning toast."

"This toast?" she said, holding out her half-eaten slice. "This toast that I made for myself?"

"Mm-hmm," he said, leaning down to nibble at her neck.

"Changing up my Vegemite-to-butter ratio is

a far bigger favour than the shirt." Her eyes fluttered closed as he rained a trail of kisses over her cheek. "What do I get in return?"

"Rub your feet every night this week."

Gracious, that sounded good. "Fine. What else?"

He moved to her earlobe, nipping the lobe, before whispering in her ear what he was prepared to do, nightly, in vivid detail. And Emerson was mighty glad he was holding on to her as her knees gave way.

And soon the kitchen bench proved itself good for something other than making Vegemite on toast.

And, right before her mind turned to starbursts, and happiness and pleasure and heat and want, Emerson smiled. A smile so wide she was absolutely certain it would never, ever come to an end.

* * * * *

*If you enjoyed this story,
check out these other great reads from
Ally Blake*

The Millionaire's Melbourne Proposal
Dream Vacation, Surprise Baby
Brooding Rebel to Baby Daddy
Crazy About Her Impossible Boss

Available now!